CAUGHT IN THE CROSSFIRE

Christine Fauconnier

www.christinefauconnier.com

To John,
my reader and my editor,
my husband and my best friend.

Acknowledgements

I would like to express my gratitude to Frank Browne of triselcommunications.com for producing the cover of this book. Frank has given his expertise and support in many ways, and I am indebted to him for his generosity and talent.

I would also like to express my gratitude to Bekah Russom for the cover photograph.

Lastly, I wish to thank John Williams for his editing and proof reading of this book. His support and encouragement were invaluable to me from start to finish.

Table of Contents

'Your children are not your children.
They are the sons and daughters of Life's longing for itself.
They come through you but not from you,
And though they are with you yet they belong not to you.

You may give them your love but not your thoughts,
For they have their own thoughts.
You may house their bodies but not their souls,
For their souls dwell in the house of tomorrow,
which you cannot visit, not even in your dreams.'

The Prophet
Kahlil Gibran

1. The Big Fight

Most families start out with expectations of happiness, but there is no guarantee of success. Distance and the self-absorption of individual members may sneak in, discontent and anger may shake things up at times. But this is the stuff of ordinary life and it does not cancel out the happy times or threaten the underlying closeness between parents and children. Some families, however, contain within themselves such seeds of destruction that when the fighting starts, they disintegrate into the chaos of catastrophic human emotions. Through no fault of her own Zoe Milton was growing up in such a family.

*

'Now you know what your father's like,' barked Leanne, glancing angrily in the rear-view mirror.

As if it's my fault, thought Zoe, slumped on the back seat, tear stains smeared down her face. Leanne was driving furiously through the narrow streets of the neighbourhood, roaring through the gears as if she needed to let the world know about her mood. Jessie sat silently in the passenger seat, shaken but also righteous. 'Typical of your family,' she had hissed into Zoe's ears moments before, when Mum wasn't paying attention. As the car drove past her school, Zoe glanced longingly at the closed building and deserted yard. Half-term. When Mum veered left and sharply right past the shops, Zoe recognised the way to Nan's house. She straightened herself up a little and stared out of the window, away from her mother and sister. An unrelenting film was playing over and over in her mind, as unstoppable as it was devastating.

The row between her parents had started the night before. It was not their first row by any means, but this one had jolted her out of her sleep, and she had listened, rigid under her duvet. Mum had just come home from the pub.

'I was there with the girls,' she shouted in her ragged after-the-pub voice, 'how many times do I have to tell you?'

'You're lying Leanne,' Dad yelled back, 'I saw Bethan and Liz walking past the house over an hour ago.'

Zoe held the pillow tight against her ears, but the shouting pierced straight through anyway, flinging bad words at her like stones thrown by nasty boys. At the sound of crashing furniture Zoe sprung up in alarm to a sitting position, with her knees drawn up and her fingernails digging through the tightly held duvet into her palms. She held her breath in the ominous lull that followed and let it out again as her mother's voice shattered the silence. 'Don't you ever threaten me again, you drunken bastard.' Zoe closed her eyes with a shudder, imagining her father's crushed face. A door slammed, then another. Mum had gone into the kitchen. Silence fell. Zoe relaxed her fingers out of their unconscious grip on the duvet but when she heard her mother coming out of the kitchen and up the stairs, she quickly dropped into bed and pulled the duvet over her head. Her mother went into the bathroom. The flush rushed water down the pipes and the door opened again. Steps trudged towards the bedroom at the front and after the door closed all sounds died down. Zoe listened for a while longer but when it became clear her dad wasn't following her mum up the stairs, she slowly relaxed and drifted into sleep.

When she woke up the following morning it was already past nine o'clock. She sat up in bed, listening, putting her feelers out for tension in the air. The house was silent, too silent. No radio on, not a single familiar sound from the kitchen. Zoe swivelled quietly out of bed and slipped on yesterday's clothes. Then she made her way downstairs, gingerly, clutching the banister and peeping through the uprights, hoping to get some idea of what she would find. The front room door was wide open, with light pouring in and she didn't bother to look there. That room, she knew, would be empty and tidy enough. As she looked down the corridor, she could see the blind was still down in the kitchen. Nobody was about. She turned to face the door in front of her and stared at it. The TV room.

She stood still for a couple of minutes, then took a deep breath and turned the handle quietly. As she slowly pushed the door open the thick smell of booze, fags and stale breath hit her nostrils, but she had been prepared for it and she pushed the door further. A ray of light was peeping in through the badly fitting curtains and she saw what she expected: her father sprawled on the couch in his shirt and jeans, lost in drunken sleep, his open mouth letting in and out a hissing flow of fetid air. The room was the usual mess, with overturned cans of beer still dripping around the edges and empty bottles struggling to stay inside the wastepaper basket. Mum's high heeled boots had been chucked across the floor, her jacket flung on the back of a chair and the plant by the window had toppled over, spilling loose soil onto the carpet. Zoe's young face looked old for a moment, like the face of a tired overworked mother. Then she went to pick up the plant and scraped most of the dry soil back into the pot. One stem had got broken and she turned the pot around so you couldn't see it was now lopsided. Her best friend's mum had a plant like that with a thick trunk like a miniature tree. A money plant she called it. This one was straggly with tiny leaves instead of the fat glossy ones in Kylie's house.

She turned away from the plant and looked down at her father again. Because she loved him she couldn't bear to see him like this. Couldn't bear to wake him up and see the humiliation in his eyes as he got reminded about yesterday's row. She didn't want him to know she had seen him here this morning nor did she want to be around when he phoned his boss to say he had a migraine. She wanted nothing to do with all this shame because she knew her father was a very different man from the pathetic figure lying on the couch now. Her father was a tall clever man who could do anything with computers and had a good job because of it, where people looked up to him and turned to him when there was a problem. She knew this because Granny had told her and Granny always wanted her to be proud of her dad, and she was. But pride was one thing and love was another. Love was about a certain look in the eyes and the feel of the arms that held you close, it was about gentle hands that could throw you up in the air just for the fun of it and a voice that was never harsh. Love was what Zoe felt when her dad was around, and he made her feel happy and safe. Zoe loved her dad more than anyone in the world.

This man lying on the couch on the other hand was the man Leanne wanted Joe to be. She had the power to turn him into a wreck and her eyes lit up with glee whenever she did it. When Zoe witnessed that she felt a deep hatred for her mother, even deeper than the hatred she felt when she got the stinging pain of one Leanne's smacks. Her mother's eyes lit up then too. Joe never smacked Zoe, but he couldn't stop Leanne doing it, even though she had heard them arguing about it more than once.

Zoe retreated quietly out of the room and headed for the kitchen where she let the light in and had a solitary breakfast. Jessie was having a half-term lie-in and Mum was sleeping off the booze. She rinsed her bowl clean over the mess of dishes and glasses left by her parents in the sink and walked softly back up to her bedroom where she settled on the floor to watch morning cartoons. Hugging Flossie the rabbit in one arm and leaning back into Bernard the bean bag dog she slipped into a world so engrossing that all dark thoughts lifted from her mind like a flight of starlings disappearing into a distant sky.

The banging of the bathroom door startled her and her eyes left the animated characters on the screen to settle on the closed silent door of her bedroom. When she heard the shower coming on, she quickly switched back to her cartoon, annoyed to have missed even a minute of the action. But her ears were now tuned into the sounds of the house in the way the ears of a mother are tuned into the slightest murmur from the cot no matter how captivating the book she is reading or the film she is watching. When Zoe heard her mother leave the bathroom, she tensed up again, but her eyes remained riveted to the telly. If her mum came in, she could just grunt a mumbled good morning. She knew her mum would be only too glad to leave her to it. But her mother didn't stick her head around the door, she went straight downstairs and sounds of water and clinking crockery drifted up from the kitchen to Zoe's room, directly above. Music burst out from the radio and Zoe reached for her remote to turn up her own volume.

Minutes later, the remote still in her hand, she turned the volume down again and half her brain disengaged from the story on the screen to pay attention to the story in the house. Her father was trudging up the stairs, heavily. She could hear the message in every step and her mouth went a little dry. On screen the boy hero was flying through the air, jumping from roof to roof in pursuit of an evil spider-like monster but she didn't fly with him, the magic was broken and she was back in her bedroom looking at the predictable antics of cartoon characters on a TV screen. She sat very still, unconsciously squeezing Flossie against her, waiting for the shouting to start again. Except that often there was no shouting in the morning and life went on as if nothing had happened the night before. You just never knew how it would go.

She had to wait ages, tensing up with every minute that went by. In actual time the wait was probably only about ten minutes, because it never took her father long to have a shower and get dressed, but those minutes rolled out of the way as if they were going uphill. At last, she heard his trudging steps heading down and towards the kitchen. She shrunk into herself and closed her eyes.

When she heard their voices, not saying much but not rising either, she relaxed just a little and opened her eyes. A new cartoon had started on the screen and she dipped her eyes into it briefly. Then back out. Listening. Hoping. Running her hands down Flossie's long floppy ears, again and again until the fur was completely flattened, then sweeping it all backwards into spiky tufts only to start again on the long slow smoothing down.

Just as her hand was leaving the bottom of Flossie's ear and about to come up to the top again, an explosion of angry voice startled her so violently she let go of her toy rabbit and Flossie dropped to the floor. It was her father's voice and although she didn't catch every word, she distinctly heard 'Fucking whore' and that flashed real danger in her mind. Shouting words like that at Mum was plain stupid. Dad didn't have a chance against Mum at the best of times, but with words like that, he was a dead man. Zoe's unsteady thumb pressed the mute key on the remote. Too late. She'd missed her mother's response. Her father was speaking in his angry voice again, but not actually shouting. Zoe reached out for Flossie and sat undecided for a moment, torn between the anxiety of not knowing what was going on and the fear of knowing. Then very slowly she got up and headed for her door.

When she opened it a fresh blast of violent words hit her like a volley of gunshot and she stopped dead, her hand clenching the doorknob. 'You apologise to me now,' her mother was shouting, 'or I'm walking out of this house and the girls are coming with me. Do you get that, you stupid moron? I don't have to put up with your shit any longer. I can just walk out.' 'I'll kill you first,' her dad shouted back, 'Watch it, I'll kill you. You're driving me to it, Leanne. You're asking for it.' Kitchen chairs scraped on the floor and Zoe pictured them circling around the table. She'd seen them do it before. Her heart was pounding in her chest and her left leg was beginning to tremble. The strange out of control trembling she had noticed a while back, when she'd witnessed their first fight. She knew there was nothing she could do about it, so she ignored it and started tiptoeing towards the stairs. Tiptoeing was stupid she realised as with the noise from the kitchen she could have run down and skipped the last three steps in one big jump as she often did, and they would have neither heard nor cared. Tiptoeing was like trembling, a strange reflex she couldn't help.

She tiptoed all the way down and then approached the kitchen in a sideways move flattening herself against the wall, as if by making herself invisible she might make the whole horrendous scene vanish out of sight and out of hearing. The door was wide open and when she got to it, she stood on the outside leaning against the doorpost. Her mother was backing away slowly around the table, dragging a chair in front of her with one hand and holding a saucepan in the other. 'You touch me,' she hissed, 'and I'm smashing your brains out with this.' Her eyes were dark with aggression but also with excitement. Joe caught a glancing sight of his daughter and stopped in his tracks. His hands dropped by his side and he shook his head the way a dog shakes water off his body. 'Sorry,' he said, his eyes brimming with grovelling apology, 'You can put the pan down, I won't touch you Leanne, I'm sorry. You know what I'm like. I lose control, but I would never hurt you.' A dog popped into Zoe's mind again, a slinking creature, curving his body sideways, with his tail between his legs, his ears flat and his eyes full of doggy shame.

8

Zoe's grip tightened around Flossie's soft body and she closed her eyes to shut out the picture of her cringing dad.

When she opened them again Mum and Dad were behaving almost normally. Mum had put the pan back in the drainer and pushed the chair under the table. She was standing with one hand on her hip and the back of the other stroking her forehead. Joe stepped closer and made a conciliatory gesture with his hand, but Leanne pushed the hand away. 'Too soon, Joe, you can't threaten me like that and expect a hug the next minute. It would be too damn easy, wouldn't it?' Her chin was up. His eyes darkened, and he said, standing tall above her, 'I was wrong to threaten you, but there is a bigger wrong Leanne, and you know it. At least I'm prepared to recognise I'm in the wrong, but you just lie.' He was staring her in the eyes, with something like courage and Zoe held her breath. 'Or can you tell the truth?' he added coldly, 'Are you capable? Just the once?' The air was thick with challenge and Leanne wavered.

The trembling in Zoe's leg spread to the whole of her left side and Flossie started shaking in her hand. Standing as they were, face to face, staring each other out, her parents suddenly looked like two cartoon characters radiating nose to nose aggression. It was comical but she knew it wasn't funny and she must not start laughing. She bit her lip, but a suppressed giggle shuddered down her back anyway.

'All right,' snapped Leanne, 'all right. You want the truth, do you?' She paused without taking her eyes off Joe's face. There was nothing comical in that tone and Zoe tensed up, whilst trembling as hard as ever from her left shoulder down to her left foot. Jessie was now standing behind her, breathing down her neck. She could sense the excitement in her half-sister who loved to see her mother on top, her mother winning against the man who was not her father. She wouldn't have been surprised if Jessie had started cheering her mother on like a football fan hungry for a goal.

Her mother took a step back and stared at Zoe's dad with an icy gleam in her eye, 'Yes, Joseph Milton, yes, I think it's time to tell the truth. Why should I protect you any longer? I do look at other men, you're quite right, and do you know why? Because my own man is a pathetic prick, eaten up by jealousy, insecure, inadequate and…'

Joe's hand had whipped through the air and caught her smartly on the cheek, killing the words. Leanne yelped and staggered. Her hand had shot up to her cheek and now involuntary tears spurted down her face whilst fury burned in her eyes. The four of them stood suspended for a moment and then Leanne spoke in a controlled snarling voice. 'You will pay for this,' she said deliberately, 'you will lose everything Joseph Milton, everything,' and she turned on her heels, grabbed the girls on her way out of the kitchen and shouted as she stormed towards the stairs, 'I've had enough of living with a psychopath.' Before disappearing up the stairs, she paused at the bottom of the banister and lay her hand on the round wooden ball. 'And the girls' she added, twisting her head towards the kitchen, 'are coming with me.' She spat the words out and tightened her grip on Zoe's arm as if she had anticipated the girl's wriggle to try and escape.

*

But Zoe knew the way home from Nan's flat and as soon as she could, she would run back and make sure her dad never let her mum take her away again.

10

They had arrived now, and Zoe obeyed the order to get out of the car, dragging her feet. Nan opened the door in a fluster of worried eyes and flapping hands. She wanted to know the story and Leanne rubbished Dad as she so often did with Nan, forgetting to mention all the bad things that she did. 'He hit me, Mam,' she kept saying, 'so that's it, best thing that could happen really, nobody will side with him now.' She shot a glance in Zoe's direction as she said that, and Zoe looked away. 'He'll be lucky to get contact,' she added coldly.

'What's contact?' asked Zoe, looking back at her mum.

'Seeing you,' replied her mum.

Zoe felt herself spinning and she dropped onto the old settee by the window. In a fuzzy distance she could hear Nan trying to smooth things over. '…rush into decisions…Joe's not a bad man… let emotions calm down…think it through…heat of the moment…' but the loud and fast beating of her heart made it impossible to grasp what was being said. What was going to happen to her? Panic tightened her gullet and she noticed her breathing for the first time in her life. The air was getting stuck, and she couldn't draw it in no matter how hard she tried. Her chest had gone so tight no air could reach it. She was gasping now, her fingers digging into the arms of the chair, her eyes ready to pop out of their sockets. Short panting breaths were making her mouth dry but completely failing to fill her lungs. *I'm gonna die,* she thought, unable to move or shout or do anything.

Just then she heard Jessie shout in a panic 'Mum, Zoe's having a fit.' Mum and Nan came rushing over, and Nan said, 'An asthma attack, the kid's having an asthma attack, quick Jessie, get my inhaler from the bedroom, on the bedside table.'

The iron hand around Zoe's chest was tightening its grip. The heads of Nan and Mum were swimming near her face, distorted masks of fear and worry. Nan had taken Zoe's hand in hers and kept repeating 'you're going to be all right love, calm down now, relax your lungs, relax your lungs. She's breaking my fingers,' she added with a glance to Mum, 'Ah, thanks Jessie, that'll do the trick, you just watch it now, open your mouth and when I say "go" take a deep breath in.' Zoe's wide panicked eyes tried to express that she couldn't take any kind of a breath in, let alone a deep one, and that was it, she was going to die. She closed her eyes to shut out the three faces zooming in on her but when the word "go" boomed in her ear she automatically opened her mouth and pulled in as hard as she could. In her head she did anyway, but her muscles didn't respond. Maybe she was already dead.

It turned out she wasn't. Miraculously, the iron hand was slowly loosening its grip. She opened her eyes in wonder and felt the immense relief of air flowing in. In and out. Her chest was gently rising and falling, and she never knew there could be such exquisite pleasure in a simple movement like that. How come she'd never noticed it before? She looked at the faces around her. Nan was smiling triumphantly, Jessie looked like she'd seen a ghost and Mum's face was back to normal, but she wasn't smiling.

'There we are,' she said bitterly, 'now the kid's got asthma, and we all know who to blame for that.'

2. Ending it All

Janet had her hands deep in flour when the sudden ringing of the phone broke her morning peace. She wasn't so good at moving fast these days and she got into a bit of a fluster trying to clean her hands and make it to the lounge in time to pick up.

'Hello, Janet Milton speaking,' she said a little out of breath, ready to give a piece of her mind to anyone wanting to sell her double-glazing or insurance. But what she heard had nothing to do with double-glazing. What she heard stopped her heart beating and tightened her fingers so hard around the phone her knuckles went white. At the other end her son, who should have been in work, was in the grip of one of his uncontrollable fits of temper, shouting incoherent nonsense about killing himself, killing his two-timing bitch of a wife and leaving Zoe an orphan to be looked after by her grandmother.

'Joe, are you at home?' interrupted his mother. She managed to keep her voice steady despite the sickness churning inside her stomach. Why had her son never learned to ask for help in any other way than manipulative anger and was this the moment when he would go beyond threats? He sounded unhinged. Out of the corner of her eye she saw her husband's head appearing round the door, a mild enquiry dancing in his eyes. She beckoned to him and said 'Joe, I can't make sense of anything you're saying, I'm handing you over to your father. Explain it to him, son.' She pushed the handset into David's hand and mouthed, 'Keep him talking, I'm going over there.' David's tall figure stooped slightly over the phone as he asked his son to start again from the beginning.

As she rushed out of the room Janet chucked the tea-towel covered in flour on her beloved settee and in one sweeping movement she grabbed her handbag, picked the car keys off the wall and pushed her feet into the gardening shoes that happened to be on the floor in the hallway. She plucked her fleece from the coat stand and tucked it under her arm. She could hear David saying, 'Yes, Joe, of course I see how you feel. Do you know where Leanne has gone to?' She pulled the door behind her quietly, jumped into her car and revved off in a most untypical way.

When she reached her son's house, she caught sight of him through the window, pacing back and forth in the front room, the phone to his ear and his other arm cutting swathes through the air. Relief flooded her. He hadn't gone and done something stupid. A moment later she was pressing his doorbell. He opened the door without a word but didn't stop her coming in and heading towards the kitchen. Her eyes swept over the empty cans and bottles, the mess of furniture, blankets and clothes on the floor but she said nothing. She didn't mention the smells either. As she got busy making tea, she noted the food debris and sticky stains on all the shelves. The cutlery drawer hadn't been cleaned for months, maybe years.

'Mum, I'm not hungry and I don't want a cup of tea.' His mother's ways grated on his raw nerves. With his elbows on the table, he cradled his head in the palms of his hands, covering his eyes to let her know he was tolerating her presence but no more. 'Have one to keep me company,' she said lightly, as if she'd called in for a friendly chat, 'I drove over much too fast and I'm a bit shaken up.' She finally discovered the biscuit tin at the back of one of the top shelves, brought it down and put biscuits on a plate. She poured boiling water over the tea bags she had dropped into a couple of large mugs and placed everything on the table. How soothing to let everyday gestures restore the ordinary tempo of life and how she would love to squeeze a good dollop of detergent on a cloth and give those cupboards a scrub. Instead, she sat down and reached out to lay her hand on her son's arm.

'Now tell me,' she said, with a light squeeze of her fingers.

'She's left me,' he said, looking up and addressing himself to the wall. 'The bitch has gone. Treats me like shit and then leaves, like I'm the one who deserves to be dumped.' His eyes smouldered in silence for a moment, and when he spoke again, his voice trembled with outraged incomprehension. 'She's taken the girls with her, Mum, said we'd discuss contact arrangements later. She can't take Zoe away from me, can she? Not when she's the one cheating on me and leaving me. They wouldn't allow that, would they?' Now he was looking at his mother and he sounded like a boy lost in a place he didn't understand, a place where he could just as easily explode into anger or sink into despair. She watched him covertly, pretending to stare into her mug. He had lit a cigarette and was blowing smoke away from her, with defiant little jerks of the head. Try to stop me smoking, he seemed to say, because if you do, I'll give you a piece of my mind about this shitty existence of mine and all the reasons why lung cancer is the least of my worries.

Janet pretended the smoking wasn't happening and kept him talking with a steady stream of short neutral questions. The facts emerged pell-mell. Leanne had been seeing someone else, as he damn well suspected, and now she had finally come clean with the truth. She might well have seen other men before that one, he'd known all along she was a two-timing bitch, taking his money and cheating on him; laughing her throaty laugh in the pub, letting them know she was available. Life in any event had become unbearable. Endless fighting. The woman was a drunk. A stirring bitch. He banged the table hard with his fist. 'If she tries to take Zoe from me, I'll kill her. I swear I will. Or I'll kill myself. What's the point of life without my family?'

If at any point Janet had half formulated the thought in her mind that Leanne's departure might turn out to be a blessing in disguise, she was now thinking again. She sat holding her empty mug, uncertain what to do next. Joe had rejected all her suggestions, including an invitation for him to come and stay with his parents for a while, and she knew it was time to leave. She stood up, pushing the chair back slowly with her legs, scrabbling inside her head for the parting sentence that would make everything feel miraculously better. Just as she was about to give up, an idea came to her. 'If you want her back Joe,' she said, 'then make sure you're in work tomorrow.' He looked up sharply, interest sparking in his eyes. 'If you want her back,' repeated Janet with the growing confidence of an angler who feels the line tightening as the fish bites, 'you don't want to jeopardise your income.' Their eyes locked in mutual understanding. Drawing deeply on his cigarette he nodded, then tapped the delicate tube of ash into the stale tea and said, 'You're right there, Mum, the steady income's always been an attraction. If her new bloke is who I think he is, then he won't last long, 'cos I know for a fact he just does odd jobs.' He emitted a short, bitter chuckle, but his eyes were almost back to normal. 'I'm off Joe,' she said quickly, 'come and eat with us tonight if you want.' He walked her to the door, opened it and stood there as she walked down the three front steps. She turned back to give her son a smile of encouragement, but the expression froze on her lips as she saw the darkness in his eyes. He was staring in the distance with murderous intensity. Could he be a danger to himself or anybody else?

She prayed he would remember her advice about his job. In the office, surrounded by colleagues who thought well of him, he would be safe.

But Joe didn't go back to the office the following day.

*

That night Joe did not sleep, and through the passing of every slow hour of darkness Leanne taunted him. At three o'clock in the morning he heaved himself out of bed and went searching the house for alcohol he knew was not there, not a single drop anywhere, not in the fridge, not in the most secret corner of the highest shelves, not even in any of the empty cans or bottles in the bins. Then he searched for cigarettes even though he remembered smoking the last one just before going to bed. It was in that moment of desperation when the world was intent on refusing his every need that he saw the way forward. He was going to stop talking of killing himself and instead he was going to do it. He took a deep breath and a new calm descended upon him as his mind focused on what he had to do. He made himself a strong coffee, sat down and worked out exactly how he was going to put an end to his miserable existence. Unexpectedly the sleepiness that had eluded him earlier in the night now started to creep up on him. He went back to bed setting his clock for six thirty.

The alarm dragged him out of a very deep sleep but when he sat up on the edge of his bed his mind was clear. He got dressed with the strongest sense of purpose he had felt in a long time and went straight out to his shed where he gathered all the tape and insulating material he could find together with old dust sheets, towels and blankets. As he walked back to the house, he felt the familiar pleasure of being in charge again, planning a job he knew he could execute successfully. Halfway down the garden however he stopped dead, insulating tape dangling from one arm and sheets from the other. A pink scooter lay on its side, abandoned in the grass. Zoe. An almighty struggle rose inside him, he could not give up his plan, not now, not when everything was so clear. But Zoe?

Zoe was gone, said a bitter voice inside his head, the bitch had taken her, the bitch would make sure he never saw his daughter again, and in any case, Zoe would be better off without the clashes and the rows and a father who was not up to the job. His insides tightened and he glanced at his watch. Seven. The corner shop would be opening now, and he could finally get that bottle of whiskey he had missed in the night. At the same time, he would post the letter he had written after getting up. He did not look back at the pink scooter in the grass.

Half an hour later Joe set to work in the kitchen.

*

18

At the same moment Janet woke up. She knew exactly what she wanted to do that morning, and she also knew precisely what David would have to say about it. 'Mind your own business.' But how could Joe's business not be her business when he was so obviously in need of help?

'Because' she heard David say in his long-suffering voice, 'you haven't been asked. Doing stuff in other people's houses when you haven't been asked is called interfering. Simple as that.'

She pressed her lips together, searching for a retort.

'Surely people can see your intention is good.'

'How would you like it,' asked David with one of his sarcastic smiles, 'if someone came over here and rearranged your house for you, according to their superior taste?'

'David,' she replied reproachfully, 'that's completely different. Joe is living in a pigsty. It's not about rearranging his house, just cleaning it up so he can feel happier and think more clearly.'

David's face was grinning back at her inside her head.

I'll go without telling David, Janet decided.

*

At eight thirty Janet told David she was off to town nice and early to avoid the crowds and he grunted back without looking up from his crossword puzzle. By that time Joe had got the doors and windows in the kitchen impeccably insulated and he was having a break and a long drink. Now he needed to think about maximising the amount of gas getting into his lungs quickly. A nice little challenge, he reflected as he sipped his whiskey, but not one to trouble him very much. He had a plan.

19

*

Janet parked in front of Joe's house and cast a fond glance at the bag of detergents, brushes, cloths and scourers on the passenger seat. But as she turned off the ignition, she was reined in by a sudden pang of doubt. Now that she didn't have to fight David's arguments against what he called interfering with their son's life, she could see the validity of his point. Was this really a good idea? She sat wavering for a few minutes, but the detergent bottles won the arguments. Whether Joe liked it or not, she was going to help her son think straight.

*

At that moment Joe was thinking straight. His mind was as clear and peaceful as he could remember. A job well done following the best decision he had ever made. The blanket was in place, the cushions were on the floor and as soon as he had downed the last drop in the bottle he would lie down, stick his head in under the blanket and turn the gas on. He could not fail.

*

Janet pulled the keys out of the ignition decisively but David's voice in her head stopped her again. 'Leave the boy to sort himself out, Jan, otherwise he will never learn.' She knew she shouldn't go. She knew she was meeting her own need, not her son's need. She knew that whatever she did in that house this morning would not help. David was right. She inserted the key back into the ignition, started the engine and drove off slowly.

As she did Joe turned the gas on.

Janet drove home thinking she would tell David the truth about this morning and they would laugh about it over their morning coffee. Her heart tightened at the thought that Joe hadn't met a nice woman with whom he could have been happy the way she was with David. Her son's tormented face appeared before her and a new thought gripped her. She should not be going home to be happy. She should be in Joe's house giving what help she could. Men didn't read unexpressed needs and she shouldn't be held back by her husband's limitations. Joe needed her. She did a quick three-point turn and drove back to her son's house. It looked empty and forlorn, crying out for attention and care.

When she opened the front door the smell of gas hit her straightaway. 'Joe!' she screamed, rushing to the kitchen door. It wouldn't open, she pushed and shoved with strength she didn't know she had and finally, in a ripping sound of sticky tape, it gave way. In a split second she took in the scene. Joe's body was sticking out from the oven with his head and oven opening covered in a blanket carefully taped all around the edges of the oven. All the windows and doors sealed with paper and tape. In a moment of heart wrenching recognition, she saw her son's methodical and careful work at hand. She rushed to the oven, tore off the blanket and dragged him out, knocking an empty bottle of whiskey over. He was unconscious, his face a light shade of blue, but he wasn't dead. She slapped him across the face, shook him, shouted his name. Then she rushed to the back door, ripped the tape off and pulled it wide open, letting the air in. Next, she came back to Joe and somehow found the strength to drag him by the shoulders into the garden. Her heart was drumming inside her chest as she cursed David for delaying her coming to the house. Men, she thought, bloody men. Stupid men. They don't understand anything, they don't understand what matters. Then she rushed back in and called an ambulance.

By the time the ambulance arrived Joe's colour was almost back to normal, but he hadn't opened his eyes. They rushed in carrying their oxygen bottle and got on with their job in a detached busy way. Janet stood around anxiously, feeling useless. She had managed in the time it took them to arrive to remove all the masking tape and rolled towels that Joe had used to seal off the room. To the ambulance drivers she repeated her story in a zombie like way. Her son had fallen asleep drunk in the kitchen after heating up a pizza and failing to properly turn the oven off. It was a ridiculous story, but the cooker was very old, and they went along with it. When they insisted on taking Joe to hospital, she didn't argue and got into the ambulance with them to make sure he didn't get a chance to tell his story. He opened his eyes as they arrived at the hospital and after a couple of hours of tests, the hospital discharged him. They caught a taxi home and sat in silence all the way, Joe with his head hanging low and Janet looking out of the window.

When they were finally on their own, standing in his small hallway, she turned on him.

'Why?' she asked, 'Why, Joe? Don't you understand what you were doing to all of us? What about Zoe? Didn't you think of Zoe?'

He looked away, a stubborn resentful look stamped on his face.

'And don't pretend,' added Janet with anger lifting her voice, 'that you wish you were dead. Have the honesty to at least say thank you.' She was glaring at him. They had drifted into the television room and Janet didn't try to hide the disgust in her voice and on her face. 'No wonder your life doesn't seem worth living any more Joe. Look at this mess. We didn't bring you up to…'

'Stop it,' he said. He was standing with his back to his mother, staring off with unfocused eyes into the mess of brambles and weeds that was his back garden. 'Stop it, you don't know what it's like to be me. You don't have any idea.' He fell silent again.

'I know what it's like to have a son who has just tried to kill himself, so don't tell me my life is simple and easy. You've had nothing but love and support from us, but you don't pay us back in kind Joe.' Her voice was quivering with distress as she faced the son she loved and hated all at once at this moment. 'Did it cross your mind how I would feel if I found you dead on your kitchen floor or if I had a phone call from the police? Did you think about that?' Her voice rose and trembled.

Joe had thought of people finding him, Leanne mainly, and he had hoped they would feel guilty. They hadn't understood him, hadn't supported him and now he was dead, and it was too late. He knew it hadn't been his main motivation, but he had enjoyed those thoughts. It was important to hide that fact from his mother.

'If you think,' she hissed in his back, 'that I would have been all weepy and sorry for my poor little boy, then think again.' Joe felt his head and neck shrink into shoulders. 'I would have had no such thoughts,' she continued angrily 'and I don't have them now. I am furious with you, Joe. Furious with you for being so selfish and weak.' She let a long breath out, looked around and screwed up her nose in disgust at smells she abhorred, not just because of the reek but because of the story they told. She had come over to clean a house that she now found was beyond cleaning. A house tainted with the smell of moral turpitude. She thought of Zoe and closed her eyes. How had a grandchild of hers come to grow up in this environment?

She spun on her heels and marched out of the house, slamming the front door behind her as she left. The minute she got into her car guilt overwhelmed her and she sat dejected, her hand limp on the ignition key. She must go back and apologise. How could she have spoken like that to her own son who had been desperate enough to try and kill himself? How could she have put her own feelings before his?

Just then her mobile rang from inside her handbag. It would be David, wanting to know if she was coming back for lunch. She flicked it open and pressed it to her ear, wondering what she would tell her husband. But it wasn't David. It was Joe.

'I'm sorry, Mum,' he said.

A weight lifted from Janet, but she knew she mustn't show it. Being angry with Joe had worked and she didn't want to lose any ground. 'We need to talk about where we go from here, Joe,' she said. 'Shall I come back in for five minutes?'

There was a silence. 'If you want to,' he said.

As she pushed herself out of the car, she knew she should have gone home and let him come to her when he was ready. Now she was being weak, but she wouldn't stay long. She breathed in deeply and turned her face into the sharp February wind.

The door was ajar when she got to it and she walked in softly. Joe was sitting in the front room, looking grim. Janet sat in the other armchair and waited for her son to speak.

'I hadn't slept all night,' he said staring off into the distance, 'I'd drunk too much, hadn't eaten, and all I could see was what I'd lost. Couldn't face life without all that.' He fell silent. Janet didn't speak either. He looked up, 'I still can't see much point to my life, but I don't want to be dead anymore.'

Janet looked down at her hands. This was as much as she was going to get in the way of a thank you, and she knew not to push her luck. 'I just wanted to agree with you who we tell about this,' she said, 'I don't see the need to tell anyone really.' She was thinking that should a custody battle develop, it would not help her son to be seen as mentally or emotionally unstable. She looked up and her clear blue eyes met his dark gaze.

'Too late Mum,' he snorted bitterly. 'I posted a letter to Leanne.'

'Saying?'

'Saying that when she read the letter, I would be dead,' he said derisively.

'But you're not dead,' replied Janet quickly.

'Exactly, I look like a complete arsehole.'

'No Joe, you look like someone who never tried.' Joe looked into his mother's eyes in silent wonder. How come he hadn't thought of that himself? 'Except for David nobody needs to know about this,' added Janet suggestively. Joe was staring at the floor and in the awkward silence that followed Janet got up to leave.

'Mum.' he said and stopped as if the thought in his head wouldn't quite form or wouldn't come out. Janet sat down again very slowly, poised on the edge of her seat.

'Mum,' he started again, 'I would be a better son to you if I was a stronger man.' Janet held her breath. 'I know,' he continued, still looking at the carpet, 'how much you help me, and I am grateful, but it makes me feel like a little boy, and I hate that feeling. That's why I'm so unpleasant.' Joe looked up at his mother surprised to find that speaking his painful truth had made him feel stronger not weaker. He felt tears in his eyes, and he let them roll down his cheeks without shame. Through the blur he thought he glimpsed a flicker of pride in his mother's eyes.

3. The Fight Begins

Seven weeks into her new life Leanne was pleased at how things had panned out for her. Leaving Joe had been a year in the making as she needed a job, a place to live and a new man. Six months ago, she had landed the job at the estate agent's, after which she was able to keep an eye on flats that were coming up for rent. One day she saw the flat right above her own office flash at her on the screen and she snapped it up, putting a deposit down straightaway. She left Joe three weeks later. Her relationship with Ivor was a few months old, and in that time, he had agreed to take on a full-time job as a lorry driver so they could move in together. He had had to accept she had no right to Joe's house because, as she explained, it belonged to his parents and he was in effect paying them rent. She had a niggling feeling she hadn't played her cards well with regards to the house, but she didn't want to think back on all that. Joe's parents had never liked her, and she had been a little bit in awe of them. The main thing was, Joe was paying child maintenance and it didn't look like there was going to be any fuss over custody. But if there was, Joe had gifted her a trump card with his pathetic letter about killing himself. A man with suicidal tendencies could kiss goodbye to custody of his daughter.

Leanne had expected trouble with Zoe because the girl was so close to her dad and her grandparents and sure enough, there had been a few rows at the beginning, but Leanne had dealt firmly with her daughter. She had also allowed her to spend time with her father and there had been visits to the grandparents. On the recommendation of a friend, Leanne had taken Zoe out on her own for some quality time together. The girl was quiet these days, but the friend had said not to worry, children take a while adjusting to a new situation and Zoe was also having to adjust to Ivor's presence. Those two didn't get on but they were learning to leave each other alone. The last three weeks in the flat had been all right, and Zoe's school report had said she was doing fine.

Such were Leanne's reflections as she packed her suitcase to go on her first holiday with Ivor, a week in the south of Spain, without the girls. Jessie was staying with her nan and Zoe was spending Easter week with Joe. *And that*, thought Leanne, *was the beauty of split families, you could have your children in your life but have your holidays without them.*

*   .

'I'm not going back.'

Zoe stared up defiantly at her father. She knew she was edging close to victory. His effort to argue with her was transparently half-hearted and in any case, the night before, she had overheard him telling Granny on the phone that he had a good mind to put up a fight and demand custody. Her heart had stopped and then sprung somersaults inside her chest as she tiptoed back to bed from the bathroom. But this morning there had been no mention of anything to do with custody and Zoe had felt tension mounting inside her until it seemed she was going to burst with it. They were well into Easter week, and she was due to go back to Mum and Ivor the day after next. It was time to act. She had started the conversation by saying she didn't want to go back and going over all her complaints about life in the flat. Her dad struggled with this, she knew, but he made her go back after every visit. This time however a whole week of happiness had strengthened her resolve and she was prepared to put up a fight.

Dad sighed and turned to look out of the window. This was a good sign. Zoe was sitting in the yellow armchair with her arms tightly wound around her drawn up knees and a hurt pout on her face. Inside her chest a bubble of hope was forming, but she kept perfectly still in case the slightest movement broke whatever spell was working on Dad. She watched his back, tall and strong, with slightly stooping shoulders like Grandad's, and something tightened in the pit of her stomach. She wanted to get up and hug him from behind and tell him she loved him more than anyone in the world, but she wasn't sure this would help her cause. Instead, she must stick with the tactics that worked, saying she hated living with Mum and that horrible man who lived with them now. That worked. She could see the angry glow in Dad's eyes when she told him about that man. Zoe's heart beat faster at the thought she might not have to go back to the hated flat where she felt she had three enemies and not one friend. At the thought that back in the flat nobody would love her she felt tears welling in her eyes.

'Dad,' she blurted out, forgetting all about tactics, 'why can't I just live here with you? It's my home. Why can't I have the life I want?' The moment the words were out, she knew it was a mistake. She'd asked these questions a million times before and the same answers came predictably back to her about children being too young to understand what's good for them… blah… blah… blah… She stared at her feet, disappointed with herself. She had also allowed her voice to go thin and whiny, and that never produced good results. She might have lost all the ground gained earlier that morning. She felt hopeless.

Dad turned around and looked down at her in silence. She met his eyes with a desperate plea in hers. With a deep sigh he ran his fingers through his curly hair and stood wavering. The bubble of hope came back. Her heart became so loud inside her chest she wondered if her father could hear it, but what really worried her was her breathing. If she had an asthma attack now, it would ruin everything. She hadn't needed her inhaler once since being with Dad and asthma attacks, she understood, counted against whoever she was with. Ripples of stress were moving dangerously towards the place where she knew her breathing got blocked. Easing out of her curled position she stretched her legs, closed her eyes and tried to relax her lungs, the way Nan had told her to do that first time. Slow breathing, in and out, just enough air to keep going, just a sliver of air slipping through, beating the blockage, in and out, her mind was now fully engaged in beating the blockage, in giving her lungs just enough air to keep going without needing the inhaler.

'All right,' said Dad, 'I'll phone and leave her a message saying you're not going back.' Before Zoe had time to open her eyes, he had marched out into the hall. She heard him pick up the phone and tap the number in. The tightening in her chest had eased, but now she was holding her breath. She straightened herself up. Was he really going to say she wasn't going back? Her heart pounded loudly in the silence. Then he started talking in that awkward stilted tone people use when they're talking to an answer phone. Zoe could also hear the controlled nervousness in his voice, and she knew Mum would hear it too. 'Hello, this is a message for Leanne from Joe. Zoe wants to stay and live here with me, Leanne. She is distressed about having to leave her home and going back to your flat, so I've said she can stay here. This is to do with what she wants, Leanne, and we should be putting her first. I hope you will see the sense in that. Good-bye Leanne.' The phone clicked back into place.

'Well, it's done,' said Dad walking back into the front room and dropping into the far side of the settee, facing Zoe. Father and daughter stared at each other in mild disbelief, searching for bearings in this baffling new reality. Zoe shifted in her chair uncomfortably, wondering if Dad had sounded just a little bit annoyed with her whilst Dad was certain he could read a doubt in his daughter's eyes. A lack of faith in him. The message he'd left for Leanne was not a good one, he was well aware of that and so was Zoe. He'd rushed it, like he rushed everything all the time. Except in work. When it came to figuring out why a computer was behaving in ways that infuriated everyone else, he experienced a profound feeling of peace and control. A challenge with a logical solution to it.

With people it was the opposite. They could churn him up inside in no time and make him want to hit out, the way some stupid people want to hit their computers or chuck the remote across the room if the TV isn't working. Leanne had done that once and when he'd laughed out loud, she had looked at him with something like hatred in her eyes. But he knew that when

31

it came to people he was just as stupid. And by the look in Zoe's eyes, she knew it too. Didn't trust him, and he couldn't blame her.

'Shall we phone Granny?' asked Zoe, confirming his suspicion.

'Let's go there,' he replied, 'she said to come over for lunch.'

In the car they were silent. Zoe knew her fight to live with her dad would only take off if Granny could be roped in. Joe knew the same. Neither of them had great faith in his powers of persuasion.

When they got to Granny and Grandad's house, nothing was said about Zoe not going back to the flat. Grandpa got a couple of beers out of the fridge and Grandma disappeared straight back into the kitchen. Zoe shot pointed glances at her father which he pretended not to see. Tension mounted inside her. How could her father be talking football with Grandpa when this enormous piece of news was making her ill with anxiety? What if Granny and Grandpa were against it? She knew exactly what would happen then. Dad would blow his top for a while and Granny would just wait for him to calm down again. And then she would start. 'Don't you see Joe the consequences of doing that?' and she would reel off one argument after another, and Dad would argue back that he was doing it anyway, and he wasn't a kid anymore, and this would go on for another half hour by the end of which Joe would be agreeing with everything she said. Zoe couldn't bear the thought of it. Yet there was Dad, talking rugby now after exhausting the topic of how Arsenal were doing. She could have screamed.

When Gran walked back in, drying her hands with a tea towel, Zoe sat up and stared hard at her father, but he avoided her eyes. She understood it was vital to bring the subject up in the right way at the right moment, and no doubt Dad was waiting for that perfect moment. She bit the fleshy side of her lower lip and followed the family into the dining room. Once at the table she gave her father a light prod with her foot, but he just pulled his leg away without responding. A large oval dish of pasta bake sat in the middle of the table covered in light brown bubbles of melted cheese, and Zoe knew that as long as her issue had not been aired, she would not enjoy a single mouthful. A sentence began to form inside her head and her heart responded with an unwarranted explosion of loud beating. It threw her. Her mouth went dry and her thoughts became muddled up. She tried to hang on to her sentence like a drowning person to a piece of wood, but it slipped away from her and she felt herself sinking. Granny was still standing behind her chair with her oven gloves on her hands, asking if anything was missing from the table. Grandpa's distant voice replied that everything looked splendid and why didn't Granny sit down and relax? Zoe knew she could not bear another minute of this tension. She took a breath and out it came, badly timed and badly worded, but off her chest.

'I'm not going back to Mum's,' she heard herself blurt out, 'Dad agrees and that's it, I'm not going back. I hate it there.' She looked up from her empty plate and, reaching out for the serving spoon in the middle of the table, she added almost innocently, 'May I help myself Granny?'

But Granny didn't reply. She was standing motionless, her blue oven gloves suspended in mid-air, her eyes fixed on her son's face, waiting for an explanation. She didn't look pleased. As for Grandad he kept looking from one to the other, as if convinced that something had been kept from him and incredulous that his wife seemed as surprised as he was. Slowly Zoe brought the serving spoon back down onto the table. She knew she had made her announcement in the worst possible way, with no tears or anything else to get anybody's sympathy and now she could see the cheese turning cold and rubbery. She hated soggy pasta. She knew she had just spoiled everything, and she would have to go back to Mum's the day after tomorrow, and that thought did bring tears to her eyes.

'She doesn't want to go back, Mum,' said Joe with a helpless shrug, 'what can I do?'

Granny's eyes came to rest on Zoe's face, and all the eyes around the table followed. The tears brimmed over and started running down with perfect unplanned timing. The three adults were silent, then looked at each other.

'Help yourself to pasta, love,' said Granny before turning away to take the oven gloves back to the kitchen. By the time she came back Zoe had a pile of steaming food on her plate and the cheese looked as if it was still soft and runny under the brown crust. She tucked in quickly. The debate would start up at some point but now Zoe didn't want to hear it. She had said what she had to say, and the adults could fight it out. She couldn't wait to finish her meal and leave the room to watch telly or perhaps play a computer game. She didn't want to hear all the arguments and she could tell that Granny had no intention of holding the debate in front of her anyway. She stuffed her mouth with pasta and swallowed it quickly. It was delicious and she told Granny so as she wiped her mouth, and at the same time asked if she could have her pudding in front of the telly. It was sticky toffee pudding, her favourite, and 'Yes' was the answer. She asked for ice cream to go with it and Granny said she would bring it over once everyone was ready. Zoe skipped out of the dining room and a moment later the sound of the television came on from the front room.

Janet helped herself deliberately to some salad, crunched through a couple of mouthfuls and then spoke.

'I don't think getting into a fight with Leanne is going to help anybody,' she said. Then she lifted a forkful of pasta to her mouth and looked at her son as she ate.

'Well, it's done now anyway,' shrugged Joe.

'What do you mean, it's done?' asked Janet more sharply than she intended.

'Left a message on Leanne's answer phone to say Zoe's not going back.'

Janet put her fork down and sat back in her chair with a quick glance at her husband before looking at Joe again. So far David was not giving anything away. Just eating. Leaving it to her.

'Mum, she hates it there, you know it as well as I do. I feel like shit every time I take her back.' He shoved a mouthful of pasta into his mouth. 'Why can't she live where she wants to live?' he said, looking down as he piled more food onto his fork.

'Because everyone believes that children should live with their mother, Joe, and you know it.' Janet leaned forward as she said this, with her hands flat on the table. 'That is what society thinks.'

'Well then let's fight that,' replied Joe looking up at his mother, 'because in Zoe's case that is wrong.'

'But is this about fighting for Zoe or is it about fighting Leanne?' Janet snapped back.

Joe was silent, mopping up the last of the sauce on his plate with a piece of bread as if nothing more important needed his attention.

'Your mother's right,' David butted in, 'fighting Leanne won't do anybody any good. It certainly won't help Zoe, and there's no way she'll ever be allowed to live with you.'

'Why not? I'm the one who loves her. Leanne never did. For some reason she never took to Zoe.'

'That's not what you told us at the time Joe,' Janet cut in, unable to stifle the irritation in her voice.

'If you two are going to gang up against me, I'm going home.' Joe had put his fork and knife down on the table and looked at his parents with a just-when-I-need-you, you're-letting-me-down sort of look. It worked. Janet reached out to him and lay her hand over his. 'You know we're trying to help, don't make it difficult Joe. You know we would do anything for you and Zoe.' Joe shrugged as if he wasn't so sure and knew as he did it that he was being disingenuous. He looked up at his parents and felt a knot of affection for them tighten around his gullet. It frightened him to feel that, made him feel weak, pathetic and horrifically close to tears. All the things a man was not supposed to feel. But suddenly he felt too tired to struggle against their love and all his defences collapsed around him, like so many cards tumbling down to scatter on the table. No more castle.

He looked up at his mum and dad. 'I know you want to help,' he sighed. 'It's just that I can't seem to cope with anything.' He paused, looking down at his hand scratching a bit of sauce off the tablecloth. This kind of confession was both painful and a relief. He looked up at his mother, then past the side of her face into an invisible distance. 'I get so churned up inside…' he shook his head, in despair at himself, 'so churned up, it's unbearable.' His eyes came back into focus and he looked at one parent after the other, with a soft apology in his eyes.

There was a silence as Janet rapidly discarded one response after another, terrified to say the wrong thing and shatter the moment. A glance at her husband told her he was struggling too, for different reasons. You don't live together for over forty years without developing connections and synapses that convey meaning without the need for language. David was clearly in the silent throes of fighting his irrepressible tendency to cringe at the sight of vulnerability in another man. He knew it was wrong to feel this, but he only knew it because he had been told, not because he really knew. The way he was gazing down at his knife as if it had become an object of sudden fascination told Janet that he was most probably going over all the reasons why he must bypass the disappointment he felt in his son and muster up some sympathy instead.

'You think I'm pathetic,' mused Joe, 'and I don't blame you. When I'm not in front of a computer or cheering for Arsenal, I feel pathetic myself. I'm sorry I'm such a disappointment to you both.' Mild hostility had crept back into his voice.

'Don't think like that, Joe.' replied David, looking up into his son's eyes. 'You've just opened up to us about your… your… vulnerability.' David paused after the effort of forcing out of his mouth such an alien word. 'That,' he resumed, 'takes courage.' He let out a short bitter laugh. 'Nothing is quite as painful as taking a long honest look at yourself. Let alone sharing the conclusions with anyone else.'

'You say that,' replied Joe, 'but I get the feeling there aren't many weaknesses to blemish the picture you see in the mirror.'

'I have doubts about plenty of things, Joe, and to give you only one example, I have doubts about the kind of father I was to you.'

'You do?' asked Joe incredulously.

'Yes.' David darted a quick, slightly embarrassed glance in his wife's direction. He took a breath before carrying on. 'I had an idea of what my son should be like and I'm afraid I couldn't stop myself wanting you to fit into it. No need to go into any details, I think we both know what I'm talking about.'

'So?' asked Joe, with a hint of challenge in his voice. Janet winced and saw David's mental hackles rise with frightening predictability. But he quickly mastered his aggressive impulse and carried on calmly, 'So I think I knocked your confidence and I feel bad about that.'

'Hell, Dad, thanks for telling me I lack confidence. That really helps.' Joe's tone was openly sarcastic, and David cast his wife a helpless glance. *See how it backfires,* he seemed to say, *when I try to do the right thing?*

'Joe…' Janet started to say in a placating tone, but her son stopped her with a raised hand.

'Never mind about all that,' he said, 'the main thing is, if you two agree that parents can damage their kids, then you should be right behind me when it comes to keeping Zoe away from Leanne and her new boyfriend. Never mind what I said in the past Mum, and let's talk about now. Leanne doesn't love Zoe, and Zoe knows it. That's why she doesn't want to go back there. She doesn't feel safe there, she doesn't feel she's got a home there. Now are we going to fight for her right to be where she's happy and thriving, or are we going to let Leanne have her way?' He looked from one parent to the other and, one after the other, they lowered their eyes to the table.

Silence descended. Animated TV voices reached them from the other room, ringing with artificial jolliness. Then suddenly Zoe's laughter broke out, true and abandoned, the simple laughter of a happy little girl falling about on the couch, her head thrown back and her body shaking with hilarity.

'All right,' said Janet with a sigh, 'we'll fight for Zoe.'

Then she got up, cleared the plates and returned from the kitchen carrying a tray with four bowls of hot pudding and ice cream. Joe picked one up and took it to his daughter in the front room. Zoe looked up at him questioningly and he winked back. Her face brightened up and she straightened herself up as she extended her hand to take the bowl. 'They agree?' she whispered. Dad nodded back, sat down next to her and wrapped his arm around her shoulders. 'It may not be easy, sweetheart, but I'm going to bring you home, I promise you that.'

But Joe had no idea what he was taking on, no idea that over the next few years he would be tested to the limit and that sadly he would, on many counts, be found wanting.

4. Child Protection Get Involved

As Leanne opened the front door to the flat on their return from the best holiday ever, she noticed the light flashing on the phone. *Work* she thought, picking up the handset whilst flattening herself against the wall to make space for Ivor to get by.

She listened to the message, slowly following Ivor into the kitchen. Something in her silence made Ivor stop and turn around, waiting to hear what it was about. When she looked up her face was white and her eyes cold with fury. 'Bastard!' she hissed, 'What a bastard, taking advantage of my first holiday away. He is going to pay for this.' The tone was familiar, and Ivor knew exactly who the bastard was.

'What's he done now?' he asked cautiously, slitting his eyes.

'He's not bringing her back. Keeping her with him.' The rage in her eyes felt as if it was directed at him.

'Why?'

''Cos she doesn't want to come back here, that's why. Can you believe it?'

Ivor thought he could believe it. The kid was utterly spoiled and determined to wreck everybody's life. He carried on towards the fridge and a much-needed drink of beer.

'Look,' he said, popping the top off one bottle, 'All we need to do is drive over there, stick the kid in the car and come back. We're not frightened of her, are we?' He put the bottle to his lips, took a long draught and set to opening the other bottle.

'You don't get it, do you?' snapped Leanne, reaching for the beer offered to her. 'We do that and play straight into her hands. If she can say we bully her, she'll have a case to live with her dad. No, I'll get the police to fetch her, first thing in the morning.' All desire to sleep had deserted Leanne and what she wanted now was to skip the night and be on that phone to the police to tell them what that bastard was doing to her. Kidnapping her daughter in effect. How did he think he was going to get away with it? She gulped her beer down, throwing her head back. The cool liquid spread wide inside her body and brought just the kind of soothing she needed. 'Bastard,' she repeated, more calmly. Ivor was leaning against the kitchen top, drinking with the intensity of a baby holding tight to his bottle. The thought made her smile. 'Perhaps,' she said, after taking another long draught, 'it might be wiser to get Social Services to go there. Then nobody can say I didn't try nicely first. What do you think?' The question was rhetorical as Leanne never had much time for his suggestions, least of all when it came to the girls.

'Interfering bastards.' he said.

Leanne looked at him twirling at a long strand of hair around a finger. 'True,' she agreed, 'but if they're going to be involved, and you can bet your life they will, I'd rather they heard my point of view first.' She knocked back the rest of her beer and set the empty bottle down on the table. 'Yes,' she mused, 'I'll go and see Social Services first thing in the morning. You could say my daughter's been abducted, couldn't you? So, she's in need of protection, isn't she?' She gave a throaty chuckle.

Ivor finished his beer without replying, burped loudly and said he was knackered and going to bed. Leanne followed him with her mind already rehearsing the following morning's visit to Social Services.

*

Gerald Crispin lowered himself carefully into his seat and placed the steaming cup of coffee in his hand on the mat by the computer. As usual he was first in the office, and he knew that being first in, ever since he started working in the Child Protection Team, had gone a long way towards getting him his promotion last July. He was now Senior Practitioner and hopefully on his way to a team manager's job, which would make his wife Karen very happy. He reached for the pile of papers in his in-tray before facing the inevitable twenty or thirty new emails in his inbox. All because he'd had to attend a stupid training event the previous day. Colleagues and secretaries had covered for him and he scanned through their notes, prioritising as he went along. The McCall family had had another alcohol fuelled crisis and the three children had gone to their grandmother's, as happened on a monthly basis – case conference needed. He put the paper to one side. Angela Richards, teenage nightmare of the decade, had gone on another rampage in the town centre and sunk her teeth in the hand of the police officer trying to control her. He shook his head and picked up the next message.

Rapid footsteps announced the first arrival in the office. Gerald looked up and Adele waved as she caught his eye. The others would follow now, one after the other, filling the space with their noise and bustle, phone calls, keyboard clatter, until his head was bursting with it. When his boss, the decisive Gail, had wanted him to work in the room with the others he had swallowed his resentment and agreed. Karen had chided him, 'If you don't learn to say no, honey, people will trample all over you.' People did trample all over him.

Just as he was starting to read the next note, the secretary rang through with the message that a woman was demanding to see someone at once. Someone senior, Linda added. The woman's daughter had been abducted by her former partner and she was very worried. Leanne Davies was her name, child's name was Zoe Milton. With a sinking feeling in his stomach Gerald gulped down the rest of his coffee, picked up his notebook and rejoiced he had put on a suit that morning. Chairing that dreaded case conference at two o'clock that afternoon was proving of use after all. He hated chairing case conferences. He also hated dealing with angry parents, but a suit helped to give him the substance he secretly knew wasn't there. Not that he was not clever, because he was, but he couldn't stand confrontation. He stood up and walked stiffly out and down the corridor towards the small interview room.

Half an hour later Linda watched Gerald and the woman with the mane of blond hair walk past her window towards the door that led out of the Social Services department. He looked manly and protective next to the small woman clutching a tissue in her hand. No doubt the father would storm through the same door later that day or the following day, shouting and bawling that he wanted to speak to someone now, this minute, and it had better be someone senior. Then the battle would start. Over the kid, but maybe not about the kid. No matter what, it would be hell for that kid, she saw it happening all the time. She expected Gerald to stop and have a word on his way back from the door, but he didn't. Didn't even look at her. She turned back to her computer.

Gerald walked straight back to his desk his mind fully absorbed by the interview he had just conducted with the upset mother. He picked up his empty mug and headed for the kitchen. A second coffee was needed. As he waited for the kettle to boil, he thought about the woman. She had been convincing, and yet something about her was bothering him and he couldn't quite put his finger on what it was. He chucked a spoonful of coffee in his mug, poured the boiling water and ambled back to his desk, still thinking. Perhaps if he stopped thinking about it the answer would come.

He picked up his phone and reluctantly dialled the police station. At the end of the day, he would, as promised, drop in on Joe Milton and ask him nicely to take his daughter back to her mother, but given the violent nature of the man, it would be safer to have a police officer with him. He sighed and sighed again when he heard that PC Harries would be the one accompanying him on this occasion. Maureen Harries was a big woman whose judgements formed and hardened before she could be bothered to hear anybody else's point of view. Particularly if the 'anybody else' was a social worker. Gerald hung up and sent his wife a text to say he would be a little late that evening. A moment later he got a text back asking him to give her a ring at lunch time. He put this second puzzle out of his mind and got on with the business of the day.

When he phoned his wife at one o'clock, she picked up immediately.

'It's about Lucy,' she said. His heart tightened. Their daughter was on a school trip to New York. 'There was an email from her this morning love, and I'm worried, I think she's homesick and I don't know…' Relief flooded Gerald and in the same instant he knew what had bothered him that morning about Leanne Davies' story.

There had not been a trace of concern in the mother's voice about her daughter's welfare. Could it be that the mother didn't care about the girl? Or was she not concerned because she knew the daughter was perfectly happy and safe with her father? But what kind of child does not want to live with her mother? He would find out later that day.

*

At five fifteen, flanked by the solid shape of PC Harries, Gerald Crispin rang the bell of Joe Milton's house, 52 Grove Road. A terraced house whose door needed a coat of paint, but which, apart from that, looked in pretty good nick compared to most of the houses Gerald had to visit in the course of his daily work. A curtain had twitched in the upstairs front room, but nobody came to open the door. The house was silent, but clearly not empty. Gerald rang again and they waited. This was not unusual. People in trouble don't open their doors willingly. Suddenly Gerald felt glad he had the policewoman with him.

Just at that moment a lock turned, and the door moved slowly inwards. The face of a little girl with light reddish hair appeared in the opening with large grey-blue eyes that examined them in silence. Steps sounded behind her and the door opened widely. A tall lanky man with curly brown hair stood behind her and asked them what they wanted. They introduced themselves and got taken into the front room. A tidy room with a large old-fashioned settee and a couple of armchairs, a few pictures on the walls and some china ornaments dotted around. The place was clean, beyond criticism. Gerald and Maureen sat on the couch and the man lowered himself slowly into one of the armchairs facing them. His daughter came to crouch on the floor by his side, snuggling up tight against his leg.

Gerald cleared his throat. 'Mr Milton, you probably know why we're here and…'

'I don't actually,' replied Joe. Hostility rippled lightly below the surface of his voice. Zoe couldn't see her dad's face, but his tone told her everything she needed to know. She pictured the scowl cutting deep lines in his forehead and felt his resentment radiating out into the room. From under her eyebrows Zoe observed the other two. The woman reminded her of Mrs Coleman in school, with hard little eyes ready to stare you out. Zoe tightened her arms around her drawn up knees. Her dad was explaining that this was the home where she had grown up, where she had all her friends nearby and where she wanted to live. He also said that her mother had left for her own reasons and he didn't see why their daughter's life should be disrupted when he was happy to look after her in her home.

'It's very unusual for a little girl not to want to live with her mother,' insinuated the policewoman, turning to Zoe. 'Can you tell us why you don't want to go home to your mum Zoe?' she asked in the artificial tone reserved for children. Her eyes seemed to nail Zoe to the floor as she said it and the girl stared back in silence, her mouth half open. The man was also looking down at her and suddenly all she wanted to do was run out of the room and hide under her bed. She looked up at her father pleadingly. *Send these people away, please, please send them away,* said her eyes.

'Zoe's a little shy,' Joe said, laying a gentle hand on his daughter's head. 'Particularly with strangers. The situation with her mother is not ideal. There are tensions with the new boyfriend and with her half-sister. She's not happy there.'

'But it would be good to hear that from the girl herself, wouldn't it, Mr Milton?' the policewoman butted in pointedly.

'Are you suggesting I'm making this up?' snapped Joe.

'We're not suggesting that, Mr Milton,' intervened the social worker. He cleared his throat slightly before continuing. 'Your partner, Ms Leanne Davies, wishes for her daughter to go back to her today. I'm sure you'll understand that Zoe is too young to decide where she lives, and it would be best if you encouraged her to go back to her mother of her own accord.' He paused and waited for Joe to respond, but the man had nothing to say. 'We hope,' he continued, 'you will listen to reason, and the matter can be resolved amicably today. A child caught in a custody battle suffers whatever the outcome.' With these words he looked down at Zoe with concern and she thought he might not be her enemy. Not like the woman anyway. But then the man looked towards the policewoman and Zoe glimpsed the nervousness in his glance. He was frightened of her, which meant that even if he wasn't her enemy, he wouldn't be much help either.

Her father's fingers had been gently resting on her head, but now they tensed up and almost gripped her skull. She glanced up at him and recognised the signs that came before an explosion of temper. She quickly looked down again, swallowing hard. Although it was good to know her father felt the same as she did about the two intruders, she feared his temper. It never produced good results. She felt a tightening in her chest and heard the air wheezing in and out of her gullet. Her father heard it too. He glanced down at her, gave her head a reassuring stroke before speaking.

'I don't think you understand Mr… err, Mr…?'

'Crispin,' said Gerald.

'Mr Crispin. My daughter is unhappy living with her mother, the new man and the stepsister. They gang up on her.' His voice was rising, and Zoe looked down at her trainers, hunching her shoulders. 'If Zoe's mum can't treat her daughter so the girl wants to be there, that's not my fault, is it? And don't expect me to tell her she has to go back, because I'm her father and it's my job to protect her. Do you understand what I'm saying, Mr Crispin? Or perhaps you haven't got a daughter, you don't know what it means to see your own child unhappy?'

'I do have…' started Gerald defensively.

'Mr Milton' interrupted the policewoman, 'you need to understand certain things too. One of them is that you have no right to keep your daughter away from her mother. We will not take Zoe forcibly today, as we have come in a spirit of conciliation, but I can assure you that she will have to go back to her mother. I daresay many children have gripes about the way their parents bring them up, and children don't like discipline. But that doesn't mean they can walk out on their parents, does it? Zoe will have to learn that she is no exception to this rule.'

Zoe was aware that the policewoman had not looked at her once as she made her little speech. This was a matter for adults to decide. Zoe didn't count. Fear gripped her chest again as she felt how powerless she was, and although she knew that her father would never stop being on her side, she also understood that she didn't have faith in his ability to be on top of a situation. Supporting her dad in a conflict was like supporting a beloved football team even when you knew in your heart of hearts that they didn't have much chance of winning.

'Is that all you have to say?' asked her father after a short silence.

'Let's just recap,' said the policewoman. 'You are not going to take Zoe back to her mother tonight?'

'No,' replied Joe.

'And you are not prepared to let us take her back to her mother?'

'No,' said Joe again.

'And you, young lady,' said Maureen to the girl, 'are not prepared to let us take you back to your mother?'

'No,' muttered Zoe in a thin voice, 'I want to live here with Dad.'

'In that case,' the policewoman declared pompously, 'I expect the matter will have to be resolved in court.'

She hoisted herself up, looked at the social worker and he stood up too, like a puppet on a string. They gave a curt little nod as they filed out of the room and Zoe's father followed them, shutting the door with a little slam as they left.

They walked in silence to Gerald's car. As Maureen curled her hand around the door handle, she spoke. 'We got the measure of the man, don't you think?' Her voice did not allow for disagreement. As Gerald lowered himself away from her eyes and into his seat, he had a few seconds to relive the moment when Joe Milton had put his hand on his daughter's head. It was such a familiar gesture that he had almost felt his own hand resting on Lucy's head and the surge of simple love that travelled straight from his fingers to his heart. He had seen that same surge travel between the girl and the father as she imperceptibly rubbed her head into the hand that loved her.

'He seemed a caring dad,' Gerald said staring ahead as he started the engine.

'Honestly,' said Maureen, with a despairing shake of the head, 'you social workers are such suckers. The man puts his hand on the kid's head and Bob's your uncle, he's a loving father. No wonder so many tragic cases slip through the net.' Gerald by now had the car out on the road and was very glad to have an excuse not to look back at her. He could not however avoid feeling the weight of her disdain on the left side of his face. 'I'm not saying he's out to hurt the child,' continued Maureen in the exasperating voice of someone with superior expertise in family interactions, 'but you saw how she had nothing to say at all. He's prepared to set her against her mother for the sake of his own revenge. I call that emotional abuse.'

The woman is a complete moron, thought Gerald as he found himself taking a round-about in the wrong lane and nervously wondering if he was going to have the nerve to push in and take the exit anyway. His eyes were riveted on the side mirror on Maureen's side and luckily the car coming up on his left slowed down and let him in.

'Nice man,' commented Maureen, 'but strictly speaking you were in the wrong lane.' She gave a rich chuckle and Gerald felt his hatred for the woman rise and fill his head.

'I cannot agree with you about the idea of emotional abuse,' he picked up after a moment of silence. 'The word abuse implies maltreatment. Maltreatment implies intention. There is absolutely no evidence in this case of any maltreatment by the father. Even the mother, angry as she was, didn't try to push that idea. Emotional abuse is a serious accusation that should not be made lightly.' Gerald reverse-parked neatly in front of the police station and turned his head to look at PC Harries with a hint of triumph at the back of his eyes. He had enjoyed the logic and accuracy of his own reasoning.

'And I say that a father who tries to alienate his daughter from her mother is maltreating her.' Maureen was wagging her finger, not at him exactly, but at whoever disagreed with her, and that certainly included him. 'What can be more important for a child's emotional health than to love both her parents? This to me is a clear case of emotional abuse.' With this she shot Gerald a superior smile, pushed her door wide open and swivelled her legs out. Once out she stuck her head back in to drop her closing words, 'If you need to go back there don't hesitate to give me a ring.' She smiled sarcastically and shut the door with a perfectly controlled little slam.

*

Meanwhile Leanne was still in the office, working late to make up for her visit to Social Services that morning. All was quiet at the estate agent's and she was able to keep an eye on what was happening in the street outside. Her flat was right above the office and she positioned herself at her desk to see her own front door even as she talked with Justine or answered the phone. The road throbbed with traffic flowing in and out of town along this main artery and the pavement was busy

51

with pedestrians passing outside the window. Women pushing buggies, men in suits, children in school uniforms and lots of students. Leanne watched these young lean bodies exuding an aura of late nights, sex, soft drugs and alcohol. Some good girls and good boys amongst them, discovering life. Watching them excited her. Landlord city, as she called the area, now had a rundown feel to it, which she liked. Cheap cafés, music bursting out of the Tavern opposite and the impersonal Spar down the road selling milk, cereals and beer to jean-clad students. She even liked the male and female oddballs in tramps' clothing who hung around the Spar's automatic doors like insects attracted to the light, hoping that an exchange of words with random strangers would break the silence of their days. Decay and young life. Booze and bedsits. Leanne felt at home here.

At four thirty she saw Jessie being dropped off by Nan and soon after she spotted Ivor's old Astra turning right to go and find a parking space in one of the back streets. She glanced at her watch. Five to five. No sign of Zoe. She grew excited at the thought of a police officer turning up on Joe's doorstep and a tiny smile tugged at her lips as she pictured him inevitably losing his temper. They would see what he was like, they would tell Zoe she had to go home to Mum, and her authority would be restored. She couldn't wait to see that police car roll up into the bus bay up the road and a defeated Zoe emerge out of the passenger door. But she would surprise the girl with kindness, take her under her wing, win her over. Especially with the police watching. Her long nails lightly beat a tune on the counter in front of her.

But the only vehicle to stop in the bus bay was the 161 into town. Three buses swung in to disgorge their passengers as

52

she watched with growing annoyance. She tried to ring Social Services but of course the lazy bastards were closed for the day. At six she left the office and stomped upstairs to the flat ready to explode with anger. Ivor met her at the door holding out a piece of paper. 'Phone number for that social worker,' he said and went back to the TV. Leanne rang the man she had labelled in her mind as the Wimp and got a convoluted explanation that was annoyingly devoid of the apology she deserved. And now he was suggesting she saw a lawyer.

'But I haven't got money to pay a lawyer,' she whimpered.

'Apply for Legal Aid. You need a lawyer to apply for a Residence Order, and that's the only way to get your daughter back,' he said for the second time.

Leanne found the will to thank him for his advice before switching off with a trembling finger. 'Bloody wimp, couldn't do the job himself,' she shouted. Jessie came running down to find out what had happened, and she followed her mum into the sitting room where Ivor was sprawled on the couch watching telly. Ivor's blank face turned towards Leanne, ready to listen and agree. He was the exact opposite of Joe, laid back to the point where sometimes you wanted to shake a reaction out of him. Still Jessie and Leanne agreed it was better than having a man who was argumentative and domineering. With his pint glass resting on his stomach Ivor waited for Leanne's fury to fill the room but it didn't happen. She lit up a fag, went to push the window open, and stood there thinking quietly, with her long hair gently lifted by the breeze blowing in.

'Anyway,' she finally said raising her chin and blowing a cloud of smoke into the cool evening air, 'that fucking wimp did give me one good piece of advice.' She gave one of her throaty chuckles. In answer to Ivor's raised eyebrows, she added, 'To see my lawyer.'

'You have a lawyer?' he asked.

'I do, a woman with the nature of a rottweiler. Lynne Savage.' She chuckled again. 'Good name, don't you think?' Ivor looked doubtful. He didn't like lawyers any more than he liked police officers or social workers. 'Believe me,' added Leanne dragging deep on her cigarette, 'a rottweiler is exactly what you want on your side when you're facing the opposition in court. Lynne Savage wins all her battles.'

*

Gerald left the office immediately after Leanne Davies' phone call, glad that a difficult day had finally come to an end. But he failed to discard work from his thinking as he drove home to the soothing melodies of Classic FM. He did not like the way Maureen, a police officer for goodness' sake, was playing psychologist and using cheap labels like 'emotional abuse'. He knew how Maureen worked. First thing in the morning she'd be on the phone to his team leader and if Gail bought the idea… his heart sank. At the same time, he was shaken by Maureen's argument. Could a child be brainwashed into not loving one of her parents? Suddenly he looked forward to being home and discussing the matter with Karen. With both children away on their half-term trips adult conversation over dinner would be possible.

When he got home, dinner was ready.

'This woman came to see me today,' he said, helping himself to mashed potatoes. Then he speared a fat sausage with his fork and dropped it on his plate, feeling his mouth water pleasurably.

'Yes?' asked Karen with a note of impatience in her voice.

'It looks like the usual thing. A woman caught up in a relationship with a violent man, a split up and a fight over the child. Nine-year-old girl.' He stopped talking to munch slowly through a piece of crisp broccoli.

'So?' prodded Karen.

'Something's bothering me about it, but I can't quite put my finger on it.' He put another piece of juicy sausage in his mouth.

'It might help if instead of keeping me guessing you told me what happened,' Karen said tartly, helping herself to more mashed potato.

'The girl spent Easter week with her dad and now the dad won't let her go back to her mum. Says the kid wants to stay with him, but the mother says he's just using their daughter to get back at her 'cos he didn't want her to leave.' He fell silent.

'Makes sense,' said Karen after swallowing a mouthful.

'Does it though?'

'The kid may well be influenced by her dad.'

'Do you really believe if that kid loved her mum the father could change that?' Gerald had stopped eating.

Karen carried on chewing on her mouthful of sausage in silence, looking down at her plate and spreading her mashed potato around with her fork. She didn't like being wrong, but as she thought of her own children, she knew her husband had a point. He read her mind.

'Do you think anybody could stop Stevie or Lucy loving you? That they'd refuse to live with you just because someone told them to?'

'No, I don't think anyone could do that, not even you. But in a nasty split-up, children can take sides. If the girl sees her dad as the victim, maybe she blames the mother.'

'Maybe. And maybe she is simply happier with her dad and that's where she wants to be.'

'Your food's going cold, love, and I'm not sure I agree with you. Nine is still very young to know your own mind.'

Possibly, thought Gerald, *but is it too young to know who you love and who loves you?* That night Gerald took a long time going to sleep. A little girl with large grey-blue eyes kept staring at him in the dark.

5. Lawyers Get Involved

The first phone call Leanne made the following morning was to her solicitor's secretary and after much wrangling and pleading she managed to get the woman to squeeze her in at lunchtime. At one twenty-five exactly she stood in front of the large, terraced house converted into offices and as she stared at her solicitor's shiny plaque, she felt the nervous beating of her heart inside her chest. She pushed the heavy wooden door and the dusty smell of old houses hit her nostrils. A smell of paper and books, like a headteacher's office. She pushed the frosted glass door with the word Reception on it and from behind her cluttered desk the tired looking secretary told her to take a seat in the waiting room. Nothing had changed here either, the same faded walls and worn chairs. It seemed to Leanne that someone like Lynne Savage should be operating within a more splendid environment. As the formidable image of Lynne Savage popped into Leanne's mind tension constricted her insides. Once again, she was reminded of the headteacher's office. Just then the secretary called her in.

Lynne did not look up as Leanne stepped into the room. She was signing a pile of letters, scanning the content before putting her illegible but elegant scrawl at the bottom. Leanne sat down and waited.

'Fire away,' said Lynne, looking up briefly.

Leanne launched into her grievances. Lynne listened with her eyes cast down, lightly tapping her pen on the blotting pad. Leanne was used to this and talked on. When she stopped Lynne looked up and said, 'Right. We'll go for an urgent interim residence order and the court will decide where your daughter lives and what contact arrangements they see fit to implement.'

'Will they say Zoe lives with me?' asked Leanne, quick to see the danger.

'I'll make sure they do,' replied Lynne reaching for the phone. She asked the secretary to bring in the required form and turned her attention back to Leanne. 'I need to know a few things,' she said, picking up her pen and pulling a large A4 notepad in front of her. Then she fired her questions. Leanne had not planned on telling her solicitor the exact truth, but she quickly found herself doing exactly that and as the picture emerged of a perfectly competent father who would never harm his daughter although he was capable of violent outbursts towards his partner, her belief in a successful outcome began to flag. The kid was asking to live with her dad, the dad was a good dad, and the mother was removing the child from her familiar environment. What hope did she have?

Lynne Savage carried on running the pen fast across the page in silence. Then she looked up.

'Emotional abuse,' she said cryptically. 'That's the line we're going to take.' The corners of her lips tugged with imperceptible scorn as she watched the woman sitting opposite her struggle to understand.

'Emotional abuse?' Leanne frowned.

'Your partner is alienating his daughter from her mother. Isn't that emotional abuse? Depriving a child of the most important person in her life?'

'But… but…' stammered Leanne, 'Zoe's saying she wants to live with her dad.' Her tone was apologetic as if she was ashamed to be telling this superior being that she had just overlooked a major factor.

'Brainwashing,' replied Lynne curtly. Then she paused and watched her client's face light up with slow understanding. The woman was not stupid, and it was important that she felt the understanding had come from within her. Lynne sat back and waited.

'Of course,' said Leanne and her voice trailed off as she gathered her thoughts. Then she added, 'and you know, it's not just him either. They're all brainwashing her. The grandparents, and that snooty sister of his, who thinks she's very superior because she's a teacher.' She snorted the word teacher, and then added, 'They've got money too. Zoe can have all she wants when she's over there. And Joe spoils her rotten. I'm the only one to bring a bit of discipline into that girl's life, Lynne.' Lynne flinched at the use of her first name, but let the other woman carry on. 'You'd think it was a sin to give the girl a smack when she deserves it.'

'I would not mention smacking if I were you,' Lynne butted in. 'Not the right image if you want to be seen as a loving mother.' Her blue eyes, cold like the sea, made prolonged contact with Leanne's.

'I know what you mean,' Leanne said quickly, allowing the picture to form of what was expected of her. She was clutching her handbag on her lap. 'It makes me angry that Joe's trying to take my daughter away from me, Lynne, but the worst part of it is he's trying to deprive Zoe of a caring mother.' The look of righteous indignation was what Lynne had been waiting for. Now she pushed the form towards her client and asked her to sign at the bottom. 'Save you coming back,' she said. 'I'll fill the form in, email you my draft and if you're happy I'll send it in.'

Leanne carefully filled the space with her large signature and stood up. She knew Lynne didn't like people hanging about a moment longer than necessary. 'When will I hear about court?' she asked.

'Soon,' was the brief answer. 'Make sure you dress appropriately.' Leanne nodded and left. Lynne watched her go, hoping she'd understood that the kind of low cut she'd been wearing today was the opposite of appropriate.

*

At two o'clock on Tuesday afternoon, just as Leanne was leaving her solicitor's office, Gerald knocked on his boss's door, ready with a well-rehearsed and carefully balanced explanation of what had happened on the visit to Mr Milton and his daughter the previous day. He had dismissed Maureen's ridiculous suggestion of emotional abuse. This was a simple case of conflict between parents and a residence order would resolve the matter. He walked in confidently and was pleased to see Gail with her head up and the shadow of a smile on her lips as she indicated for him to sit down.

'I understand it's a clear-cut case of emotional abuse,' she said, putting her pen down from signing a pile of minutes. She leaned back in her chair, peering at him with mild interest. Maureen had got there first and although he had been prepared for this, he had not expected Gail to be so blunt in her assessment before he had a chance to say a single word.

'It does look as if the father may be trying to influence the child,' he conceded, 'but the girl was too frightened to say anything to two complete strangers. She needs to be interviewed in a more congenial environment.'

'Quite,' replied Gail, pushing her fringe back, 'with her father nowhere in sight. She's not going to say in front of him that she loves her mum and wants to live with her, is she?' There was a note of sarcasm in her voice as she eyed her colleague with commiseration at his lack of insight. It takes women to see through these things, she seemed to be saying.

Gerald saw the father's hand on the girl's head again, the fingers gently stroking through the hair, the head tilting imperceptibly into the hand, the current of love passing discreetly between the father and the daughter, the trust and the hope contained in that simple gesture. He looked at the childless woman sitting opposite him behind her large desk and thought that perhaps she just didn't know anything about children, or perhaps she didn't like them, or didn't like to think she was missing a certain kind of love that other people had. Or perhaps, he went on to consider, she hadn't had children because she was a hard-hearted bitch who had nothing to give to anybody. What he said was: 'You're right, we must talk to her away from any outside influences. Would you like me to do it, or do you have someone else in mind?'

'It's your case, Gerald, you pick the best person for the job.'

A wave of hatred rose inside Gerald. Had he suggested someone for that delicate interview, she would have had an immediate objection and a ready alternative. But had he said he would do it she would have tilted her head to the left in that falsely pensive way of hers and asked whether he didn't think a woman might connect better with a little girl. Gail was a master at making people feel weak and incompetent.

'I'll give the matter some thought,' he replied evasively, getting up before she had a chance to dismiss him. As he put his hand on the door handle, she spoke again, stopping him in his tracks.

'Whoever talks to the girl needs to understand the point is to uncover emotional abuse. An unfocussed chat will be a waste of time. Kids are very good at protecting their parents, and she won't volunteer anything that might make her father look bad.' She paused. Gerald dropped his hand from the door handle and turned around, waiting. 'The answer I want from that interview is how the father has managed to make his daughter reject the mother. We need to expose the root of the emotional abuse.'

At that moment Gerald knew that he should have grabbed the expression 'emotional abuse' and twisted its neck once and for all. Let's never hear that nonsense again. I saw that father and I saw that daughter, he should have shouted, and I saw a man who loved his daughter and a daughter who felt safe with her dad. But if he said any of this, he knew exactly what he would read in Gail's eyes: *Don't be so ridiculous.*

He was defeated. He didn't have it in him to slay that dragon and so he let the dragon twist his mind instead and he began to think that perhaps there was something unnatural about a daughter not wanting to live with her mum. He straightened himself up and laying his hand firmly on the round knob of the door handle, he said, 'I'll do it myself, Gail, I have children, I know how to talk to kids. I'll get the truth out of that girl.' He emphasised the last words with a couple of eloquent nods, smiled his good-bye and left.

Gail watched him go and as the door closed her contempt for the man broke through on her face. *The girl will twist him around her little finger,* she thought with a scornful smile, *just like she's doing with her father. I can see the whole thing so clearly. Mum is strict, Dad is a soft touch and understandably our little madam prefers to live with a soft touch. Dad wants to get back at Mum for leaving him and encourages the girl to think she has the right to choose where she wants to live. In so doing he alienates the girl further from her mother and is prepared to deprive his daughter of a mother for the sake of his own revenge. That's where the emotional abuse comes in.*

A little smile played on Gail's lips. It was pleasurable to suss out a situation, and even more pleasurable to know that you were in a situation of power where you could make sure that your understanding of events would prevail.

*

From two different offices on that Tuesday the expression 'emotional abuse' took on a life of its own and went marching into the unsuspecting lives of Joe Milton and his daughter.

*

By Tuesday afternoon Joe had had time to dwell on the events of the past few days and he felt torn by second thoughts on the wisdom of allowing Zoe to have her way. The sudden invasion of his life by the police and social services had unsettled him. He had committed no crime and yet there they were, at his door, with the right to come in, ask questions, meddle. It was scary. The visit had churned him up and although he hated to admit it, the big policewoman had frightened him. Perhaps they had a point, perhaps it wasn't worth it and not in Zoe's best interest to get tangled up in a custody battle. He was sitting at the kitchen table with his daughter, having quickly put together an evening meal of beans on toast.

'Are you sure you don't want to go back to Mum's?' he asked at last.

'I'll go if it's going to avoid a load of hassle for everyone,' she said, looking miserable.

'I don't want you to hate your mum, Zoe.' Joe paused and absent-mindedly lifted a forkful of baked beans to his mouth.

'I don't hate her,' replied Zoe, 'I hate living there. There is nothing good about my life when I'm there.' She doodled with her fork amongst the beans.

Joe understood that feeling. Now that Leanne had left him there was nothing good about his life either. He understood the emptiness and the loss that his daughter couldn't quite describe.

'What I hate there,' continued Zoe, staring at the wall, 'is feeling lonely.' The beans and toast were going cold and soggy in her plate, but Joe realised this was not the moment to tell her to eat up. There was a little frown of concentration on her forehead as she continued, 'Sometimes I think I'm wrong, Dad, I think I'm being silly. Being with mum isn't that bad and I see you at the weekend and I see Granny and Grandad as well, so I'm OK really. But then I go back to the flat after school and I feel lonely again and I know that if I was here, I wouldn't feel lonely. That's what I hate.' She paused, took a deep breath and with a sheepish look creeping into her eyes, added, 'Sometimes I wish she would beat me up so then I wouldn't have to stay there. But she doesn't, she just looks at me and her eyes pierce me, they don't love me.'

'Your mum is not a touchy-feely sort of person Zoe, but it doesn't mean she doesn't love you.'

Zoe shook her head in despair and sudden tears rimmed her eyelids. Joe laid his hand over hers and said, 'I know sweetheart, I know exactly what you mean.' Zoe's tears rolled over the edge and her father brushed them off her cheeks with the tip of his fingers. 'It's just that I think you might get on better with her later, like Jessie does. I don't want you to miss out on that. My parents also got me down at times, but obviously I wasn't going to leave home, so it passed and now they're very important to me.' Joe was surprised to hear himself say this, as it was a truth he mainly denied because his parents also made him feel inadequate and not quite grown-up.

'I don't care about later,' replied Zoe, sniffing up the snot coming out of her nose, 'Mum is always saying bad things about me, like my hair isn't nice, and I've got a temper, I'm moody, I think I'm always right, and then you know what she says, she says I'm just like you. It's like she hates me because I'm like you. And Jessie's also got long lists of what's wrong with me and it's the same as what's wrong with you too. And I hate Ivor. He calls me a spoiled brat and you know what else he says? He says that as long as I spend time with you and Granny and Grandad, I'll carry on being a spoiled brat.' Her tears were flowing again, angry now. 'When he says that, I shout at him to stop saying bad stuff about my family, and I tell him he's not my family and I hate him.'

'And then what happens?' asked Joe, who was surprised Zoe hadn't told him any of this before.

'I get smacked on the legs.'

'By him?' snapped Joe.

'No, by Mum. Or I get sent to my room, and Jessie brings me my food. But I'd rather eat there anyway than eat with them.'

'That's terrible,' said Joe clearing the table in a loud clanking of plates and cutlery. 'I can't believe you've never told me any of this.'

'I told you I hate living in the flat,' protested Zoe.

'But you didn't explain the reasons,' said Joe, stroking his daughter's head whilst handing her a yoghurt.

Zoe stared silently at the strawberry yoghurt in her hand. It was true that she hadn't told her dad or anyone else the reasons she hated living in the flat, and she knew why too. Telling adults anything was a waste of breath. For instance, you told your parents you didn't like school and next thing they were telling Granny how you loved school. Or you told them you didn't like something, like Brussel Sprouts or homework, and their answer was that you should like it, 'cos it was good for you. And that's why Zoe never bothered to tell her parents or any other adults how she felt about anything. But now something different had happened. Her father had listened, and he hadn't told her she was wrong to feel what she did.

'So, I'm not a bad person for hating living with Mum?' she asked tentatively, dipping her spoon in the pink yoghurt.

Her father was washing up with a great splashing of water and scraping of pans. Now he turned around, snatched the cloth hanging over his shoulder and started drying his hands, finger by finger. Then he chucked the cloth back over his shoulder and said, 'Zoe, don't ever think that you're a bad person. That is the last thing you are. And from now on I want you to tell me everything unpleasant that happens to you when you're staying at your mother's.' He was leaning against the sink, looking at her with caring eyes, but she glimpsed the anger smouldering right at the back of them. 'We will go to court,' he added deliberately, 'and we'll see what the judge has to say about your story.'

The fight was on again and Joe had forgotten the warnings from the policewoman and the social worker. The sense of rightness inside him and inside his daughter was so powerful they had no doubt a judge would see it as clearly as they did.

How wrong they were.

How painful the lesson they were about to learn.

*

Two days later Joe had a letter in the post from Leanne's solicitor telling him his ex-partner was applying for an interim residence order. His insides tightened. He remembered with painful clarity Leanne's descriptions of her rottweiler of a solicitor and knew that his own pleasant and mild-mannered lawyer would not stand a chance against a woman who was, as Leanne used to put it, savage by name and savage by nature. He read the letter again and headed for his computer upstairs. The internet gave him all the information he needed about interim residence orders, and although it sounded as if the court took the child's wishes into account, he feared that, in

67

the real world, people didn't. People believed that a child belonged with her mother, and that was the impossible battle he'd taken on.

Court happened a week later, and Zoe was told that her presence would not be required. She would phone her father at lunch time to find out the outcome. Her morning in school dragged by interminably. All Zoe could do was glance at her watch every few minutes. At break time she joined in a game of touch and her competitive nature got the better of her worries so that for a good ten minutes she forgot about the hearing. When the bell broke the spell, she glanced at her watch again. 10.45. As she followed Kylie towards the classroom, she pictured her dad waiting outside the courtroom, getting into a darker and darker mood. Would her mum be in the same waiting area? Would they manage not to get into a screaming row? Zoe shuddered. One good thing about the separation was the end of the fighting. They still shouted at each other on the phone, and complained loudly about the other in their absence, but the actual face to face fighting was over. She had escaped from the noise that split her head, from the gusts of hatred and the waves of violence, but what she had now, when she was away from her father, was a hostile, silent place.

Kylie was astonished when the teacher didn't tell Zoe off for failing to produce a single answer on her Maths worksheet. Kylie shot her friend the occasional concerned glance, but didn't try to talk to her, not even when the teacher was fully occupied separating James and Brian who had started one of their fights. Zoe cast them a distracted glance and turned her eyes back to the window. Only fifteen minutes left to lunch. She slipped her hand inside her bag and felt for the reassuring shape of her mobile. In fifteen minutes, she would know, unless court wasn't over, of course. If it wasn't she would phone again and again throughout the lunch break. Her heart started beating fast and her head felt strangely light. Maybe she was going to faint. She had never fainted in her life and felt a twinge of curiosity, but then quickly dismissed it. She didn't want to faint, she wanted to know what the judge had decided. She felt fear, but she felt hope too.

At long last the bell went, and all the children rushed out without waiting for the teacher to say they could. The young woman stood there looking half amused and half despairing as she followed the jostling children with her eyes. Then she noticed Zoe fumbling with her mobile and remembered what the grandmother had told her on the phone that morning.

'Do you want to phone from here Zoe?' she asked helpfully. 'I'll be in the storeroom.'

'Thanks Miss,' replied Zoe as she clamped the little phone to her ear and watched the teacher's back disappear round the door.

The phone rang three times and her father said 'Zoe?' The defeated tone of his voice said it all and her insides began to slide as she waited for the details. 'Sweetheart,' he said in his gentlest voice, 'I'm afraid they said you have to go back.' They were both silent.

'Zoe, there's other not very good news.' He paused.

'What Dad?' she asked in small voice.

'They've given me contact, but…'

'What's contact?' Zoe butted in tensely. She remembered her mother using the word but wasn't sure what it meant.

'It's the time we're allowed to spend together.' He sounded deflated, chastened, with all the anger beaten out of him.

'What do you mean Dad?' asked Zoe with anxiety tearing at her voice. 'I can't just come and see you when I want?'

'No sweetheart. It's not split evenly anymore, but you will be allowed to stay over, and Leanne will be only too pleased for me to have you when she wants to go out or go away, so we'll see plenty of each other, same as before I reckon.'

Zoe was quiet. This felt like the worst punishment she had ever received in her young life and yet she couldn't see that she had done anything to deserve it. Just wanted to live with the person with whom she felt happy and safe. In a tiny voice she said goodbye and slipped the phone inside her pocket. Miss Brown came quietly out of the storeroom, and the look in her eyes destroyed Zoe's determination not to cry.

The tears came and it felt as if they would never dry up.

6. Joe's Big Mistake

Zoe had to go back to her mother that very afternoon after school. She packed her things with her father's silent help. The look of deep gloom on his face was so distressing that she cheered up for his sake, and this helped her in turn face the ordeal of being confronted in the flat by the gloating and sarcastic eyes of the three people in her life she was fast coming to hate. But now she was ready for them, except they didn't know it. She had a long-term plan which they would discover as the weeks went by. She was going to be silent, hostile and rude; she would not do what she was told, she would annoy Jessie endlessly and provoke rows between her mother and Ivor. She had a pretty good idea how to achieve all that, and then they would know how much she didn't want to be there, and perhaps the day would come when they didn't want her there either. A good plan she thought.

Sure enough, things went gratifyingly from bad to worse over the next couple of months and Zoe enjoyed her sense of power. She was going to win this battle, she could feel it coming, Ivor had already threatened twice to move out if Zoe was allowed to carry on as she was, and Jessie expressed growing resentment against their mother for being soft on her sister. And yet it was Zoe's plan, successful as it seemed, which was going to lead to a disaster that she could never have foreseen. Not even an adult could have foreseen it.

Because Zoe's behaviour was driving everyone mad at home Leanne resolved to seek Joe's help. Her call stunned him. Apart from catching glimpses of her when picking Zoe up or dropping her off Joe never saw his ex-partner anymore and had given up hope that he ever would. The thought of meeting up with her sent his heartbeat soaring and until the day of the appointment he could think of nothing else. When the moment finally came and he opened his front door with a trembling hand, he thought he might faint at the sight of the real live woman who had been inhabiting his dreams. She came in, they talked, and he promised to have a word with Zoe. It was a surreal conversation in which the words coming out of his mouth were utterly disconnected from the thoughts in his head and the feelings in his heart.

*

After Leanne and Ivor had moved in together Joe's life had become a struggle. He couldn't stop imagining his family sitting around their kitchen table and talking amongst themselves as if he didn't exist. He pictured the short stocky man standing right where he should be standing, casting a proprietary eye over his woman. He fought the image of Leanne and this man together, knowing a stream of others would follow, like a tsunami of dirty pictures sending in wave after wave to torture him, unstoppable, monstrous, filtering into his mind and spreading there like a disease that no medication could cure. The doctor had suggested antidepressants, but Joe had said no. He nearly told the doctor, 'I've got my own drugs, thank you, and although they've got their drawbacks, they're my friends and I can handle them.' Then Joe had felt he was beginning to lose control over his friends. They weren't turning into his enemies yet, but he had seen the concern in his mother's eyes and his father had hinted about going for a whole day without alcohol. But after the debacle of going to court Joe had regained control and was doing better. Leanne's visit, however, changed all that, and a week later Joe started stalking his ex-partner.

It felt like an innocent pastime. His way of dealing with his loss. Remaining close to Leanne whilst gradually learning to let her go. In the comfort of this explanation, Joe took to frequenting the pub that was almost exactly opposite Leanne's flat. His old student pub, now raucous with a new generation of scruffy young men wearing their jeans halfway down their arses. The latest trend. As there was no question of hanging around the bar with these young men, Joe would go and sit at a small table in the window. This window happened to be part-stained glass, part frosted glass, with a perfect crescent of clear glass affording him an excellent view of Leanne's flat.

On his third night sitting alone at the little table, Joe had just finished his first pint when the brown door opened, and Leanne walked out. Joe gave his lips a quick swipe with his sleeve and jumped to his feet. He ran across the main road without waiting for the lights to turn red, oblivious to the clamour of angry hoots, and disappeared down the street Leanne had just taken. He ran to the next corner and as soon as Leanne appeared in his line of vision he slowed down and followed from a distance. He felt alive now, with his heart beating pleasantly inside his chest and his eyes taking ownership once again of the slender, lightly swaying body that had come to inhabit his brain. She walked briskly, hugging her handbag on her right hip, sashaying prettily on her high heels. Every so often her left arm lifted, and her fingers ran lightly through her hair, sending deliciously painful vibrations through Joe's insides.

He could feel his own fingers running through that golden silk. He imagined his hands sliding down to her hips, pulling her towards him. She resisted gently but that was only to make her surrender more exquisite later. Shivers of excitement ran through him as he walked carefully from tree to tree, concentrating on remaining invisible. He followed her down to the left and up the hill and then right into the road where her regular pub was. She walked to the door, swung it open and disappeared. Joe closed his eyes. Every man inside looked. Eyes travelled up her legs to the hem of her short skirt, hovered there, knowing they were welcome. Slowly Joe's fingers clenched into fists.

Now he was hooked. In control once again and part of Leanne's life. On Saturdays she would take clients out to visit houses or flats and as he trailed her carefully, he felt like a private detective on the chase. He watched her from a distance opening doors, showing people in, letting them out again, shaking hands, smiling. As soon as they'd disappeared in their cars, her face would harden as she watched them go, thinking she'd wasted another hour of her life. He felt a kind of fondness for her at those moments. He also felt protective towards her once again because of her innocence, her unawareness that she was being followed.

But he was wrong about that. Leanne knew. She was annoyed but she was also flattered and decided to have a bit of fun at her ex-partner's expense. She only meant a bit of fun.

Leanne's opportunity came one balmy evening in late June when Ivor was away, and the girls were staying with Nan. Before going out she dressed with care, checking in the mirror that her little black dress looked as good as she thought it did. She plucked at the shoulders, changed her bra to a more uplifting one, slipped the dress back on and posed like a model in front of the mirror. She looked good. She brushed her long golden hair thinking how Joe used to love watching her do that. A quick spray of perfume. Her sexy gold handbag in her hand. Time to go.

She closed the brown door behind her without a look across at the pub, but she didn't need to, she knew he was there waiting. Slowly she started walking down the road, her dress caressing her silky body in the breeze. Thong and a bra. She gazed casually into the distance and kept walking, taking pleasure in the light swinging of her hips. She felt a little drunk on the summer fragrances of the night, and more than a little excited with her plan. She paused to cross the road and a rapid glance at the traffic enabled her to check that Joe was following behind. She was pretty sure she recognised the tall silhouette half hidden by the trees lining the road. As soon as she had turned the corner, she dived into a small side alley and stood waiting, with her heart kicking unaccountably. She heard his footsteps approaching and then they stopped. She smiled to herself as she pictured his surprise on meeting with an empty street in front of him. Predictably he broke into a long-legged fast stride and sailed past the alley. Leanne stepped out and called his name in mocking surprise. He stopped and swivelled round. They stood and stared at each other with every muscle in their bodies alert and tingling.

'What do you think you're doing, following me like that?' hissed Leanne. 'Do you think I'm stupid? Do you think I haven't noticed you, following me in the car, on foot, everywhere, all the bloody time?'

'Don't you like it?' replied Joe slowly, his eyes drinking her in. 'Don't you love attention from men?' He stepped forward, coming too close to her, but she stood her ground, unfazed.

'I like attention from some men, Joe, but you're not one of them.' Her voice dripped with sarcasm.

'Who are they then?' he murmured, stepping so close they were almost touching. 'You have one man, you shouldn't be open to any others, should you?' He was still not touching her, and she wasn't stepping back or pushing him away. A strange trance like immobility had descended on both.

'You look very beautiful, Leanne,' he said softly. His gaze sent her eyes straying to the ground, but she didn't stop his hand when his fingers lightly brushed along her shoulder and up the slender curvature of her neck. 'Very beautiful,' he repeated.

Leanne felt a tightening of her insides. She had not expected this. It took her back ten years ago when he first uttered those words with that same entranced look. She had felt worshipped then, and she couldn't help feeling it again now.

'I'm following you,' he said quickly, 'because I want to discuss Zoe with you.' He put his hand up in answer to the sarcasm in her eyes and added, 'I know, I can never bring myself to do it. I feel you're just going to say no, go away, so I just follow you instead and wait for the next opportunity. But now,' he said, holding her eyes, 'now we can do it. Let's go back to your flat. I'm asking for half an hour, then I'll give you a lift to the pub. You'll hardly be late at all.' His voice was sweet and convincing catching Leanne off balance. She had anticipated the look in his eyes, but she had not expected to feel melted by it. Having planned to laugh in his face and threaten to call the police if she ever caught him following her again, she was now tempted to spend the next half hour with him. What harm could it do? For the sake of appearances, she protested that she didn't want to do that, they could walk along and discuss Zoe as they walked, but they both knew that she was going to say yes. Ten minutes later they were back in her flat, with a bottle of wine between them on the kitchen table. The fire escape door was wide open, letting in the warm evening air. A couple of flies buzzing around the room failed to annoy either of them. Leanne reached for clean glasses out of the cupboard and handed him one with a consciously sweet movement of her arm and wrist. His eyes made her feel alive and beautiful.

Memories flooded Leanne. She downed some wine, felt the alcohol course through her veins and looked at Joe through confused eyes. Her rational mind tried to kick in. There was no going back. She had left Joe for good reasons. His irritating, domineering ways. The boredom of living with him. His jealousy. The fighting. But most of all, what had done it had been the absence of that loving look in his eyes. She mustn't be fooled by the reappearance of that look. It was a sham. Love was dead. In her it was anyway. She looked up at him and asked in a business-like voice, 'So what is it about Zoe you want to discuss?'

'I still love you Leanne,' he said, ignoring her question. 'Nobody will ever love you more. I know I wasn't showing it in the end. But now I've had time to think things over, and I wouldn't make those mistakes again. I want you back Leanne.'

His eyes gazed into hers and she gazed back with her lips curling provokingly.

'You know that's not going to happen, Joe, forget it. I've moved on…'

'You like the way I look at you, Leanne, don't deny it. You dressed for me tonight, didn't you? You wanted me to find you beautiful, and I do. Look at you. A twenty-year-old with golden hair.'

She pulled a packet of cigarettes out of her bag, offered him one and plucked one out for herself. He had his lighter ready and lit them both. They sat back and locked eyes in a haze of bluish spirals, inhaling deeply, sharing the pleasure. They drank their wine in silence, letting alcohol and tobacco mingle in their blood creating lightness. Joe was leaning back in his chair, in a dreamy distant trance of his own. Never had he thought the stalking would lead to this, and now with hope surging inside him he felt transported, like a surfer finding his delicate balance on the foaming edge of a big wave. Leanne's eyelids drooped seductively, and she was peering at him through pensive slits. Weighing things up, he dared to hope but had the wisdom to keep silent. Leanne took one last drag on her fag and crushed the end in a saucer on the table. Then she looked up at him and smiled. Her glossy lips held a silent invitation. Was she suggesting what he thought she was? Her hand went lazily up to her exposed cleavage and her fingers rested there, where the breasts came together in two soft mounds of milky flesh. With tremendous effort he looked away and up at her face again. The smile was still there, taunting him, daring him to touch. Very slowly he raised his hand and without letting go of her eyes, in case the message there suddenly changed, he followed the cut of her dress with light fingers, just brushing at first, then stroking, then gently sliding under the flimsy black material, entering forbidden territory. Still she smiled, and imperceptibly leaned forward.

Slowly his finger traced a line from her breast up her neck, along her cheekbone and onto her lips. She caught his finger lightly between her teeth and bit it. It hurt without hurting. It was part of the excitement. Leanne had always liked to mix pain and pleasure, and he had learned to find that arousing. He was aroused now, and she stared at him provocatively, holding his finger between her teeth. His heart pumped and his veins pulsed with excitement. All Leanne did was hold his finger in her mouth, playing around it with lips and tongue. For a fleeting second the image of a cat playing with a mouse flashed through his mind. Then Leanne's lips, soft and baby like, encircled his finger, and push-pulling, sucked on it, sending ripples of pleasure deep into his body.

Still Joe made no move. He was bursting with hope as much as he was bursting with lust, and his fear to lose that hope kept an iron grip on his body's clamouring needs. To Leanne he was a man possessed by a self-control she knew he didn't have. Wanting to see him fall, she kept pushing. She reached for his other hand and cupped it over her breast, still sucking with wet lips around his finger. Tension mounted in her as it mounted in him, and now they fixed each other with hardened stares, like two children in a staring game where the one who loses is the first to look away. Her nipples responded to his touch, jutting out firm and hard into his palm. Their bodies started to ooze the sweet tears of sexual arousal and they could smell it on each other.

Without letting go of each other, they slowly hoisted their bodies from the wooden kitchen chairs and in a strange slow dance got closer and closer. Then they lost all control. They rushed and stumbled into the front room and onto the big sloppy couch, their hands and lips crazy with reawakened passion. It was only at the very end, just after Leanne's exploding moment of ecstasy that from a great distance he heard a muffled sound that made no sense but by then he was lost to the world, thrusting fiercely and hoping she could feel how much he loved her. His climax was of another dimension, followed by a flow of uncontrollable tears as he buried his head in the hollow of her neck.

Then she pushed him away, her eyes full of cold resentment, her lips taut with contained rage. She looked contemptuously at the man sitting next to her, his shirt dangling open and his body naked except for the ridiculous socks on his feet, his erection still there. She snatched her dress from the floor and slipped it over her head.

'What's going on Leanne?' he asked sharply.

'You know exactly what's going on, Joe Milton, so wipe that dumb look off your face.'

'I don't know what you're talking about, Leanne.' He grabbed her wrist.

'Let go of me, you bastard.' As she said this, her eyes filled up and silent tears ran freely down her cheeks. He dropped her wrist.

'If I hurt you, Leanne, it was an accident, I swear…'

'It was no accident,' she blurted between sobs, 'You forced yourself on me, Joe Milton, and you know it. You heard me say 'no', you felt me pushing you away and you just squeezed harder. Don't say you didn't.' She was a hurt little girl now, but he was only too familiar with the cold calculating woman behind that little girl.

'You bitch,' he hissed softly between his teeth, 'you nasty lying bitch.'

He picked up his clothes and pulled them on with angry, jerky movements. He fumbled with the buckle on his belt, trembling with indignation, aware that she was watching him.

'You stalked me Joe, you got me back to the flat and then you raped me, and I know what Ivor will say when I tell him. He'll say, report it to the police.' She shot Joe a look from under her eyebrows, and looked down again, sniffling.

'You've got to tell Ivor that, to protect your back, haven't you?' He sat down next to her and lifted her chin, forcing her to look at him. Her gaze had gone dead and cold. 'But you and I know the truth. You wanted to get fucked as much as I wanted to fuck you. But that gives me power, doesn't it? I could tell Ivor, couldn't I? So, you tell him you got raped and the power's back in your court. Well, do it. Report it to the police and I'll see you in court. I'll tell my story and we'll see who they believe.'

Her eyes slid down to the floor and her mind jumped to another conclusion that would not occur to Joe until much later that night, as he lay in bed unable to sleep. For now, his brain was all taken up by furious outrage and cruel disappointment. He looked down at the small woman in her crumpled little black dress with her beautifully dishevelled hair and felt a sharp pang of longing. Despite everything.

'Come back home, Leanne,' he blurted. 'Bring the girls back with you, let's be a family again, it's the only way we can all be happy.'

She stared down at her delicate little feet with pretty red nails, and spoke in an icy cold voice, 'I'll never come back to you, Joe. What you did tonight is exactly why I don't want to live with you. You're a violent man. You can't be trusted. I didn't go back to the first violent man in my life, and I won't go back to the second either. I'm not that kind of woman.'

Joe sprung up and looking down on her, said, 'And has it occurred to you, Leanne, that you could be the kind of woman who makes men violent? With your lies and your sly underhand behaviour, and your need to have all the power all the time. No doubt you'll be on the phone to the police the day Ivor lets rip, and bear in mind, when he does, he might not be as restrained as me.'

Then he left. Slamming the door behind him. As he marched through the warm air towards his car parked in one of the side streets behind the pub, he convinced himself that Leanne's threat had been empty and spiteful, but she wouldn't do it. Too risky for her. He brushed some sweat off his forehead with the back of his hand. He also realised that his anger failed to dampen his desire for her. He wanted Leanne more than ever. He felt ashamed, knowing exactly what everyone would think of him if they knew, but he didn't give a damn about other people. They didn't understand and they had no right to judge. He clicked on his remote and watched the car flash back at him obediently. The doors would be open when he got to them. If only it were that easy with people.

It was only much later that night, as he lay awake on his bed with all the covers thrown off, that Zoe popped into his mind. He sprung up like a wound-up toy and sat staring into dark space. Zoe. How had he not seen it sooner? How had he not seen the bitch plotting her victory against him from the moment she stopped him in the street? Or had she? Maybe she had only scented victory coming her way, in the way gifted generals seem to know just how to move their troops on the battlefield, with premonitions of success, and had gone with the flow, knowing the right move would come to her at the right moment. That was it. Instinct, not intelligence. He fell back onto his pillow and groaned aloud. Once again, he had let his daughter down. What man accused of rape will ever be granted custody of his daughter?

7. Zoe's Anger

After Joe left the flat Leanne had a long shower and then sat in the kitchen smoking and drinking coffee. She had just won a big victory over Joe, she knew that, but now she had to think carefully about the next steps. How would she handle Ivor, the police and Zoe? By the time Leanne went to bed her plan had formed and she was confident she could make it all work to her advantage. She switched the light off and went to sleep.

The following day Zoe came home from school at her usual time of quarter to four. She opened the brown door with her key, hoping it wouldn't stick, as it often did, which meant she had to go into the estate agent's and find her mum or someone else to help her open it. But the door opened, and she entered the cool of the staircase going up to their landing. As she closed the door behind her she stopped to listen thinking she'd heard something. Yet at this time nobody could be home. She stood tensely at the bottom of the stairs, her head cocked to one side. All had gone silent again, and she thought it must have been jackdaws on the roof. It was surprising the racket they could make considering they were only birds. The heat grew as she trudged up the stairs and she headed straight for the kitchen to get a cold drink. She pushed the door open and stopped dead. Her mum and Jessie were sitting there, their eyes ready for her.

She stood in the door looking from one to the other. Something bad had happened, she could tell, and they couldn't wait to spill the news to her. She felt the familiar tightening in her chest and tried to breathe calmly. Her mum shot a pointed look at Jessie, then extended an arm towards Zoe who shuffled slowly forward and stood by her mother's side, looking at her in the way a mouse might look at a cat. Her mother's arm came to wrap gently around her shoulders, drawing her close whilst Jessie stood by, looking annoyingly important and protective.

'I have something difficult to tell you, chicken,' said Leanne, looking Zoe in the eyes, 'something about your father. Something that happened last night when you and Jessie were staying at Nan's.'

Zoe tensed up, casting her mother and sister a distrustful look. Leanne looked down at the floor, coughed lightly and started to tell her story. In no time at all Zoe stopped listening to the words, they didn't make sense, wrapped as they were in a fog of things impossible to comprehend. What Zoe was highly tuned into however was her mother's tone of voice. It was gentle. No shouting, no raving and ranting, no insults. A crawling chill ran down Zoe's back. What was coming? She looked from her mother to Jessie and Jessie's wide excited eyes warned her she was about to hear what her father had done. Had he tried to kill himself again, or was it worse than that? She looked back at her mother, breathing through her open mouth, and when the loaded sentence came at last, she knew this was a triumphant victory for her mother, but she did not understand what it meant.

What she had just heard was that her father had raped her mother. She knew, of course, that rape was one of these bad words that make adults go pale and silent, but she also knew it was to do with bad strangers you must never talk to. That word couldn't have anything to do with her parents, hostile as they were to each other. She scrabbled in her mind for the beginning of her mother's story. Something about Dad following her in the street, they had argued, well they always argued so that wasn't surprising, but he had wanted to talk about Zoe, so they'd ended up in the flat. But how had they ended up in the flat? Why had Mum let him in if he was going to do this terrible thing? Mum must have known he would do it because Mum knew everything. She was the clever one. Zoe had never seen Dad have the better of Mum. Not once. She stared blankly down at the table.

'I know it's impossible for you to understand, Zoe,' continued Leanne, 'you are too young. All you need to know is that you father did that very bad thing to me and I have had to report it to the police, I did consider…'

'I don't believe you,' interrupted Zoe, pulling sharply away from her mother, 'you're always saying stuff about Dad, and it's just lies…' Spinning on her heels she ran out, straight to her bedroom where she buried herself into pillows, duvets and soft toys. 'I hate them,' she sobbed to Flossie, 'I hate them, I hate them.'

When Jessie knocked on her door a couple of hours later to say food was on the table, Zoe shouted back that she wasn't hungry and when Mum pushed the door open to tell her she had to come and eat, she buried her face in her pillows and clutched at the bedclothes around her to show that if they tried to drag her into the kitchen, they'd have to take half the bedding as well. Mum came to sit on the bed and put her hand over her daughter's back, saying, 'Zoe, I wish you'd stop taking your father's side all the time. What's happening between me and him is grown-up stuff which you can't understand. Keep out of it. But I'm not going to protect Joe just because he's your dad. If he does bad things, then he's got to pay the price.'

Zoe flounced over to face the wall, grabbing the side of the duvet and pulling it on top of her. There was a long silence before her mother spoke again in a sharper tone of voice. 'Right, Zoe, that's enough of that now. I want you to get up and come and eat your food. Now.' She stood up and waited. Zoe didn't move. Then the threats came. She would be grounded, not allowed to play with Kylie, no roller skating, no TV. Zoe didn't move. No visits to her grandparents. With a hateful look at her mother Zoe got up and taking Flossie in the crook of her arm, strode out of her room. In the kitchen she sat down in silence and nibbled at the chicken salad that lay limp on her plate. Her mother poured herself a coffee, then sat down at the table. Jessie was engrossed in watching Neighbours on the small TV jutting out from the wall and her mother's vacant eyes settled on the screen too. When Zoe had finished eating, she pushed the plate away to the middle of the table, scraped her chair back and headed for the door. But she was smartly reminded to clear up her plate, which she did in silence. Jessie shot her a sideways glance and as the adverts came on turned to her mother to complain that if she behaved like that, she would get a right telling off and how come Zoe was getting away with it. 'It's not as if she's got a good reason to act like that,' she added, 'after what her dad's done.'

'My dad's done nothing,' shouted Zoe, whirling round to glare at Jessie. 'You're just jealous 'cos you haven't got a dad.'

'I'd rather have no dad than a dad who's a rapist,' hissed Jessie back.

Zoe went flying at Jessie and the girls lashed out at each other as if years of jealousy and resentment where suddenly erupting into this torrent of hot rage. Jessie was taller but Zoe was more of a fighter and she had her sister on the floor within seconds. 'I hate you,' she spat at her, 'I hate you both,' she added looking up at her mum who sat transfixed in her chair. Then she ran off again into her bedroom slamming the door behind her. Moments later she heard her mother's angry steps approaching. This time instead of hiding under the bedclothes, she sat leaning against the wall and stared at the door ready for her mother's entrance. The door flew open and mother and daughter locked eyes.

Tension mounted in the silence, with Jessie's whimpering still audible from the kitchen. Finally, Zoe's mother spoke in a harsh, low voice, 'I don't know why I want you living with me, you're a wicked child, Zoe, a nasty wicked child.'

'Good,' replied Zoe, 'then let me go and live with dad. That's all I want.'

'Never,' hissed her mother, 'do you understand? Never. Even if I don't want you here, I'll make damn sure you and him never live together.'

'And that's why you called him a rapist, isn't it?' shouted Zoe, a red flush spreading across her cheeks, 'just to stop me seeing him. And that's why I hate you.'

Zoe's mother stepped forward and looking straight into her daughter's eyes, she lifted her hand high in the air and brought it down hard on the girl's bare thigh, just below her short summer skirt. A white imprint of her hand appeared there against a rush of blood under the skin. Zoe didn't flinch. Her mother pivoted on her heels and left the room closing the door hard behind her.

That night Zoe made up her mind to run away.

*

As soon as Zoe walked through the school gates the following morning, Kylie dropped out of the skipping game with the other girls and ran over to meet her friend who was looking dark and distant. Zoe's life was not unlike the soaps Kylie liked to watch on TV, and it seemed unreal that through her friend she should be involved in such entanglements herself. Her father couldn't help showing some hostility towards a friendship he feared might have a bad influence on his daughter, but Kylie's mum frowned her disapproval at this attitude. 'Zoe needs support,' she would say sharply, 'not more rejection just because her parents are behaving badly. The kid can't help that.'

Kylie knew she had a great family life but the very smoothness of everything was the reason she was powerfully attracted to the wild streak in her friend's personality and to the powerful emotions that tore her life apart on a regular basis. Being with Zoe was exciting. She was quick to get into fights, made friends with the naughty boys in the class, played football in the yard and rode faster on her blades than anyone Kylie knew.

Kylie would never forget how they had become friends. It was the first day at school and Kylie had cried and protested all the way, very nearly getting her mother to give in and keep her home. But what she had said instead was that Kylie must try it for a week and if at the end of the week she was still very unhappy, they would think again.

Kylie had spent the first couple of hours in the classroom fighting the choking feeling building up inside her gullet. The dire consequences for the children unable to contain their tears focussed her mind on this battle. By breaktime that first morning the class was divided between the cry babies and the superior people who moved in the new environment like fish swimming in water. Kylie kept a very low profile, aiming to make herself invisible. When the teacher said they had to sit on the floor with their knees folded and theirs heels tucked under, a fresh surge of tears assaulted her eyes. She hated sitting like that. She blinked furiously and looked around to see how the others were doing. Suddenly her eyes widened, and her heart stopped. A girl with light reddish hair was sitting with her legs crossed. Kylie glanced at the teacher. What would happen to that girl if the teacher noticed? But the teacher never noticed.

At break time Kylie mustered the courage to walk across the noisy playground and up to the girl with the light reddish hair. She was squatting on her own by the railings, observing some ants filing in and out of a little hole at the edge of the concrete. Kylie squatted next to her and watched in silence. The girl shot her a glance and went back to her ants.

'You sat with your legs crossed,' said Kylie.

The girl looked at her nonplussed. Then she said, 'I hate kneeling.'

'But the teacher said we had to kneel,' Kylie insisted, as if probing one of the great mysteries of the planet.

'My aunty told me I didn't have to be frightened of school,' replied the other girl, 'because the teachers are not allowed to smack us.' She prodded a group of ants with a twig. The tiny insects scattered in disarray and the girl chuckled.

'I saw a boy hit another boy,' continued Kylie, expressing one of her other fears.

'If someone hits you, you hit them back,' pronounced the squatting girl, still staring at the ants with her arms wrapped around her bent knees.

'I've never hit anyone,' Kylie whispered, swallowing hard and staring intently at the ground, so the other girl wouldn't notice the tremble in her lips.

The other girl gave her a long look and asked, 'Do you live on Grove Road?' Kylie nodded, biting her plump lower lip. 'Me too,' said the girl. 'If anyone hits you,' she added, 'tell me. I'll hit them back for you.' Then they heard the teacher calling them in and they wandered off together towards the slowly assembling group of children. They learned each other's names later, when the teacher called every child to her desk, one after another. They both thought the other had a nice name. Nobody hit Kylie that day, or any other day after that and now she had a friend, she forgot all about not wanting to go to school.

*

Today, however, her friend looked as gloomy as she had ever seen her, and Kylie wondered if Zoe would tell her what the problem was. 'The worst thing ever has happened,' Zoe whispered, glancing around in case someone might be within hearing. Just as Kylie's lips parted to ask the next question, the bell rang.

'Tell me quick,' urged Kylie, as they walked slowly towards the forming lines. 'We've got two minutes.' Zoe shook her head and said, looking Kylie in the eyes, 'I can't tell you Kylie, I can't tell anyone.' Something wild and desperate hovered at the back of Zoe's eyes. Curiosity was killing Kylie, but she knew she would have to wait. They walked into class and sat together at their usual places in the second row and Kylie noticed that Zoe didn't listen to a word the teacher said. She let her copy all the Maths answers, wondering how long it would be before Miss Brown told her friend off. The teacher looked at Zoe a couple of times, but nothing happened, and when the bell went for break, Miss Brown gave Zoe a funny kind of look, like she felt sorry for her.

The two girls walked away from the others and Kylie pressed her friend, 'You can tell me, I promise I won't tell anyone, honest.'

'If I tell you,' Zoe said, 'will you promise you'll still be my friend?'

'What have you done?' blurted Kylie, looking worried.

'Nothing, it's my parents again.' She shrugged and looked away.

'Why should I stop being your friend because of your parents?' Kylie asked, feeling a little dishonest as she knew exactly how her dad felt about her friendship with Zoe, and she knew that Zoe was aware of it. One day, out of the blue, Zoe had said, 'Your dad doesn't like me, does he?' and they had both known that Kylie had struggled to answer.

'Will you still be my friend?' repeated Zoe.

'I'll never stop being your friend,' replied Kylie, 'and anyway my mum says you shouldn't drop your friends just because they're in trouble.' The lower rim of Zoe's eyes glistened, and a couple of tears slowly rolled over and down her cheeks. With a quick brush of her arm, she got rid of them.

'My mum says my dad raped her,' she blurted, looking down at her feet.

Kylie's jaw dropped in astonished confusion. Without understanding what 'rape' meant she knew it was a very bad word, and she knew something else too. If her dad heard about this, he was not going to like it. 'I won't tell my parents,' she said quickly, and saw from the relief on Zoe's face it was what she had wanted to hear. 'But I don't get it,' she continued, looking at her friend with a puzzled frown, 'how could he do that to your mum?'

''Exactly,' Zoe shrugged. 'She's a liar and I know she's lying about Dad, but it's bad for Dad anyway.' As Zoe said this, Miss Brown's concerned face popped into Kylie's mind. *Yes,* she thought, *it must be bad.*

'Will he go to prison?' Kylie asked, unaware of the effect this question would have on her friend. Now it was Zoe's jaw that dropped. She had not thought of that possibility.

'I don't know,' she replied, with panic flaring in her eyes.

Kylie tried to backpedal but it was too late. Zoe was now convinced her father would end up in prison. 'If he does,' she said, 'I'll never talk to mum again.' This time Kylie knew better than to ask if she would do that even if her dad was guilty, but Zoe's next sentence answered that question as if she had read her mind

'Even if Dad did something bad,' she said, 'I'm sure she made him do it. He only does bad stuff when she's around. She winds him up.' Zoe had heard her Granny say this, and although it was not her own thinking it summed up her experience perfectly. 'It's always her fault,' she added brushing more tears away. The bell rang, putting an end to the difficult conversation. Kylie was relieved. At lunch time both girls joined a game of touch and Zoe got right into it. In the afternoon she seemed to get on with the Science worksheets. Kylie relaxed. Perhaps things weren't as bad as they had seemed.

But the following morning Zoe was not in school.

8. Zoe Disappears

When Miss Brown called out Zoe's name, Kylie replied 'absent' and their eyes met. In answer to her teacher's silent question about the reason for Zoe's absence, Kylie gave a helpless little shrug meaning 'No idea'. Miss Brown finished calling the register, then wrote a note on a post-it, stuck it on the register and asked James to take it to the secretary. When he came back, he gave Miss Brown a note in reply which she read quickly with a frown on her face. Kylie guessed the note said there hadn't been a phone call to say Zoe was ill, but they would check straightaway with the parents. Everyone in school knew that's what happened if a child didn't turn up. When Miss Brown said to go and pick up the geography projects they had started the day before, Kylie followed the others and gathered what she needed but then sat at her desk staring blankly at the map and colouring pens. Miss Brown was sitting on a little chair next to Samantha when a knock at the door made everyone look up. The secretary came in and Miss Brown walked quickly over telling the children to carry on with their projects, which nobody did obviously. The two women talked in whispers with their heads close together and no one could hear a thing, least of all Kylie who sat near the window on the other side of the classroom. The secretary left saying, 'I will let you know if I hear anything.' Kylie managed to do some mindless colouring on her map and Miss Brown left her alone, but when the bell rang for break the teacher came over to Kylie and sat down next to her, asking if she could have a word. Kylie's heart started beating fast even though she knew she had done nothing wrong. She looked down at the table and waited nervously.

'Nobody seems to know where Zoe is, Kylie, I wonder whether you might have an idea?'

'No Miss, Zoe never said anything,' replied Kylie, her eyes glued to the geography project which lay unfinished in front of her. Kylie liked Miss Brown, but she was keen not to say anything that could get her friend into trouble and the safest bet was to remain silent. Miss Brown said Kylie could go and play but just as the girl put her hand on the doorknob, ready to run out into the yard, the teacher's voice reached her again, 'If you can think of anything, Kylie, anything that might have upset Zoe, you will come and tell me, won't you?'

Miss Brown, with the mindreading ability of teachers had just plucked words out of Kylie's secret thoughts and spoken them out loud, as if they were perfectly innocent words that had a right to dance around in the open. Kylie stood paralysed for an instant with her hand on the doorknob, then quickly nodded without looking around, opened the door and ran out. She went straight to the girls' toilets where she could lock the cubicle and not talk to anyone. Kylie knew only too well what had upset Zoe because she had done it, asking if her dad would go to prison. Every time she thought about that stupid question, she felt a little sick, and now that Zoe had disappeared, she knew it was her fault. Sitting on the toilet lid with her arms tightly wrapped around her drawn-up knees, she closed her eyes and thought of her mum. Kylie's mum could make the worst problem turn into a minor difficulty that had an easy solution, she could stroke your cheek and stop your tears and she was also good at keeping secrets. But there was no point thinking about her mum because today Kylie was on her own. Not only did she know why Zoe had disappeared, but she also had a pretty good idea where she was. But that was a secret, and Zoe would never forgive her if she talked. After school she would go and find her friend, and she would do it without her mother knowing. This felt strange, but not altogether bad.

*

At ten past nine that morning Leanne was in the office ready to take a husband and wife on a promising house visit when she noticed Justine trying to catch her eye. She excused herself and went over to her colleague, trying not to look annoyed. What a time to take her away from a client.

'There's been a phone call from school,' whispered the young woman.

'Which school?' snapped Leanne under her breath.

'Zoe's school. She didn't turn up this morning and they want to know if she's ill.' There was a big apology in Justine's eyes as she said this. Leanne's face had gone white, and indecision was tearing her apart. She glanced back towards the couple who stood waiting by the door. The woman was talking, arguing against the pricey house, Leanne could just tell. With an enormous weight of regret in her heart, she turned back to Justine and asked if she would take them. If the house sold, they would share the commission, but Leanne had little faith in Justine's ability to win a client over. Anger with Zoe surged inside her, the girl was doing this just to spite her. Typical. Then she felt guilty and picked up the phone.

She phoned the school first. Then she phoned Joe's house. No answer but that didn't mean anything. If Zoe was there, she wouldn't answer the phone. She phoned her mother on the off chance she knew something, but Nan hadn't heard from the girl. Finally, she phoned Joe in work. For once they had a conversation devoid of hostility. They reassured each other their daughter must be either at his house or with his parents, he would check both places and phone her back. Leanne waited unsure whether to feel worried or annoyed. The odds were the girl would reappear in the next couple of hours, unharmed, having alarmed everyone in such a way that instead of reaping the anger and punishment she deserved, she would get sympathy and Leanne would get the blame. In a rare moment of emotional honesty Leanne allowed herself to feel the pain of having a daughter who was so hostile. She had done nothing bad to this daughter. Tried to bring her up with the same combination of firmness and fun that had worked so well with Jessie, but this child had not taken to her from the start. With Zoe it had always been about Daddy. A sudden tightening in her throat took her by surprise and she blinked hard to get rid of the rush of moisture around her eyelids.

Just then another thought popped into Leanne's mind. Do nine-year-olds kill themselves? Teenagers do, she knew that, but nine-year-olds? Should she be worried, or was this just emotional blackmail designed to hurt her? She could not completely extinguish a flicker of guilt at the back of her mind. Should she have told Zoe her father was a rapist?

98

*

As soon as Joe switched his phone off, he felt panic mounting inside him and knew he was at risk of being engulfed. Images were crowding in with Zoe lost in a strange area somewhere, Zoe having an asthma attack without her inhaler at hand, Zoe calling him when he couldn't respond. He felt himself beginning to hyperventilate and thanked his lucky stars he was alone in the office. He closed his eyes and tried to enter the mindset he found readily available when there was an IT emergency, like that terrifying cyberattack six months ago. His heart slowed down, and a miraculous sense of calm came over him. One thing at a time. He picked up his phone again and called his parents, aware that he should break the news gently to them. He was glad when his father answered and they were able to keep calm. He asked him to look everywhere in the house, garden, garden shed, everywhere Zoe might have found a hiding place. 'I'm sure we're going to find her at your place or mine. Call me back as soon as you've looked everywhere and don't worry. It's her way of saying she doesn't want to live with her mum, it's the usual thing, Dad, nothing more than that.' But as he came off the phone Joe felt anxiety grip the pit of his stomach. Despair had driven him to do something extremely stupid and now he couldn't stop thinking Zoe might be following in his footsteps. She got churned up by emotions just the way he did, he saw it all the time.

He turned everything off in the office, locked the door and stopped by his boss's secretary to explain he'd be gone for an hour or so and would work late that afternoon to make up for it. She gave him a friendly smile, aware it wasn't easy being Joe Milton these days.

Joe ran to his car and drove off too fast. Fifteen minutes later he left his car parked badly in front of his house and rushed in. He ran all over the house shouting Zoe's name but met with silence and emptiness. He knew his daughter's hiding places and looked in all of them, and because she had fooled him many times before when playing hide and seek, he looked again and again, even in spaces that seemed much too small for a girl her size. Then he opened the back door into the garden and went straight to lift the little ceramic frog on the patio wall. The key to the shed was there undisturbed, still a bit wet from the latest rain. Disappointed, he picked it up anyway and went to search the shed, which was as empty and quiet as the house had been. He looked in the little metal box where he kept a spare key to the house and found it lying there, exactly as it always did. Zoe didn't need that key anyway, she had her own, but his hope of finding some trace of her somewhere was stronger than his logic. He slumped down onto the stool by the workbench and leaned on the rough wooden surface. His daughter's disappearance had opened a crack in his defences, and he could see himself now, as if he were looking at another person, unshielded by excuses and denials, someone who had let his daughter down in the most unforgivable ways. He shuddered and tried to dispel the vision, but the vision stayed. 'Zoe,' he said aloud, 'Sweetheart, I'm sorry. I cannot tell you how sorry I am.' The words did not have the magic to make Zoe reappear, but they were not completely useless either and when he got up, he felt a little stronger and more determined.

As he walked back into the garden, he heard voices and glimpsed his parents coming through the back door and up the overgrown path that meandered towards the shed. They met half-way and stood looking at one another in silence.

'You looked everywhere at your place, the house, the garden, the shed?' he asked, despite knowing the answer. They nodded and all three of them walked back to the house and went to sit in the kitchen and make coffee. Joe phoned work, then Leanne and then the police. They said to keep looking and phone them back if the girl hadn't shown up by dinner time. Janet phoned Emma who said, 'What about asking Kylie?' She wondered if her niece might have gone somewhere familiar, somewhere she was used to playing with her friends.

'Emma's right,' said Joe with new energy, 'there's a lot we can do. Mum, could you go home and stay there in case Zoe turns up at your place, and Dad could you go to the front and have a look round there?'

'Yes,' said David, 'and I'll go to the place where I take Zoe birdwatching. The tide is out this morning and if she's walked out there, there won't be many people around to worry her.' David suddenly had a good feeling about this. Zoe loved spotting curlews and oystercatchers on the edge of the faraway water and in his mind, David could see the shape of his granddaughter, small and lonely in the vast expanse of wet muddy sand. He would find her, and he would bring her home.

'What are you going to do?' Janet asked her son, trying to keep the anxiety out of her voice.

'I'm going to stay here in case she comes home, and I think that's the most likely outcome, and I'm going to phone the school and see if the teacher could speak with Kylie. I'm also going to ask Kylie to come over after school. Kylie is our best bet I reckon.'

*

At lunchtime Kylie had the unpleasant surprise to find that Miss Brown wanted to speak with her again. Zoe had not turned up and everyone was now extremely worried. Shifting in her seat Kylie asked if people had looked down the front where Zoe and her friends played and rollerbladed, and Miss Brown said the grandad had been there and not found her. Kylie shrugged as if to say she had nothing else to contribute.

'Children often have dens or hiding places, could you think of anywhere down the front where Zoe might be hiding?' asked the teacher.

'No Miss,' replied Kylie, looking her teacher in the eyes, 'there's nothing like that, we just rollerblade or have an ice-cream in the café. We don't play hide and seek.' Kylie's eyes were transparent with truthfulness and Miss Brown sighed and let the girl go. Then she remembered there was something else and ran after the child. 'Kylie,' she said as she caught up with her, 'Zoe's dad would like you to pop round to his house after school. Is that all right?' She had expected the girl to be reluctant, as she had been with her, but Kylie said cheerfully, 'Sure, I'll go and see Joe.' Miss Brown felt defeated. She was usually good at getting children to open up to her, but when she most needed that talent it had eluded her. She watched Kylie join her friends in a skipping rope game. And suddenly she glimpsed something important: Kylie, who was a worrier, did not seem the least bit worried about her friend.

Kylie could not believe her luck. She had racked her brain all morning trying to find an excuse to run out the back as soon as she got home, and now Miss Brown had just given it to her. Zoe's dad wanted to see her. She would go to his house the back way and first go straight to find Zoe in their den, which is where she was bound to be. Where else could she be? Miss Brown had been right about a den, but fortunately she thought the den was down the front which had made it very easy for Kylie to dismiss the idea.

Nobody knew about Zoe and Kylie's den because parents would have forbidden them ever going there and they didn't want to share their secret with other friends. The den was an old shed in the garden of an empty derelict house. At the beginning they had explored the house itself, and some boys had played there too, but one day they had found all the windows and doors boarded up. The shed however made a very good den and when they were in it, they could lock the garden gate and keep everyone out. They had put some old rags and towels on the ground, a few cushions stolen from Zoe's attic and there was a pile of old comic books in a corner.

When Kylie finally made it out into the back alley, she fully expected to find the gate locked and to have to climb over the wall, which was risky if someone saw her. Her heart was beating fast as she got to the gate and pushed, but to her surprise it swung open without resistance. She rushed to the shed door and pulled it open, ready to see her friend sitting on the cushions, waiting for her to arrive. The shed was empty. Kylie stood in disbelief, scanning every inch of the empty space, and now she felt a little sick. If her friend wasn't here, where was she? She should have told Miss Brown, she should… Kylie's eyes stopped on a tiny bit of something glinting from under a cushion. She grabbed the cushion and found a Whisper wrapper under it. A Whisper bar was what

Zoe had in her lunchbox every day. Kylie looked around the shed again as if expecting Zoe to materialise now she had proof of her presence.

At that moment Zoe was standing a few feet from her friend, motionless amongst weeds and brambles between the back of the shed and the garden wall and barely breathing. She had her rucksack in one hand and her inhaler in the other. So far, her plan was working.

The figure of Zoe's dad waiting for her in his house loomed in Kylie's mind. She put the wrapper back under the cushion and fled out of the rundown garden and into her own, as fast as she could down the path, into her kitchen and her mother's arms where she burst into tears.

'I don't know where she is Mum, I don't know where she is,' she hiccupped between sobs.

'It's all right, darling, nobody expects you to know. Did Zoe's dad say something to upset you?' Kylie's mum was brushing her daughter's tears away and pushing wet strands of hair out of her face, trying to look into the girl's eyes to find an answer to the mystery of this upset.

'No, I haven't been to see Zoe's dad,' she hiccupped again, 'but I thought I knew where she was, but she's not there.' Now everybody would find out about the den, there would be reprimands and disappointment, and Kylie's life felt more miserable than she had ever known was possible. Her dad would say she wasn't allowed to play with Zoe anymore, at which thought her crying redoubled, and then her thoughts focussed on Zoe again, and she knew she must stop crying and help the grown-ups look for her.

Five minutes later Kylie's mum and Joe were discovering the derelict house, the overgrown garden and the shed. They didn't make any comments, just looked around the garden and tried the doors and windows into the house. Nobody thought of looking amongst the brambles behind the shed and although Zoe was gone by then, one of them might have noticed a patch of trampled weeds and a couple of broken brambles and been reassured that the girl had been there not long ago. Joe might even have recognised his daughter's way of playing hide and seek, moving silently from one hiding place to another, fooling the adults searching for her and never showing up until they had given up in loud voices.

Kylie and her mum went back home, and Joe carried on searching the alley. He opened unlocked gates, peeped into gardens and talked to all the neighbours he could find. Nobody had seen his daughter. His phone had not rung and there was no point phoning his parents to be told they were no wiser. He went home to make himself a drink. He filled the kettle and sat down at the table, waiting for it to boil. The police had said children who run away usually turn up again by teatime. He looked at his watch, but it was only just after five. His breathing was shallow with anxiety and his limbs weighed a ton. When the kettle stopped boiling, he didn't move, he didn't even notice that it had stopped. Dark thoughts were going round and round in his head, driving him crazy.

'Dad,' said a voice coming from behind. Joe froze and then started to turn around on his chair, very slowly as if a sudden movement might frighten the voice away.

'I don't believe what Mum said about you', the voice continued, 'but I wanted to ask you anyway.' Zoe stood there, dishevelled and ragged, with her rucksack dangling from one hand and her eyes looking straight into his. It was the most beautiful sight, and he wanted to pick his daughter up and squeeze her in his arms, he wanted to tell her off for frightening him so much, he wanted to cry, and shout for joy, and scream with relief, and ask a million questions, but instead he sat where he was and extended his arm for his daughter to come close. When she did, he took hold of her hands and said, looking deep into her eyes, 'Zoe, what your mother said about me is not true, I did not do what she said, but I am very sorry that what happened that night led to you being upset. I am very sorry about that Zoe.'

Zoe climbed onto her father's lap and snuggled into his arms. 'I knew it,' she said, 'I knew she was lying.'

Zoe showed no sign of wanting to move from her position and although Joe knew he must make all the necessary phone calls, he didn't move either. *Let her recharge her batteries*, he thought, *because her life is not going to get any easier,* and he tightened his hold around his little girl.

*

The following morning Kylie's head was bursting with questions as she waited for her friend to show up in the schoolyard. The moment she spotted her walking down the pavement, her heart started beating. Would Zoe want to talk? She ran towards her and her friend smiled, with a hint of triumph in her eyes.

'You'll never guess where I was when you were looking for me in the den,' she said.

'You saw me?' asked Kylie

'I heard you coming, and I hid behind the den.'

'In all those brambles?'

Proudly Zoe extended her scratched arm to prove the point.

'I didn't want you to find me, but I knew you'd come straight to the den. You did well not to tell your mum. I knew you'd go and tell your mum when you couldn't find me, so I sneaked out and went to hide in Dad's garden, behind his shed. When he came out to look at the den with your mum, I got the key to his shed and hid there.'

'How did you know he wouldn't look there?'

'He would have looked before, and grown-ups don't look again in the same place.'

'Did you get told off?' asked Kylie, moving to the next pressing question on her mind.

'I didn't, not even Mum,' replied Zoe, unable to make sense of this unfathomable mystery. The girls pondered this in silence for a moment and then Kylie told Zoe there was something she didn't understand either. Her mother had not said a word to her dad about the den. 'I was scared all evening,' she said, 'waiting for it, I thought I'd never be allowed to play with you again, and then nothing.' She shrugged.

'Same here,' said Zoe, grabbing her friend's arm, 'Dad said nothing about the den to anyone, just said I'd been hiding in the back alley. Can you believe that?'

Just then the bell rang, but Kylie wasn't quite done, and she held Zoe back.

'Why did you wait till five thirty to go and see your dad? Everyone was really worried.'

Zoe shrugged, looked a little stuck and then said, 'That's when I was ready to ask him my question.' She paused and added, 'Also I got hungry.'

The two friends joined the line of children waiting to walk into their classroom and Miss Brown gave them a long look.

Kylie thought that against all the odds it seemed to be a friendly look.

9. Zoe's New Offensive

The postman on Grove Road was an early riser which meant Joe could expect to hear the soft thud of his mail landing on the doormat whilst he was munching on his breakfast cereal. In the ordinary run of events the arrival of the post barely got noticed as most communications now came by email. But this changed the moment Leanne reported Joe's alleged rape to the police. All through breakfast Joe's ears were now tuned in to the possible click of the letter box and when it came, he would stop eating, slowly put his spoon down and make his way to the front door with a knot of fear tightening his insides. It didn't take long to shuffle through a few familiar envelopes, but there was no peace in not finding the letter that was coming to bite him, because every day that it didn't come just added to his mounting anxiety, knowing that one day an envelope with a different look would lie on his floor and he would pick it up with a trembling hand.

The day the letter came was exactly a week after Zoe had run away. He stared at it long and hard, and when he found the courage to rip it open, he saw immediately it wasn't from the police. It was from Social Services. He tried to read but it all blended into an incomprehensible blur, so he stuffed it in his pocket, went upstairs to brush his teeth and left for work. He didn't look at the letter again until his lunch break. He read it quickly then in disgust. They were asking him to attend a Case Conference regarding the safeguarding of his daughter following the allegation of rape reported to the police by his ex-partner. An explosive mix of fear and anger filled his head, and he stuffed the letter back in his pocket. It felt to Joe as if a cold and indifferent world was closing in on him, and he was trapped.

The case conference took place four days later.

Until that day Joe had had no idea a bunch of ordinary people like teachers and nurses, led by the report of a completely biased social worker, could have the power to rule over the lives of other ordinary people like him. Yet on that day, that is precisely what happened. The Chair sat at one end of the table, like a judge, and along one side, Zoe's Deputy Head Teacher, the school nurse and the social worker in his suit accompanied by his manager, a thin woman with cropped black hair. The wimp hadn't had the bottle to come on his own. The big policewoman was there too with her small piercing eyes and a couple of other people sat along from the secretary, but he didn't catch who they were. The meeting started and to his astonishment, his whole life was gaily spilled onto the table, with everyone in turn discussing his family, their relationships and how best to protect his daughter from her dreadful parents. Dreadful father actually. Never had he felt so angry and nervous all at once, so unable to put on a good show. Leanne sat next to him, her usual alluring self, cool as cucumber as she talked coyly about 'what had happened between them'. When the discussion turned to whether it was safe for Zoe to spend time alone with her father, Joe banged his fist hard on the table and shouted that the allegation was a lie and surely, he was innocent until proven guilty, and in any case he had never done any harm to his daughter, never smacked her, never shouted at her and there was no reason to stop her seeing him, they couldn't do that.

But they could and they did. As long as the allegation of rape stood Zoe would not spend time alone with her father. When Leanne agreed to Zoe spending time with her grandparents in order to give the girl some stability in her difficult young life, Joe turned to look at her in disbelief. The caring mother. The fucking caring mother. He scanned the faces around the table, couldn't they see all she was interested in were her free weekends?

No, they couldn't. And now Joe had to break more bad news to his daughter.

*

The anxious wait for the arrival of the letter from the police resumed, but now he also had Zoe asking him on the phone if the letter had come so he could clear his name and she could stay with him again. No letter came but a couple of weeks later the secretary in work told him there had been a phone call from the police and could he ring them back. He tried to stop his hand shaking as he took the post-it note she was holding out for him and with a curt nod he turned and made for his office. His colleagues were already busy at their computers and he had to go out again and phone from his car. He got through quickly and the woman asked him to call at the station before the end of the day but would not say anything more. The matter must be dealt with in person. Joe's mouth was now completely dry and his insides dangerously loose. He could not take any more time off work and decided he would go at four thirty. The day passed extremely slowly and yet when four thirty came if felt as if it had flown by and he wasn't ready, not the least bit ready.

At the police station they kept him waiting fifteen sweaty minutes, before a pleasant young man in uniform called him into his office.

'I have good news for you, Mr Milton,' he said as Joe was taking his seat, 'the rape allegations have been dropped.' The young man was leaning forward on his desk, looking at Joe with a friendly but uncertain look in his eyes. He knew that this sentence could bring anger as well as relief and he was reading Joe's face to prepare for what was coming. But Joe sat there motionless looking blank. This also happened. A moment was needed to take the news in, and then the emotional reaction came. But the conflicting thoughts and feelings in Joe's brain were silencing him. After a while he asked 'She can do that? Just like that, no explanation, no apology?' The young man nodded in sympathy. Joe felt so completely drained he wondered if he would be able to make it to his car and drive home. The young man got up and he did the same, saying thank you and goodbye automatically, and when he finally sat down behind his wheel, he did not know whether to scream in anger or shout for joy. Zoe was spending a couple of weeks of her summer holiday with his parents and he trembled with impatience at the thought of arriving there and announcing his news. But first he must go and have a shower to wash away the sweat still clinging to him.

*

112

Joe pressed the bell at his parents' house and tried to suppress the little smile tugging at his lips. His daughter had seen him through the window, and now he could hear a lot of shouting and rushing on the other side of the door, but would he be able to keep them hanging for just a minute? The door opened, Zoe jumped into his arms and his parents and sister stood staring at him questioningly. Visits normally had to be arranged and reported to Social Services, so this could only mean one thing, but they didn't dare believe it. His little smile turned into a big grin and then they believed it.

'She dropped the charges?' asked his mother.

He nodded and they all walked into the living room, sat down and listened to Joe's story. When he finished the four adults looked at one another expressing with their eyes what they could not say outright in front of the child. 'The bitch,' said the eyes, 'the sly cunning bitch.' Then they all moved into their own separate thoughts with Janet worrying that this might ultimately fuel her son's anger, leading to more fighting and more pain for Zoe whilst David wondered how the woman could be punished for what she had done to his son. Emma scrutinised her brother's face for signs that the veil had finally dropped from his eyes in relation to the nasty cow he had so hopelessly fallen in love with.

Zoe was sitting silently in her father's arms and Joe looked down at her wondering why she wasn't showing more enthusiasm. She was all coiled up, like a spring gathered unto itself, and her lips did not smile.

'What's up, sweetheart?' he asked

'So, she gets away with it does she?' replied Zoe angrily. 'Tells a great big lie, stops me seeing my dad for weeks and then says, "Oh, sorry, I lied," and that's the end of it?'

Joe's arm tightened around his daughter, but not one of the adults could find anything to say. They agreed with the girl but also understood the importance of not fuelling her anger. Like it or not she would have to live with her mother. And yet, had they expressed their own felt truth at that moment, they might have helped Zoe to move on. Instead, she remained stuck in a lonely place where nobody understood her, and her anger did not get a chance to become diluted in the flow of shared emotions.

Later that evening, after Zoe had gone to bed, Joe and his family were finally able to share their thoughts.

'You'll never guess how she explained dropping the charges,' he said. They looked at him and he continued, 'She's doing it to protect Zoe, so the girl isn't known as the kid whose father is a rapist.' His voice was bitter now, all joy drained from his eyes.

'Like she hasn't done the damage already,' snorted Emma.

'Yeah, and more to the point, Emma, like I am a rapist.'

'She's making damn sure the mud's going to stick,' muttered Joe's father.

'This is worse than mud, Dad, much worse.'

*

When the time came for Zoe to go and spend the rest of the summer holiday with her mother, Joe met with the usual resistance. 'I don't want to go, Dad, please.' Watching her eyes fill up, he hugged her in his arms, hating the sight of those tears. His lips brushed against her hair as he tried to be reassuring. 'It'll be okay,' he said soothingly, 'you'll see. Mum will be glad to see you after two weeks, and anyway you can spend most of your time with Kylie.' All meaningless nonsense, he knew, but what else could he do but try and twist the truth into a more acceptable shape, for both their sakes?

But as soon as Zoe walked into the flat the following afternoon, she knew that things would not be okay. At first it was just the way they all looked at her. Then the words came.

'Look at this sullen face,' snorted Ivor over tea. 'We were hoping for some gratefulness from the little madam after her dad was let off the hook.' He pulled his enormous mug of tea to his lips and stared at Zoe over the rim. She pushed a mouthful of pizza into her mouth and stared back, munching.

Leanne extended her hand and laid it over her daughter's arm. 'I did it for you, chicken, you know that don't you?' Zoe met her mother's eyes coldly and asked, deadpan, 'Did what?'

'Not press charges against your dad,' replied Leanne.

'It was a lie anyway,' said Zoe. 'You lie all the time.' Her mother lied easily, with wide candid eyes and Zoe had always been surprised when she was younger and very naïve, to see other adults, whom she credited with supernatural powers of knowledge and understanding, completely taken in. Lying was just part of the business of living for Zoe's mum, and she had no qualms about it nor did it trouble her that Zoe and Jessie were regular witnesses to her deceitful methods. The rape accusation was just another example, but this time her mother had gone too far.

Zoe met her mother's eyes brazenly, then Ivor's and then Jessie's. Go on, hit me, was the message in her eyes, let's get on with the war and see who wins. Leanne sent Ivor and Jessie a warning glance, then turned to her daughter and said coldly, 'Go to your room, Zoe, and don't come out until you're ready to apologise.'

'Never,' shouted Zoe, as she left the room with her chin up, 'You're the one who should apologise.'

*

After the rape allegation was dropped the Milton family closed ranks, freshly united by their anger against Leanne and newly determined to find a way of bringing Zoe home to her father. It was Emma who came up with the idea that if Zoe had her own solicitor a case could be built to overturn Leanne's residence order. Zoe was taken to meet a nice lawyer called Mr Fowler but as she explained her situation, she saw the surprise in the young man's eyes at a girl not yet ten years of age being so wise to the ways of adults and the enforcements of the law. He didn't like her very much, she thought resignedly, used as she had become to that feeling, especially when she mentioned rape allegations and residence orders. It reminded her of when, as a very little girl, she had told clueless adults on the beach that what they had just called a seagull was actually a black-headed gull, except that in winter it didn't have its black head. But then the looks from the adults had been full of admiration, whereas now they were wary, as if she had become a creature people couldn't quite place and found a little disgusting.

Zoe described her life to Mr Fowler, hoping he would agree it was quite intolerable and the time had come to go back to the judge for a different decision on where she should live. But he didn't. Nasty words and smacking were perfectly legal according to him, and this led Zoe to conclude that if she wanted a case against her mother, she needed to get properly hurt. Someone had to hit her in a way that was not just a smack, and there was one person in that household who'd been dying to do just that to her for a very long time.

Two weeks without Zoe had been an eye-opener for Ivor. Life with Leanne could be good. Fun. Relaxed. But now it was turning sour again. The brat was back, hardly talking to anyone, complaining that she didn't like the food, didn't want to go out with the family, and ignoring him when he made the mistake of addressing her. He was desperate to take things in hand, teach her to be polite, forget all the nonsense about pussyfooting around the little madam in case she made a complaint to her newly acquired solicitor. What kind of fucking nonsense was that? A nine-year-old threatening to write to her solicitor if she wasn't happy with the treatment she got from her parents? From her parents, for fuck's sake! But Leanne wouldn't hear any of it. Not that Leanne seemed to love the girl, forever likening her to the ex-partner she hated, so why not let the brat go and live with her dad and be shot of her? Ivor was not a violent man, but what was the point of all his strength if it couldn't be used to make a child behave? The girl wasn't frightened of him, she was cheeky in her sullen provocative way and there was nothing he could do about it except seethe inside and make his ulcer burn.

Until the day he could hold back no longer.

It happened on a hot afternoon in August, when Leanne was in work and he had been back a couple of days from a long drive to the South of Spain. The day was sultry with dark blue clouds hanging low above the roofs, threatening to explode in a fanfare of thunder and lightning. Slouching on the couch with his bare chest and shoulders glistening with sweat, he held a cool beer in one hand and the remote in the other. He was flicking aimlessly through channels when he heard Zoe coming down the stairs.

'Zoe,' he called, 'come here a minute.'

She came to stand in the doorway, a distasteful look in her eyes and her lips a thin sullen line. He half twisted his big torso to face the door, smiled pleasantly as if he hadn't noticed her expression and asked if she fancied a lift down to Kylie's. Zoe shook her head, 'No thanks,' she said and made to head for the kitchen again.

'Wait a sec,' called Ivor, stretching his arm over the top of the settee. 'It doesn't have to be Kylie, could be any friend, or your Nan. I'm easy. I just don't want to be stuck in the flat all afternoon.'

'I want to stay here,' replied Zoe her large grey blue eyes holding his gaze.

'Well, you're not staying here. Know what, kid? Today it's just you and me, so for once it's going to be the adult who decides what happens. And what happens is I'm shooting off to the pub where it'll be a damn sight cooler and the company will be more cheerful.' He hoisted himself from the couch and pulled his baggy shorts up to fit around his waist. Zoe looked up at him silently, then turned and started walking away saying, 'I'm not going anywhere. I can stay here on my own.'

In a swift movement forward, surprising in one so bulky, Ivor caught up with her and grabbed her arm.

'Don't walk away on me, you little brat. You may have your own solicitor but you're too young to stay on your own, so decide where you want to go.'

Zoe shook her arm free and carried on walking. He grabbed her shoulders and spun her round, but she went slack in his grip, letting her head loll about as if she were a rag doll. Ivor

118

wiped the sweat off his forehead with the heel of one hand and looked down at the girl the way he might have looked at a spider before squashing it with one foot. She looked straight ahead, through his body, her eyes dull with boredom.

'Where do you want to go?' he asked again, trying to control his temper. 'Your friend's or your nan's? That's the choice.'

'Mum didn't say I had to go anywhere,' replied Zoe, her eyes sliding to the floor, 'so I'm staying here. You can do what you like.'

'You little brat,' said Ivor, bending over and lifting her chin up, forcing her eyes to meet his, 'you're doing this on purpose aren't you? Winding me up. Well, you're going to learn one thing today Zoe, there's a limit to what I'm gonna tolerate from a manipulative little bitch like you.'

Zoe looked back at him, her wide eyes unafraid. 'My mother's a manipulative bitch,' she said, 'and you tolerate loads from her.'

Ivor was taken by surprise, like a judo player thrown on the mat by a much smaller person. He stood still for a few seconds, his hulk of a body balanced in the void of indecision, and then slowly his hand moved. It went back like the racket of a tennis player before a well-aimed forehand and swung forward making perfect contact right in the middle of the girl's left cheek. It was a well-executed shot, not too hard but hard enough to spring a joyful note in his heart. At last. She got what she deserved. He had on his face the satisfied look of someone who has just accomplished a task that had been postponed for far too long. But his moment of triumph didn't last. With widening eyes, he saw the girl as if in slow motion put her left hand up to her cheek as if to test that the cheek was still there and then sway sideways and, like one of those

119

diving bastards on a football pitch, project herself against the edge of the doorframe behind her. The whole movement was performed with an almost graceful sideways rolling motion so that her forehead hit the wood rather than the back of her head. The impact was loud, and she shrieked as she collapsed in a crumpled heap on the floor, straight into the foetal position, screaming 'Don't touch me, don't come near me.'

At that moment Ivor knew he'd been set up. A nine-year-old had had the better of him. Sweat broke all over his face, and it wasn't because of the heat. His great bulk had gone limp as he watched the hateful girl writhing on the floor. He was lost. Thoughts clashed inside his head, leading to paralysis of both body and mind. He knew he'd fucked up and Leanne's anger would be something else. Yet he also knew he had been provoked beyond endurance. The girl had wanted him to hit her. His hatred of her rose inside him and at that moment he would have happily stepped on her as if she were a spider. Got rid of her. Out of his life. Out of their life. Which she was ruining. And Leanne couldn't see it. A scream of frustration choked in his gullet as he watched the girl carry on with her act.

'Call an ambulance,' she was crying, holding her head and hiding inside her doubled-up position. 'I've got brain damage, I'm sure I have. There's blood on my hand.'

Ivor tried to control his heaving chest and asked to see her head. She carried on screaming from the floor that she didn't want him near her. He took a couple of deep breaths and went to the phone. With a shaking hand he picked up the receiver and dialled the GP's surgery. When the receptionist answered he explained the situation as best he could without giving away his part in the fall. The woman said it was probably safer to take the girl to casualty and check her out. The sweat was now pouring off him and his hand was trembling. Child abuse. He'd heard stories about kids being removed because of violence at home. Had he in one stupid move lost Leanne's battle for her? Would that spell the end of their relationship? He stood numb by the phone, desperate to put the clock back. How the mind lets you down when it cannot give up on the idea of turning the clock back, when it takes you step by miserable step back to the point where you could have acted differently, where all the options were still open, where, if you concentrate hard enough you might still be able to make an alternative choice. Ivor could hear his heart pumping.

He turned slowly around and contemplated the girl crying on the floor. Her sobs were getting more and more forced, but he knew he now had to try and recover something out of the fucking disaster. He went to her, dropped on his haunches and asked in a falsely concerned voice if her head was getting a little better. He dragged a mumbled apology out of his knotted throat and told her he would take her off to casualty. She parted her hands just enough to cast him a malevolent look and reminded him that she wasn't going anywhere with him. She then wailed that she wanted her father or her gran to take her and curled up again into a ball of fake sobbing. Ivor was at a loss. He stood uncertain what to do next and finally decided to phone Leanne and risk her wrath if she was with a client. As luck would have it, she wasn't but her anger came travelling down the phone line all the same and as he felt the sharp edge of her voice knifing into his skull, he considered just packing his bags and saying goodbye to the goddamn mess of a relationship. He sighed, agreed to everything and hung up.

Ten minutes later Leanne walked into the flat and took her protesting daughter to casualty. Zoe was found to be all right, except for a bump and a small cut on her forehead which would not leave any traces the doctor assured her. The skull is remarkably hard he explained reassuringly to her mother, and the knock had no doubt felt worse than it had been. He then cleared his throat and lowered his eyes before saying in a soft voice that was meant to be out of Zoe's hearing that smacking children on the face carried a risk and if physical punishment was needed, a slap on the legs or hands was the safe choice. Zoe heard anyway and noticed that the doctor didn't like to look at her mum as he talked about smacking. But her mother gave the doctor her biggest smile, said all the right things in a humble tone and wrapped a motherly arm around her daughter as they got up to leave. The doctor nodded understandingly, looking quite reassured.

As soon as Zoe got home, she shut herself in her room and phoned her father. He phoned the police. They phoned Social Services. A new offensive had been launched.

10. Leanne's Counter-Offensive

Zoe had every reason to be pleased with herself. In the planning and execution of her campaign to escape from life in the flat, she displayed strategic talent and bravery she hadn't even known were in her. She felt she had won already and would soon be allowed to go and live with her dad. But children are novices at life, and they play their moves one at a time, without predicting, and therefore pre-empting, the many moves hiding up the sleeves of the opposition. Zoe knew her mother well and yet she failed to see that Leanne would quickly launch a counter offensive built around her superior ability to manipulate people and situations.

The first move that took Zoe by surprise was that on the night of the 'assault' Ivor packed his bags and took himself off to a friend's flat. This should have been a gratifying moment, but Zoe watched him go with a sinking heart, grasping immediately that she no longer had a case to refuse to stay in the flat. How could she not have seen that coming? What she did not see coming either was that Leanne, unlike Zoe, was not about to sit back and think that because she won one battle, she had won the war. Leanne understood perfectly the importance of never half-killing your enemy, and in this case the enemy was the idea that she was failing to protect her daughter. She made an appointment to see Gerald Crispin the following Monday.

At four thirty on that Monday Leanne was shown into a small room with a round wooden table in the middle and four chairs around it. When Gerald walked in a few minutes later, Leanne got up from her chair and extended her hand. As he responded to her smile Gerald knew he would mention that smile to Karen in the evening. Too much, too friendly, as if they knew each other of old and were in this together. He stiffened very slightly and took his eyes away from her generously exposed cleavage.

They sat down and Leanne launched into her explanation. He had perhaps already heard of the incident between her new partner Ivor and Zoe? He agreed he had. She was here to explain what had happened in case he got the wrong idea. She talked of her partner as a man of many qualities but not used to children, particularly a child like Zoe who could not accept the presence in her home of any man other than her own father. She smiled a lot, with nuances of regret, sympathy and understanding colouring her words. Here was a mother doing her best for everyone. Ivor, she explained, would move out until such a time as Zoe was able to accept the presence of another man with her mother. It was a sacrifice they were both prepared to make for the long term good. 'It's not easy for him, Mr Crispin, and he is devastated by what he did. Can't understand it to this moment. And still, he will not blame Zoe. If I say to him, she wound you up, and you know what girls are like, Mr Crispin, they can be very clever at winding people up, if I say that to him, he won't accept it. No, Leanne, he says, I'm the adult, I shouldn't have let my temper get the better of me. And that is the difference between Ivor and Joe. Never would Joe recognise that he is in the wrong. Never would he admit that his temper got the better of him. With Joe it is always somebody else's fault, Mr Crispin.'

She went on to explain that Ivor wouldn't spend the night at the flat when Zoe was there, nor would he ever be in sole charge of her. It would make life difficult, but Leanne understood that a split up between parents is not easy for the kids and Zoe was reacting badly. They would all have to fit round her for a while, until things settled into their new routine. She smiled with the confidence that they obviously would settle down in the end. And then she played her master card.

'Are you happy with these plans, Mr Crispin, or would you like to suggest anything else? Social Services are the experts in these matters, and I am here to take your advice.'

Gerald couldn't help enjoying the flattery. He knew the woman was being supremely clever in every move she made and every smile she pulled, yet he was convinced. She had painted a picture of a mother who loved her daughter and was prepared to put her first at this difficult time, and that was the picture he saw. He saw the painter at work, but he believed the picture. She added her last touch with the hint of a tremble in her voice, 'You see Mr Crispin, I love my daughter. I want her to be happy. I would never try to take her away from her father, but I don't want her taken from me either, and at times it feels like there's four of them out there trying to do just that against one of me.' She looked down and paused, as if to give her emotions a break, and raised her eyes again as she added with a reflective smile touched with sadness, 'Life isn't easy every day for a single mum.'

Gerald had watched Leanne as she spoke. The woman didn't have a beautiful face, her eyes being too small and close together and her nose too strong, but when she smiled, she was attractive, and she made the most of a good figure. Her hair was amazing. But what the woman had above all was a certain presence that made a man want to look again. Her smile was engaging, her attraction of the alluring kind. Gerald could well understand why a man like Joe Milton could not let her go. She must have brought riches to his life he had never dared to hope for.

'Mrs Milton,' said Gerald, looking straight into her eyes, 'the new situation sounds perfectly satisfactory to me, but we will have to call another case conference and put an official stamp on the arrangements you have just described. Before that I would like, if I may, to have a chat with Zoe on her own. When I saw her at home with her father, she was perhaps too intimidated to say anything, as you know there was a police officer with me, and children can be awed by a uniform.'

*

Leanne's mother was looking after the girls in the flat that Monday afternoon and she left as soon as her daughter got back. Zoe was watching TV in her room and came down reluctantly when called to dinner. She expected nothing good to come from her mother's meeting with Social Services, but when she saw the hint of triumph in Leanne's little smile, she trembled to think what might be coming. She watched her mother drain the pasta, mix it with the sauce and finally dish it out onto their plates. Jessie was engrossed in her phone and Leanne was in no rush to speak. Zoe ate slowly, struggling with the knot of tension in her stomach. Still Leanne said

126

nothing. A few more mouthfuls went down, and finally Leanne spoke.

'I had a very good meeting with Mr Crispin,' she said casually, 'and now he would like a meeting with you Zoe, on your own.' She wrapped a big coil of spaghetti around her fork and showed her pleasure as she munched through her food. Zoe meanwhile felt that the contents of her stomach had just come straight back up her gullet. She managed to carry on eating the next small mouthful as if she didn't care, but she did care. Her brilliant move against Ivor had led to something she needed like a hole in the head. A vivid picture popped up in her mind, she was playing chess with Grandad and he had shaken his head as he took her queen. 'Sweetheart,' he'd said, 'it's not enough to think of your own move, you have to look at what you're opening up for your opponent.'

Zoe was beginning to feel very small and very lost.

Three days later she was taken to the same small room where her mother had had her meeting and Mr Crispin was there waiting for her. She wanted to turn around and run away, but Leanne was standing right behind her, ready to grab her arm if she tried to escape. She went in dragging her feet and sat down determined to say nothing. But Mr Crispin surprised her. On his own he turned out to be nice, and she quickly found herself happily telling him about school, about Miss Brown, about rollerblading with her friend Kylie and about visiting her grandparents. He listened nodding his head and wanting to know a little more about everything. Then he popped a different kind of question. 'What is it about your dad, Zoe,' he asked, 'that makes you so keen to live with him?' He was watching her closely. Her eyes searched the walls for something to focus on whilst she thought about her answer, but she met with blankness. I love him and he loves me, was the simple answer, but it sounded too much like a stupid gushy song and wasn't convincing when talking about your dad. Her eyes dropped to her feet and stuck there, on her new trainers. Even though it was Mum who had bought them, Zoe loved her new trainers. Mum had hit the jackpot with those and there was no denying it. She looked up and said, 'When Dad puts his arms around me, I feel safe". Mr Crispin nodded, and Zoe felt she had said the right thing.

'What about Ivor,' he then asked, 'are you frightened of Ivor?'

The girl gave him a long look before replying. Then she said slowly, 'Yes, I'm frightened of Ivor, he's nasty,' and Gerald knew she was lying.

'What about your mum, Zoe,' he asked leaning back in his chair and pretending to be casual about this question, 'you've complained of getting smacked. Are you frightened of her? Is that why you don't want to live there?'

'No,' replied Zoe, 'I'm not frightened of mum, but…'

Just then there was a knock on the door and Gerald spun around with annoyance. But when he saw Gail pushing her head around the door his expression changed to a polite welcome and he told Zoe this was his boss who was keen to hear her story. Zoe stared at Gail, doubting this woman was in any way interested in her story. Gerald sat back and watched his boss destroy all the good work he had achieved in the last twenty minutes. But that wasn't the worst of it, because he was also watching the girl making an enemy of a person who had a lot of power over her young life, and he was powerless to do anything about it.

128

'You see, Zoe,' Gail pronounced sanctimoniously, 'saying you're not happy living with your mother is not a good enough reason. Nobody is happy all the time. Happiness is all about compromise and taking others into account. Your mother wants you to live with her, by all accounts she's a perfectly good mother and we can't take you away from her just because you're saying you're not happy. What if next week you're not happy with your father, where will you go then?'

Zoe stared at Gail thinking she had evil eyes.

'You see, you have no answer, have you?' insisted Gail.

'Mum left dad because she wasn't happy with him so why can't I leave her because I'm not happy with her?' replied the child with the faultless logic of the young.

There was a stunned silence. Gerald looked down at his feet and Gail stared at the cheeky girl with the extreme annoyance of someone whose authority has just been flouted yet fails to find the cutting reply needed to restore it. Zoe recognised the look on Gail's face and couldn't suppress a smile. It was the disbelieving look of a tennis player who thought his shot had won the point but sees the ball coming back at him from an angle that shouldn't exist. Gail looked round to Gerald like the tennis player in a doubles game looking at his partner as if to say, 'why didn't you get that one back? That was your shot.' Gerald cleared his throat and came up with nothing better than some bland remark about things being different for children and adults, and you couldn't apply the same rules.

'Why not?' asked Zoe, encouraged by her previous success. But now Gail had had time to recover her wits and her reply was cutting and final. 'Because, young lady, children are dependent on adults for everything. The house you live in, the clothes you wear, the food you eat, your TV, your music,

129

everything in your life is provided by your parents and has been since the day you were born. And that, Zoe, gives them rights. Bringing up your children is a duty, but it is also a right. Your mother who carried you, gave birth to you and then looked after you has the right to bring you up and unless she is seen to harm you, she will have our support in upholding that right. Now do you understand that, Zoe?'

Zoe was dimly aware that she had gone far enough and yet she couldn't let the woman have the last word.

'My dad also has the right to bring me up,' she retorted, 'and he provides more money than Mum.'

The woman looked as if she had completely stopped breathing and was about to explode. Mr Crispin must have been worried too, because he put his hand out as if to smooth things over and looking sternly at Zoe said, 'That's enough answering back, Zoe. Mrs Anderson and I are here to help you and your parents resolve a difficult situation and we will get nowhere if we just argue. We have been listening to you, Zoe, and you also need to listen to us. As Mrs Anderson explained before, finding solutions is all about compromise.'

That was the moment Zoe gave up on Mr Crispin. Like all adults he sided with the other adults, not with the child even if she was right, and Zoe felt that Mr Crispin knew she was right. The meeting ended and Leanne took her daughter home but failed to get a word out of her. Zoe went straight to her room and phoned her dad who was still in work. Joe listened with mounting anger to the story of an interview he hadn't even been notified of and half an hour later he was standing in front of the receptionist and demanding to see Mr Crispin immediately.

Gerald could have told Linda that Mr Milton needed to make an appointment, but he decided to face the unpleasant situation now rather than let it hang over him for a day or two. Linda told Joe Mr Crispin would spare him a few minutes now. A few minutes would be fine replied Joe. She showed him into the interview room and closed the door. As she headed back towards her office, Gerald emerged out of the staff room looking weary.

'You've got one angry man waiting for you in there,' she whispered.

As Gerald walked down the corridor towards the interview room, he felt a familiar burning sensation in his stomach. He tried to straighten his back and square his shoulders as he pushed the door open and greeted the tall man who stood looking out of the window.

Joe spun around, ignoring the hand that had been extended towards him. His face was taut and his eyes threatening. 'What right do you think you have to try and get information out of my daughter without even letting me know about it?' he said, 'Without her solicitor being informed?' His finger had shot up, pointing directly at Gerald. 'The girl may only be nine, but she has rights you know, just like you and me.' His voice was too loud, his body too tense and his eyes too aggressive. Why did people have to be so unpleasant?

'Please sit down, Mr Milton,' said Gerald, backing around to the other side of the table and lowering himself into a chair. He waited for the other man to take the chair opposite before carrying on. 'Zoe's mother was happy for me to have a chat…'

'Leanne doesn't give a damn about how Zoe feels about anything,' said Joe with a dismissive wave of the hand. 'But her boyfriend assaulted my daughter, that's what we should be talking about.' Joe slammed the flat of his hand on the table. 'You had no right to subject Zoe to an interview without…'

'Mr Milton, if a child appears to be at risk Social Services have every right to find out what is going on, indeed it's not just a right, it's a duty. As you rightly said your daughter had been taken to hospital after receiving a slap and although…'

'But you didn't ask her anything about the assault, did you?' Joe butted in. 'No, you tried to wheedle god knows what out of her. You were manipulating a young child, but she's not stupid you know, she could see what you were doing. I've got a good mind to put in a complaint against you.' Red blotches stained Joe's pale cheeks and his eyes were black under his thick eyebrows. Recoiling slightly, Gerald clutched at one idea after another to try and pacify the man. How could he tell him that a complaint to Gail would be the worst possible outcome for his daughter, how could he get the man to understand that he, Gerald, was the only person on Zoe's side, the only one interested in knowing what was going on in the child's mind. He took in a long breath, aware that Joe was waiting like a cat ready to pounce. 'Mr Milton, please believe me,' he said, 'there was no ill intent, I have no hidden agenda, no desire to take sides in this conflict, I only wanted to hear what Zoe had to say without any adult influence around her. I agree that I should have informed you and I'm sorry I didn't.'

Joe relaxed. 'What did she tell you?' he asked.

'There is no doubt you are very important to your daughter, Mr Milton,' replied Gerald, understating the truth of Zoe's love for her father because he was by now very annoyed with Joe, 'but is that a good enough reason for her to refuse being brought up by her mother as well?'

'It's her life and she should have the right to decide where she wants to live,' replied Joe bluntly. His face was tight with resentment and hostility and Gerald looked away towards the small window overlooking the street. He forced his mind back to the moment in Joe's house when, with his hand on his daughter's head, the father had looked down at the anxious child and a gentle smile had transformed his face. Even though Joe Milton was not going to show that side of him to anyone in authority, it was important not to forget it because that glimpse of love between father and daughter explained everything. If he only showed his angry self to people like Gail and PC Harries, they would fail to see how his daughter could possibly prefer him to her smiling mother. Brainwashing or bribery would be their ridiculous explanation.

As Gerald's eyes returned to Joe, he felt a stab of pity for the man sitting opposite him and unexpectedly his sympathies shifted wholly to him and away from the mother. It was a gut feeling. It happened when you watched sport and found yourself cheering for the underdog, shouting for Fiji to beat the All Blacks or for Cameroon to kick that equaliser past the Argentinean goalkeeper. But you had to be careful not to lose sight of reality when allowing your emotions to ride with the underdog, because the underdog invariably lost. With Joe Milton it wouldn't do to take his side just because the man was a loser and the woman a sharp little weasel and Gerald shouldn't gun for him to have the daughter. Given Gail's view of the matter this wasn't likely to happen anyway, but he must not be swayed by the underdog phenomenon. He didn't know for sure what was right in this case and he must let things unfold without taking sides.

Gerald straightened himself up in his chair with renewed confidence and assured Joe that Zoe would have a say in the matter of where she lived. The Children's Act said so, and the Children's Act guided all decisions related to children. The anger slowly waned from Joe's face and the two men eased out of hostilities and into the kind of neutral exchanges that take a meeting to its conclusion. Gerald assured Joe that from now on both parents would be kept religiously informed of anything concerning their daughter and he also emphasised that the child's welfare was at the heart of everything that happened. They shook hands as they said goodbye and Gerald returned to his desk feeling pleased and relieved at the way he'd handled the situation.

As he drove home, he reflected that his involvement in this case could prove difficult if he allowed himself to care too much. He wasn't responsible for these people's lives and whatever they brought upon themselves was not of his doing, nor was it his job to explain the world to them. In most people's eyes a mother is a good person and a girl who rejects her own mother is therefore a suspicious character. To compound the girl's problems her mother had superb instincts for self-preservation and victory, her father had none, and Zoe herself was like her dad, all confrontation and no diplomacy. There was nothing Gerald could do about any of that and as he swerved into his drive and turned the engine off, he felt justified in thinking that when a judge ultimately ruled on where Zoe should live, he would not have to bear any burden of responsibility.

The following morning, with the shadow of Gail hanging over him, Gerald Crispin drafted his report which described two warring parents and a child caught up in the conflict. By

Zoe's own account the problem in the mother's home was between the boyfriend and the girl, not between the mother and her daughter, and this problem was being addressed sensibly and voluntarily by the mother and her new partner. The father's wishes to bring up his daughter alone were unreasonable and there was no reason to alter the existing terms of the residence order. Gerald read it over, pleased with his flowing English and the fairness of the content. Gail would like it and hopefully this family would now settle down. With the boyfriend out the way the girl wouldn't have any more reasons to complain of bad treatment and the case might be closed in a couple of months.

Little did Gerald realise that what he had witnessed so far were no more than skirmishes and the war itself had barely started.

11. A New Ally Lets Zoe Down

With Ivor out of the way, there was no longer anything to stop Leanne and Joe shouting their anger down the phone at each other. Sometimes Leanne phoned Joe, sometimes he phoned her. From behind her closed bedroom door Zoe heard every word of every row. She heard her mother scream at her father that she was going to stop Zoe spending any time with him or his fucking family because all they did was poison her mind. She guessed that her father still pleaded for them to get back together when her mother shouted back, 'Never, you must be off your fucking head to even suggest it. Zoe doesn't need us to be together to be happy. What she needs is to be allowed to be happy with her mother. And that's what you and your bloody parents will not allow. If you weren't all twisting her mind, the kid would be fine with me, like Jessie is.' The phone got slammed down and above in her bedroom Zoe jumped and tightened her clutch on Flossie's long floppy ears.

This shouting and screaming went on and on until one day Zoe felt she could take it no more. After hearing the phone slammed down once again, she pushed herself up from the floor and snatched her rucksack and pink jacket from her chair. She slipped the jacket on, chucked her inhaler and purse in the rucksack, stuffed Flossie in as well, apologising for carrying her in this undignified way, but Flossie would understand. Flossie understood everything. She slipped her mobile in the back pocket of her jeans, hitched the bag on one shoulder and turned the sound of her TV up. Then she crept down the stairs, freezing where a board creaked and holding her breath as if the sound of breathing would carry into the front room where her mum was now talking to Nan on the phone, complaining about Dad. The smell of cigarette smoke drifted from under the door. Zoe tiptoed along the landing and down the second lot of stairs, her small hand holding on to the banister. She turned the lock handle carefully and managed to pull the front door open quietly. Reassured by the sound of her mum still talking away on the phone, she slipped out and pulled the door behind her gently. Even so the clicking of the lock sounded awfully loud. She pressed her ear against the door. No sound of footsteps coming after her. She was safe. A glance up at the bay window confirmed that her mum was not looking out.

Hugging the walls, Zoe walked briskly up the road with her head down. Once she got past the point where she could be seen from the flat, she stopped to slip her left arm into the second strap of the rucksack so that it sat squarely on her back. Then she got going again at a slower pace. Deep down she knew she would achieve very little by going to her grandparents now and they would probably bring her straight back to the flat, but at least she was out of there for now, no more shouting, no more bad stuff about her dad. Her head felt light and a little smile tugged at the corners of her lips.

Just then a hand of iron dropped on her arm and froze her to a halt. She stopped breathing. The hand spun her round and her mother was standing above her looking down with eyes as sharp as knives. Zoe managed not to look away.

'And where do you think you're going young lady?' hissed her mother into her face, her hand still clamped around her daughter's small arm.

'To Granny's,' replied Zoe bravely.

'To Granny's,' repeated Leanne, shaking her head. 'And what makes you think you can just go where you please without a word to your mother?' Leanne was bending over so her eyes were just above her daughter's. People passing by slowed down, heads turned, eyes sneaked stealthy looks. Zoe glanced at the people then at her mother as if to suggest having the argument in this public place might not be a good idea. Leanne also looked around but something like glee lit up her gaze, as if to say, you want to watch? Fine. Watch. Watch this girl getting a good telling off in front of everyone. Help me humiliate her. Help me batter her into submission. She wants war? Let her find out what it's like to fight me. Leanne was wearing a tight T-shirt and cropped trousers which made her look good. She was happy for people to watch. Her thick hair was held on the back of her head by a claw-like barrette and enough strands had come loose to give her what she knew to be an attractive look just on this side of wild.

'I wanted to get away from all the shouting,' replied Zoe, trying hard not to shrink away from her mother's face. Nails bit into her flesh and there would be little point in trying to shake her arm free.

'Well, you failed, kiddo,' shouted her mother, 'cos there's going to be a lot more shouting and this time it's going to be directed at you.' She yanked her daughter's arm in the direction of the flat, 'get moving,' she snapped, 'home.'

This time Zoe pulled her arm back sharply. 'I'm not going back if you're going to shout at me. I'm going to Granny's because I hate the shouting and it gives me asthma.' Zoe gave her mother the sly look of someone who knows that all along she had this winning card up her sleeve. An old couple had stopped to watch but Leanne shot them a filthy look and they moved on. Then she turned her eyes back to her daughter and grabbed her arm again. 'You think you've got power over me, don't you? But you're going to find out how wrong you are.' Zoe let herself be dragged back. She could have gone limp and collapsed on the pavement, she could have put on an asthma attack, she could have carried on arguing. But there was something good about being dragged back by force. It showed her mother had run out of arguments and when adults ran out of arguments they resorted to their superior physical strength, and although for the child it meant taking the punishment, there was also a sense of victory. The adult had nothing left, just the fact they were bigger, and that wouldn't last for ever.

But Zoe was soon reminded that for the time being her mother did have power over her and there would be no sense in ignoring that fact of life. Once they were back in the flat, Leanne marched Zoe into the kitchen and sat her at the table. As if to keep the suspense up, she deliberately lit a fag, dragged deep and slowly blew long strands of smoke out of the open window. Then she rounded on her daughter. 'If you ever try to run away again to your father or your grandparents,' she hissed, 'I'll get the judge to say you're not allowed to go there at all. Now do you understand that, little madam?'

Zoe held her mother's eyes with a dark, resentful stare.

'I know your game Zoe, don't think I've been fooled,' continued her mother coldly. 'You think if you make my life miserable enough, I'll let you go and live with your dad. I will never do that, but I won't keep you here either. There are places for children like you, and that's where you're going to end up.'

Zoe tried not to show the cold fear she suddenly felt. 'I don't care,' she said with a shrug. But she did care and that night she couldn't go to sleep. This time she knew the adult had had the last word.

*

Leanne's threat to have her daughter taken into care had the desired effect and Zoe stopped running away. Her unhappiness, however, was unchanged. There were new accusations against her father. He was, said Leanne, stalking her and threatening her. Joe told his daughter it wasn't like that, her mother was lying, she was the one calling him and winding him up. Charges were made, charges were dropped and screaming rows on the phone carried on being a part of life. If I was living with Dad, thought Zoe, none of this would happen. Then Ivor moved back in and although Zoe complained to everyone about this, he stayed. Through the winter the girl had endless minor illnesses.

On one cold February morning, almost exactly a year after the Big Row, she woke up with a tight knot of pain in her chest. It wasn't asthma, but it was in the same place and the least movement or cough provoked a stab of pain. She lay in her bed without moving, hoping the tightness would go away.

Her door flew open and her mother stood there, dressed for work and ready to go.

'What's keeping you, Zoe?' she asked with irritation in her voice.

'I'm not feeling well,' whined Zoe from under the bedclothes.

'What's the matter?' asked Leanne thinking she had an appointment at 9.15 that morning.

'I've got a pain in my chest. I don't want to get up.'

'An asthma pain?' asked Leanne, as concern replaced irritation in her voice.

'No, a different pain.'

'Have you tried your inhaler?' Leanne's body stiffened as she glanced at her watch. If the kid was ill now, she would have to phone in, and her boss wouldn't be pleased. People in work had little sympathy about colleagues' illnesses, but when it was your kid's illness then hostility was palpable.

The inhaler didn't work, but Leanne made her daughter get up anyway and after breakfast and a hot drink, the pain in Zoe's chest had eased. She went off to school but the air outside was so cold it seemed to stab her every time she breathed. Her chest got tight again, and the pain grew and grew until she couldn't hold it any longer. A scary coughing fit shook her, and she found herself spitting out phlegm on the pavement with tears running down her face. A lady stopped to ask her if she was all right and the concern in her eyes made Zoe think that she was most definitely not all right. She nodded, walked on and quickly pulled her mobile out of her coat pocket. She dialled her dad's number and waited whilst his phone rang and rang. She had almost given up when he finally picked up.

'What's up sweetheart?' The sound of his voice brought tears of relief to Zoe's eyes. Between sobs she told him about the pain in her chest and that mum didn't believe her. He told her to wait outside the school gates and that either he or Granny would pick her up in a few minutes. She switched her phone off and walked on slowly, breathing in a controlled way to avoid coughing. Anticipation bubbled inside her at the thought of snatching a bit of time with her dad, perhaps even a few days if she was ill in bed. And surely it would bring Dad back to his senses. If she was ill, he would listen to her, and she would tell him all the shouting must stop. She concentrated on her pain, making sure it was as bad as she thought it was, willing it to get worse.

As she stood by the school gates the knot in her chest started to threaten again. She was holding the cough back when Dad pulled up a few feet away and jumped out of the car. When she tried to speak the knot exploded in her chest and sent her spitting and spluttering as her father rushed to her with a handkerchief snatched out of his pocket. Zoe gripped his arm and smiled between her tears. Out of the corner of her eye she noticed other schoolchildren casting her surprised looks. Dad was wiping her face down and once she'd confirmed with a nod that she was okay, they got in the car.

'We're going straight to the surgery,' said Dad. 'Granny will meet us there and then she'll take you home and look after you until I get home from work.' He turned his head to give his daughter a reassuring smile. He hated to see her in pain, but if Zoe was ill and Leanne had neglected to care for her properly this could be his chance to have her back.

'Can't you stay home just for today?' pleaded Zoe. 'If I have to go back to Mum tomorrow, we'll hardly have any time together.'

'Can't take today off, I'm afraid. It was difficult just coming out now, we've got a lot on at the moment. Anyway, let's hope you'll be with me for more than one day.'

When they walked into the doctor's surgery Granny hadn't arrived yet, so it was Dad who went in with Zoe. She sat on the high bed looking so frail and vulnerable Joe had to look away to stop tears coming to his eyes. The doctor bent over, pressing his stethoscope against her chest, but when he asked her to cough, she shot her father a worried look.

'She gets a fit when she coughs, doctor, she finds it frightening.'

'Do a little cough, I need to hear the sound of it.' He listened closely to the controlled rumble that came out of her chest, stood up and folded his stethoscope away. 'A chest infection is what you've got Zoe, and with your asthma, you want to be careful. Bed and plenty of hot drinks for a few days.' He looked round at Joe and added, 'antibiotics should deal with this fairly quickly, but keep her in and warm until the course is finished. All right young lady?' he added signalling the end of the consultation.

'How many days in bed?' asked Zoe, pulling her clothes down over her chest.

'A couple and then…'

'Only a couple?' said Zoe, sounding disappointed.

The doctor shot a surprised glance at Joe who pressed his lips together in a kind of apologetic smile that said he couldn't really explain but there was a good reason for the child saying that. She was now standing next to her father and his hand had shot to her shoulders as he drew his daughter to him protectively. The doctor screwed up his eyes as he looked from parent to child and recalled the information he'd been given about this family when he had been asked to attend a case conference. He hadn't been able to make it but remembered, as he tapped out the prescription on his computer, a battle between parents and a girl who wanted to live with her dad, not her mum. Unusual. He pressed print and as the printer made its preliminary rumble he smiled at the girl and gave her a friendly wink. She looked back at him with her large serious eyes and then, suddenly a beautiful smile lifted her face. After the printer spewed out the prescription the doctor scribbled his signature on it and handed it to Zoe's father. The girl slipped her little hand inside her dad's and they left.

Doctor Ian Bates watched the father and daughter walk out hand in hand wishing he had attended that case conference a few months ago. He liked the girl with the serious eyes and the sudden smile. The affection for her dad had been obvious, but he had also seen pain in the back of her eyes and being a doctor, he felt a strong urge to help soothe that pain.

Yet when Doctor Bates was given his opportunity to help, he let both himself and Zoe down in the most unpredictable way.

*

Zoe did get to spend a few days with her father whilst she was recovering from her chest infection, but this led to more bitter rows between the parents and another child protection conference was called. This time Dr Bates attended, and now of course he had a view on the case. After seeing the father and daughter together he did not believe the child was at risk. He was also interested to see how Anne King was going to handle these volatile parents. Anne had become the

144

independent Chair a few years back and her non-judgemental approach had been a revelation to Dr Bates. Whereas in his experience case conferences were a stage for explosive battles between the authorities and the families of children at risk, with Anne they became an opportunity for communication. She had a knack of listening to parents which got them to open up and even face up to what was unacceptable about their behaviour. When they did, social workers knew they could count on their cooperation. Dr Bates had a lot of respect for Anne King.

But the first thing he noticed as he walked briskly into the conference room, at five to ten on March 11th was that Anne King was not there. He recognised the local authority lawyer in his pin stripe suit and PC Harries who gave him a nod from across the table. He sat next to a young woman and when she told him she was the school nurse he remembered meeting her before. Just as he was about to say so, a commotion from the far end of the room attracted their attention.

'Now you tell me this!' The male voice boomed loud and angry and in the same moment a door flew open at the back of the room and Zoe's father emerged, shouting that he had been set up and there was no point in him staying a moment longer. His curly hair stuck out in corkscrew strands and despite the suit he was wearing his appearance was one of slight neglect. Two other men in suits came after him, intent on pacifying him, and behind them came a small woman with blond hair. This must be Zoe's mother, thought Ian, not an unattractive woman. She had put some effort into dressing for the occasion with her hair neatly tied back in a thick bun. The frilly blouse she wore under her smart navy suit gave a hint of vulnerable femininity.

Somehow Joe agreed to stay, and everyone sat down. One of the men walked to the Chair's seat at the end of the table and introduced himself as Phillip Wright, Team Manager for one of the Childcare Teams. Dr Bates' disappointment was sharp, and he struggled at first to take in the report being read out by the social worker, Gerald Crispin. It was, however, better written than most social workers' reports he had heard, and he became absorbed. It expressed concerns about the emotional wellbeing of a child torn between warring parents and put the blame on the father, accounting for the child's wish to live with her dad by alleging that the paternal family had managed to influence the girl against her mother. There was concern that the father was using his daughter to get back at the woman who had left him, and this could be construed as emotional abuse.

Dr Bates found himself in disagreement with the man's assessment. He was a doctor; he had seen the father and child together and there was no doubt that love had flown between them. This was not a man prepared to damage his daughter in order to hurt his ex-partner. It came back to him how the girl had hoped to be confined to her bed for a few days so she could stay with her dad a bit longer. He shook his head at the social worker's ineptitude, but it didn't surprise him. That profession, as far as he was concerned, was full of second-rate people. With some exceptions, of course, Anne King being one of them.

The social worker ended his report with the recommendation that the child be placed on the Child Protection Register and that an application be made to the court for a care order. This, Dr Bates understood, would mean the local authority, advised by that pompous social worker, would decide where and with whom the girl should live. And that of course could mean foster carers. Indeed, the report had hinted at the need for a neutral environment. No wonder the father was enraged.

As if reading his thoughts, Joe Milton exploded at that very moment. 'It's outrageous,' he shouted slamming the table with the flat of his hand, 'Mr Crispin never led me to believe that…'

'Mr Milton,' interrupted the Chair, 'I have not asked for your views and I advise you to keep quiet until I give you permission to speak.' He met the other man's eyes and held the stare with the cold pleasure of someone who knows his authority will prevail. The father went to speak again, hesitated and instead let his hand flop down on the table and bowed his head. The mother was perfectly still, her eyes safely cast down.

The Chair turned to the social worker's Team Manager, a slim woman of sharp features with short black hair and piercing eyes. Ian listened to her spouting off about emotional abuse and pooh-poohed every word in his head. The little hand slipping into the big hand was still vivid in his mind and he started to think about introducing his own contribution with that image. His heart was beating a little faster than usual. He wasn't nervous about speaking in public, but it looked as if he was going to disagree with the majority and he needed a well prcsented and forceful argument. A lawyer was speaking now in a dull tone, hiding any personal views behind legal jargon.

Dr Bates was preparing himself to steal the show around the table with his greater understanding of people, his perceptiveness and his compassion. He would tell them just what he saw in that little girl's eyes, and because he was a doctor, he knew his word would carry weight. His heart was beating louder, and his mouth was just a little dry, but he knew that the moment the adrenaline kicked in he would be all right. PC Harries was making a strong case for the girl not spending a moment longer with her dad and she obviously didn't care that the dad was there listening to every word. But PC Harries had a big impact. People nodded in agreement and the Head Teacher, sitting next to her, looked like someone who had lost his way.

The chair asked him for his view and Dr Bates willed him to speak in favour of the father. His heart was now beating a drum in his gullet, almost stopping his breathing. He focussed on maintaining a calm exterior. The Head Teacher inclined his head to the right and said thoughtfully that he had always had a good relationship with both parents and that Zoe was doing well in school despite her difficult home life. As he had no cause for concern, he would abstain from the vote and with these words he leaned back in his chair.

Dr Bates felt a few beads of sweat pearling on his forehead. He was about to disagree with everybody around that table and make a fool of himself. The Chair was looking at him. Everybody was looking at him. His head felt as if it was going to spin out of control. Was he so sure that the girl wouldn't suffer harm if she continued in the present arrangement? Wouldn't it be safer to remove her from the terrible tensions that were tearing this family apart? They were waiting for him to speak. He clutched at the only straw that made him feel safe and important, his medical expertise. He launched into a talk about asthma. The well-established link between asthma and the emotions. Illness as a cry for help. Particularly in children who are not always capable of expressing their genuine feelings. Ian was doing a good job of convincing himself and derived much comfort from the nodding heads and approving eyes around the table. He warmed to his own voice and came down fully in favour of placing the girl in a neutral and peaceful environment. He too sat back in his chair, thinking he had had more courage than that headmaster who had just opted to sit on the fence.

A voice was clearing itself on his left and he half twisted his body to look at the young school nurse who was getting ready to speak. His patronising smile asked, 'Well now, what can a young female nurse have to say of any use on this matter?' The eyes of all the other people present reflected the same sentiment, with the hope she wouldn't take too long over what was now of no interest to anybody.

'I have come to know Zoe well,' said the young woman clearly, commanding immediate attention as she made quick eye contact with everyone in the room, 'because of her asthma. My experience is different from what I've just heard, and I believe I can tell when a child is telling me her truth.' The young woman paused briefly, as if choosing her next words. 'What I see is a warm and loving relationship between father and daughter, and I think Zoe could suffer serious emotional damage if she was no longer allowed to spend time with her dad.'

There was a stunned and slightly embarrassed silence. PC Harries was looking across the table as if to ask how come the nurse failed to see what a fool she was making of herself. Ian's mouth had gone dry again. The little hand slipping into the larger hand burst into his mind and took up all the space in there, refusing to budge. The young nurse had ripped through a veil and he could see the truth again. He looked down at the floor, flooded with shame.

'What about the mother?' asked the Chair dryly. 'Does she talk about her mother?'

'No,' replied the nurse, 'she doesn't talk about her mother.'

'Don't you think that's odd?' asked the Chair.

'No. It's not unusual for children to speak a lot about a parent, or a grand-parent. It tells me that person matters a lot to them. Some people use the expression "the significant other" and I would say that Zoe's significant other is her father.'

Now the father in question could no longer contain himself and started shouting that the school nurse was the only one who had listened to Zoe and the rest of the people in the room had no right to make decisions about a child they didn't know. 'Bloody typical of Social Services,' he kept repeating. The Chair brought order back to the meeting and then rounded on the father with a bunch of heavy criticisms which made Dr Bates wince. He saw Anne's compassionate blue eyes and imagined how she would have dealt with a man who was now behaving as badly as could be expected of a loving dad who was about to lose his daughter and was being told it was entirely his fault. He was standing up again, shouting his outrage and brandishing one fist. His fingers worked wildly through his hair so that it looked even more disorderly than when he had first come in. His gaunt face was all sharp angles and angry lines.

'You have only yourself to blame, Mr Milton,' barked the Chair in a second attempt to re-establish his authority.

'No, I don't, I have the people in this room to blame.' He pointed at one person after the other with his fingers in the aggressive shape of a gun. 'People who have decided to side with her,' he added pointing at his ex-partner sitting beside him. 'Because she licks your arses and plays your little games. And I don't. And I never will. But nobody will take my daughter away from me.' He kicked his chair back and stormed out of the room.

The mother looked up with eyes full of apologies for the behaviour of the man she kept telling them was violent and dangerous and now they could see just what she meant. She was struggling, Ian thought, to contain her satisfaction at the way things had unfolded, but she did an excellent job of appearing distressed and compliant. Not my type, he reflected, but you could see why a Joe Milton would find it difficult to let her go. Ian also noticed that she hung around at the end, like the worst swat in the class, making sure there was an opportunity for a confidential word with the Team Manager.

Ian left with the school nurse and as they walked down the corridor he said in a self-deprecating tone of voice, 'You were braver than me.' She shot him a questioning look and he sighed, shaking his head. 'I thought the same as you, but somehow the wrong words came out.'

'You don't know the girl like I do,' said the school nurse kindly, 'if you did you wouldn't have found it difficult to speak out.' They were standing outside, and a cold wind was blowing in from the sea, whipping the young woman's hair all around her face in a wild and attractive way.

'You give me more credit than I deserve,' Dr Bates replied looking out towards the sea.

He knew he had let himself down, and worse than that he had let the little girl down. He felt sad and guilty, wishing

151

foolishly he could turn the clock back and have another chance.

He would get another chance, but not for a while.

12. Emma Keeps Hope Alive

'What?'

Zoe was looking up at her mother with incomprehension swimming in her large grey-blue eyes. The girls were sitting at the kitchen table, having their tea. Zoe's mouth had been open, ready to take in a mouthful of chips, but now her fork stopped midway from the plate to her mouth and she just stared at her mother. Leanne shot Jessie a warning glance to keep quiet and repeated what she had just said.

'Social Services are applying for a care order and that means they can put you with foster carers if you keep complaining about living here.' Leanne turned to the sink where the pans were waiting to be washed.

'I don't want to live with foster parents, I want to live with Dad,' cried Zoe.

'You'll have no choice,' replied Mum as she squeezed washing up liquid over the pans. Zoe stared with hatred at her mother's silent, inflexible back. 'That's what you get,' Leanne added with a note of smug satisfaction in her voice, 'for acting up the way you've been doing, running away and saying your life here's unbearable. Don't say I didn't warn you.'

Zoe slammed her fork back down in her plate, splashing tomato sauce all over herself and the table. 'If they try to take me to a foster family, I'll run away or I'll kill myself.'

'You're impossible, Zoe,' said Leanne, turning around, 'just like your father. Let someone else see how they can cope with a difficult kid like you.'

'Then let me go and live with Dad,' screamed Zoe. 'He can cope.'

'Never.' Leanne pulled a chair out and sat down at the table to face her daughter eye to eye. 'You're my daughter, I will never let you go to Joe. That's just what you want, isn't it,' she snorted contemptuously, 'the two of you getting your way against me. Making me look like the failure. The woman who couldn't look after her daughter. But that's not the way it is Zoe. The reason I've had enough of looking after you is because of your bad behaviour, not because I'm a bad mother. I'm a good mother. Ask Jessie.' She jerked her chin in Jessie's direction, giving permission for a supportive intervention.

'You're the best mum,' chipped in Jessie on cue, with a snide look at her half-sister. 'My friends all think I'm really lucky.'

Zoe ignored Jessie's remark. 'You just want to spite me and Dad,' she shouted, 'but I will never say I want to live with you, I'd rather live with strangers. At least they won't smack me and tell me I'm a bad person all the time.'

She pushed her plate away, scraped her chair back against the worn lino and ran upstairs to her bedroom where she snatched her phone from the windowsill and threw herself on the bed. She tried her dad, but angry as he was, he didn't want to hear that she hated her mother. Nor did Granny, who just tried to be reassuring, saying it would never come to that. Then Zoe started dialling Kylie's number, but her thumb stayed suspended over the 8. Kylie didn't understand. Couldn't understand. Not with her perfect family life. In despair Zoe pressed menu and started going through her contacts, as if a magical name might pop up and answer her prayers. She scrolled down slowly, postponing the moment when she would get to the end of the list and realise that there was nobody she could really talk to. And then she froze, thumb in mid-air, as she stared in disbelief at the highlighted name. Why hadn't she thought of her before? Of course. Aunty Emma was the person who wouldn't bullshit her with one thing when she thought another.

She selected the number and put the phone to her ear. It rang and rang. Zoe was clutching Flossie against her, holding her breath. Her need to speak to Aunty Emma became acute, but Aunty Emma wasn't there, or didn't have a signal wherever she was, or was busy with other things. Zoe snapped the flap shut and stared at the phone in her hand. Just as she was contemplating how she might go about killing herself, it rang. Emma, it said on the little screen. She pressed speak.

'Aunty Emma,' she cried, 'I was thinking of killing myself. Thank god you phoned.'

'I've just heard the latest Zoe. Foster parents! I think I'd want to top myself too if I were you.'

An enormous weight lifted from Zoe's chest. 'You would, would you?' she checked again, in case Aunty Emma hadn't really meant it.

'I would Zoe, although it doesn't mean I would do it. But this is so unfair, like they want to punish you when you've done nothing wrong.'

Zoe's mind grabbed that idea and settled inside it like it was the place she'd been looking for this last hour. A perfect fit.

155

'I've been telling Gran and Dad that they all hate me in Social Services. They say I'm wrong, but I know I'm not wrong.'

Emma was silent. 'Emma?' asked Zoe, wondering if they'd lost the connection.

'I'm still here sweetie, just thinking. Why do you think they hate you?'

'They hate me because I don't want to live with Mum, and they think I'm a freak or something. So now they want to punish me for being a freak.'

'That's really interesting,' said Emma thoughtfully.

'Why?' asked Zoe, intrigued. She couldn't remember when a grownup had sounded as if they genuinely found one of her ideas interesting.

'I had another explanation,' Emma continued, 'but it could be you're spot on with that idea. People who don't conform do get hated and refusing to live with your mum is certainly unusual.'

'Emma, am I a bad person because I hate Mum?'

'No sweetie, that doesn't make you a bad person, but it certainly makes her a bad mother.'

'How come?' Zoe was holding her breath. Would Aunty Emma convince her, or would it be another disappointing ploy by an adult to make her feel good with an untruth?

'Because,' Emma replied in a matter of fact tone that didn't belong to the adult repertoire of voices specially put on for 9 year olds, 'children want to love their parents. So much so that they often love parents who don't deserve it. So, if a child doesn't love a parent, it must be that the parent is doing something wrong.'

Zoe fell silent. Then she said, 'So maybe I'm not a bad person.' She paused, before adding, 'Are you sure, Emma?'

'I am,' replied Emma. 'Nor do I believe…'

Zoe's door flew open, giving her a nasty jolt. Her mother stood in the doorway, bearing down on her with angry eyes. 'Who are you talking to?' she snapped.

'Kylie,' replied Zoe. Her first instinct had been to shut the phone guiltily, but she was fast emerging out of the simple reactions of childhood into the more complex and sly reasoning of adulthood. Shutting the phone too quickly would be an admission of guilt and leaving the phone on had the added advantage that Aunty Emma would hear how her mum spoke to her.

'Don't lie to me,' barked Leanne, 'I heard you say Emma.'

'Why do you ask if you know?' challenged Zoe.

Leanne swooped down on Zoe and snatched her phone away. 'Emma?' she asked.

'Yes Leanne?'

'You are not to talk to my daughter, do you understand? I know exactly what you're up to. Setting her against me.' Her voice rose dangerously, 'So leave her alone will you, and mind your own fucking business.'

Emma snapped her phone shut and made a mental note of what Leanne had just said to her in case it could be used one day as evidence against the woman. In the meantime, Emma would do her best to support her niece because things didn't look good and although her parents and brother loved the girl, they also gave her mixed messages, telling her one minute she should love her mum and listen to her, and arguing the next that the woman was an alcoholic with no maternal feelings whatsoever. Good job I'll be around, thought Emma as she headed towards the kitchen to make her tea, the next few months won't be easy.

157

Emma was right about that, but little did she suspect that she should have been thinking years, not months.

*

When Zoe said she would rather live with strangers than with her mother, it had been a lie. The thought of living with strangers preyed on her mind and every moment of her life was now tainted by the fear she could be whisked away and thrown into a terrifying unknown. A tight knot formed in the pit of her stomach whenever the thought popped into her mind, making her feel slightly sick.

'When will I know if I have to go to foster carers, Granny?' she asked every time she saw her grandparents. She didn't ask her father because that kind of question could put him in such a dark mood their whole time together was ruined. It was a bit ruined anyway because the question was on both their minds, but as long as it remained unspoken, they could still enjoy some good times together. Granny on the other hand was okay with the question and keen to soothe her granddaughter's fears. Worrying served no purpose, she said. But one day she said something else too.

'Hopefully you will never go to foster carers, sweetheart. The judge may not give social services a care order, and if he does, I don't believe they'll ever use it. And now you're going to have a Guardian, you know that don't you? That person will listen to you and make sure your interests are protected.'

Zoe nodded, unconvinced.

Yet when the day came to meet the Guardian, she could not squash a flutter of hope and excitement. Granny gave her big smile as she let go of her hand when the secretary came to fetch her.

The guardian's name was Byron Wood, which was not a nice name, but that of course didn't mean anything. Zoe held her breath as she waited in the now familiar little interview room in social services and when the door was pulled open, her eyes quickly swept past Gerald seeking the other figure walking behind. She saw the whole of him in a flash. Old, bald, a bit fat, with a stern suit on and small critical eyes. The breath she had been holding was let out and her heart went silent. This man had already decided he didn't like her and as he conducted his interview his eyes cut into her as if he was looking for proof of the wickedness hiding deep in her heart.

She came out of the interview with tears lining her eyelids and grabbed Granny's hand without looking at her. As soon as they were safely in the car with the doors closed Zoe burst into tears.

'I said all the wrong things, Granny, I know I did.'

'His job is to be on your side,' replied Granny, 'so don't worry love, everything will be all right.'

But everything was not all right. Joe received the report a week later and took it round to his parents on his way to work. 'Didn't have time to read it', he said, 'but I'm not holding my breath. I'll phone you at lunchtime.' Janet took the large brown envelope and her hands trembled as she pulled the report out and started scanning the pages. It was an off-putting document full of convoluted language in the image of the man who had written it and Janet rushed to the back page and the conclusion. She read it quickly with a beating heart. Then she read it again more slowly. What Zoe needed, the report advised, was a neutral environment where the girl, away from all influences, could rediscover her love for her mother and repair that broken relationship. Janet let her arm drop with the stapled sheets dangling from her fingers and looked up at David who had just walked in from the garden.

'Bad news?' he asked.

'Without using the words foster carers, that is basically what he's recommending.'

She handed him the papers, pointing to the conclusion. David read it slowly, at arm's length as he didn't have his glasses with him. Then he came to sit down next to his wife on the settee and took her hand in his.

'They've made up their minds, love' he sighed. 'All this fighting is just making things worse. If Zoe had put up with spending some time with her mother, which was fair, we wouldn't be looking at this now, would we? Have you wondered if we're not encouraging her to be unreasonable? And we both know why, don't we?'

Janet lowered her head. David had always chided her for taking too much of a dislike to Leanne. He pressed her hand and she looked up at him with wet eyes, but in all that tearfulness David saw no weakness, only a greater determination to stick to her chosen road. This was about her son, and her son's daughter. A mother would do anything for those two people, and Janet was a mother with bells on.

'All right, we'll fight it.' he said. 'But I'm not sure where we go from here, and I'm not sure we've got the money to do it. The solicitor's bills are already mounting up and although our pensions are adequate, we're not rich. We could well end up with no money in the bank.'

'You wouldn't put money before Joe and Zoe, would you?' exclaimed Janet indignantly, but secretly pleased that he'd given her such an easy argument to rebuff.

'No, no, but we still need to make sure it's worth spending money we may not have. It would seem a pity to get into debt for a lost cause.'

'I don't believe it's a lost cause, David. Anyone with any sense would see the stupidity of trying to protect Zoe's emotional well-being by removing her completely from both parents.'

'And in fact, Leanne won't want it either, so we may not have to fight anything,' said David with relief.

'Oh, Leanne will want it. It'll suit her down to the ground and what's more, it'll prove what I've always said, the woman doesn't love Zoe and never has. You just wait for it; she'll go right along with this.'

'Why would she want Zoe with carers? She's been fighting to have her with her.'

'David, you are too naïve. Leanne's been fighting for Joe not to have Zoe, and for Zoe not to have her way. As long as Zoe is not with her dad or with us, Leanne won't give a monkey's where she is. To her this will be victory.'

David was silent. Janet could be cynical about people and she had always had it in for Leanne. Hopefully she was wrong about this. He got up to go and put the kettle on, get back to his latest Ian Rankin novel and forget about the Zoe business for a while.

The following evening Joe and Emma came over to their parents' place. Joe informed them all that Leanne was perfectly happy with the idea of foster carers and Janet refrained from shooting her husband any kind of a glance. At that moment she wished he had been right. A despondent silence fell over the room which was at last broken by Emma. They must carry on fighting, she declared, people had always

161

fought fights against the odds, and if they hadn't then slaves would still be slaves and women would still be another kind of slave and gays would still be looking at prison sentences for being who they were and …

'All right Emma,' interrupted her father with a wave of his hand, 'you don't need to take us through the history of humanity's fights against injustice. We're only talking one child here.'

'But that's how it starts,' replied Emma hotly. 'Remember Rosa Parks. One black woman refuses to give up her seat to a white man and it's the end of segregation in America.'

'But Emma,' Joe butted in with irritation, 'we're not talking of a fight to liberate children. Dad's right, this is an individual case. No other kids need Zoe to stand up and fight for them, 'cos no other kids are in that situation.'

'I disagree,' replied Emma, nodding yes to her father's offer of a glass of white wine. 'The next freedom fight will be for children. Society has a downer on young people. Just listen to people speaking about youths. Youths this, Youths that, it's like they're talking of the scum of the earth.'

'Emma, you're exaggerating,' said Janet from the kitchen, 'ordinary youngsters get treated perfectly well…'

'They don't Mum,' interrupted Emma. 'Tell me, do you smile and say hello to a youngster, the way you would to someone your age?'

Janet didn't answer.

'People don't feel youngsters deserve respect,' continued Emma, 'and Zoe is just an extreme example of that fact. She shouts from the rooftops that she wants to live with her dad, and they all shout back with their authority guns pointed at her that she doesn't know what she's talking about because she's only a child. Isn't that wrong? To deny people their basic rights to make decisions about their own lives?'

Emma's mother had emerged from the kitchen, tea towel in hand and the young woman stared at her audience of three. They stared back. This was her hobby horse, feminism, animal rights, children's rights, and they were marginally bored with the predictability of her arguments, but they were also, in a funny kind of way, proud of her. She was the thinker in the family, the one who took the moral stance. At the age of six, when she had discovered where meat came from, she had immediately declared that if that was the case, she wanted to be a vegetarian.

'Their point is Emma,' replied Janet, 'that if Zoe is allowed to live with Joe, it also affects Leanne who is deprived of her daughter.'

'Weren't you just telling me that Leanne is happy for Zoe to be with foster carers?' asked Emma after taking a long sip of white wine. Janet shrugged. 'So,' continued Emma, 'if Leanne is happy to be without her precious daughter when it comes to foster carers, how come she's not happy when Zoe asks to be with her father? How come nobody's putting two and two together?'

'You don't need to convince us, Emma,' said Joe, 'we can all see that.'

'So, what are we going to do?'

'Fight them,' replied Joe.

'Good,' said Emma with a nod. "The one thing that will keep Zoe through all this is hope. As long as we fight there is hope.'

Had they known what the consequences would be for Zoe of keeping hope alive they might have changed their minds.

13. Stefan

'Nobody understands,' complained Zoe to Kylie. She was sitting on a bench facing the sea and rolling her blades back and forth on the soft grass underneath. It was the end of the Easter holiday and although the girls had just spent a pleasurable hour rollerblading along the front, Zoe could not stop thinking that she was going back to her mother's flat the following day.

'I understand,' replied Kylie reproachfully. She felt she couldn't have been more supportive, more patient in listening to her friend's problems and crazy plans, and it hurt when Zoe dismissed it all with one wave of her angry hand.

'I'm not saying you don't do your best,' said Zoe, 'but you can't understand what it's like to have a horrible mother, specially you, with the best mum in the world. But there's something else you can't understand. Something I can't even tell you.' Zoe fell silent.

'What?' asked Kylie, holding her roller blades straight out in front of her on their back wheels and admiring the perfect white and pink boots.

'Can't tell you.' Zoe retreated behind a pout, but Kylie knew that her friend wanted her to get the information out anyway.

'I'll never tell you any of my secrets then,' threatened Kylie.

'You haven't got any secrets. Nothing bad anyway.'

'I have.' Kylie racked her brain to try and come up with something, but as she couldn't she thought she'd make something up. A good starting point would be Georgina, who really bugged her at dance lessons, with her two admiring friends boasting all the time she was the best in the class.

'All right,' said Zoe, 'you tell first and I promise I'll tell you after.'

'I'm planning to trip Georgina up in a dance routine so she breaks a leg and can't come to lessons anymore.'

Zoe stared at her friend in disbelief. This was so unlike Kylie it was unbelievable she could come up with it even as a story. The two friends burst out laughing simultaneously, and Kylie admitted between giggles that she wasn't really planning to do that, but she liked the idea. Zoe could have said Kylie's bogus secret didn't count but she didn't. She just stared down at her roller blades in silence.

'So?' pressed Kylie.

'I hate my mum,' blurted Zoe fast and under her breath.

'Like I don't know that?' mocked Kylie.

'I haven't told you before,' protested Zoe.

'Like it isn't obvious?' Kylie stuck her face in front of her friend's making a do-you-take-me-for-an-idiot face, squinting her eyes and pulling a wide toothy grin. Kylie could do very funny faces and this was one of them. They both giggled again.

'Look,' exclaimed Zoe, 'that's Stefan Hopper.' She was pointing to a fair-haired boy rolling along on his skateboard, pushing with a strong left foot and then bringing it up onto the board as he freewheeled past dogs, walkers and little kids toddling along. 'He looks good.' Stefan was a boy from school who didn't mix much in the playground, but there was something attractive and grown-up about him. He did have friends, but he didn't seem to need them.

'I bet he's going to the skateboard ramps,' said Kylie.

'Let's go and see how good he is,' exclaimed Zoe pushing herself off the bench and waddling clumsily across the grass on her blades. As soon as she touched the tarmac, she thrust with one leg and eased into a fast glide. Kylie would struggle to keep up with her, but Zoe had to admit that whilst her friend didn't have great speed, she did have the elegance of someone who's been doing dance since she was four. The girls reached the skateboarding area just as Stefan was starting his first descent. He went down and up again, landing neatly at the top of the ramp. Then he started practising some new trick which he couldn't quite do and kept coming off the board. He hadn't noticed the girls. When he did his face was a picture of conflicting emotions. Annoyance that he couldn't practise freely without an audience, but also pleasure that he had an audience. With her long silky hair Kylie was one of the prettiest girls in school and although Zoe was not exactly pretty, there was a touch of wild about her that he liked.

Kylie waved and shouted, 'Hi Stefan!'. In school she wouldn't have looked at him. He was tempted to show off a couple of his best tricks, but the risk was that the girls might get bored and leave. This was too good an opportunity to waste on some pointless showing off. He picked up his board and came to meet them.

'I was going to get an ice-cream from the café,' he lied. 'Want to come?'

Ten minutes later the three of them were sitting on the low wall facing the sea with their legs dangling and tongues busy licking ice-cream. Inevitably Kylie was in the middle and the other two had to lean forward to address each other, which they did increasingly as they got into a debate about the respective merits of rollerblading and skateboarding. In the end Stefan admitted, as he crunched into the cone of his nearly finished ice-cream, that he would quite like to try roller blades, but it was out of the question as only girls did it.

'That's rubbish,' disagreed Zoe, 'the best skaters along here are men, they're brilliant. The other day I saw one do a jump, turn in the air and land backwards. Then he kept going really fast, just looking over his shoulder, you know.'

And then somehow, before Zoe knew how, they were talking about their families. It started with Stefan saying that his dad was actually a good skater, both ice and blades, although when he was a kid, it was roller skates, with four wheels. Then Kylie had asked if his mum did too, and he came out with the stunning reply that he didn't have a mum.

'She died?' asked Kylie under her breath, as if this was something you shouldn't say.

'No,' replied Steven, 'but I only see her about once a year, so it's easier to think I haven't got a mum.' He stared off into the dull greyness of sea and sky merging into each other. Kylie detected the hurt behind the pretence of not caring but Zoe heard nothing except the loud voices inside her own head.

'I wish I didn't have a mum,' she blurted out.

'You don't know what you're talking about,' replied Stefan in a voice tight with anger. He picked up his board and turned to get off the wall.

'She didn't mean it like that,' said Kylie, quickly grabbing the boy's arm. Stefan froze at the touch of Kylie's hand and his heart beat faster. He stopped and turned back slowly. He didn't want that hand to move. Kylie was looking at him with a soft apology in her eyes and Zoe's face was twisted with pain, regret and confusion all in one. Kylie looked from one to the other and in that moment of suspended reality, the most basic rules of friendship dissolved from her mind. 'You see,' she said to Stefan 'Zoe hates her mum.' The moment the words were out, they exploded into Kylie's ears with the enormity of what she had just done. Zoe was staring at her in disbelief and tears of shame spurted out of Kylie's eyes as she blurted, 'Zoe, I'm sorry, I'm sorry, Stefan, I shouldn't have said that, please say you never heard what I said, please, please.' Her hand was back on his arm, gripping hard now, but he didn't want her to stop.

'I promise I'll never tell anyone.' He looked at Zoe as he said this and suddenly felt tears welling into his own eyes. He blinked a couple of times and then said quietly, 'I should hate my mum, but I don't, I just wish she would come back.' Zoe remembered what Aunty Emma had said to her about children wanting to love their parents no matter what. After a silence Stefan added, 'I say my parents are split up, but it's not like that. She just left one day, and that was that. What kind of a mum does that?' A couple of breakaway tears rolled from his eyelids and he let them dry quietly on his cheeks.

The three children sat in silence staring at the grey sea and then Stefan turned his head towards Zoe, and leaning forward he asked, 'Why do you hate your mum?' It was as if his tears had just sealed a new friendship which gave him permission to ask the unthinkable. The girls understood.

'My parents are split up and I want to live with my dad, but she won't let me.' replied Zoe. 'She even wants me to go with foster carers. What kind of a mum wants that?' she added, echoing Stefan's own sentence, as if to say, 'if you think you're in a bad way, listen to this'. His eyes widened in surprise at finding someone who seemed to be worse off than him. 'She smacks me,' added Zoe, 'and she likes my stepsister much better. They gang up against me. And I hate her boyfriend Ivor.' Zoe didn't mention loving her dad. A nine-year-old child might admit to loving a dog or a cat, but it would not be cool to say that about your parents.

Some kid went past behind them asking his mum in a wailing voice if he could have an ice-cream and when she replied not before lunch, Kylie glanced at her watch and was horrified to see it was nearly half-past twelve. Her mum would be waiting to pick them up in a few minutes. They said goodbye, see you on Monday, when school started again after the Easter holidays and Stefan went back to the skateboarding ramps whilst the girls skated away as fast as they could. None of them was worried about how they would face each other on that Monday morning in the playground. They didn't even have to think about it. Playground rules were simple: boys and girls ignored each other.

But Stefan could not forget the feel of Kylie's hand on his arm and Zoe could not forget the tears in the boy's eyes. Kylie thought it was nice to have a new friend. Perhaps they would meet up again on the front and have another ice-cream. For all three of them school became a more interesting place because the others were there, but for Zoe, Stefan was a constant reminder that a child could live with his father, and if he could, why couldn't she?

*

In the next month Zoe ran away three times.

169

The first time was after a weekend spent with her father. On the Saturday she had gone rollerblading with Kylie, and they had met up with Stefan again. This time they had all skated along together and because Stefan took the same shoe size as Zoe, they had done a swap and she had had a go on the skateboard whilst he tried rollerblading. He had been surprisingly good, and Zoe had felt a pang of hurt as he and Kylie went off ahead while she tried to keep up on the stupid skateboard. Then Stefan complained the rollerblades were hurting his feet and the girls made fun of him saying he was ashamed of wearing a girl's blades. Stefan had given Kylie a mock push on the shoulder, pretending to be annoyed, and Zoe had known in that instant that Stefan fancied Kylie. Fancy meant to like in special way, between a boy and girl, and it also meant that when the three of them were together it turned Zoe into a bit of an outsider. She had carried on laughing with the other two but inside she had felt lonely.

When she walked into the school playground the following morning and saw Kylie and Stefan chatting by the railings, an instant thought crystallised in her mind. After school she would go to Dad's, and she didn't care about the consequences. She got two days with Dad out of it, and then the judge ordered Joe to return Zoe to her mother.

Dad took her back to the flat and watched as she let herself in, making sure she was safely in before he drove off. She waved and closed the door behind her. As she walked up the stairs, she heard their voices and her heart contracted. She knew how it would be up there. The three of them sitting around the kitchen table, half-way through their meal because they couldn't be bothered to wait for her, three pairs of hostile eyes ready to meet her as she walked in. Ivor might say 'Here comes trouble' and Jessie would glare at her and somehow shift her chair just a little to get closer to her mother. Mum would demand a kiss and send Zoe to kiss Ivor on the cheek. Zoe would make sure that her lips only ever kissed the empty space next to his cheek and then she would sit down with her nose in her plate and answer any questions in monosyllables. She would get told off for being antisocial and rude, and she would only relax when she was finally able to disappear into her room. This time would be worse of course because she was coming back after going to her dad's when she wasn't supposed to.

The next time Zoe ran away was only about a week later and this time she complained of being bullied and assaulted by Ivor. The medical examination failed to find any marks on the girl, and she was once again returned to her mother. A week later she ran away again, this time to her grandparents' place, complaining of wrenching pains in her stomach. Once again, the hospital failed to find anything wrong with her and the paediatrician who examined her put the problem down to stress. As the girl was pulling her clothes back on, the nice woman in the white coat turned to the grandmother and asked if there was any way that the girl could possibly spend a little time out of the conflict, by staying with one or other set of grandparents for instance. With her heart leaping into her mouth, Granny said that they would be only too happy to have Zoe for a while. The consultant nodded and said she would write to Social Services. Zoe and Granny could hardly believe their good fortune as they drove back to the house.

A week later Zoe was called back to the hospital and Granny took her. The woman in white explained she wanted a chat with Zoe on her own if the grandmother didn't mind. Zoe looked questioningly at her gran who smiled reassuringly and patted the girl on her way to the consulting room. The room they went into was child friendly, with posters of farm animals on the walls and lots of toys on small tables. The tall doctor managed to sit down on a low stool and Zoe took one of the little chairs. The woman started out with questions about Zoe's best friend, and it was easy to talk about that, she even mentioned her new friend Stefan and launched into an animated description of the differences between rollerblading and skateboarding. The woman listened with a smile on her face and then surprised Zoe with an unexpected question about her mother.

'Does your mother know your friends, Zoe?' she asked, fiddling with the pen in her hand.

'She knows Kylie,' replied Zoe.

'But not Stefan?' asked the woman.

'No,' replied Zoe, suddenly nervous that she was giving the wrong answer and that this was turning from a nice chat into a kind of test. She stopped smiling. 'I've only just got to know him.'

'But you do talk to your mum about your friends?' asked the doctor, peering encouragingly into Zoe's eyes.

Zoe suddenly understood what was going on. This woman was trying to make her say that she got on well with her mum and then they could all forget about Zoe staying with her grandparents. A hole opened in the pit of her stomach. It was vital to make that doctor understand that she didn't get on at all well with her mother and didn't want to go back there. Her little face closed and her eyes glassed over.

'I don't talk to my mum,' she replied flatly, 'I don't get on with her.'

'Why is that?' asked the doctor. 'Little girls usually get on well with their mums.'

Zoe panicked. She knew this voice. It was the voice of a disapproving adult pretending to be nice. 'It's not my fault,' she replied sullenly, 'she tells me off and she smacks me. I don't want to talk to her.'

'Sometimes parents have to tell children off, don't you think?'

'Dad doesn't tell me off and he never smacks me.'

A look fleeted over the woman's face telling Zoe she wasn't convinced by that argument and it was in a desperate attempt to convince the doctor that the girl uttered the statement that was going to have such a devastating impact on the rest of her childhood: 'Dad thinks mum is wrong to smack me, and so does Granny. And also, I've been assaulted by Ivor.'

The doctor looked up sharply and Zoe knew she had said the wrong thing.

When the paediatrician's report came, it said that Zoe Milton was being brainwashed by her paternal family into hostility towards her mother. This was apparent in the flat emotionless style of talk adopted by the girl when talking about her mother, using adult words like 'assaulted', and in contrast to the lively childlike voice which was her own and which she used when talking of school and friends. Her recommendation was that Zoe should be moved to a neutral environment until a psychiatric assessment could be carried out.

Two days later Social Services were granted an interim care order and the following day Zoe was taken to the home of foster parents Jean and Owen Tinsley. She clung to Granny when they came to get her, she cried that she didn't want to leave but Granny whispered in her ear it was better to do as she was told, and it wouldn't be for long anyway, just a few days until the report was done and then Zoe would be back with her parents. Granny didn't say which parent and Zoe didn't probe. The other thing Granny didn't tell Zoe, because at that moment she couldn't bear to add to her granddaughter's distress, was that during the stay with the foster carers there would be no contact with any of the family. The purpose of the placement was to keep Zoe in a completely neutral environment so that she could recover from the bad influence of a paternal family intent on damaging her relationship with her mother. That was what Joe had been told and that was why he wasn't here today to say goodbye to his daughter. 'Better if I'm not there, Mum, or I might lose my cool and end up in prison. That wouldn't help Zoe, would it?'

Janet managed to hold her tears as she watched her granddaughter being taken away, with Flossie's ears flopping over the girl's arm as she was dragged towards the police car parked outside the house. But her undoing came when her eyes strayed from Zoe to Zoe's pink suitcase held firmly in PC Harries's right hand. The suitcase that had gone on many happy holidays was now dangling in the worst possible hand, heading for the worst possible destination. When her eyes collided with the little sticker of a smiling sun that Zoe had put there two years ago before the family's last holiday together, the tears could be checked no more. They poured silently down her wrinkled skin and onto her navy-blue cardigan, where they stopped and spread into two dark patches. When Zoe managed to turn around one last time, she saw the tears and in a superhuman effort broke free to run back to her gran. PC Harries caught up with her swiftly but just as her arm was being grabbed, Zoe saw something in grandmother's eyes that stopped her own tears. Granny was not looking at her properly. She was hiding something from Zoe, and Zoe wanted to ask what it was, but the policewoman was pulling on her arm and telling her off. Just before being pushed into the car, she managed to duck under the uniformed arm and standing on the pavement, she shouted, 'What is it Granny? What is it?'

14. Zoe in Foster Care

It was Jean Tinsley who told Zoe what Granny had not had the courage to say.

Zoe had not long got there, and Jean had taken her round the house, showing her where everything was and going over the rules of what was allowed and what wasn't. There was a TV room for the children, and Jean explained that at the moment Zoe was the only foster child staying. She would have to ask permission to watch what she wanted and if they were children's programmes, Jean said reassuringly there wouldn't be any problems, although she didn't believe it was good for children to watch too much television. She had then shown Zoe the computer in the lounge and said Zoe would be allowed to use it for school purposes. As Zoe had determined not to talk to this woman she didn't ask if she would be allowed to do emails. She figured she could always pretend she was doing schoolwork and do emails instead. She hated everything about the house. It was so tidy and neat you felt you'd get told off for sitting down and messing up the cushions.

As if Jean had read her mind, she asked Zoe to sit down in one of the two big armchairs and she sat on the settee next to it, turning sideways to face the girl. Zoe stared blankly back, unsmiling. She hadn't smiled once since arriving and she wasn't planning to smile ever again. This woman with her stupid rules had no right to be so cheerful at having Zoe staying in her house. She shouldn't have agreed to it. She should have said, 'No, I'm certainly not taking in a little girl who has a family who want to look after her.' Orphans yes, and perhaps children whose parents couldn't look after them because they were ill or something, but surely not someone who had a father and a mother, and grandparents. For the first time ever, Zoe longed to be in her mother's flat. She thought of her bedroom where everything was familiar, and she could do what she wanted. She imagined being there now and her eyes welled up. She quickly looked down, determined not to give the woman the pleasure of seeing her cry. She was the kind of woman who loved to see you upset so she could feel important comforting you and giving you cuddles you didn't want. Zoe kept her eyes firmly glued to her red and white trainers so the woman couldn't read what was going inside her head. There was a silence and then the woman spoke.

'You know, don't you Zoe, that you won't be seeing your family for a while now?' The voice was enjoying itself. This sullen little girl won't look at me, but I have the power to get a reaction anyway.

Zoe's eyes shot up and went so wide they seemed to eat up her little face.

'What?' she asked with eerie calm.

Jean repeated what she had just told her, adding that a doctor called a psychiatrist would do an assessment on her and it was important she didn't get influenced in the meantime by either set of parents.

Zoe went very quiet and then her breathing stuck inside her lungs. There were no lungs anymore, just an enormous pillow taking up all the space in there, blocking and stifling everything. She opened her mouth, but no air passed her lips, in or out and she felt her head spinning as if she were in the worst fair ride whirling her round and round until she was so sick she would die.

'Zoe, Zoe…' an unknown voice was calling her name and two hands were holding her head, shaking it gently. 'Zoe, where's your inhaler love, where? Owen, look in her rucksack, for goodness' sake hurry.'

'I want to…to… die, leave me… alone, …die' panted Zoe, pushing away weakly at the helping hands. A familiar sensation sent a shiver through her body and she felt the rush of air into her lungs. The pillow dissolved and pathways opened. She was alive. She opened her eyes and looked straight at the face hovering two inches from her own. 'I hate you,' she said and closed her eyes again.

Two hours later Zoe woke up in a strange room with flower-patterned wallpaper and yellow curtains. The flowers on the wall were blue and yellow on stupid stems that didn't look like flower stems at all. Even Zoe could have drawn better flowers than that, and Zoe wasn't even good at drawing. The room smelled of polish, like school on a Monday morning. School. Zoe's eyes filled up. Kids running, chairs scraping, rucksacks banging down, loud arguments, stifled giggles, the smell of food at lunchtime. It was hard to believe, but school now felt like home. Zoe's insides tightened with longing. Kylie whispering in her ear. Stefan winking from across the yard. Stefan who fancied Kylie but had been impressed when Zoe had made the skateboard jump onto the pavement and down again without falling. Zoe's heart had done a few somersaults inside her little chest. No asthma then, but clear happy airways and only the need to hide her excitement at being able to impress Stefan. Now she might impress him with her story of being kidnapped from her family by the very people who were supposed to protect her. She pictured his serious green eyes widening as he listened to her story and heard his typical response, 'You're kidding me,' which he said just like his dad. A couple of tears rolled down Zoe's cheeks. She wouldn't be going to school either. She wouldn't go to school the following day, or the day after, or the day after that. Wouldn't eat, wouldn't drink, wouldn't do anything until she was returned to her family.

Perhaps Miss Brown would come and rescue her when she heard what had happened. Or better still perhaps she would tell the headmistress, and Zoe knew what a scary person the headmistress was because even her parents were frightened of her. Two years ago, Zoe had found out on the first day of school that she wasn't in the same class as Kylie so her parents had said they would go and talk to the headmistress. But it was obvious they didn't want to go. They discussed in advance how they were going to play this, who would say what, and had asked advice from Aunty Emma. Zoe had watched them go with a sinking heart. Yet against all the odds, they had come back victorious, and Dad had said, 'You can thank your mum for this, Zoe, I was useless, couldn't string two sentences together. But your mum said all the right things, Zoe, and the woman changed her mind. Your mother's a star, kiddo.' Dad had smiled proudly at Mum, putting his arm around her whilst she pushed him away laughingly as if he was talking nonsense. But that of course was before the day of the big row. Still, it

179

showed how frightened people were of a headmistress. Zoe thought the social worker might well be frightened of her because he was a wimp, but she didn't think the policewoman would be frightened. Not one little bit.

Zoe pushed herself to a sitting position in her bed and looked around at the ghastly room. Her attention was soon diverted from hating the room to feeling the twist of hunger pains in her stomach. She wondered how bad it would be not to eat day after day. Her mouth was dry, and she wanted to pee. She swung her legs out of the bed, noticing that someone had taken her jeans off. They were folded tidily on the foot of her bed. Very quietly she tiptoed to the white door, pushed the brass handle down and pulled. The door creaked loudly, and she froze. Through the gap she heard some steps downstairs and a voice shouted up, 'Zoe are you up? Do you want some food love?' She didn't reply. They wanted her to eat, they wanted to be nice and that gave her a sense of power. She could say no to all of it.

Silently she slipped out of her room and looked rapidly at all the doors on the landing. The bathroom had a sign on it, and she quickly locked herself in there. A big weight lifted as she revelled in the feeling that she was safe. Nobody could barge in on her. Away from these horrible people who had agreed to keep her in prison cut off from her family. The word prison brought Aunty Emma into her mind and as she sat on the toilet enjoying the relief of finally emptying her bladder, she decided she would get her mobile and come back in here to phone Aunty Emma. Maybe she would come and rescue her. She got off the toilet and went to the sink without flushing. She let a rivulet of water run over her fingers and quietly made her way back to her bedroom.

Her mobile was in the side pocket of her rucksack, which was on the floor leaning against the chest of drawers. Her hand dived into the pocket and she froze. The pocket was empty. Someone had emptied her suitcase and she could see some of her stuff on the table by the window. She searched frantically but all she found were her library book, her see-through pencil case, her spiral address book that she had for her last birthday, and along the back of the table, all her animal friends, Flossie, Blackie and Brownie the dogs, Croakey the frog and Pat the tortoise. Her two favourite Barbie dolls were there too. Her heart was beating fast now. There was no phone. She must be wrong. She must have missed it, looked too fast. She lifted and searched everything again and then went back to the rucksack and plunged her hand in amongst her school things. Her fingers didn't find the familiar shape. She turned the rucksack upside down and just as books, lunchbox, and water bottle were falling into a messy pile on the floor, her bedroom door opened softly, and she looked up into Jean Tinsley's smiling face.

'How are we doing?' asked the woman, stepping into the room.

'I've lost my phone,' replied Zoe forgetting she wasn't speaking to the woman.

'I've got your phone,' said Jean, crossing her arms across her chest.

'Did I leave it downstairs?' asked Zoe, relieved. She stood up in her knickers and looked expectantly at the woman.

'No, I unpacked your things while you were sleeping and I'm afraid I took your phone Zoe. I've been told you're not to have a phone. You see, you're not allowed any contact with your family until…'

'I want my phone back,' shouted Zoe, 'you have no right to do this. I'll tell my lawyer, I'll take you to court for this, you're stealing my property, I…'

'I haven't stolen anything Zoe and you will have your phone back as soon as this assessment has been done. I'm just doing what I've been told. Surely you can live without your phone for a few days.'

'No, I can't. I don't want to. How can I phone my friends, how can they phone me, I must have my phone. Give it back to me. I'll smash everything in the house if I don't have my phone back.' In a quick move, she pushed the woman out of the way to run downstairs to find her phone, but she wasn't quick enough.

'Well, well,' said Jean grabbing her arm with a surprisingly firm grip, 'your mother did tell me what a difficult little madam you were.'

'You know my mother?' snapped Zoe, turning around and wrenching her arm out of the woman's grip.

'Yes, I worked in the pub with her for a while.'

'Then I'm not staying here. It just shows Dad is right about a conspiracy. They say I must be in a neutral environment and then they put me with my Mum's friend. Call that neutral?' she shouted, her little face ugly with rage.

When Sally Walker from the fostering team had phoned looking for someone to take Zoe in for two or three weeks, Jean had said yes enthusiastically. She enjoyed fostering. She liked being helpful and she also liked controlling other people's lives, although she wouldn't have put it quite like that herself. Bringing order into disorderly lives, cleaning up these poor little things, folding their freshly washed clothes tidily in drawers, choosing what they should wear, perhaps even buying them clothes, although you couldn't do too much of that or you'd be left with no income. In principle the money was for the children, but everyone understood that some of it must be left for the foster carers or else who would do it?

What Jean liked best of all about fostering was setting out rules. Children needed rules. This was what was wrong in today's society, no rules, no boundaries. The children who came to her were told the rules as soon as they arrived and after that all went swimmingly. 'Swimmingly,' she told her friends when they complained about their own children being rude and difficult. 'Rules,' she would say, wagging a finger at them with the look of the wise in her eyes. They argued it was different when the children were your own, but Jean shook her head and laughed, knowing that her method worked perfectly. She had been brought up with rules herself, and it had done her the world of good. True she didn't take any children older than twelve, and she preferred girls to boys, but she had had success too with younger boys.

Jean realised things might not work out swimmingly with Zoe when the girl used the word conspiracy. Words like that had no business in the mouth of a nine-year-old. The girl even seemed to know what it meant. It had sent a shudder of revulsion down Jean's spine. Two seconds later the girl was rolling out the words 'neutral environment' with as much ease as she might have said 'chocolate ice-cream', staring at her with defiant eyes. Jean's own eyes had shifted away uncomfortably, and they had both known whose little victory that had been. As she closed Zoe's door and walked ponderously down the stairs, Jean made up her mind to phone Sally Walker the following day and hand Zoe back to Social Services. Their problem. But when she told Owen this, his succinct reply took her by surprise. 'Wow,' he said, taking his eyes off the football on the screen, 'I've never known you to give up so easily.' Jean stiffened and carried on knitting without answering.

The following day Zoe refused to get up, refused to eat, refused to speak. Jean didn't phone Sally Walker. Instead, she phoned Zoe's Gran. They talked for a good while, then Jean took the phone up to Zoe and left the girl alone to speak with her grandmother. Half an hour later the girl came downstairs and handed the phone back to Jean, and though her eyes did not flinch, her hand trembled. With hunger probably. She looked a small frail thing with her tear-streaked cheeks and her damp matted strands plastered around her face.

'Shall I make you some breakfast?' asked Jean in a neutral voice.

Zoe nodded.

'And shall I phone school to say you'll be back tomorrow?'

Zoe nodded again.

That morning Zoe wrote her first letter to her grandparents. 'Write to us,' Granny had said. So, she did. As her ballpoint made its uncertain way along the page, Zoe discovered the unexpected comfort of spilling her feelings onto a silent page and after she read over her finished letter, she paused in disbelief, stunned that written words could have such power. When they read this her grandparents would know how she felt. Then they would come to rescue her.

But when her grandparents received her letter all they could do was cry.

*

184

Zoe's letter dropped on Janet and David's mahogany floor the day after it was posted and when Janet came to pick up the mail, she instantly recognised her granddaughter's childish writing on the back of a pink envelope. Janet's morning backache was forgotten as she bent swiftly down to pick up the mail. She chucked the printed letters on the hall table by the peace lily and walked briskly to her habitual armchair by the window in the living room. With trembling fingers, she clumsily tore at the top of the envelope and extracted one small sheet of folded pink paper. Before flipping it open, she closed her eyes and made a small prayer to a God she knew she didn't believe in. 'Please let her be all right,' she mouthed silently. Then she opened the letter and read. It didn't take long. Afterwards she sat with her eyes closed and her hands clasping the pink sheet in her lap. She needed to get up and show this to David, but she couldn't move. Her heart had become a lead weight inside her chest. She willed David to walk into the room.

But David was busy in the garden and had no reason to be walking into the house just then. He was giving his lawn its first spring feed and carefully spreading granules at the rate of 72 grams to a square metre. In the old days of being a fussy gardener David used to measure out the square metres with sticks and string in order to achieve accurate dosage, but now he felt he could do it by eye alone. The thing was to concentrate and not get interrupted in the middle, forgetting what he had covered and what he hadn't. Which was why, when Janet called him from the back door, he neither turned around nor replied, but kept on scattering his granules like a peasant sowing his seeds.

'David!' shouted Janet again, with an angry tremor in her voice.

David paused and slowly straightened up. Then he turned his head without moving his body, so he could resume exactly where he had left off.

'Janet, can't you see I'm in the middle of this,' he said reproachfully. 'You know I need to do it in one go.' Then he stopped as he took in his wife's decomposed face and the pink piece of paper between her fingers. A letter from Zoe. He took a deep breath and stepped out of his gardening crocs, leaving them at an angle to remind him where to start again later. He then walked back towards Janet in his socks.

'Read this,' she said to him, handing out the letter.

Standing in the weak sunshine on the patio, David plucked his glasses from his breast pocket and read. Then he looked at his wife, put his arm around her shoulders as he directed her back into the kitchen and said, 'Janet, don't forget that Zoe is an emotional child. She wants us to understand how she feels, and so she uses the strongest words she knows.' Janet snatched the letter back and read it again, sitting at the kitchen table.

Dear Granny and Grandad,
Please come and get me. I hate it here.
It's like being in prison.
Please please come and take me back
home.
They've taken my phone away and I'm
not allowed to phone anyone.
If I can't phone you or my friends, I'll die.

*If they don't give me my phone back I'll
stop eating.
I love you and I love Dad and I want to
come home. If I have to stay here I'll kill
myself.
I love you,
Zoe*

David had put the kettle on and was washing his hands with care, working the foam into every fold of his skin.

'I disagree with you David,' said Janet with a tremble in her voice, 'If Zoe is emotional, it's because nobody listens to her. Even you want to brush this under the carpet and say it's just an overreaction by an emotional child.' Janet was angry as well as upset. Of all people she expected her husband to be with her on this and she couldn't quite cope with the fact he wasn't. It felt like betrayal.

'Janet,' he replied throwing a couple of teabags in the pot, 'children are not the same as adults. They're not rational, their brains are not fully developed, and they can't see the whole picture. It would do Zoe no harm to learn to be patient when things are not exactly as she wants them to be. She…'

'So, you think,' interrupted Janet hotly, 'that taking a child away from all the people she loves will teach her a useful lesson and help her brain grow to its full potential?'

'I'm just saying children cannot have their own way all the time.' David sat down and placed the two mugs of tea on the table. 'Nor can we,' he added, 'it's a lesson we all need to learn.' He lifted his mug to his lips and took a long sip.

'So, you think it's all right to bully a young child to make her obedient? Take everything away from her until she caves in. You think that's right?'

David sipped his tea in silence. He trusted Janet's emotions more than his own, and her sense of right and wrong too. She had been against the invasion of Iraq at the time, and he had secretly been in favour. She had been right too about Leanne being okay with Zoe going to foster carers. And now she was right again, he knew, even though he couldn't quite let go of the idea that children should do as they're told. It had done him no harm to grow up with rules he hated, and punishments dealt out by parents and teachers, that method had produced a fine generation of people. He sighed.

'No, I don't think what's happening to Zoe is all right, love.' David reached across the small round table and his large hand folded over Janet's fingers. She pressed his hand back and two tears rolled down her cheeks.

'Good,' she replied, 'because if I had to fight you as well as the rest of the world, I don't think I could do it.'

'But we have to be patient Janet. They said a couple of weeks. If we try to break the orders and contact Zoe, we won't be doing her any favours.'

'I know,' Janet nodded.

David was right, as became evident when Joe defied the judge's order and arranged for a friend to meet Zoe after school and let her use his phone so they could speak. They did. It warmed their hearts just to hear each other's voices. But a couple of days later, in the heat of an argument with Jean, Zoe made the mistake of shouting that nobody could stop her talking to her dad if she wanted to. It was the glint of triumph in her eyes that alerted Jean. Moments later Zoe was floundering under the scrutiny of superior adult questioning and the truth was extracted out of her. Gerald Crispin was informed, and Joe's image was blackened again. If Zoe ended up in care for longer than necessary, warned Gerald, it would be thanks to her father's irresponsible behaviour.

But the truth was, and the whole Milton family could see it, that Social Services were simply failing to organise the psychiatric assessment. In fact, it was beginning to look as if they were doing it on purpose. Two weeks had passed, and nothing had happened. The consultant psychiatrist had supposedly left for another job and they were waiting for the new appointment. Janet pleaded with Gerald to let Zoe go back to her parents at least until the new appointment was in place, but he wouldn't hear of it. The placement was working, he said. Janet pulled some of the girl's letters out of her bag and asked if he could sleep at night when for no good reason a nine-year-old girl was being deprived of the love and affection of her family?

'There is a good reason, Mrs Milton. Zoe needs protection from the emotional damage her family are inflicting on her.'

'Gerald,' Janet shouted, banging at the table with the palm of her hand, 'you are not protecting her, you're hurting her. She hates being in care. Read her words.' She pushed the letters forward angrily.

'Children can be very manipulative, Mrs Milton,' replied Gerald without glancing down at the pink sheets of paper in front of him, 'and Zoe knows how to tug at your heartstrings.'

'Mr Crispin, with respect, I know my granddaughter better than you do. She is desperate. In almost every letter we've had she's talked of killing herself.'

'That's what she says to you, Mrs Milton. But I am told she's doing well in school and she is seen talking and laughing with her friends, not the behaviour, you must admit, of a child about to commit suicide.'

'Yes, Gerald,' replied Janet in a controlled voice, 'I know Zoe is all right in school. It is the one place that is keeping her sane.'

'Which goes to show she is not as unhappy as she makes out. Children…'

'…are very resilient, I know,' interrupted Janet. 'Gerald, that is all you seem to know about children. They are also very fragile, they need love, and they need their homes, and if you take these things away from them in the cruel way that you are doing, you do them untold damage. They may well survive, but who knows the impact it will have on their health later on, mental and physical? What if it were your children Gerald? Snatched from their home and dumped with strangers. . .'

'I am not here to discuss my children, Mrs Milton,' interrupted Gerald dryly.

But after Zoe's grandmother had left, he went back to his desk and sat there lost in thought. He couldn't push away the memory of his daughter telling them, when she came back from her school trip to New York, that she had been homesick. He remembered her young face suddenly crumpling as she recalled her unhappiness at certain times, particularly just before going to bed. She had been twelve then. This little girl was nine.

The room around Gerald was a bustle of noise, conversations, phones ringing, computer keys clicking away, but for once he took no notice so completely absorbed was he by the conflict inside his own head. He had allowed a question to filter through and now the words were dripping away at him, drip, drip, drip, 'Are we doing that little girl untold damage?' Drip, drip, drip. An image burst through and forced itself into his field of vision. Joe sitting in his front room, his hand on his daughter's head, gentle and reassuring. He knew what he had to do next.

He opened Zoe's file, leafed through it quickly and homed in on Joe's mobile number. He picked up his phone, punched the numbers in and waited. He wanted to meet with Joe again, in a calm environment, and get the man to relax and open up. He felt excited. This was what made the job exciting, getting to the bottom of things, finding out the truth, having an impact on people's lives. Joe's phone was still ringing, and Gerald had a sinking feeling that he wasn't going to answer. Sure enough, the voice mail came on, and an instinct of self-preservation stopped Gerald leaving a message.

Half an hour later he was thanking his lucky stars he hadn't left that message. Gail was on the phone to him and although she wasn't calling to discuss the Milton case, which as far as she was concerned was done and dusted, her cold snappy voice came just in time to remind Gerald why phoning Joe Milton would prove a poor decision, one that could lead nowhere except into a minefield of problems. As he put the phone down, he also put all thoughts of Joe Milton out of his mind. He had reached the proverbial crossroads where the direction you take transforms everything forever after and he chose safety for himself. Had he instead left a message to invite Joe Milton to a friendly meeting after work that day, he might have taken the anger out of the man and averted the next disaster in Joe's long line of calamitous decisions.

What Joe did that night left even his own mother distraught and appalled.

15. Joe Gets Violent

As Joe's mobile was ringing away in his empty office, Joe himself was sitting in a meeting. He hated all meetings, but particularly the kind where he got invited because some self-important arsehole wanted a sizeable audience to boost his ego. This meeting had been organised by the Health and Safety manager and Joe sat resentfully in the back of the hot room thinking of all the work he could have achieved in those precious two hours. People were pulling blinds down against the sun. Soon into the meeting his mind switched from resentment against his present situation to resentment against the world in general. Joe felt he had good reason to be aggrieved. The world was in a conspiracy against him, and it had all started with Leanne leaving him. His eyes appeared to follow the power point presentation flashing one tedious point after another, but his mind had long left health and safety issues to follow the ineluctable path that led to Leanne. The bitch. Joe's eyes darkened as he thought of Zoe with foster carers, deprived of contact with the people who loved her. The only reason Leanne was doing this was to hurt him. He pondered that thought for a moment, looking down at his pen lying idle on the table, and looked up at the board again. No point taking notes, he reflected, looking in commiseration at the people around him dutifully bent over their papers, scribbling away like swots. A power point presentation invariably came with a handout, he would photocopy the handout and pass it around his colleagues. The copies would end up in the bin, unread.

He sagged in his chair a little, extending his long legs under the chair in front of him and finding a more comfortable angle for his back. His mind focussed on Leanne again. He liked the fact she wanted to hurt him. It gave him hope. They were still connected and although it was a negative connection, Leanne wouldn't let it go. He hadn't seen her for ages and as he pictured her in his mind with her long flowing hair and that cheeky look in her eyes, he felt a sudden urge to see her. He sat up and leaned forward, easing the discomfort in his back. It was time to go and see her again. All he needed was a reason. His mind worked away at that problem until he heard the welcome sound of people pushing their chairs back and gathering their belongings. One or two of the swots walked to the front to ask further questions. Things never changed. Joe, however, didn't have any questions to ask. He had used his time far more profitably than worrying about rules which, behind their well-meaning ethos, only had one aim in mind and that was to protect the back of the employer. As that back became more and more aware of its own vulnerability, so the rules sent their tentacles out into every avenue of life stifling all sense of responsibility in everyone. Joe wanted nothing to do with any of it. He didn't need rules to protect him, he had his own brain for that. He shuffled out of the room behind a group of stout middle-aged women and headed past them towards his office, his eyes aching for a glimpse of Leanne's slim figure.

At half past five he walked into his parents' home. His mother asked him immediately if he was all right, but today her concerned look failed to raise his hackles. His mind was on other things.

'Any more letters from Zoe?' he asked, trying to sound natural.

'One this morning,' replied his mother, 'but you're not supposed to see it Joe, and frankly you'll just get upset.'

'Mum, it's the only contact I have with my daughter, let me see it for Christ's sake.'

'Will you please not swear in front of your mother,' snapped his father from the armchair where he was doing his crossword puzzle, his glasses poised on the tip of his nose.

'C'mon Mum,' pressed Joe with a pleading look in his eyes.

Janet walked to the sideboard and opened the middle drawer. From under a pile of placemats she pulled a green folder. Inside were Zoe's letters. She opened the flap and rifling inside, pulled from the back what she recognised as the latest pink sheet. She handed it over to her son and stood watching as he read. 'Bastards,' he muttered. His lips drew a thin angry line across his jaw. Janet extended an open hand to be given the letter back. She noticed his reluctance to hand it over but waited in silence with her hand held out. Finally, the letter was placed back in her hand. She nodded slightly, inserted it at the back of the little bundle, and brought the flap over firmly. It was a message to Joe, and he understood it perfectly. These are not for you. His mother replaced the folder in the drawer and pushed the drawer closed. As she walked back into the kitchen Joe shot his dad a glance. Seemed absorbed in his crosswords, but no, this was not the moment for the execution of his plan.

The meal was chicken, broccoli and potatoes tossed in olive oil, herbs and garlic and grilled to crispy perfection. He made a show of enjoying his food and talked about work. The atmosphere appeared to relax. Joe went on his mother's laptop to check his emails, Emma phoned, and Janet took the call in the kitchen. She didn't want Joe to hear any more about the letters and risk upsetting what seemed to be a reassuringly settled mood. By the time her son left to go home Janet was feeling more optimistic. It was the first time Joe hadn't raved and ranted, the first time they'd had something like a normal family meal, chatting about easy stuff, being together pleasantly. No bad vibes. What a relief.

What Janet didn't know was that Joe had had the narrowest window of opportunity when she was on the phone and David had left the room to go to the toilet. It was only a pee, David had thought, aware that the drawer must not be left unwatched, but Joe was busy on the laptop and David would keep his ears open from the downstairs cloakroom. But these days David took just little longer to have a pee and his gait was now slower than he realised. Nor was his hearing very sharp anymore, but he didn't admit to that either. Joe, on the other hand, had been like lightning. He knew how long it took his dad to have a pee, and with his heart beating madly, he had managed to silently open that drawer, pull the green folder out and snatch a letter out. Only one, and not the last one, in case Janet checked before going to bed. It had taken him two minutes exactly. When his father shuffled back towards his armchair, Joe was sitting on the couch with the laptop on his knees in the same position he had been for the past half hour. Janet was still chatting away behind the kitchen door.

With the folded piece of pink paper tucked safely in the back pocket of his jeans, Joe left his parents' house and drove to Leanne's flat. Rain was falling densely over the town and he had to peer through his fast-moving windscreen wipers to see anything. He found a parking space on the main road from where he could see the flat. A glance at his watch told him it was too early for Ivor to have already gone out to the pub. Joe knew the habits of the inhabitants of the flat very well. He decided against running across to the pub in the rain and sat in his car instead, happy to wait. Slowly a wet mist rose on the inside giving him just the kind of cover he needed. He lit up a fag and slid down the car seat into a more comfortable position. Fifteen minutes passed and he lit up another fag. Another fifteen minutes passed, yet Joe had no desire to move from where he was. Near Leanne, where he might see her, even if it was only as a silhouette in the window. That silhouette would send his heartbeat soaring.

But tonight, the curtains had been drawn and there was no sign of anyone coming out. His eyes never left the door of the flat, but he stopped expecting to see it swing open. It wouldn't be his night and he had the weather to thank for that. He felt the letter in his pocket, thinking he would come back another day, and reached for the key in the ignition. Just then Leanne's front door opened slowly. Joe shot up in his seat, his heart racing. Mechanically he stubbed his cigarette out in the little ashtray. Would it be Ivor on his own or would it be the two of them? Now that Zoe was in care, Leanne was a lot freer to do as she pleased, and nobody kept an eye on how Jessie got looked after. A black umbrella was pushed open out of the door and Ivor stepped out under it. Then he pulled the door behind him. Joe watched with fascinated eyes but failed to notice the carrier bag in Ivor's other hand, hidden by the bulk of his body. Ivor was not going to the pub, just to get a six pack from the Spar.

The rain was easing, and Joe jumped out of his car and ran down the road to the flat door. He rang the bell once and waited with shoulders hunched up against the weather. When it opened, he pushed his way in and by the time Leanne had realised it was Joe not Ivor, it was too late, he was already walking up the stairs, saying he needed to talk to her about Zoe. She followed him up. He went straight down the corridor into the kitchen where he spun round on his heels to face her.

'You can't stay away, can you?' she said sarcastically, crossing her arms and leaning against the tall white fridge, with one hip thrown slightly out, provocatively.

His eyes took her in the way a man dying of thirst takes a long draught of water. The narrow shoulders, the perky breasts moulded to perfection by the tight green tee-shirt, the small waist and hips in the sexy jeans, but more than anything the seductive look in those eyes, taunting him now as they taunted him in his sleep and in his waking hours, whenever he allowed his mind a free rein.

'You look fantastic, Leanne…' his voice trailed off, as if he was overpowered by the force of what he saw.

'You're wasting your time, Joe. Why are you here?' Leanne's words dismissed him, but he felt that her eyes didn't. Her eyes wanted him right where he was, looking at her in just the way he was looking. Her eyes could never quite say no to his adoration. She shifted her weight from one foot to the other, as if giving herself a little shake. 'If you have nothing to say then I want you to leave,' she added firmly.

'Oh, I have something to say,' snapped Joe, coming out of his trance. 'Are you aware what you're doing to our daughter?'

'What I'm doing to our daughter?' she mimicked mockingly. 'I'm doing nothing to our daughter, Joe, she's not here in case you haven't noticed.'

'Exactly. She's not here. She's not where she should be. At home.' His anger was rising again now, in the familiar pendulum movement between hope and anger that was set off by Leanne's presence, or even just by her presence in his mind. When hope faded, anger flared.

'Well, well,' replied Leanne with a sarcastic smile, 'I thought this wasn't home for Zoe and never could be.'

'No, I want her at home with me, and I want you there too, you know that. But now she's with strangers Leanne. Strangers. Don't you care about that?'

'It won't do her any harm and it'll make her appreciate her real home when she comes back. And it's working, isn't it? You just said she should be here. You wouldn't have said that a month ago.' Leanne pulled one of the kitchen drawers open and fished out a packet of cigarettes. She plucked one out for herself and offered one to Joe. He shook his head. She lit hers and leaned against the kitchen surface, throwing her head back as she inhaled the smoke.

'You know damn well what you're doing to Zoe. She's lonely, she's homesick and there you are, not giving a shit. And you want custody. You don't know what it means to love a child Leanne, you don't know what it means to love anybody. This proves it. Your daughter is breaking her heart in a strange house and …'

'Breaking her heart!' snorted Leanne, 'the girl's rebelling, as she does all the time. It's all she knows. And it needs to stop Joe. She needs to be taught a lesson and …'

'Read this,' shouted Joe, pulling out Zoe's letter from his back pocket and shoving it under Leanne's nose. 'Read this if you don't think she's breaking her heart.' His own heart was thudding. She pinched the piece of pink paper between her fingertips as if she wanted as little contact with it as possible. Her eyes scanned it quickly as she sent a dismissive plume of smoke up to the ceiling from the corner of her mouth. She looked up at Joe, her lips curling into an attractive pout, the cigarette tucked in the corner at an angle. She dangled the paper from her fingertips for a reflective moment and then a slow smile broke on her face. Her most provocative smile. Her eyes held his. And very slowly her right hand moved up to join her left so that the fingers of both hands held the paper, and then in a swift downwards rip, she tore the letter in two, and then again and again until it was reduced to tiny pieces which she let drop like confetti to the floor. The smile didn't leave her face, not even when she saw the familiar darkening at the centre of Joe's pupils.

'That's what I think of that,' she said. Her eyes still riveted to Joe's, she took her cigarette out of her mouth and blew more smoke to the ceiling. Then she made a mistake. She took her eyes off Joe to find the ashtray on the kitchen surface and the next thing she knew her head was reeling from a powerful blow to her left cheek. Then two hands grabbed her shoulders, and she felt her head hit the cupboard behind her as her whole body was shaken out of its skin.

'You fucking bitch,' Joe hissed at her, 'I'm gonna kill you, that's what I'm gonna do.'

Neither of them heard the front door closing.

'Stupid bastard,' hissed Leanne back, freeing her hands and pushing frantically at the much stronger body threatening to smother her.

Joe caught her wrists easily and pinned her against the wall. With his back to the door and his heart hammering in his head, he never heard a thing behind him. It was Leanne's sudden eye movement that alerted him and as he turned his head to catch sight of what she had seen, he just had a glimpse of the fist coming at him. The force of the blow sent him flying to the floor. He lay there senseless for a few seconds and then the pain kicked in. Between shallow pants he heard Ivor asking Leanne if she was hurt, if they needed an ambulance. Slowly he raised his hand to his face as if to check it was still there. It was. A mass of fleshy pain oozing warm liquid. He didn't need to check the colour of the liquid. His left eye wouldn't open. His skull was thudding with pain and inside it his brain seemed to have been shaken loose. He daren't move. Then he heard Ivor's voice floating down to him. 'I've been wanting to do this for a long time.'

The hospital dismissed Leanne within an hour of examining her. The brain scan showed there had been no damage and apart from a shadow on her cheek and a bump on the back of her head, she had been more frightened than hurt. They kept Joe a little longer. He needed stitches above his eyebrow and was told there would be a scar where Ivor's ring had sliced neatly into the flesh. There was nothing they could do about his eye or broken nose. His face would heal in time, said the A&E doctor reassuringly. When he hobbled out of the little room where the nurse had cleaned his face, he found his parents sitting in the waiting room, and although he knew someone had to drive him home and he should be grateful for their presence, all he could feel was resentment. Resentment that they must always be there to make him feel like a little boy.

It was the foster carer who told Zoe what her father had done, over breakfast the following morning.

'Your father is a violent man, Zoe,' she said in her sanctimonious voice, not noticing the darkness gathering around the girl's eyes. 'I really don't understand why you say you want to live with him.'

'He's not violent!' shouted the girl banging her spoon loudly on the table.

'That is no way to behave, young lady,' snapped Owen, lowering the pages of his newspaper. 'In this house we will not have children shouting at adults. Do you understand that?'

'Then don't say bad things about my dad,' retorted Zoe, unfazed by the man's stern voice. She knew he would never touch her, and if he did it would be the end of the placement which was fine by her.

'Jean didn't say bad things about your dad, she said the truth.' Owen was leaning forward now, boring into Zoe's irritatingly level eyes. 'He is a violent man and he got what he deserved. A punch in the face and a broken nose. He wouldn't have attacked someone bigger than himself, would he? So, he's a coward as well as a violent man.'

In one swift movement Zoe stood up, grabbed her cereal bowl and threw it crashing to the floor. Milk and cereals all over Jean's clean floor. Good. 'I hate you,' she shouted at Owen as she spun on her heels and ran out of the room. She raced up the stairs, kicked her bedroom door shut behind her and dived on her bed, grabbing her pillow to hold and hug and cry into. Pain shook her, breaking her up into fragments of shattered illusions. Her dad had let her down again and she hated the world for it. 'If he loved me…' she thought, burying her head into her pillow, but the rest of that sentence was too painful to contemplate, and Zoe banished it. 'He does love me,' she sobbed into Flossie's soft little body, 'it's just that he can't control his temper.' She knew that wasn't the whole truth, but it was the only one she could live with.

It was at this wretched moment in Zoe's life that a new expert entered the scene: the psychiatrist. Would Zoe be able to make this person understand that she loved her dad, that he loved her back, and that she desperately wanted to spend the rest of her childhood with him?

16. The First Visit

When Zoe heard she was going to be assessed by a person called a psychiatrist her heart sank. She had by now been interviewed by two social workers, a policewoman, a lawyer, a guardian, a paediatrician and not one of them had listened to her. Instead, they had turned her words against her, called her a bad person and taken her away from all the people she loved. She did not know what a psychiatrist was, and she didn't have Granny or Aunty Emma to ask but google told her it was to do with mental health and mental health was to do people who wanted to kill themselves. The difficult words danced in front of her young eyes on the computer screen, whilst she kept herself on high alert in case Jean walked in and caught her in the act of googling things. Zoe knew she had said she wanted to kill herself, but in her case, there was a simple answer. If they let her live with her dad, she wouldn't want to kill herself anymore. Her heart beat hard as she read about mental health and wondered if the psychiatrist would understand why she wanted to kill herself. Zoe knew it was his job to understand these things but a few days later, when she walked into yet another interview room with colourful posters on the walls, her mouth went suddenly paper dry with the fear of saying the wrong thing. All she wanted to do was run out of the room and away from the stranger holding out his hand to say hello.

The man in question had also done his research before carrying out this assessment and had made up his mind long before meeting Zoe. The reports and minutes of case conferences he had read all sang the same tune in almost perfect unison, with only a minor variation, but he attached no importance to what a school nurse had to say when she was in a minority of one. Now he had Zoe in front of him and as he asked his questions, he saw the girl shrink more and more into herself. Her eyes avoided his, her answers were monosyllabic, but what disturbed him most of all was how she would not be critical of her father in the face of his bad behaviour. She would not admit he was letting her down. 'Unhealthy', was the note made by the psychiatrist in relation to Zoe's relationship with her dad.

Trapped in a room with this stranger, Zoe felt despair. This man thought that because her dad had let her down, he didn't love her. He didn't say it exactly like that, but it was obvious what he thought, and she didn't have the words to explain to him that letting her down could coexist with loving her because the human heart is a complicated place. After that failed exchange Zoe said very little more and the man felt his pre-formed judgement had been correct. A couple of weeks passed before he had time to write his report, which was sent to the Child Protection team manager with a copy to the Senior Practitioner who sent copies to Joe and to his parents, as had been agreed.

The first person to read his report was Janet.

By now school had broken up for the summer and Emma was sitting in the garden with her mother enjoying the first warm sunny day since back in June.

'It breaks my heart to think it's the first day of school holidays and Zoe's not here with us…' Janet's voice trailed off as she felt her gullet tightening. Emma was silent, soaking up the sun with her eyes closed under her hat. Her mother continued, 'I'm hanging all my hopes on that psychiatrist. His report should come any day now.'

'I wouldn't trust a psychiatrist,' said Emma. 'Zoe's not mentally ill, is she? So, what's a psychiatrist got to do with it?'

'I suppose you're right, Emma, but that report is all I've got to hang my hopes on, and I need hope just to survive, one day at a time.'

Emma's heart constricted as she heard the pain in her mother's voice. The heartache, she knew, was not just about her beloved grandchild being caught up in this situation, it was also about her own shattered dreams. All her mother had ever wanted in life was a happy family. Which was what all mothers wanted, weaving around themselves cocoons of human warmth and measuring their success by the size, cohesion and harmony of the final product. Was that why some deep, almost primitive instinct, led everyone to feel that Zoe belonged with her mum and not her dad? To deprive a mother of one of the essential components of the cocoon was sacrilegious whereas the man wasn't losing anything vital because his purpose was of a different nature.

'Mum, I know what you're like,' said Emma from under her hat, 'hope or no hope, you'll never stop fighting.'

'You're right Emma, I don't think I will. It's about Zoe, but it's about all of us, isn't it?'

'What do you mean?' asked Emma, lifting the hat to look at her mother.

'I mean,' said Janet meeting her daughter's eyes, 'it's about the family name. Our pride in ourselves.'

Emma turned her face to the sun again without replying. She didn't agree with any of it, but there was no point in upsetting her mother with an unnecessary debate. She put the hat back on her face and closed her eyes. The only sounds were the buzzing of bees in the flower beds and the slow flicking of magazine pages. Her mother had started to read again. Emma felt herself dozing off.

The distant jangle of the doorbell broke the dozy silence. Emma opened her eyes to the shuffling sound of her mother pushing herself up from her seat. How sad it was to see this active woman stiffening up and slowing down, showing advance glimpses of the old person she would ineluctably become. A knot tightened Emma's gullet. She heard her mother's steps echo down the tiled kitchen floor then fade as she stepped onto the runner in the hall. A faint voice at the door, probably the postman. She lifted herself to a sitting position and turned around to catch sight of her mother returning. Sure enough, there was a pile of mail in her hand. As Janet stepped into the sun and blinked against the sharpness of the light, she glimpsed her daughter's upturned face and questioning eyes.

'I think it's the report,' she said, sitting down and rushing to tear open a large white envelope. She pulled it out with a lightly shaking hand and scanned the accompanying letter from Gerald Crispin. It didn't say anything. She handed the letter to her daughter and turned to the report. She couldn't stop the light tremble in her hand and her eyes struggled to make sense of the words. If only Emma hadn't been there scrutinising her face. She tried to control her features as she took in the gist of the meaning behind the tortuous sentences. Her heart was tightening painfully in her chest and her lower lip wobbled like a little girl's. She didn't want Emma to witness her moment of weakness, nor did she want to see the inevitable message in her daughter's eyes, 'I told you so.' It felt as if it was Emma's fault. She dropped the stapled sheets on the table and stared off into the garden, saying not a word.

'I'll go and get Dad,' Emma muttered, leaving quickly for the greenhouse where her father had been pottering all morning.

When they returned Janet had collected herself. She looked up at her daughter with a grateful little smile and handed the report to David who lowered himself next to her at the table. He held the report with one hand and placed the other over his wife's wrist, gently stroking it between fingers and thumb. Emma sat on her lounger, looking down at her feet, giving her parents space. When David finished, he took the glasses off his nose and lay them on top of the report. Then he looked at his wife, at his daughter, and back at his wife. They waited, suspended.

'So,' he said, 'what's new? Another idiot has joined the gang. That's not going to stop us fighting for our granddaughter, is it?'

Relief swept Janet's face. She pressed her husband's hand back.

'Of course not, dear,' she said. They beamed at each other and David handed the report to his daughter. The bees still buzzed amongst the flowers and the sun was hot on her back, but summer oblivion seemed a distant thing now. Her mind was back in thinking mode. She tried to control her anger as she read.

'At least he says there's no way Joe would be violent with his daughter,' she said looking up, the pages dangling from her fingers.

'But he doesn't rule out emotional harm, does he?' Janet took the report from her daughter's hands and pointed to where it said Joe's extreme expression of feelings needed to stop before the girl could stay with him.

'I'm not sure Zoe is damaged by that,' replied Emma, 'but Joe would do well to take note. What's the point in saying he wants Zoe living with him if he can't behave in a way that makes it possible?'

'Your mother's told him often enough, Emma,' David butted in, 'and so have I. We get nowhere. I don't know where all these emotions come from, Joe seemed such a quiet boy.' He sighed and shook his head, looking helpless.

'Still,' said Emma, 'Zoe wants to be with Joe, so who is that psychiatrist to say she shouldn't want that? And after her dad, you two are the people she wants to be with. These so-called experts make me mad.'

'He's not just a psychiatrist,' said David, 'he's a consultant psychiatrist.'

'That just goes to show that a consultant psychiatrist can be wrong.'

'Trouble is Emma, people will think with that kind of a title, he must be right.'

'I know,' replied Emma, 'we really are up against the Establishment with a capital E.' Then she snorted a short burst of amused laughter and added, 'I bet you two never thought you'd be fighting the Establishment.'

'You're right,' replied David quickly, 'nor did we ever think our children and grandchildren would turn out to be such a rebellious bunch, or that we'd have to spend our retirement years getting them out of trouble.' His stare held his daughter's eyes unflinchingly. He would do everything in his power for his family, but he wouldn't let them make fun of him.

Emma was chastened. She looked down at her bare feet and up again at her parents, 'You've been very supportive,' she said, 'I don't know where Joe and Zoe would be without you…'

'Same place they are now,' interrupted David, 'we've achieved nothing.'

Emma's parents exchanged a knowing glance, then looked away from each other as if leaving it to the other whether to speak or not. It was Janet who spoke.

'Do you have any idea, Emma, how much we've already spent on legal fees?'

'No,' replied Emma, mildly embarrassed.

'Ten thousand pounds.'

Emma's eyes widened. 'Ten thousand pounds?' she whispered in disbelief.

'Think about it,' said David, 'Joe's solicitor, Zoe's solicitor and our solicitor. It soon mounts up, and that's only the beginning. Given this piece of rubbish,' he added picking up the report and flapping it angrily through the air, 'there's only one avenue open to us now, and that's to go back to court. But this time it won't be solicitors' fees we'll have to pay, it'll be barristers' fees. And that's a different ballgame altogether.'

'Wh…why,' stuttered Emma, 'will you be going to court?'

'Because on the back of this report,' replied her father slamming the bundle on the table, 'the local authority will now be applying for a permanent care order. What they have at present is still the interim care order, placing Zoe with foster carers pending the psychiatrist's report. Now they will go the whole hog, and if they win, it means they in effect become Zoe's new parents. Can you imagine that bunch of morons in complete charge of Zoe's life? So, we're going to oppose it. Apply for residence orders ourselves. Apply for every goddamn thing we can think of.' He leant back in his chair, his eyes brimming with grim determination. But as Emma watched her father's face closely, she uncovered a different story. Yes, he would go through those motions, for his wife's sake, for the family's sake, and even for his own feeling of being the provider and the protector. As for the fight, he had already accepted there was no hope of winning it.

*

Zoe meanwhile had not stopped hating life away from her dad and grandparents, but it was her summer holiday and there were things to enjoy in spite of everything. Rollerblading down the front was one of them, and Owen was always prepared to take her down and pick her up. One day she was greeted home in an unusual way.

'I have good news for you,' trumpeted Jean from the kitchen.

Zoe pushed the front door shut behind her without answering. She had long stopped believing in good news and nothing irritated her more than watching Jean doing her mother-hen act, fussing and flapping like someone who knew just how to win over difficult children. Zoe dumped her rollerblades on the floor and looked up blankly as Jean came scurrying into the hall.

Zoe was on the defensive. She had made mistakes with Jean in the recent past and she was not about to repeat them. The first humiliating incident had taken place in ToysRus about four weeks before when Jean had taken her and Kylie on a shopping trip. Zoe had been chatting away with Kylie, the two girls just ahead of Jean walking past piles of soft toys on the shelves, when Zoe spotted a small grey rabbit with floppy ears. She froze. Flossie. A smaller Flossie. Losing all sense of where she was and who she was with, she reached for the adult arm next to her and shouted excitedly, 'Look Mum, that could be Flossie's baby.' Hot shame flared in her cheeks, but it was too late to backtrack. Looking radiant Jean quickly skittered off to buy the cute little rabbit and for the rest of that day behaved like she'd won the lottery.

Then Zoe got caught again. Twice. The day of the pedal boats and the day of the ice skating. Twice she hadn't been able to stop herself shrieking with laughter and enjoying herself as if Jean and Owen were her best friends. They had looked chuffed to bits and Zoe had seen something in Jean's eyes that she didn't want to see there. Something reserved for Dad or Granny. Now Jean had that look on her face again. But Zoe was geared up and Jean would not get a smile out of her. They held each other's gazes, patiently, like two poker players convinced that they are about to win the showdown.

'So?' asked Zoe at last. And to show she had no interest whatsoever in the answer, she turned to the mirror on the wall and became absorbed in rearranging her hair into a neater ponytail. Jean watched her with a mixture of irritation and amusement. The girl had grown her frizzy hair as a rebellious

212

statement, but Jean had to admit the result was attractive. Different. Never mind what Leanne would say when she saw it. Thinking of Leanne brought her piece of news back to the front of her mind. She took a light breath and with her eyes fixed on the girl's profile, blurted out excitedly, 'You're going to start seeing your family again. Tomorrow if you want.'

Zoe spun around with her mouth half open and her eyes wide with incomprehension. The ponytail was forgotten, and a mess of hair dropped on her shoulders.

'What do you mean seeing them?' she said accusingly. 'They said I'd be going back after that report.' Her voice trembled. Jean heard the anguish, read the hurt behind the anger and in a flash saw the world from the girl's point of view.

'I'm sorry, Zoe,' she mumbled. 'I don't know why I thought this would be good news, of course it's not what you wanted to hear.'

Zoe burst into tears. Uncontrollable waves of pain ripped through her, reaching deep into her most secret hiding places, crashing against her defences, whipping away her anger and leaving her naked. Jean dropped to her knees and Zoe fell into her arms. Tears and snot mingled on Jean's shoulder, spreading stains of desolation on her clean cardigan. At long last Jean had Zoe in her arms, but it felt like defeat, not victory. The girl had nowhere else to go. If resentment followed Jean would have to be sensible about it, but for now Zoe was showing no signs of wanting to leave her arms. Jean held her, ignoring the numbness in her legs and the ache spreading up her back.

Finally, Zoe spoke between her abating sobs. 'I want to go home,' she hiccupped, without taking her head out of Jean's shoulder. Jean tightened her arms gently around the girl without saying anything. Zoe kept on repeating her mantra, and in her desperation to help, Jean made a mistake.

'You can, Zoe,' she said, pushing the girl out in front of her by the shoulders and peering encouragingly into her eyes, 'just tell them you'll get on with your mum and …' It didn't seem a big deal to Jean, just an easy simple solution that would take Zoe straight back to her parents, but Zoe's tears dried up and her face shut down.

'I don't get on with my mum. I hate it there,' she said with all the familiar hostility flooding back into her voice, 'and you're on their side, trying to make me do what they want. Nobody understands, nobody listens. I might as well be dead.' She turned on her heels and trudged up the stairs towards her bedroom.

'Zoe,' called Jean after her, 'shall I make that appointment to see your grandparents tomorrow?'

'Don't care,' said Zoe without turning round.

'Does that mean yes?' asked Jean.

'Don't know.' Zoe carried on walking upstairs.

'All right, Zoe, I'll make the appointment. See how you feel tomorrow.'

Then Jean went straight to the freezer and fished out Zoe's favourite pudding.

*

In bed that night Zoe lay on her side facing Flossie. 'Tomorrow,' she whispered, 'I'm going to see Granny and Grandad.' She looked deep into Flossie's eyes. 'But I'm not allowed to see them in their house. Just in some stupid room somewhere. Can you believe that?' Then, timidly, she allowed images to form. Granny walking into the room, with her soft

214

white hair and gentle eyes. Granny's hug. She trembled slightly at the thought of Granny's hug, and pushed it away in case something came up before tomorrow to stop it happening. Then she closed her eyes and let the hug creep back in. Granny's arms around her, her lips on her head, everything familiar and right. Tears hurt the back of her eyes. She blinked hard and held Flossie close. Now was not the time to start crying. Only when Granny was there to kiss her better could the tears come out. She shut her eyes, but sleep did not come for a long time. Despite everything it felt as if she would never see Granny again.

At ten o'clock the following morning a woman came to pick Zoe up and take her to the room where she would see her grandparents. She was short and chubby, with smooth black hair and a lot of make-up on her eyes. She introduced herself as Elaine and her mouth gave Zoe a smile, but her eyes didn't. They peered at her, with critical interest. In the car the woman made conversation, but it came from far away, through a fog, and Zoe didn't pay attention to any of it. Fortunately, like most adults, the woman was not interested in what the child had to say and kept talking on her own. The car stopped in front of an old building with a sign on the door saying Family Centre. They walked in, along a dark corridor and stopped in front of a blue door that had another sign on it, saying Children's Room. Zoe's heart stopped beating. A wave of fear rose, as if to crush her. Holding the handle, the woman looked down at Zoe and said, 'I believe your grandparents are already in there, Zoe.' Zoe's mouth was dry and her legs too limp to move. The door was pushed open and all the pictures in Zoe's head shattered and instantly reassembled into the amazingly real presence of her grandmother. Then she ran.

Just as she had imagined it. The open arms, the soft lips, the lavender fragrance, and the tears. 'I thought you wouldn't be here,' sobbed Zoe, clinging to her gran.

'I am here,' whispered Granny in her ear. 'Can you feel my arms around you and my lips against your ear?'

'Yes, but I felt them in my dreams too, and now I don't know if this is a dream or if it's true.' And they both burst out laughing, and Grandad, who was still waiting for his cuddle, joined in, and the three of them were mingling tears and laughter in their disbelief at being together again.

'Can I come and live with you?' asked Zoe, wiping the joy off their faces in one quick swipe.

'Sweetie,' replied Gran, 'we are doing everything we can.' Her eyes did a quick shuttle between Zoe and something just behind Zoe, as if to warn her granddaughter of a mysterious danger. Zoe's head spun round, and she was taken aback to find the woman with the peering eyes standing there, a few feet away.

'I'll just sit over here,' said the woman, pointing to a blue plastic chair against the wall, not very far from the little table where her grandparents were sitting. 'I need to able to hear what you say.'

Zoe frowned and turned an enquiring face to her grandmother.

'They haven't explained?' asked Granny, not surprised that the dirty work had been left to her.

'Explained what?' asked Zoe with new tension in her voice.

Granny sighed, glanced at her husband and turned her concerned eyes back to Zoe. 'All visits are to be supervised Zoe. This lady is here to listen to what we say to you.'

'Why?' protested Zoe, 'it's none of her business what you say to me.' Her eyes had flared up with indignation.

'She's here to make sure nothing bad is said about your mother.'

'You never say bad things about Mum,' exclaimed Zoe, tightening her grip on her grandmother's arm. 'I don't want that lady here when I see you. It's not the same.' The tears were coming again, bitter liquid salt.

'There's nothing we can do, love. We'll have to enjoy our visits anyway. It is better than no visits, isn't it?'

'Will it be the same when I see Dad?' asked Zoe tensely.

'I'm afraid so, sweetheart,' replied Granny. Her hands went up to cup the girl's face inside her palms and she gazed into those young eyes with gentle persuasion. Then she wrapped her arms around the girl and held her close.

She had rehearsed this scene a thousand times, but now she couldn't say what she had planned to tell Zoe. Joe would have to tell his daughter himself what he had decided in relation to these visits, because Janet could not bear to see any more tears in her granddaughter's eyes.

17. A Pact with Stefan

The visit with Dad was scheduled for the following Saturday morning and Zoe couldn't wait. He would share her feelings and wouldn't tell her things were all right when they weren't. And there was no doubt in Zoe's mind that these stupid visits were not all right.

After the first half hour with her grandparents, they had run out of things to say, and that was after discussing the latest episodes of Coronation Street and East Enders. School had been exhausted in all of five minutes, friends took another five, and moans about life with the foster carers had been gently stifled by Granny's pointed looks. Never before had the three of them sat around a table trying to make conversation. This, they now realised, was not the way grandparents relate to their grandchildren. There is a need for freedom of movement, with information emerging in short bursts in the middle of activities like baking ginger-bread men and making tiny chairs for the doll's house. But that kind of togetherness had now been wrenched from them and they were left with this inadequate, awkward package that left them feeling bored, frustrated and mildly guilty. It was like food without the taste.

The visit with Dad went differently.

Despite her bitter disappointment after finding out what supervised visits were like, Zoe still let her anticipation mount as the moment approached to see her father after seven weeks of separation. And when it finally happened it was better than anything she had imagined. When she saw him standing there, tall and perfectly himself in his black jacket and faded jeans, the room disappeared, the spy woman disappeared, everything disappeared, and a whirlwind took her straight into her father's arms where she stayed crying quietly for a long time. He sat down awkwardly on one of the blue plastic chairs and held her in silence, stroking her hair, her cheeks and whispering gently into her ear. 'It's ok, poppet, it's ok, I'm here now, everybody's working on the problem, we'll soon be together again. Trust me.'

Then he said, 'Look, I've brought you some presents.' Disentangling one arm he picked up a bag from the floor and Zoe fished out one thing after another. A couple of books by Jacqueline Wilson, which he said Aunty Emma had recommended, a couple of difficult bird puzzles still wrapped up in their tight plastic sleeves, a book of coloured stickers and a bag of chocolate éclair toffees. She spread out her treasures on the table and then snuggled back against her father's body. His lips were on her hair and she closed her eyes, listening to the soft whisperings in her ear.

'Could you speak up Mr Milton,' butted in the supervisor. 'As you know I will have to write up notes of what's been said during the visit and if I can't hear you, I can't write my notes.' She smiled pleasantly enough, but there was also self-importance in her voice at this not unimportant amount of power she had been given over two other people.

'What do you think of these visits, Zoe?' Joe asked in a loud clear voice.

Zoe looked up at her dad trying to figure out from his expression what game they were playing. Annoying the woman, or worse than that? A dark cloud had descended into his eyes.

'I hate them,' responded Zoe. 'I hate the room, I hate not being at home, and I hate someone listening to everything we say. It's like being in prison.'

'Have you made a note of that?' snapped Joe at the woman. Then he turned back to his daughter and said, 'I agree, the whole thing is hateful. How was your visit with your mum yesterday?'

'I'm sorry, Mr Milton, but I have been instructed not to allow any talk about Zoe's mother.' With her pointed chin up in the air, the woman stared at Joe disapprovingly.

'I'm not talking about Zoe's mum, I'm asking my daughter how the visit went.'

'Still out of bounds,' snapped the woman back, clutching her pad of paper and pen as if to gather strength from them. She had obviously been warned that this man could be difficult and had probably said with great confidence that she wouldn't be troubled by that, she knew how to deal with difficult people.

'And how are you going to stop me?' He uttered one of his slightly crazed chuckles and Zoe tensed up on his lap. Immediately his arm tightened around her reassuringly. But she wasn't reassured. Maybe her dad would end up in real prison if he disobeyed all the rules and this horrible woman told on him. Zoe looked up at him pleadingly and he looked down at her with a wicked smile. Watch this, said the smile.

220

His eyes turned back to the woman and he said mockingly, 'Are you going to fight me? Try and stop my mouth with your hand. Because that's the only way you will stop me. I'm going to say exactly what I want to say, and you can write it all down in your silly notes. I'm here to talk to my daughter after not being allowed to talk to her for seven weeks, and I'm going to make the most of this.'

'Dad,' Zoe butted in tentatively, 'what if they don't allow any more visits?'

'Your nine-year-old daughter has more sense than you Mr Milton. That is exactly what will happen. No more visits. That's your choice.'

'And I don't give a damn. Visits like these, with someone snooping and watching are not worth having. They're degrading. It says it all about Social Services that they call this child protection. And people like you,' he added with anger seething in his voice, 'are just like the concentration camp officials who followed orders. Can't you see how wrong what you're doing is? Can't you see nobody should agree to a job like that?' He was shouting now, and Zoe patted him on the shoulder, saying soothingly, 'Dad, stop shouting Dad.'

'I've finished shouting Zoe,' he said, turning round to her with a big smile and his gentle voice back on. 'I won't see you again in this room. I can't do it sweetheart, I'm sorry. But I'll keep on fighting for us, and we'll carry on with the letters. Don't cry now,' he added brushing her tears away. 'When you get back to the house, you do those puzzles and let me know how long they took. I bought this one,' he said pointing to the one of seagulls flying amongst the clouds, cormorants drying their wings by the seashore and little sanderlings running at the edge of the lapping waves, 'because you know all the birds on it. I thought you would like that.'

Zoe nodded, brushing away the saltiness from her face with the back of her hand. 'That's a good one, Dad, and it won't be easy because the herring gulls are almost the same colour as the clouds.'

'Good,' said Dad, 'it'll keep you busy tonight. Remember Daddy took special care buying this puzzle just for you, and also that book.' He pointed to the book with the pink cover and two girls on it arm in arm. Zoe peered at him and when he winked twice with his back to the supervisor, she knew he was trying to tell her something. When he had said 'just for you' he had squeezed her arm. Just for you. This reminded Zoe of treasure hunts organised by Granny where you had to understand secret clues.

'Thanks, Dad,' she replied, 'I'll do the puzzle all on my own.' Their eyes met and she knew the puzzle would tell her something.

'That's my girl,' said Daddy in just the way that Granny said it when Zoe had done something good. This thought brought more tears to run down her already streaked face. Dad bent over and kissed her on both cheeks.

'Now,' he said, 'I want you to know that what these people are doing to us is very wrong, Zoe, and if they ever try to tell you that your father is damaging you, it's a lie. They are doing the damage. They are stealing your childhood. I'll never stop fighting to have you back living at home with me, but in the meantime, we have to say goodbye. You can see these visits are no good, can't you, with a woman watching us and writing down everything we say. You can see they're making it impossible for us to see each other, can't you sweetheart?'

Zoe nodded, with the tears going into free flow. She threw her arms around her father and clung to him. The room went silent, with the afternoon sun streaming in, reminding them it was summer, and this should have been a happy holiday time. Then Dad got up, put all the presents back in the bag and handed it to his daughter as if it were a precious treasure. He patted her little hand holding the bag, spun around without a look at the supervisor and stalked out of the room. Zoe watched his back disappear round the door and although her tears wouldn't stop, she was also proud of him. And somewhere amongst the presents there was a message for her, she was sure of it. She would just have to be very careful not to give anything away. Her fingers tightened around the handles of the plastic bag. In a daze she followed the woman to the car and was driven back without a word being said. When they got there the woman and Jean shut themselves in the kitchen on the pretext of a cup of tea. Zoe headed for her bedroom with her heart beating fast. She went in and stood undecided by the door. Closing it felt safer but leaving it open meant she could hear anyone coming up. Owen was watching football downstairs, but that didn't mean he couldn't come up for a pee and decide to pop his head round the door to see what she was doing.

She briefly considered shutting herself in the loo to open the puzzle box, but if she was caught it would arouse suspicions and whatever plan her dad had concocted might be ruined. So, she left her bedroom door wide open and pulled the puzzle out of the plastic carrier. She pushed her nail against the thin plastic film that wrapped the box and ripped it off. At Christmas two years ago, Zoe had found an MP3 player inside a wrapped puzzle box and she wondered what she was going to find today. Her heart was thumping now, and she glanced towards the door, listening hard before taking the next step. The football was still on and if Owen was going to leave the room it would be during the adverts, not in the middle of the game. No sign of Jean and the woman emerging from the kitchen.

She pulled the lid off the box and in one swift scan took in all the contents. Nothing. Just a jumble of grey and blue puzzle pieces. She scattered them around with her hand but there was nothing else. Then she noticed the number. Written neatly in one corner of the box. 49. It could be the number of pieces, but Zoe had recognised her dad's handwriting. What could it mean? Her heart was thudding even though there was no danger because if someone walked in all they would see was a little girl looking at the scattered pieces of her new puzzle. Owen's voice still startled her when he asked what she was doing.

'Doing my new puzzle,' she muttered back, without turning around. She was staring at the figure 49, cursing her dad for not giving her a better clue. Thankfully Owen left, but what if she couldn't make sense of the number? She brought back to mind her father's words. 'Just for you,' he had said, and she had known that to mean 'don't show it to anyone else'. He had pointed at the puzzle and, she struggled to remember, had mentioned something else too. The book, that was it. One of the two brightly coloured books. Brilliant colours, trust Aunty Emma to pick something good. Maybe there was another clue in the book. She glanced around over her shoulder and pulled the pink one out, with two cartoon girls smiling at her with big shining eyes, one sweetly, the other wickedly. They had their heads close together, like two friends, but something told

224

you that other things were going on, and that's what made you want to read the story. She bent the book and let the pages flip rapidly from end to end. Nothing hidden in there. As she watched the page numbers fly by, an idea struck her. 49. She quickly opened the book on page 49 and her breathing stopped. Quickly she snapped the book shut again. The empty bottom half of that page was covered in her dad's neat handwriting. In pencil. She looked around again, clutching the book in her hand. She couldn't have taken her puzzle to the toilet, but a book was different. Jean and Owen had a little shelf of books and magazines for that very purpose and although Zoe had never understood the point of reading on the toilet, it came in very handy that nobody could question the fact that she was about to do just that. She grabbed her rucksack from under her bed, fumbled inside for her pencil case and her nimble fingers soon found the smooth shape of her eraser. She stuffed it in her pocket and got up.

At the door she stopped and listened. The football was over, but the telly was droning on and the kitchen door was still closed. Forcing herself not to rush Zoe made for the bathroom and when she got there, she probably closed the door a little too sharply and pushed the lock in a touch too fast, but there was nobody around to notice. Then she took a deep breath and, sitting on the edge of the bath, she went to page 49. Her dad had a plan. Of course, he had. Of course, he wasn't going to just stop seeing her, she should have known. Hers eyes smarted just a little. She read the plan over and over and when it was perfectly clear to her, she pulled her rubber out and erased everything from page 49. She blew all the rubber bits from the page into the loo and decided that later she would do a drawing there to cover up any marks. She flushed the loo and came out. Jean and the woman were now saying goodbye, sounding as if their cup of tea had marked the enthusiastic beginning of a new friendship. All because they'd been gossiping about Zoe and her dad. But then Zoe herself knew that she never felt as close to Kylie as when they agreed Michaela was a sly cow, so it was probably the same with grown-ups.

That evening, against all the odds considering what Elaine had reported to her of Zoe's visit with her dad, Jean found the girl more friendly than usual. Perhaps she was beginning to understand that it was time to go along with the decisions of others and be grateful for what she had.

How wrong she was!

*

The following day Zoe asked permission to phone Stefan and arrange to meet down the front. When Jean asked if Kylie would be coming too, she was ready with her answer that Kylie had said she was spending the day with her Nan. This was a lie, but Zoe didn't want Kylie there that day, and it wasn't just because there was something sweetly exciting about arranging to meet with Stefan on his own. Dad's instructions were to find a friend she could trust. He had probably thought of Kylie, but Zoe knew that Kylie struggled to keep stuff from her mum, and nice as Kylie's mum was, she certainly couldn't be trusted not to talk to Kylie's dad, and Zoe knew exactly what Kylie's dad would do with Zoe's secret. So, she had settled on Stefan. A little thrill sent Zoe's heart fluttering when she thought of asking Stefan if he would keep a secret for her.

She dialled Stefan's number and stood nervously looking out of the window in the lounge, conscious of Jean's hovering presence behind her. Jean was nosy and that was one thing Zoe couldn't stand about her. Always wanting to know everything, her small eyes peering at you, ready with the next question. But as Zoe needed Jean to take her down the front, she suppressed her irritation. Finally, the boy answered.

'He's already down there,' Zoe told Jean, banging the phone down into place. 'Can we go?'

But when they arrived at the skateboard ramps, Zoe had to make an enormous effort not to show her disappointment. Stefan was there, but he wasn't alone. Jean, however, was happy to see that Zoe would have friends to be with and she arranged to pick her up at the garage at lunchtime. This gave Zoe a couple of hours, but with Oliver and Richard hanging around with Stefan, she may not be able to move the plan forward at all. She watched them going down the ramps and up again, shouting out tips and insults. Impatience was tying knots inside Zoe as she failed to see any way of speaking to Stefan on his own and she felt tears of frustration wetting her eyes. She turned her back on the ramps and sat in the grass to put her blades on. As she was tightening her laces, Stefan's voice gave her a jolt. He was standing right beside her talking about his dad getting him some blades for his birthday. Zoe's hands froze with the laces taut between her fingers. Stefan on blades. Dizzying images of tricks, races and crazy fun reeled in her mind, but all she said, as quickly and quietly as she could, was, 'I need to talk to you alone.' Then she looked down, pulling at her laces to make them as tight as possible. Stefan hadn't reacted. Maybe he hadn't heard. She looked up, he glanced around. Oliver was calling him to watch his latest feat. Oliver was forever wanting to impress the other boy.

'I've twisted my ankle,' shouted Stefan. 'I better stop for a bit.' He winked at Zoe and she smiled back, impressed. She had chosen the right person for her secret. Her heart was beating fast as she deftly tied her double knot. Stefan flopped down onto the grass next to her and bent over to massage his ankle.

'Can you keep a secret?' whispered Zoe.

'Depends what it is,' replied Stefan with a light frown.

'I can't tell you unless you promise never to tell anyone, not even your dad.'

Stefan fell silent. Zoe stared at her rollerblades, feeling a pit of anxiety opening in her stomach. She had failed to prepare for the possibility of Stefan saying no.

'I can't promise never to tell my dad,' he said at last, and that little sentence sucked all the life out of her. Stefan glanced at her and quickly launched into an explanation. 'It doesn't mean I will tell him, just that if I was worried about something, I could tell him. But that would only be if I was really worried, and I can promise you that my dad would never get you into trouble.' Tempting stuff. But not good enough. She sighed and looked out at the dull sea under low hanging clouds, wishing she could talk to her dad. It must be a secret, he had written, and he was right. Zoe knew exactly what happened when people didn't keep a secret. They told one person, swearing them not to tell anyone, and that one person told one person, and on and on until everybody knew. She shook her head, blinking hard to send her tears back inside her eyes. She would have to try Kylie.

Now Oliver and Richard were jostling out of the skateboard rink and running down towards them with their boards dangling from under their arms. She gave her eyes a quick swipe with the back of her wrist. Oliver asked from a distance if Stefan's ankle was bad, but instead of replying, Stefan blurted at Zoe, 'All right then, I promise.' Their eyes met and a new breath-taking pact was sealed. Zoe dived over her blades to adjust her laces again. Oliver and Richard dropped to the ground, chucking their skateboards to one side, quite unaware of the tension in the air. Stefan was now as impatient to know the secret as Zoe was to tell it, but Oliver and Richard were on form, cracking one joke after another about wimps with bad ankles. On another day Zoe would have enjoyed herself. She liked the company of boys and was as quick as any of them to come up with a good insult or a smart retort. They liked her too. For a girl, she was okay. She accepted this. As a girl you had to because girls were second class citizens in the eyes of boys, and that was how it was. But today she was silent, incapable of joining in the boys' banter. She looked at her watch a few times, feeling the knot inside her stomach get tighter as lunchtime approached. She bit her lower lip until she felt the shocking taste of blood in her mouth. She licked the little crack and stopped biting.

At long last Richard and Oliver got bored and headed back towards the ramps. Zoe watched them go with her heart leaping inside her chest. She took a deep breath. The plan was simple, but it went against the ruling of a judge. How would Stefan cope with that? She launched into her secret, and when she finished, she concentrated on twisting a dandelion stem around her fingers. Stefan was silent. A light breeze was blowing in from the sea and the familiar screech of gulls tore through the air. Zoe sneaked a glance at the boy.

His face was serious. Grown-up serious.

'All right,' he said. 'I'll do it.'

'Really?' she asked holding her breath.

'They shouldn't stop you seeing your dad,' he said, as if speaking to himself. 'That is just wrong.' He was staring off in the distance.

'No, they shouldn't,' repeated Zoe. Her heart was beating hard and fast.

Stefan took his mobile out of his pocket and handed it to Zoe. As their fingers touched something gripped her deep inside. With a trembling thumb she tapped in her father's number. Then it all happened very quickly. Dad spoke to Stefan and the boy had that serious look on his face again but didn't change his mind. Said yes to everything. Zoe could barely breathe. She was going to have a mobile again, and Stefan would look after it for her. And then the secret visits would start, and Stefan would be part of that too. Tightening her arms around her drawn up knees, Zoe listened to the hammering of her heart inside her chest. How could it be so loud and Stefan not hear it?

Stefan pocketed his phone and looked at Zoe with shining eyes.

'This is the most exciting thing I've ever done,' he said. 'It's like being in a film.' The serious look was gone, and he was grinning, looking forward to this adventure. Relief swept through Zoe. Now she could believe in the future. A few drops of rain splattered on her arms, thick and fat, warning of worse things to come. Dark clouds were rolling in from the sea, but Zoe didn't care. She wanted to laugh and cry and run madly on the beach.

'Com'on,' shouted Stefan, 'we're gonna get soaked.'

Richard and Oliver had already whizzed past on their skateboards, and Stefan and Zoe raced after them. But the rain got them and when they joined the other boys in the garage forecourt, they were dripping and laughing, slightly exhilarated. By the time Jean pulled in to pick Zoe up, the shower had passed, and Stefan declined a lift home. His ankle was better he said, and the three boys were larking about now, pushing and shoving each other off their respective skateboards. As Jean drove off with Zoe sitting quietly in the back, she shook her head and sighed. 'Boys,' she said, 'it takes them so long to grow up, doesn't it?'

Little did she know that nine-year-old Stefan had just taken the kind of mature decision many adults fail to ever take in the whole of their lives. He had decided to follow his own sense of right and wrong against the voice of authority. He wasn't sure where the decision would take him, but he didn't think nine-year-olds went to prison for helping a friend. He felt a little sad to be keeping something from his dad, but if there was a loss there was also a gain. Something to do with growing up.

As he walked home later that afternoon, carrying his board most of the way as it was mainly uphill, his mind kept returning to Zoe's grey blue eyes looking up at him and he wondered at the funny way his insides tightened when he thought about that. This, he suddenly realised, would be the second secret he would be keeping from his dad.

18. Secrets Visits and a Film

Three days later, on a sunny August morning, Zoe got dropped off at Kylie's house. She rang the bell and when the door opened, she waved at Jean and stepped into the house. Kylie's mum stepped aside to let her in, but the look on her face was one of mild surprise.

'I thought Kylie had told you…' she started.

'I know Kylie's out, I thought I'd drop her book back in case she needs it, then I'm going over to Michaela's.' Zoe pulled the book out of her rucksack and handed it to Kylie's mum with a sparkling smile. 'Can I go out the back?' she added innocently, 'it's quicker that way.'

Once in the back-alley Zoe dropped down on a little pile of breeze blocks just outside Kylie's gate and fiddled with her trainers until she was confident Kylie's mum would be safely back in the house and unaware of which direction Zoe had taken after leaving her. She stood up, pulled her hood over her head and walked along the walls with her eyes to the ground. Her heart was racing and all she wanted to do was break into a run, but Dad had said to act slow and cool. No running. Kicking little stones out of her way, she progressed along the alley without meeting anyone except for Mrs Evans' white cat. When she reached her dad's back gate, her heart's pounding got louder, and her breathing got fast and shallow.

With the sense she was doing something wrong screaming inside her head she pressed on the latch with two fingers and watched the lock lift out of its rusty groove with a loud click. A glance reassured her there was nobody about to take any notice. She pushed the gate open, slipped in and shut it again carefully. She cast a worried glance at the windows of the neighbouring houses, hoping no one was looking. Then she proceeded quietly through the mess of weeds in the garden and found the backdoor key where Dad had said it would be. 'The door will be locked, to be absolutely safe,' Dad had said, 'and don't forget to lock it again as soon as you're in.' But now Zoe's hand was trembling so much she couldn't get the key to slot in and thought Dad must have put the wrong key out. With tears threatening she now felt a great fear. Fear that the key wouldn't turn, the door wouldn't open, Dad wouldn't be there or if he was, the policewoman would be knocking at their door within five minutes and sending them both to prison. Her heart was hammering, and her breathing faltering.

Then the key turned, and the door opened. She stepped in and paused, overwhelmed by the poignant familiarity of everything. Home. She locked the kitchen door and headed for the study on the second floor, tiptoeing all the way up. Dad had said he would wait for her up there so neighbours wouldn't hear anything through the walls but Zoe still felt unsettled by how quiet the house was. On the first floor landing she paused and looked at the door to her bedroom. Her gullet constricted. Would she ever be back in her bedroom? She set off again, walking softly up the second flight of stairs. Her dad had said he would be working from home that afternoon, so she could come any time, but was he really going to be sitting at his desk, ready to swivel round on his chair and take her in his arms? Her heart was knocking as she reached the top landing and she stopped to catch her breath. She could see the study door was ajar, but it looked dark in there and she paused again wondering if this was the right time and the right day. What if the room was empty? She broke into a run, pushed the door open and stood ready to face the worst disappointment in her life. But there was Dad, solid but dreamlike, sitting in his swivel chair and facing the door, his face tight with emotion.

Another run and everything went from silence to noise, from peace to whirlwind, arms, lips, kissing, crying, laughing, hands, clinging, holding, jumping up and down, 'I made it, I made it!' Dad was laughing too, shushing his daughter, pretending he needed to blow his nose, but the tears were there, she saw the tears, just like her tears, tears of anger, tears of joy, we beat the policewoman, we beat them all, here we are together, the doors are locked, we're safe, safe, safe. We can talk, play computer games, get a drink from the kitchen, and chocolate biscuits of course, and then more games, more talk, more cuddles.

'Thank god you're here,' said Joe burying his head in his daughter's hair, 'I was so nervous I couldn't do any work at all.'

'Will you be in trouble with your boss?' asked Zoe with a frown bringing lines to her young face.

'That's the least of my worries,' laughed Joe, throwing his head back, 'but have no fear, I'll catch up tonight.' Father and daughter sat looking at each other in wonder and delight. He stroked her face with the tips of his fingers, lifting her curls with gentle hands and she patted his shoulders and arms as if to check they were real.

'What if we get caught?' Zoe asked in a nervous little voice.

'They can't hurt us more than they've already done, sweetheart, so you needn't worry about that. But the longer we make it without getting found out, the more we see of each other. So, we will have to be careful, and not make loud noises in the house,' he added, making a face at the thought of the noise they had just made. 'I don't want the neighbours asking questions.'

'Do Granny and Grandad know?'

'I haven't told them, but they may suspect something.'

When they had remonstrated with him for losing his temper at the very first supervised visit, he had replied sharply and pointedly, 'I will only see my daughter on my terms. But that doesn't mean I'm giving up on seeing her for the next five years.' They had looked at him curiously, then at each other, then Janet had gone off to make a cup of tea and not another word had been spoken on the matter.

'Still,' added Dad, 'it's important you carry on writing your letters and complain about not seeing me.'

'That'll be easy, Dad, 'cos I'm not seeing you properly anyway, am I? I have to hide, sneak around, and we can never go anywhere together. I can't have my own mobile...' but her voice trailed off and her eyes got lost in some private thinking of her own.

'Is Stefan proving a good ally?' Joe asked, and when her eyes lit up, he couldn't help a little pang of jealousy. He put his arm around her again and hugged her tight. Neither of them moved, and then it was time for Zoe to leave.

As she walked in the back alley heading towards Michaela's house elation rose up inside Zoe. She had done this bad thing and she'd got away with it. She was free. She chucked her hood back and walked tall in the direction of her friend's house. Over the next few weeks Zoe became an expert at spiriting away the odd half hour out of her days in order to see her father. She saw Aunty Emma too. The first time was in her dad's house, but the second time she worked up the courage to venture to Emma's flat, having asked Stefan to cover up for her. From Emma's attic room, level with the treetops in the park across the road, they watched the squirrels taking improbable leaps from tree to tree, as if about to commit squirrel suicide. Zoe held her breath, mesmerised, but Aunty Emma just laughed because she knew the squirrels never missed the other branch, even though it looked unreachable.

'Isn't it amazing what little creatures can do?' said Aunty Emma wrapping her arm around her niece's shoulders, and she added, looking down at her with a smile, 'and what little people can do.'

Aunty Emma believed children were amazing people who didn't get the treatment they deserved, even by well-meaning adults.

'Talking of the amazing things little people can do,' said Aunty Emma, 'I've got a film for you.' Zoe looked up and took the DVD her aunt was putting in her hand. 'Watch it with a friend,' she added, 'not at Jean's place.'

'Why?' Zoe asked, intrigued. She looked down at the cover and strange title, screwing up her nose. 'A film about rabbits?'

'It's not about rabbits, it's about two little girls, about your age. Email me to tell me what you thought of it.'

Zoe tucked the slim plastic case in the front pocket of her rucksack and said goodbye. It was time to rush off and pretend to the world she had spent that Saturday afternoon with Stefan. Now she had a new secret to keep, and a mysterious film was burning another hole in her world of interdictions. She couldn't wait to watch it.

But when she suggested watching it with Stefan at his place he looked down at his trainers, kicked a few loose stones through the railings and then glanced vaguely around the schoolyard. 'We could ask Kylie to come too,' Zoe added quickly.

'What film?' asked Stefan. Rollerblading with Zoe and Kylie was one thing but watching a girlie movie with them in his house was another.

'It's a film about children, my Aunty gave it to me. She says it's really good, but it's boring to watch it on my own…' Zoe didn't want to give any more details. The strange title might put her friend off, and she couldn't tell Stefan it was about two girls, 'cos boys just never wanted to watch films about girls. Which was very unfair, seeing as girls were forever watching films about boys, but anyway that's the way it was.

'Okay,' said Stefan without enthusiasm. 'Saturday?'

'I've got contact with my grandparents at two,' replied Zoe. 'Sunday?'

'Kylie won't be allowed on a Sunday, and I'm supposed to visit my mum. What about the Saturday after next?'

'We could do it after school one day.' suggested Stefan, feeling a growing interest in this mysterious film.

Zoe looked embarrassed. 'Kylie's always busy after school,' she said quickly.

'Okay, Saturday after next then. What's the title of the film?' asked Stefan.

Just then the bell cut through the school yard noise and Zoe blurted out 'Rabbit Proof Fence' before escaping quickly to

237

join the girls in her class. She had not wanted to discuss 'after school' with Stefan because every Tuesday at four o'clock she had to go to therapy, and she would have died of shame if anyone in school had found out; and she liked to keep the other days clear in case her dad was working from home and she could go and see him. Zoe caught up with Kylie and whispered in her ear about the film as they walked past Miss Brown on their way to their table. But Kylie looked uncomfortable and whispered back that her mum might not allow her. 'Don't tell her, just say we're going to Stefan's house to play computer games.' Kylie gave her friend a long look and opened her Maths book. The following day, however, she said she would be coming to Stefan's house.

The ten days leading up to the day of the film dragged by with Zoe having to face one frustration after another. Only one secret meeting with her dad could be arranged, and they only managed to snatch fifteen minutes to spend together. They spoke on the phone most days, but never for long as Stefan had to hang about whilst she made the call. Supervised contact was getting Zoe down and she hated the sight of the spy-woman looking at them without any shame throughout the visit. The family centre had been closed for the last visit and they had had to go to the Leisure Centre instead. They sat around a small round table in the cafeteria and Zoe felt a deep shame that some of her schoolmates might see her there, with the spy-woman making her notes.

She poured her frustration into her letters. Desperate letters to her grandparents, begging them to rescue her, threatening to harm herself if she had to spend another day in care but also telling them about her life and how much she loved them, which she couldn't do with that stupid supervisor watching over them. She also wrote to her father and sent him letters to pass on to the doctor, to her solicitor and even to the judge who had sentenced her to this miserable existence. She wanted the world to know just how she felt about her life and she made a point of showing the letters to Jean.

'That's what I've written,' she would tell Jean before putting the pink sheet in the envelope.

One day she overheard Jean talking to Mr Crispin on the phone. 'Her letters are just manipulative Gerald. Zoe is not a child about to harm herself.' Then there was a silence whilst Mr Crispin replied, and Jean continued, 'She's happy enough, Gerald, I know, I live with her. You should see how quick she is to snap out of a bad mood if a friend phones, especially Stefan,' she added with a chuckle. Zoe felt a wave of pure hatred sweep through her. Another silence followed and Jean replied saying she couldn't see any signs of Zoe missing her dad very much. Zoe had a little smile when she heard that but soon after she showed Jean her calendar with every day crossed out in red going all the way back to August 11th. When Jean failed to see what this was about, Zoe told her 'That's the number of days I haven't seen Dad, from August 11th to October 15th, and you don't even care.'

'It's his choice, Zoe, he can see you if he wants.'

'No, he can't, not properly. How would you like it if you could only see Owen with a spy-woman listening to every word you say? How would you like that?' she shouted, leaning forward and going red in the face. Then she turned around and ran up the stairs, slamming her door shut behind her.

At long last the day came when she was going to discover what the mysterious film was about. Aunty Emma hadn't given it to her for no reason, she knew that much about Aunty

Emma, the film was going to tell her something, and now she couldn't wait to know what that was. She told Jean that she was going to watch a Harry Potter film over at Stefan's because his dad had just bought a huge plasma screen and watching Harry Potter on it was going to be amazing. Kylie told her mother the same, and Jean gave them both a lift to Stefan's place. Zoe watched the houses going by and grappled with her mounting excitement as they approached Stefan's house. Stefan, with his light-coloured hair and serious green eyes; his mocking smile; his graceful hip movement on the skateboard. Her heart beat faster.

As Jean's car rolled to a stop in front of the small terraced-house, Zoe saw Stefan's dad open the door and walk out towards the car. Her heart stopped beating as she watched the man approach and then lean over to talk to Jean. Zoe couldn't breathe, clutching the door handle and waiting for the words 'Rabbit Proof Fence' to burst out and destroy the afternoon. But all Stefan's dad said was that he would give the girls a lift back. Zoe started to breathe again but she wasn't moving, and Kylie had to shake her arm to bring her back to life. Stefan's dad pulled the door open for the girls and they all walked to the house together. Zoe had now recovered from her shock, but she was about to have her second one very quickly. Stefan's dad went off to the kitchen to get his coffee and the girls walked into the lounge where Stefan, remote in hand, was ready to show off the new plasma screen.

'Dad's going to watch the film with us,' declared the boy as if nothing was more natural.

'My film?' mouthed Zoe in disbelief.

Stefan shrugged and spread his hands, as if to say, 'don't blame me, couldn't do anything about it.' Zoe felt crushed by disappointment. This was going to spoil the whole afternoon for her. She watched Stefan's dad lowering himself into the one armchair in the room and to add to her misery, Kylie flopped down onto the settee next to Stefan so that Zoe was relegated to the far side. She felt a smarting in her eyes and wondered if Stefan would be pleased about having Kylie next to him. She handed him the DVD and then said lightly, looking at Stefan's dad, 'Jean thinks we're watching Harry Potter.' She gave a forced giggle.

'Why did you tell her that?' asked Stefan's dad, looking around at Zoe curiously.

'She bugs me,' replied Zoe, 'she's always asking questions about everything, so I don't tell her what I'm doing if I can help it.' She remembered her grandmother using that expression and she thought it added adult weight to her decision not to tell Jean about the film.

'Fair enough,' replied Stefan's dad, as if he couldn't care less, which was unusual for a grown-up. 'Anyway,' he added, stretching his legs out in front of him, 'I'm looking forward to this film, it's supposed to be really good.'

Zoe curled up at her end of the settee, fighting her resentment against Kylie for snatching the middle seat when this was her idea, her film and she hadn't even needed to invite Kylie. And fancy Stefan talking to his dad about the film and then letting him watch it with them. The presence of adults changed everything. The trailers they were forced to watch did nothing to alleviate her bitterness and when the film finally started, she had lost all desire to watch it.

A few minutes into it however changed all that and she forgot everything. Where she was and who else was there. She forgot about social workers, foster carers and cruel judges.

She forgot how much she hated her life, because now she was a little girl in a hot dusty village where everyone was running and screaming. She was running too, with her sisters, away from the nasty men who were chasing after them and trying to catch them. Her skin was dark, her eyes black and her hair was thick and crinkly. She was small but she was strong and wilful. She screamed and fought and clawed at the men and when they finally threw her in the van with the other children, she wailed and shouted for her mother who stood in the middle of the hot dusty road with tears flooding her face.

An arm that felt a little like her dad's arm was wrapping around her shoulders, shyly, as if to say, 'I'm here if you want me.' In a daze she glanced around and saw that Stefan's dad was now sitting next to her and Stefan was in the armchair. Kylie had moved up. Stefan's dad was looking down at her kindly. Her face was wet with silent crying and he gently pulled her against him. She let him, even though it was the wrong body and very much the wrong arm. But she soon forgot about that too, because now she was in an orphanage. She felt horribly lonely and homesick, and she hated all the white people who bossed her around and told her she was going to have new parents and she would be much better off with them, because they were white and educated. Pain, indignation and hatred were tearing at her insides. She wanted to kill them all. She wanted to run away. But running away was impossible. They had taken her miles away from her home. Australia was a huge country, full of dangerous animals, and she wouldn't have any food. She wanted to die. Dying was the only way out.

And then, miraculously, she found herself running away with her sister. It was good not to be alone. Zoe sat up again, tense and alert, only vaguely aware of a hand stroking her back. As she faced one danger after another, Zoe twitched, jumped, tensed up, relaxed and dug her fingers into whatever human flesh happened to be next to her. Once or twice her fingers were gently released from their grip, but she barely noticed. As she made her escape by following the fence that would take her back home, she came to understand the strange title, 'Rabbit Proof Fence'. By the time she got back to her mother, Zoe had walked 1500 miles. When the film finished, they all sat in silence watching the credits rolling down the screen. It was an excuse to catch your breath and get over everything that had just happened to you. Then Zoe turned round to Stefan's dad and asked, 'Graham, is it really a true story?'

'That's what they said,' he replied.

'It just doesn't seem possible that two girls would do that.'

'Especially girls,' Stefan butted in, keen to bring some lightness back into the atmosphere. He had felt the threat of too many tears during this film and couldn't wait to put that behind him. Zoe however did not respond. Her eyes were faraway, lost in a world were running away in the most hostile circumstances had taken a daughter back to the parent she loved. She had been wiping her face dry, and so had Kylie, and neither of them seemed to care. Stefan's own dad was unusually silent, and the boy wondered if he too was allowing the choked up feeling to pass before he ventured to speak.

When Stefan's dad finally extricated himself from the settee to get some drinks and biscuits, Zoe asked Stefan if she could use his computer to send an email. The email was not to her dad, as Stefan had assumed, but to her Aunty Emma. She typed quickly, using her two index fingers.

Thanks for the film Aunty Emma. I loved it. It's the best film ever. If those girls could walk across Australia to be with their mum, then I can run away a thousand times, until they let me live with dad. I love you. Zoe.

19. The Christmas Lights

A month and a half later Zoe ran away. This time it was about seeing the Christmas Lights with Granny and Grandad on December 1st.

About a week before the end of November one dinner time, Jean and Owen told Zoe in happy voices they would take her to see the Lights on December 1st. The girl's response was to shrug as if she didn't care one way or the other but inside her head a voice was screaming 'No way, not with you, that is something I do with Granny and Grandad and nobody else!' Whilst she carried on eating the food on her plate, Zoe's mind worked furiously. Now that the Christmas Lights had been mentioned she knew she had to see them with Granny and Grandad, anything else was intolerable. She felt sure she could arrange it, like the secret visits. She could say she was going with Kylie or Stefan, and then meet her grandparents instead and drive around with them. Stefan was a better bet because Kylie's parents wouldn't go along with a lie, but would Stefan's dad agree to lie? Grown-ups were always against lies, even though they didn't seem to mind when it suited them. Zoe concluded sadly that Stefan's dad would not agree to lie, even if he felt sorry for her.

'What are you thinking about Zoe?' asked Jean, giving the girl a jolt, 'you haven't eaten a mouthful in five minutes.'

Zoe promptly resumed eating whilst carrying on with the thinking. But she was stuck, no plan was emerging to save the day and all she could do was imagine Granny and Grandad alone in their house, not going out to see the lights, maybe not even bothering to put up the Christmas tree, because that was Zoe's job every year. Zoe felt tears coming and panicked. If Jean saw tears there would be no end of questioning. The girl got up quickly and ran to get a tissue, apologising when she came back because she had needed to blow her nose. Then she thanked Jean and Owen and said it would be very nice to see the Lights. It was important they didn't suspect anything because Zoe had just made another dangerous decision. She would run away to her grandparents' and it would be amazing. She didn't care about the consequences. She didn't realise it was easy not to care when you didn't know what the consequences would be.

She told her dad what her plan was, and he didn't try to stop her but said he would let Granny know, and not to worry, Granny would not turn Zoe away from her door. The next few days were exciting and scary all at once, but Zoe was used to these emotions by now.

On December 1st she told Jean she would go to Kylie's after school and phone her later when she needed a lift home. Instead, she walked all the way through the park in the cold and over to Granny and Grandad's house and although her heart was beating fast and loud inside her chest, she was not frightened. She enjoyed her feeling of freedom and didn't allow thoughts of consequences to spoil her excitement. Through her grandparents' front window, she saw the flickering lights of the Christmas tree and she trembled with excitement. She pressed the bell hard, and Granny opened the door so quickly it felt like she must have been waiting behind. Zoe rushed in and stopped dead in front of the biggest Christmas tree they had ever had. All the decorations were new, red and silver and white and under the tree were piles of presents wrapped in gold and silver paper with strings of red metallic ribbon forming long curls. She burst into tears and ran into Granny's arms, and it was hard to have a cuddle because she still had her anorak on, and her rucksack was on her back. Still, she stayed in Granny's arms for a long while before taking her coat and bag off.

'Granny,' she said, 'please don't let them take me away this time. Please.'

Granny drew her into her arms again, 'If only I had the power to keep you here with me, sweetheart, you know I would.'

Grandad appeared in the doorway, with a sad kind of smile on his tired face and Zoe ran out of Granny's hug into his arms, but that was only for a couple of minutes and then she was back with Granny and although they weren't outside or crossing the road or anything like that, Zoe's little hand slipped into her grandmother's and showed no sign of wanting to let go. They headed for the kitchen hand in hand, and whilst Granny was making tea and cutting the chocolate cake she had made that afternoon, Zoe had to let go of her hand, but she held on to her by the waist and Granny managed to do everything with Zoe wrapped around her. Zoe didn't even want to cut the cake, or carry the plates into the lounge, or do anything that would take her arm away from her grandmother's waist. On the settee she ate her cake and drank her squash cuddled up to Granny.

'Granny,' she said after swallowing a mouthful of cake, 'if I asked to live with you instead of Dad, maybe they would let me, what do you think?' Her eyes turned up hopefully towards her grandmother's face. Granny ran her fingers through the girl's soft hair without answering. 'Do you think Dad would be upset if I did that?'

'No, Sweetheart, Dad wouldn't be upset at all. In fact, your grandfather and I have applied for a residence order, and Joe is perfectly happy with that.'

'A residence order? Didn't Mum have a residence order?' asked Zoe, screwing up her face as she tried to get her head round these difficult words.

'She did. Then the Local Authority got an interim care order, and that's why you're now with foster carers. That's because the Local Authority has the power to decide where you live…'

'I hate them Granny,' Zoe butted in with feeling. 'I hate living with foster carers, it's like being in prison.'

'I know, love,' replied Granny hugging Zoe close to her and giving David a heartbroken look. 'That's why we're applying for a residence order.'

'They'll never give it to you, Granny,' said Zoe in the disillusioned voice of a much older person, 'they hate us. They'll never do anything good for us.' She inched closer again to her grandmother, so close that any closer and she would have had to climb onto her lap, and she couldn't quite bring herself to do that, although she would have liked to. But ten-year-olds were not babies, and Zoe had some pride left.

'It's a shot in the dark,' said Grandad, 'you're right there Zoe. Your dad is applying for one too. He's even less likely to win. But we have to try everything. We've written to our MP, and to the Children's Commissioner.'

'Who are they then?' asked Zoe. The word MP was vaguely familiar, but not the other one. Grandad explained as best he could, and Zoe asked if the MP would be talking to the Prime Minister about her. Her grandparents laughed and although she was a little offended, she laughed with them. It was good to be laughing together again.

'Isn't it good,' exclaimed Zoe after she stopped laughing, 'not to have that horrible woman listening to everything we say?' Granny pulled her close again and kissed her hair.

The three of them were doing a good job of pretending that there was nothing out of order about Zoe's being there visiting her grandparents. What could be more normal? A grandchild having a nice time with her loving grandparents. Just before Christmas. Happy times. The kind of happy times any child is entitled to. But an outsider listening in on the conversation between this particular grandchild and her grandparents would have been taken aback. Zoe was now talking of writing to her MP herself, and she said she was also going to write to the judge about the residence order and to the Children's Commissioner. She stumbled over the word Commissioner a couple of times, but after that she rolled it off her tongue confidently. She also asked her grandparents if she could have a different Guardian as Byron Wood was a waste of time.

'Granny, he says I'm too young to understand what's good or bad for me, but I know when I'm happy and when I'm not. And when I'm with you I'm happy. So how can that be bad? Anyway, I don't get this thing about emotional damage. What do they mean?'

Just then the bell rang and all three of them froze. Both Granny and Zoe shot a look at Grandad, and when the bell

249

rang again, insistently, he got up slowly and made for the front door. At that moment the strident ringing of the phone gave Granny and Zoe another jolt. Granny left Zoe's arms and went to pick up the phone. Zoe stared hard at her, as if she were trying to read the words of whoever was at the other end on her grandmother's face. She quickly gathered it was her dad, and he was on his way. Her heart constricted as she looked up to her gran with anxious eyes.

'Your father's coming over,' she said, walking back to the settee and they both turned their ears to the front door. A cold draught was blowing in, carrying with it the sound of indistinct voices. Three voices. Grandad, another man and a woman, approaching. Zoe and her gran stood up and Zoe wrapped her arm around her grandmother's waist. They were standing in that defensive position, with the Christmas tree standing poignantly behind them, when Grandad walked back in, followed by Gerald and the woman with evil eyes. Zoe's arm tightened around her grandmother's waist. Grandad muttered something about taking a seat, but nobody did. They all stood in hostile silence and then the woman spoke.

'We've come to take you back to your foster home, Zoe.'

'I'm not going,' replied Zoe, clutching her grandmother's woolly cardigan in her clawed fingers. She stared back at the woman, thinking she looked like a witch with her hair sticking out from the wind.

'I'm going to have to ask for your cooperation, Mrs Milton. Your granddaughter…'

The doorbell cut through her sentence and left it hanging. Everyone froze, and then all eyes turned to David, again. His shoulders sagged, but he did his duty and made for the front door once more. The door opened and a fresh gust of cold air blew in. Zoe's head peeped from behind her grandmother's back to check this was her father. She hadn't seen him for a whole week and now she was ready for him, and ready to make her point to Gerald and the Witch. Grandad walked in first followed by Dad, rubbing his hands from the cold. Zoe let go of her grandmother and flew past the Witch straight into her father's arms.

'Dad,' she shouted, 'Dad, I love you Dad, take me home, please take me home.'

Joe picked his daughter up and held her in his arms with her legs wrapped around his body and her arms tightly knit around his neck. As she dropped a little, he hitched her up and got a more secure and comfortable grip. Then he stared challengingly at Gerald and Gail. Zoe breathed in the cold from outside on her father's jacket and snuggled tightly in the comfort of his arms.

'Well,' said Gail with dry sarcasm, 'quite a family gathering. It looks as if…'

The loud ring of the doorbell interrupted for the second time, but this time the door opened by itself, and Emma flew in bringing another whirlwind of cold air with her. She was out of breath, in her running gear, looking wild and flushed, a beautiful fairy with long flowing hair come out of the night to rescue Zoe.

'What's going on?' she asked as she stopped dead inside the door and looked around at all the people.

'Zoe ran away to come and see us,' said her mother pointedly. 'When a child is locked up away from the people who love her, the only way to be with them is to run away. It's what anybody would do. Especially when there is no good reason for the child being kept away from the people she loves.' Granny looked straight at the Witch as she said this, and Zoe wanted to cheer. At last Granny was telling it as it was.

'Scenes like these are the very reason why supervision is needed with Zoe's paternal family,' replied the Witch cuttingly. 'The paternal family are making things difficult for Zoe, making it impossible for her to settle down and establish good relationships with her foster carers and her maternal family. Because of…'

'I don't want good relationships with the foster carers,' shouted Zoe, 'I hate them, I don't want to live with them, that's why I'm running away.'

'Don't you interrupt me little madam,' snapped the Witch back, 'you may get away with that kind of behaviour with this family, but you won't with me, and you don't with Mum or with the foster carers, do you? You want to be where they spoil you, don't you? But we can see through all that, and we're the ones who decide what's good for you and what isn't. So, you're going to come out of your daddy's arms and walk out to the car with me and back to Jean and Owen who have been very worried wondering where you'd been. But you didn't give them a second thought, did you?'

'Why should she give them a second thought?' Emma butted in, stepping forward to come face to face with the Team Manager. 'You are forcing my niece to live with these strangers, so don't try and make her feel guilty, when you're the ones who should feel guilty for destroying her childhood.'

The Witch looked as if she was going to choke on her own breath. Gerald stepped in and in his usual wimp's way tried to calm things down.

'Miss Milton,' he said, 'you are letting your temper run away with you and if you carry on, you will just make everything worse for everyone including Zoe…'

'Yes, and that's the way it goes, isn't it? Supposedly your job is to protect the child, but actually you use the child to punish the adults if you don't like the way they speak to you, and …'

'Emma,' intervened Grandad with a stern voice, 'let's not get into a slanging match. Gerald,' he added turning to the social worker whom he knew extremely well by now, 'Zoe wanted to see the Christmas lights, she wanted to see our tree, surely that's no great crime for a ten-year-old. Let her stay with us tonight and she will be back in school and with Jean tomorrow. I know you have children of your own and you must know what Christmas lights mean to them.' David knew Gerald was the one to appeal to, but it enraged Gail to be ignored in this way and as she sensed that Gerald was about to be swayed, she rushed in with the authority that was hers.

'Don't even think about that Mr Milton. What kind of message is that for the girl? Reward for bad behaviour. Run away and you get to spend the night with your grandparents? No, Mr Milton, there is a care plan in place, and I expect Zoe and her family to respect it.'

'Why should we respect your care plan,' butted in Emma whose anger had had time to ripen and rise again. 'The plan doesn't care for Zoe. It doesn't take her needs into account, it doesn't take her wishes into account, it treats her like a bad person who needs to be punished. Let's punish her for not behaving the way we think she should. Let's punish her for having a mother who treats her badly. Let's punish her for loving her dad whom we don't like. You are doing untold damage. You…'

253

'That's your partisan opinion Miss Milton,' retorted Gail, cutting through Emma's speech. 'Funny how the rest of the world takes a different view. Funny how the rest of the world, judges, psychiatrists, psychologists, lawyers, doctors, all professional people who deal with these situations day in day out, funny how they all think the Milton Family is doing untold damage to Zoe. Even Zoe's own Guardian believes the same. Everyone except yourselves can see it. And that's why the care plan is there to protect the girl from emotional damage. To protect her from exactly this kind of scene.'

Zoe felt a tightening in her father's muscles, and she could hear his heart hammering inside his chest. She slipped down out of his unconsciously hard grip and stood by his side, holding his hand, hoping to calm him down. She held her breath and looked down at her feet.

'Without you here,' he shouted, 'there would be no scene. Without you here there would be a happy child enjoying the day of the Christmas lights with her family, as she has done every other year of her life. Without you in our lives, there would be no emotional damage. Zoe would live where she wanted, and she could see her mother as much as she wanted, and if she didn't want to see her, then that would be her mother's problem…'

'Nonsense, Mr Milton,' snorted Gail contemptuously, 'Utter and complete nonsense. She would never see her mother, and you would make sure of that. You have poisoned your child's mind and…' startled she turned around sharply. Gerald had had the temerity of laying a cautionary hand on her arm and she was now about to explode at him. Zoe looked on mesmerised. Perhaps the Witch would hit Gerald. Her breathing stopped, suspended as she waited. Unfortunately,

Granny picked this moment to find her wits again and calmed things down by attracting attention to herself.

'Could we all put Zoe first for just a moment,' she said, 'and stop frightening her with all this shouting. The child is white as a sheet and I'm concerned she's going to have an asthma attack.' Everyone looked at Zoe, who buried her head in her father's waist. 'If you let Zoe stay, I promise you that Joe and Emma will go back to their homes, Zoe will spend the night here quietly and go back to her usual arrangements in the morning…'

'I'm not going to be bullied by bloody social services, they can fuck off out of my life,' shouted Joe, out of control.

'There you are Mrs Milton,' said Gerald, feeling the need to assert some authority in line with his manager, 'you can see that we cannot expect cooperation from your son and that is why Zoe will have to come with us now…'

'No,' screamed Zoe, letting go of her father's hand and running off to the bathroom where she locked herself in.

Gerald and Gail exchanged a glance and Gerald shook his head. His boss, he could tell, was thinking police, but he knew that without a recovery order from the judge they wouldn't be able to remove the child. It wasn't worth it. His eyes told Gail as much, and she knew it anyway. It was hard for a woman like Gail to accept defeat and that night her resolve to have the better of this family hardened into rock. She might even take the case over herself in case her spineless colleague failed to punish them as they deserved. Pure white hatred was what she felt just now, particularly as she detected a hint of cheeky triumph in the eyes of the brother and sister.

'If the girl isn't back in school tomorrow, and with Jean straight after school, we'll be back, but this time we'll have the police with us. As for your language, Mr Milton, it will give me a nice bit of evidence against you when we go to court.'

'Court?' asked Janet with a frown. She had thought this would be the end of it.

'Of course, Mrs Milton, you don't think we're going to allow this kind of behaviour without seeking greater powers, do you? If a family refuse to cooperate with the Child Protection Plan, the child can be removed. That is the power we have. We do all we can to get cooperation, of course,' she spieled off in her best politically correct voice, 'but if that fails and the child keeps running away, we move the child to another town. What will happen now is that we will go to court to get a Care Order, giving us full powers over Zoe.' Now the glint of triumph was in her eyes.

Janet's own eyes went straight to her son and daughter with a severe warning. They must have recognised the moment when their mother could be much stricter than their father and they held back, watching the two social workers leave the room behind their father.

Gerald followed Gail to her car with a sinking feeling in his stomach. '*Poor kid,*' he thought, as he slid into the leather seat on the passenger side. They pulled their seat belts on in silence, and Gail leaned forward as she started the engine. He glanced at her profile and saw the anger in the set of lips. '*What a dumb family,*' he thought, '*every move they make is dumb, everything they do sinks them into deeper shit. But should a child be punished for having a dumb family?*' He sighed quietly, but not quietly enough.

'Feeling sorry for them, Gerald?' Gail snapped.

'No, I was just thinking how dumb they all are, and how much work it's going to mean for the rest of us. They're fighting us as if they think they can win…' his voice trailed, in apparent despair over the stupidity of some people. Gail was reassured and her voice was almost amicable when she asked him if he was going to take his children to see the Christmas lights that night.

*

Whilst locked in the bathroom Zoe had curled up against the side of the bath, sitting on the cold tiles and waiting for her asthma to start playing up. She didn't have her inhaler with her and wished for a bad attack that would take her to hospital in an ambulance and frighten everybody so much that they would let her stay with her grandparents for fear she might die. While willing her lungs to close up on her she strained to hear what was going on in the living room. The voices came to her in blurred snatches of words she couldn't make out. Then she heard a door opening and the sound of footsteps marching away towards the front door. She got up and went to the bathroom door. She pulled the small bolt quietly out of its hole and pressed the door handle down without making a sound. Her heart was racing and she held her breath as she tiptoed from the bathroom to the kitchen window where she caught a glimpse of Gerald and the Witch walking down the path with their tails between their legs. Victory exploded within her, but she stayed perfectly still in case the least movement dispelled the magic. She felt rather than heard a presence behind her and turned around slowly, not sure what to expect from the adults around her. She knew she was causing them a lot of trouble. Her eyes met her granny's gentle eyes, and she ran into the extended arms trying not to think about the sadness she had seen on her grandmother's face.

"They've gone,' said Granny hugging her granddaughter close. 'Now we'll go and see the Christmas lights. Your dad and Emma have had to leave, but we'll pick them up on the way. These people are not going to stop us doing what is right for you.' Zoe's arms tightened around her grandmother's waist. Granny's voice had been strong and made the child feel that her grandmother had the power to protect her, as she had always done from when Zoe was a baby. Running away had worked. A few moments later Zoe was sitting in the car surrounded by all the people she loved, excitement was in the air and nobody seemed to mind that she could not stop talking, pointing, exclaiming and repeating endlessly that this was the best night in her life. Which it was, because the contrast between months of dark loneliness and these few hours of brightly lit joy made it so. That night Granny slept in the other single bed in Zoe's room as they all understood that not a moment of togetherness must be lost, not even during sleep.

Togetherness however came to an end, and it didn't take long for Zoe to realise that running away hadn't worked all that well after all. The following day she said a tearful goodbye to her grandparents as she got out of the car in front of the school. At 3.30 Jean was waiting outside the school gates her face frozen with disapproval. They drove to the house in silence, but when they got there, Jean rounded on the girl with a torrent of angry words, 'How could you? Making us look bad. You wilful naughty child. Can't be trusted for a moment. But you're going to pay for this, mark my words. No more playing with your friends, no more walking to school on your own, no more…'

'I hate you,' shouted Zoe, blocking her ears. Jean flushed a deep red and her lips trembled slightly. She too hated this child for turning her into a failure. Never before had she had problems with a foster child, never before had her skills been defeated and for the first time her hand itched to hit out at the smaller person in front of her. She knew not to do it, but she lashed out with her tongue instead, 'No wonder your mother smacks you. You ask for it, Zoe, and you shouldn't complain when you get what you deserve. I shall tell the judge myself.'

'What judge?' asked Zoe, taking her hands from her ears in surprise.

'There's going to be a court case, Zoe, and by the end of it it'll be the Local Authority who decide what happens to you, and I don't mean just for a few weeks, I mean for good.' Jean looked down on Zoe in what felt at last like victory. The girl's defiant face had crumpled into a mass of twitching muscles fighting against tears. 'The judge will want to hear what we all have to say, and let me tell you something young lady, we will all say that you're a difficult spiteful child. Your dad won't,' she added as Zoe's face turned ready for another fight, 'or your grandparents, but they don't matter, Zoe, nobody will listen to them.'

Zoe spun on her heels and ran upstairs to slam her door against the world and collapse on her bed sobbing her rage into her pillow.

Jean's predictions turned out to be true in other ways too. 'No more secret visits,' Dad said on the phone, 'it would be too risky during the court case. Could jeopardise everything.' This was another new word added to Zoe's vocabulary. Jeopardise. She had heard it before, now she didn't need an explanation to understand what it meant. Phone calls could

259

jeopardise things too and Zoe heard that they would be limited to virtually nothing.

In the grip of this unforeseen disaster, Zoe clung to the possibility that the judge would take her side, but she knew deep down she was most probably kidding herself and in her worldly-wise little girl's heart emotions were coloured by fear, not hope.

20. The Court Case

Four days after the incident of the Christmas Lights Joe and his parents received letters informing them that Social Services were applying to the Family Court for a Permanent Care Order in relation to their daughter / granddaughter, Zoe Milton. If granted, this Permanent Care Order would give the Local Authority parental responsibility for Zoe and whilst they would consult with the parents as to the best living arrangements for the girl, they would have the power to make the final decision based on protecting the child from suffering significant harm. The child's wishes would be considered, as per the Children Act, and so would the conclusions of the psychiatric assessment indicating the ability of the child to form her own opinions.

Such was the gist of the letter and after reading it Janet and David looked at each other in silence while their cups of tea went cold and their toast lay half eaten on the small breakfast plates. It was a heavy price to pay for taking Zoe to see the Christmas Lights, and yet, with the girl's happiness still fresh in her memory, Janet couldn't bring herself to wish they hadn't done it. She kept it to herself, however, knowing David thought otherwise, and now she could read the worry in his eyes about the cost of the barrister they would have to hire in order to oppose the application in court. With a heavy heart she pulled a pink envelope from the little pile on the table and said, 'There's this too.' David nodded and waited for his wife to read out Zoe's letter. These letters from his granddaughter were breaking his heart but they were also an unintended burden on his old shoulders. How could a man like him have become so powerless, so unable to care for his family? He bowed his head as Janet started to read.

'Dear Granny and Grandad,

It was brilliant seeing the Christmas lights with you. I can't stop thinking about it. I loved sitting in the front of the car. I am so happy we could do that, even tho there was a big row before.
Thank you thank you thank you and sorry for running away and causing trouble to everyone. I love you more than anyone (except Dad).

Do you think the judge will say I can come and live with you?
If he doesn't I'll kill myself.

I hate it here. Jean and Owen bug me. They tell me I should be nice to Mum all the time. What about Mum being nice to ME? It's her fault if I can't have Christmas with you.
I want to run away again so I can have another night in your house.

Could we all run away and live in another country?
I love you loads,
xxxxxxxxxxxxx
Zoe

Janet folded the letter carefully with a tremble in her hands.

'I can't bear it anymore,' she uttered in a small voice, 'Christmas on her own…'

'She will be with her mother,' said David.

Janet sighed deeply, resting her eyes in the distance. 'You know what I think of that,' she said.

'I know, but Leanne is her mother and …'

'Leanne doesn't give a monkey's about Zoe's happiness. Sometimes I think it pleases her to…'

'Let's not go into that again,' interrupted David. 'We now have a court case on our hands,' he added, jerking his chin in the direction of the letter lying by his plate, and we will have to keep our cool.' His eyes plunged into his wife's eyes and she nodded reluctantly. How could one keep one's cool about a woman like Leanne?

The court case started a week later and then dragged on for three months. Three endless months of delays and adjournments. Of actual days in court, only twelve, with armies of barristers and solicitors standing up, sitting down, voicing objections, arguing, appealing to the judge, but most of all quizzing witnesses. Zoe's family knew they would be quizzed and understood they had to be prepared. Hiring a young barrister called Hannah Campbell, who was affordable but with a growing reputation, gave their confidence a boost. The young woman was positive, clear and full of compelling

263

advice. She was expensive however, and because they felt in need of much reassurance and support, they also consulted their own solicitor as well as Zoe's solicitor, and even though the bills mounted, their hopes also rose.

They had family planning meetings, they told each other what to say, what not to say, how to get the better of these sharp barristers, how to get on the right side of the judge. They wouldn't badmouth Leanne; indeed, they wouldn't talk about her at all. They would concentrate on themselves. How much they loved Zoe. How much she loved them. How well they had always looked after her, and how well they would look after her if she was allowed to live with them. Which was her strongest wish. They would make sure she saw her mother. Once she was happy and living where she wanted, she was much more likely to renew her relationship with her mother, and they all agreed a child needs a good relationship with both parents. They would ensure this happened. They had listened to the advice poured into their ears by the experts, they had nodded, they had understood and now they were prepared. They knew exactly how to play their cards.

What they hadn't prepared for was to be faced by other players who were in a different league altogether. Players who seemed to juggle with the cards, and come up with trumps every time, players who shuffled the cards so quickly you lost track of what you had just seen, forgot whose turn it was to play, put the wrong card on the table, and ended up so flustered that you no longer knew what the game plan had been. And as you looked down at what was in your hand the cards became blurred and panic took over, so you no longer even knew what game you were playing and what the rules were. And in that moment of panic, you looked up at the opposition, and they smiled a nice reassuring smile that gave you confidence, so you looked down again at your cards thinking this is all right, of course I know what I'm doing, I just need to put down the cards I know are the right ones. The ones that ring true, the ones that come from the heart, the ones that everyone will see are the winners. And with the evaporation of the game plan, a new clarity formed. Easy. Based on one's deepest convictions and knowledge. The truth jumped out. With gusto. Proud to show itself to this audience. Look, Your Honour, look at the truth. Here it is. The truth. My truth. Beautiful, clear, undeniable, flying off my chest and giving me such relief, I can feel my confidence growing with every word. The man in front of me is leaning forward, interested, he wants to know what I have to say, he's nodding me on, smiling, his eyes full of the most wonderful comprehension, at last someone is listening.

This explains how Janet Milton, who had felt no fear of the witness stand, came off it in an agony of confusion. She gripped the banister as she stumbled down the three steps that took her to the solid floor below and stood there unable to let go of it. Her face had aged ten years in the last few minutes and the skin seemed to droop in folds around her cheeks. David saw the wild tears at the back of her eyes and willed her to move and come to sit safely by him, but she wasn't moving, just standing there paralysed, like a swimmer who has just come dripping out of the sea and stands forlorn, all bearings lost. David looked angrily at the barrister for not helping her back to her seat, wasn't he pleased that he had so utterly destroyed her, did he have to add insult to injury and watch her collapse in a heap of tears on the floor?

Janet's own barrister sprung to the rescue and led her by the arm towards the empty seat between David and Joe. Janet looked down at the woman holding her arm and whispered pitifully, 'I said all the wrong things, I'm so sorry.'

'You spoke your truth, Mrs Milton,' replied Hannah Campbell, 'don't worry about it, it's my job to make the most of what you said. You have done nothing wrong.' She gave Janet a reassuring smile and squeezed her arm to let her know she wasn't angry with her, not even disappointed. And it was true. The young barrister was used to people collapsing in the witness box. The first time it had happened she had reeled from the shock and her own performance had suffered badly. She still trembled with shame at the memory of it. But now she knew that thoroughly primed clients were perfectly capable of walking up those three steps and then shooting themselves in the foot with gay abandon. With this family she had expected it and she had known the grandmother who appeared sensible and level-headed in conversation might prove to be the weakest link. Too attached to her truth. She had said all the wrong things. Now the rest of the family would be shaken and the whole damned edifice might crumble in one swift sweep and leave her with precious little to defend their cause.

But at least she had foreseen it. At least she had a line of defence ready. A family in despair, and was not that despair the very sign of their love for their granddaughter? Who could hear them crying for help with such a genuine mix of indignation and pain without seeing that all they wanted was to rescue their little girl from a life of unhappiness? She knew she could speak convincingly, people had said she had a gift, she knew how to carry an audience, and her heart raced with anticipation. But as she glanced across at the old bulldog of a judge, she also knew she didn't have a hope. This judge, she felt, had walked into the court with his mind made up. The reports had done it. All the professionals singing from the same hymn sheet and the old judge had heard the tune and any deviation from that tune grated on his ears, she could just tell by the way he pursed his lips and narrowed his eyes when he didn't like what he heard. The witnesses who sang the right melody on the other hand had his nodding approval.

Hannah Campbell saw it through however, producing her best in the face of hopeless circumstances, and she left the court with her head high. She hadn't let anyone down, neither herself nor the family, and now it was all in the hands of the judge who would deliver his verdict in due course. Her work was over and already the next case on her list was moving in to take up the space inside her head.

*

During the weeks of the court case Zoe's life became even more miserable than usual. Given her dad's refusal to have supervised contact with her she no longer saw him, and they only got to have very quick chats on the phone once or twice a week, with Stefan hanging around, waiting to take the phone back and look after it safely. Contact with Granny and Grandad also deteriorated in ways that Zoe couldn't quite grasp. They seemed distant and distracted even when they were being warm and loving, and Zoe's questions about the court case never got the kind of honest answer that she was used to with her grandmother. Instead, there were hesitations, pauses, quick glances between her grandparents and denials that they were keeping anything from her. 'It's all very complicated, sweetheart,' was their cover-up for not telling her the truth. Zoe could see them struggling and felt a mounting combination of guilt and anxiety. Even contact with Emma turned out to be a disappointment, with the young woman no more able to tell Zoe anything useful than the rest of the family. The presence of the spy-woman became almost unimportant because the visits themselves had become stripped of real emotions and honest conversation.

But worst of all were the visits to Mum. Because Mum was positively glowing, and Zoe didn't like that glowing. It was the kind of glowing you sometimes saw in your opponent's eyes in a card game, when they've just picked up their cards and although they try very hard to keep an indifferent face, they can't quite manage it and you just know from the suppressed sparkle in their eyes that on this round you haven't got a hope. That was the kind of face Mum was wearing all the time these days, and she didn't seem at all tense or worried about the judge's verdict.

'I believe the judge will come out with the right decision, Zoe, so I'm not worried. Whatever he says, I'll go along with it. And I hope that you'll do the same.'

Zoe had been sitting at the kitchen table and leaning wide on her elbow when Mum said this, her head cupped in her small hand. She didn't volunteer the information that she had written to the judge herself to leave him in no doubt as to her wishes. She was silent, except for the scratching of her fork against the plate. Playing with her baked beans. Unable to eat. Mum wouldn't be saying this if she thought the judge was going to say that Zoe could go and live with Dad. Her heart constricted with anxiety and she had to take her ventilator out of her pocket. For days after Zoe could not dispel the memory of that secret glow on her mother's face.

*

In the meantime, David and Janet were struggling to recover from their excruciating memories of their day in court. Janet could not shake off the despondency that gripped her insides every time she thought back on her performance at the witness stand, and she seemed to think back on that miserable episode in her life through most of her waking hours. The memories pursued her right into her dreams. How could she have let her family down like this?

'David,' she would suddenly ask over coffee, 'did I really say that Leanne was an alcoholic? Or am I dreaming that?' At other times, on waking up or just before going to sleep, she might ask if she had volunteered the information that Leanne smacked Zoe too hard and too often, or that Leanne had never loved Zoe, not really loved her. It went on and on.

'Well,' David would clear his throat uncomfortably, 'I can't remember exactly, love. I don't see the point in going over it endlessly.'

'David,' Janet would insist, appearing calm and collected, 'I need to know. Best to know and then get rid of it. Otherwise, it'll just plague me to the end of my days.'

She looked composed, keen to know, capable of dealing with it. So, he would tell her that yes, she had said something along those lines and then the tears would spring from her eyes and the pain that swam amongst those tears would break his heart and he would swear to himself that he wouldn't be caught again. But she did catch him again and again. She was punishing herself and although he hated to see it, he also understood she had to put herself through this.

'Look,' he said one day, taking hold of her hand as they sat on the settee pretending to watch the news, 'stop fretting. The judgement isn't going to depend on one witness.'

'I know that,' she replied calmly.

'So, stop blaming yourself.' He tucked her hand under his arm and squeezed it affectionately.

''It's just that the rest of you didn't exactly do brilliantly either, did you?'

'We didn't?' David was taken aback. He had felt pleased with the way he kept his cool under the barrister's fire.

'You probably did the least damage, but you still criticised Social Services and you more or less said that Leanne had no idea how to bring up a child.'

'I didn't say that,' replied David letting go of his wife's hand.

'You did. Would like me to repeat exactly what you said?'

'No, I wouldn't Janet. I want to forget about it all and just see what the judge has to say when he comes up with his ruling. Then we can move on.'

'I doubt there'll be any moving on,' muttered Janet bitterly.

'What do you want me to do?' snapped David, getting up in exasperation and walking to the window where he stared vacantly at the blue tits doing their ballet all around the nut holders.

'Joe and Emma made a complete mess of their statements too, but I seem to be the only one aware of my failings. Fancy Emma getting carried away with her views on how children get treated in this dreadful society. Now how's that going to help Zoe? And Joe endlessly blaming Leanne for leaving the family. Going round and round the argument like a hamster inside his wheel. Can't he see nobody's interested in that anymore? Can't he see the damage he's done behaving the way he has? No, everybody else seems to think they're perfect, and I'm taking the blame for everything.'

David spun around in astonishment at hearing his wife coming out with all this bitterness against the whole family. Tears were running freely down her face and her pain stopped him from remonstrating with her. This was getting too much for all of them. As he sat down next to her and wrapped his arm around her shoulders, he couldn't stop his mind grabbing in mid-air the thought that he had an appointment with his accountant the following day, and he knew what the man was going to say. Take a mortgage on your house. 'Never,' David had said before, 'not at my time of life.' It was a matter of pride to him that he was the owner of a beautiful house and that it was his entirely and not half his and half the building society's. A mortgage was too much like going back in time. Giving up his pride and sense of achievement. Yet he knew that tomorrow he would have to stop being irrational and agree to it. There was little hope that the judge would take the costs away from them, the barrister had explained that, and he couldn't carry on paying extortionate interest rates.

He hugged Janet and reached over to take her hand in his. 'Let's not talk about this again, Jan,' he said. 'Let's wait for the decision. Judges don't become judges without being clever and wise. They see through things. This old judge has years of experience, he's not going to just swallow everything he hears. He's not going to be taken in by Leanne just because she dressed in her Sunday best. He's a judge, for God's sake, he's going to want to know why a ten-year-old girl doesn't want to live with her mum. There's a Children's Act these days. Emma

271

read out to you the bits that say they must take the child's wishes into account. Do you remember?'

Janet nodded like a child, tears streaming down her face, and David felt he loved her so much at that moment his heart might burst with it. He hugged her closer and whispered, 'You're a beautiful, strong woman Janet, and I love you more than I can say.'

She nodded again, as if there was nothing unusual in this gushing statement from her usually taciturn husband, but David, with another pang of love for his wife, understood that she had only heard him from a great distance, from the faraway place where all she could see was the pain her son and granddaughter were going through. She dried her face with a tissue from her cardigan pocket and looked up at her husband.

'Do you really think the judge will see through things?' A tiny flame of hope flickered at the back of her eyes.

'I do,' he replied with such conviction he almost persuaded himself. 'That's what judges are for, to see through stuff and not be taken in.'

She squeezed his hand back and looking suddenly brighter, said, 'Good. I better get on with lunch.' And off she went. David followed her with his eyes, amazed as he invariably was to see the womenfolk in his family rebound in seconds from the depths of emotional trauma. When Janet had first demonstrated this uncanny ability, David had felt she was a fraud. A row had blown up into unbearable emotional turmoil and just as he felt he was about to drown in it, she had perked up and talked about going shopping to cheer themselves up. He could have killed her. Emotional turmoil left him drained and battered for hours. So, they had had a further row in which he accused her of putting it on to get her way. Instantly

272

she had been crying and shouting again, as if to show him that yes, she could put it on at will. Up and down, on and off. But now he knew better. Her feelings were real enough, but she could snap out of them and he couldn't.

David picked up his paper from the table and went to sit in his armchair. As he leaned back into the firm cushion, stretching his legs out in front of him, his mind jumped back to the judge. Janet had been hard on him about his witness statement, but that was because she hadn't seen the way the old judge had looked at him. David recalled the moment and dwelled on it pleasurably. Through the slits of his bulldog's drooping eyes he had looked at David with sympathy. There was no doubt about it. Their eyes had met, and the unspoken message had been, 'Yes, I believe you, and I like what I hear. You and I understand each other, same gender, same generation, same way of looking at the world.'

Suddenly David felt a wave of positive anticipation sweep through him. Let that judgement come. Janet might have a surprise after all.

21. The Day of the Judgement

The court case had started on December 5th 2005, and the judge announced he would be ready to deliver his judgement on March 4th 2006, at two o'clock in the afternoon. By then Zoe's parents had been separated just over two years and she had been living with foster carers, against her will, for nine months. Given the history of these last two years, the Milton family should have seen what was coming, but they went to hear that judge like lambs to the slaughter. Joe and Emma left work early and the four of them gathered in front of the court, exchanging muted but hopeful looks. Surely that wise old judge was going to give them some good news. Perhaps not all they hoped for, but something at least, and never mind that Leanne over there looked like she was very full of herself.

The doors opened and slowly, reverently almost, people filed in. The room was light and simple, with two rows of modern wooden tables and chairs facing the platform where the judge would sit behind an imposing desk. Above his head, on the wall behind him was a Royal Coat of Arms, symbol of authority and reminder to the people that they were here as subjects who would have to obey the ruling of the judge. The lawyers took their places in the front row, talking amongst themselves. Leanne made her way to the end of one table, and sat behind her solicitor, the formidable Lynne Savage, while

Joe and his family sat close together at the other end of the same row. In front of them sat their solicitor and their young barrister Hannah Campbell. The back wall of the small court room was lined with chairs and that is where Gerald sat, alone, near the door. The court stenographer settled herself at the bottom of the platform and finally, arriving from his own door, the old judge walked in and made his ponderous way up the steps and to his seat. His face gave nothing away and when he started speaking a hush fell over the room. Janet's eyes were riveted to the judge and her heart was pounding. David's warm hand enfolded hers and she gave his fingers a light squeeze. Very soon after, however, she gripped that same hand with unconscious force, her nails digging into the flesh.

A ten-year-old girl, the judge was saying, is too young to know who loves her and who doesn't love her. Too vulnerable, too susceptible to influence. Janet's heart stopped beating and her mouth went dry. She felt a little sick and wondered if she should leave the court now and find the toilets, drink a little water, get some fresh air outside. There was no point in staying to hear any more except to prolong the pain, but a glance at her family told her they hadn't come to that conclusion yet, they were still listening, attentively even. She stayed, holding on to her husband's hand.

The old bulldog of a judge was droning on about love. It went without saying that a mother loved her children. Didn't she carry the child for nine months, feed it, clothe it, push it around the park in its buggy whilst the father was doing other things that have nothing to do with loving a baby? Isn't that obvious? As for the child who rejects her devoted mother, there must be something wrong with her. There is need for experts. There is need for treatment. Psychiatrists,

275

paediatricians, psychologists, child protection workers. Teams of people need to come together and work on this. Special multi-agency meetings will be called. Minutes will be taken. Plans will be implemented. Progress will be closely monitored. Everything will be done to rehabilitate the daughter to the person she has forgotten she really loves, and she will be kept safely away from the people who have brainwashed her into believing she did not love her mother. The people who are doing her untold damage. Let the professionals come to the rescue. The girl will learn to love her mother and she will come to understand that her paternal family had her under a spell. A malignant spell. She was a means for revenge against the woman they saw as an enemy, her own mother.

'It may take a little while for Zoe to understand all this,' said the learned judge in his summary, 'but everyone involved in this case can see it. All the professionals. The mother and her family. The foster carers. I have formed a very good opinion of these witnesses. By contrast the father, his sister and his parents have failed to produce convincing evidence. They have been poor witnesses.

I am aware that the Children Act, in its section on safeguarding and protecting the welfare of children, recommends taking the child's views into account. If possible. This is the crucial word. In the case of Zoe Milton, it is not possible to take her wishes and feelings into account given that the child is under the influence of the paternal family and therefore her true wishes are not known.' The old judge paused for just a moment to refresh his mouth with a sip of water. As he lifted the glass to his lips and felt the cool liquid trickle down his dry throat the memory of Zoe's letter to him flashed through his mind. A little perturbed by the girl's plea for help and happiness, he had shown it to his wife, which he realised was a little unprofessional, but worth it given Ethel's invariably insightful views. Consistently identical to his own. They praised each other generously for their superior understanding of cases and whenever he gave a verdict, Ethel's green eyes shone in the back of his mind giving his delivery the assurance of the wise.

On this occasion Ethel had held the small pink sheet delicately between finger and thumb whilst lifting her coffee cup to her lips. Dinner was over and they had retired to the comfort of the expensive leather suite in their spacious lounge. She had given the letter her full attention and after a thoughtful pause had looked up with a disdainful pout. 'What is she up to?' she wondered aloud. 'Trying to manipulate you? Trying to bully you?' He nodded encouragingly and she continued, 'a nine-year-old never wrote this, darling, or if she did a grown-up was whispering in her ear, don't you think?'

'My thoughts exactly,' he had replied, relieved not to have to think about it anymore. The pink letter went back into the folder, where it lay squashed and forgotten between the reports of experts.

The judge drank a little more water and set the glass down again, carefully, on the little paper mat placed in front of him.

'Then,' he continued, 'there is the question of the paternal family. The European Convention for the Protection of Human Rights states the right of the father and of the grandparents to family life. Reduced contact will constitute an interference with that right. But the safeguarding of Zoe's welfare must come first, and at the core of Zoe's welfare is the improvement of her relationship with her mother so that mother and daughter may become reunited in the future.' He looked up from his papers and down at his audience to measure the impact of his words so far. He then moved gravely to his conclusion. 'My decision,' he said loudly and clearly, 'is to give a Care Order to the Social Services of this Local Authority, so it is now for them to determine where the child should live. This order will last until the child is eighteen. From my understanding it is in the best interest of the child to continue living in a neutral environment in the hope that one day she may be able to live with her mother.'

The courtroom greeted these words with a moment of complete silence as people took in what they had heard and what the implications were for themselves. As the judge got up to leave, the room came alive with a light bustle of talk and activity. Leanne turned around to catch Gerald's eye, but he pretended not to notice and left quickly. He had no wish to examine his feelings regarding the judgement and luckily for him another matter was taking up his attention. He needed to rush back to the office and catch Sally of the fostering team to let her know Zoe would now be staying with Jean and Owen indefinitely. His heart sank at this thought, because he was almost certain they would say no. And then what? Judges were prompt to allocate children to Foster Carers because it didn't fall to them to find the said Foster Carers. He wondered if Leanne was now going to agitate to have her daughter back, and if she did, he would go along with it for the simple reason that the Local Authority didn't have any spare long-term Foster Carers. That he knew for sure.

Lynne Savage smiled triumphantly at Leanne as she got up, but didn't hang around for a chat, she had better things to do. Leanne, however, was not feeling a hundred per cent triumphant. She hadn't been disgraced like Joe's family, and she could savour the taste of their discomfiture, but it had been a bit of a shock to hear her daughter was now in the care of Social Services until she turned eighteen. She had believed the judge would vindicate her in the eyes of the world and say that the right place for Zoe was with her mother, for the simple reason that she was a good mother. The judge had spoken well of mothers in general, but he hadn't said a word about her. Instead, Zoe was staying in care as if both sets of parents were equally bad. This was not the outcome she had hoped for and she needed to put pressure on Gerald to turn it around. What she desperately wanted was to tell her friends and colleagues that she'd won her daughter back. As she left the courtroom, she started planning her meeting with Gerald, hopefully the following day, with a view to achieving the desired outcome. Once Zoe was back with her, she could hold her head high again. No more looks from anyone on hearing her daughter was in care.

The Milton family sat in their seats as if they would never move again. Their solicitor had gone quickly after a few mumbled words of regret, but Hannah Campbell, the barrister, was still sitting in front of them, pretending to fiddle with her papers. She knew how they felt, she knew they weren't ready to talk, but she was not going to leave until she had expressed some words of support and commiseration. What they had just heard about themselves was so deeply hurtful that they were paralysed, couldn't look at anyone or at each other. The wound to David's pride was making him bleed inside and the pain was clutching at his heart. His old heart. Thoughts of cardiac arrest and strokes flashed through his mind as he felt the bitterness of his disappointment in the old judge. He controlled his breathing, trying to recover a measure of calm but didn't look at Janet. She didn't look at him either. The judge's words were crashing and banging inside her head. Poor witnesses. Emotional damage. Emotional harm. Need to safeguard the child. Need to protect the child from her father. From her grandparents. From their malign influence. Had he said 'malign' or was she imagining that word? It was what he meant anyway. He had painted a picture of them as evil people, out to use Zoe to do damage to Leanne. He had formed poor opinions of all of them, he told the world. As she thought of her love for Zoe and of all she had done to be a good grandmother, hot tears of rage burned her eyes. A few of them rolled down her cheeks. She wanted to scream at the injustice of every word she had heard, and sob at the wrongness of a sentence that punished a little girl who was only guilty of getting caught in the crossfire of other people's hostilities and prejudices. She couldn't look at Joe, she couldn't add another drop of pain to her already full cup. She looked down at her hands in her lap and noticed how old they looked. Her eyes welled up again.

Joe was sitting still, apparently lost in thought, but Emma, observing her brother from the corner of her eyes, knew better. His eyes were as dark as she had ever seen them and she held her breath, ready for an explosion of rage. It didn't come. Mysteriously Joe held it together and was the first to make a move. 'Let's get the fuck out of here,' he whispered to his sister, leaning against her so she would get up and they could all leave. Hearing movement, Hannah Campbell turned around to express her disappointment, hoping to find words of comfort for her clients. She met with a scene of such emotional disarray, however, that she couldn't speak. Their eyes met, they shook hands, and she finally managed to utter a heartfelt but useless 'I am so sorry.' She then left and they followed.

*

By the time the Milton family returned home Janet had recovered her composure. The others had not. They were on an ascending flight of anger and hatred towards a system which was twisting and crushing them in its implacable cogs. David's rage in the face of the humiliation he had experienced would, a few weeks ago, have been honey in Janet's cup. At last, he was reacting on his own behalf and not just to indulge the rest of the family. Now she looked on as if watching an episode from EastEnders rather than a slice of her own life. She had dropped into David's armchair and it gave her a strange feeling of detachment to be observing her family from a different angle.

Emma had rushed into the kitchen to put the kettle on, quickly slipping into the role of carer for the family whilst her mother was out of action. Janet read panic rather than concern in the eyes of her family. Was Mum about to lose it? Was the rock under their feet about to disintegrate? The rock they had taken for granted for so many years. She was pleased to see their fear, pleased to see the recognition of her importance in their eyes. David, who always seemed to be the strong calm one, but knew damn well he would be lost and alone without her to take care of the emotional side of things; Emma, who strutted her intellectual stuff around the place and patronised her antediluvian parents for not understanding the big issues; and Joe. Joe too was panicking. She could see it. Joe had always used her to get his way. He had known her love gave him that power. She fought his battles, suffered his

281

pain and was there for him no matter what. All the while, he could pretend he didn't really need her. Yes, that was Joe. Who, in the past, had routinely taken Leanne's side against his mother.

Yes, Janet saw her family with a rare clarity of vision, and she knew with equal clarity that once the vision had dissipated everything would return to normal and they would all slip into the well-oiled grooves that directed the course of their relationships. But from inside her suspended moment of insight Janet recognised that she was enjoying her family's distress. Let them glimpse a world where she wasn't there to care, listen, advise, help out, lend money, give money, make tea, Sunday lunch and Christmas dinner. Let them stop for just a moment taking her for granted. She sat in David's chair watching their antics, listening to their shouting and their indignation, talking all at once, reinforcing each other's rage, wanting to burn that judge's house, wanting to kill everyone in Social Services, wanting another judge, one who would be fair, one who would listen, one who would see the light.

Janet looked upon them as if from another planet. Floating free. Under no obligation to feel their pain or solve their problems. Floating without a care. Like the girl she had once been, when life had been light and easy.

Except of course that it hadn't.

Girls didn't have much freedom in those days, and she had resented her parents' old-fashioned ways. She remembered talking to her mother in the exact condescending tone of voice Emma sometimes used with her. And as she heard her younger self sounding so much like her daughter, her anger fissured, cracked and split open revealing the simple contents of an ordinary life. Life repeating its cycle with minor variations, tricking every creature into thinking they were so different and so special. Not a muscle on her face moved, but inside she smiled. She looked around again, coming back to the present, noticing her family shooting sideways glances at her, wondering what storm was brewing, what new disaster was about to hit them. She knew her moment of freedom was coming to an end. She was about to re-join the imperfect world where love gets all tangled up with dark emotions and selfish impulses, so tangled up sometimes that you think it has disappeared altogether. She was about to speak to them, and yet again to sort them out with motherly care and authority. They would be relieved, and they would resent her at the same time, because people want your help, but they also want to be independent. They want your love, but they also want to be free. They want you in their lives and sometimes they want you out of it.

'Mum, you haven't touched your tea,' said Emma tentatively, with so much loving concern in her voice Janet thought she might burst out crying, and it would be all right because they would all think she was crying about the judgement and not because for just a moment she had stopped loving them. She had wanted to be rid of their needs and their problems, and their bad behaviour. For just a moment they had been nothing but a burden to her. But Emma's voice, sweet with unusual gentleness, dissolved her resentment and brought her back to what gave meaning to her existence. Her family.

She shifted and straightened up, then reached forward to pick up her cup of tea. It had gone cold.

'Shall I make you a fresh one, Mum?' asked Emma.

'Would you darling?' replied Janet, lifting cup and saucer and holding them out to her daughter. Then she slumped back into the chair, not unhappy to let them see how tired she felt. Tired to her old bones. She sighed deeply and as Emma placed the fresh cup on the small glass table by her side, she ran her eyes steadily from one to the other, and when she felt she had their undivided attention she spoke, reminding Emma of a teacher in a classroom.

'This raving and ranting against everyone and everything needs to stop,' she declared, in the voice of that same teacher Emma had conjured up. 'What happened today is our own fault.' A stunned silence greeted this verdict. For the second time that day the family had been judged and found wanting, but now it was Mum who was pointing the finger.

Janet lifted her cup to her lips, aware of the attention she had managed to command. Like a general regrouping the troops after a defeat she wanted to deliver her message in a way that was guaranteed to convince. She understood what had gone wrong and she was clear about the new strategy they needed to adopt. She was also acutely aware that the troops would not like what they heard. She took a long silent breath, put her cup down neatly in the saucer and looked up. They were listening.

'We have been stupid,' she said, 'and Leanne has been clever. That's why she won, and we lost. The world does not reward the truth or the better person, the world rewards the person who has what it takes to win.' Her family kept silent. She continued, 'Leanne played the sweet game and we, idiots that we were, shouted at the people who had power over us, as if that was going to win them over.' Emma was looking out of the distant window, the men seemed to be examining their shoes. 'We've got to stop being angry with Social Services,' she continued, 'and stop treating them like they're a bunch of idiots who don't know what they're …'

'But Mum,' interrupted Emma, 'they are a bunch of idiots!'

'I know that,' snapped Mum, 'but that doesn't mean we should tell them, does it? If you want something from someone, you play nice.'

'Forget it Mum,' butted in Joe. 'If you think I'm going to go and lick arse in order to get Zoe back…'

'Are you telling me you don't care that much about Zoe?' snapped Janet, turning on her son.

'No,' he shouted back, 'don't start distorting everything I say, you're always doing that to me…'

'Joe, stop it this minute,' hissed Janet, hitting her armrest with the flat of her hand. 'You're going to have to listen for a change. And you're going to have to look at yourself. Look at your part in all that's happened to Zoe. These people are not entirely wrong. You have not put Zoe first. You've put your emotions first. You've put Leanne first. I'm not saying you didn't love Zoe at the same time, but Joe,' she added more gently as his face decomposed, 'you have not put her first.'

'Nor has Leanne,' he shouted back, 'she's been far more selfish than me, and yet she's won, so you're talking crap Mum, sorry to tell you. And I can't believe you're suddenly siding with those bastards, on a day like today of all days.'

Oh, my beautifully manipulative son! Janet watched him and her head swam. If only she didn't love him, she could just tell him to fuck off out of her life and take all his crazy notions with him. Instead, she took another deep breath.

'Yes,' she said with as much strength as she could muster, 'I do agree with some of what that biased judge said. He was right that your extreme emotions have been damaging Zoe,

285

and he is right that you have refused to cooperate with anybody and that you have fuelled the fire. He is right about that, and I'm not going to be blind to that truth just because I'm your mother. We need to go forward now, for Zoe's sake, and the only way forward is to change our ways.'

David had been silent during this exchange, all the more uncomfortable because he wasn't sitting in his usual armchair. His lower back was aching, as so often happened these days, and the settee was not giving him the support he needed. He got up and went to the window to stare at the blue tits flitting around the nut holders. He felt weary, he felt he was experiencing what it would be like to be a hundred, should he live to be that age, perish the thought. He had gone along with the children's anger and indignation, had raved and ranted with them, carried by a desire to feel togetherness with his family. But the truth was he had been disingenuous. Deep down, after the shock of hearing his family so utterly condemned, there had been relief. This was now over. There was nowhere else to go, and the fighting could come to an end. An inglorious end, but so be it. They would all have to do as they were told, and although it would not be a pleasant future, it would be an easy one. Accept the situation. Make the best of things. Stop thrashing against currents that were much too strong for you. He had misinterpreted Janet's silence, fearing she was about to breakdown in the face of her cruel disappointment, but not for a moment thinking she was quietly taking in the new situation and finding ways to carry on with her battles. Stronger than ever. So strong she was tackling Joe in a way she had never done before. He felt proud of her, but he also felt he couldn't carry on. There was no hope. Admirable though Janet's spirit was it was also foolish. She was prepared to take the family into years of fruitless wrangling with a system that was too big, too strong and too hostile. Gerald, he felt, was not obtuse, but he was weak, careful to protect his back. David knew all about men like Gerald, men who would appear to be on your side but who would let you down in the meeting with the bosses. It had been their bad luck that Zoe's social worker was one of those. Intelligent and spineless. A mouse. With a sharp-clawed feline for a boss. What hope was there?

Now it would be his duty to lead the family away from this crazy warpath. Even Zoe would be better off abandoning hope because she would also then abandon despair, and whilst not completely happy, she could stop thinking of killing herself. They had encouraged her on that road. Had they all said in the beginning, Zoe, you have a mum and a dad and you're going to have to learn to live with both of them, and that's all there is to it, the kid would probably be happier now than she was, and she would at least be spending half her time with her father. Janet, Joe and Emma were still arguing bitterly over who had been right and who had been wrong, and he felt his head was about to burst with the clashing of words and emotions. How could it have got to this? How could his family have so utterly lost all sense of proportion?

He turned around from the window, squaring his stooping shoulders and lacing his hands behind his back. 'Will you stop shouting, please,' he snapped.

It worked. The other three froze, looking as surprised as if he'd come back from the dead. Joe had been pacing the room and gesticulating, Emma sitting on the edge of her seat waving her hands at her mother, and Janet was still sitting with her back straight against the back of his chair, and that was exactly why he liked that chair, it was a bit old fashioned, but it supported your back like no other chair he knew. Now they were looking at him and in different circumstances he would have burst out laughing, their expressions of surprise were so identical and Emma in that moment was raising her eyebrows exactly like her mother, and to see the raw power of genes never ceased to amaze him. But he didn't laugh, didn't even smile. He had his 'no more nonsense' look on his face.

'Janet,' he said, 'I admire your tenacity, your courage and your energy, but all those qualities are taking us down the wrong road. There comes a point when we must recognise that the road is not leading where we wanted to go. It's taking us to worse and worse places. We must stop now and make the best of where we are. I agree with what you've said about our mistakes. You all know I've had my doubts about what we were taking on, but now, I for one am going no further.' He stood there, tall and strong, feeling a rush of power through his veins as his family looked at him and listened to the voice of authority.

Except they were not doing that at all. He should have known better. They let him have his say, they allowed a short pause as they let their own emotions and thoughts rebound from this setback, and then they all started speaking at once. No way were they going to give in now. There was nothing to lose any more, things could not get worse, and you might as well keep going. Bowing to those bastards? Never. They might not agree on the exact way forward, but they agreed on going forward. 'In any case,' declared Janet 'there is no question of letting Zoe down now. It's going to be bad enough for her to hear the news, if she feels we're deserting her as well, she might well kill herself. Children do, David.

When children talk about killing themselves, you can't afford to shrug it off. The only thing that's keeping Zoe going now is hope, in the knowledge that we're all behind her.'

'I agree with Mum,' said Emma.

Joe was silent. Standing behind his mother's chair and gripping the ridge of it, he was staring down, not particularly at his mother sitting there below him, but looking into an emptiness he feared to fill with an honest appraisal of his own behaviour. He had defended himself against his mother's accusations, and he hadn't done a bad job of that, but now could he convince himself that she hadn't been right in much of what she had said? He reached for the packet of cigarettes in his pocket and pulled one out which he stuck between his lips. He felt instantly better. When the smoke hit his lungs, he would be able to think clearly again.

'I'm going to have a fag,' he muttered, pulling his lighter out of his shirt pocket and stalking out towards the kitchen and the back door.

Janet looked across at David and they locked eyes for a moment, then he looked away. She always had the emotional advantage and they both knew he couldn't bear to see her unhappy. She expected his support and he wanted to give it to her. He wanted her to feel his love, but he also knew it would be wrong to give in to emotions. Someone had to keep a cool head here. They had a forty-thousand-pound mortgage on the house now, but it wasn't about the money. He wouldn't quibble about the money. Emotional destruction was what he feared. How many more court cases were needed before Janet could see the world was against them and nothing would change that. Every professional out there was against them. Leanne had won. Janet was right about that. She had outplayed them, and that was because for her it had been nothing but a game.

He straightened up, bracing himself. He must be strong. Argue the rational case. Take the lead, be the head of the family. Make them listen. His adrenaline kicked in. Just as his lips parted, ready to impart words of wisdom, Janet's voice cut in.

'David,' she said calmly, 'in case you're thinking we're not going to fight this anymore, save yourself the trouble of an argument. Nothing will stop me. That judge has put me right back on track, and we just need to agree, as a family, how we go forward.'

David almost heard the whistling sound of a balloon deflating inside his chest. 'Fine,' he said without turning around, 'given that nobody's interested in my views I'll go and do the lawns.' He marched rapidly to the door, stepping aside to let his son back in and then turned sharply round and shot a scathing look at each of them in turn. 'No doubt I'll become of interest again when cheques need to be signed.' He disappeared through the kitchen and the back door shut noisily after him. There was an uncomfortable silence in the room. Joe sat down and stretched his legs in front of him, staring at his smart working shoes. He had felt he should dress smartly to go to court, fool that he was. Dressing up like a schoolboy for Prize Day, knowing damn well there were no prizes for him. No prizes for the likes of him. At that moment he hated the whole world, and he hated his father in particular for reminding him what he owed him. His father. The successful one. With the happy marriage, the money in the bank and one of the nicest houses in town.

At that moment the phone burst into shrill ringing from its little base on the side table next to Janet. 'Zoe,' said Janet glancing down at her watch. She looked at Joe questioningly, he nodded and extended his hand, 'I'll speak to her,' he said, looking grim. Before speaking he walked briskly away into the kitchen, closing the door behind him.

22. Zoe's Choice

That morning in school Miss Brown watched out for Zoe. The girl's grandmother had been in touch to explain about the court case, saying Zoe might well be distracted during her lessons today. Miss Brown was glad to see Kylie walking very close to her friend as they came to stand in line. The boys were pushing in behind the girls with their inevitable roughness and Miss Brown was annoyed with Stefan for joking loudly with Max and Joshua as if he didn't have a care in the world. She had noticed Stefan and Zoe often enough in the playground to understand theirs was a special friendship. When she snapped at Stefan to sit down and be quiet the boy gave her a surprised look in which she saw a flash of distress. She smiled at him kindly. Emotions hid inside boys behind the fighting and the joking, but it didn't mean they weren't there.

Stefan sat down feeling he had been picked on unfairly. He banged his bag on his desk and spilled the contents. What was the point of picking on him and then smiling at him, like nothing bad had just happened? Stefan was enjoying being angry at Miss Brown because it saved him being angry with himself, which was the real problem today. He too had noticed the way Zoe looked that morning and he knew damn well he hadn't been a good friend to her in the last few weeks.

292

He felt anxious whenever her eyes met his as if they expected something. Like a coward he had avoided her. But today he felt bad. Today of all days he should have been nice to her, yet this morning he had watched her walk into the playground, with her eyes lost and lonely, and he had quickly turned away to crack jokes with Max and Joshua.

'Stefan,' said Miss Brown with high pitched surprise in her voice, 'you haven't even started on your English comprehension! What's the matter with you today? Come on, stop dreaming and get on with it.'

The words of the story swam in front of Stefan's eyes. Miss Brown had laid a gentle hand on his shoulder as if she had read all his thoughts and knew exactly why he couldn't understand a simple little story today. Her sharp voice had been for the rest of the class, the gentle squeeze on his shoulder was for him alone, but the trouble was some stupid tears had come into his eyes now and he certainly didn't know what to do with those. He blinked furiously and quickly focussed on Arsenal's latest win and the magical goal scored by Thierry Henry. Passing three players and kicking the ball sweetly in the corner just out of reach of the goalie. Him and his dad had sprung from the settee screaming their joy in perfect unison, and his dad had said 'That was a beauty.' Stefan had thought he would remember that expression to use with his friends. Sounded very grown-up. He heard Miss Brown's footsteps heading towards him again and he swiftly buried his head in his English workbook.

At break time he summoned up all his courage and walked towards the railings where Zoe was standing talking with Kylie. On reaching them he stood awkwardly with his hands stuffed in his pockets, determined to see this through.

'When will you hear?' he asked.

He thought he saw reproach in Zoe's eyes, but it could just have been anxiety or something else nothing to do with him. She looked away to the empty street and said, 'I'm hearing after school. I know I won't be allowed to live with Dad, I just know it.' Then she turned her eyes back to meet his with distant sadness and he was seized by a powerful impulse to put his arm around her shoulders and give her a hug. Fortunately, they were in the school yard and it was very easy to resist that kind of an impulse.

'You don't know,' he replied, pushing his hands further down his pockets, 'maybe they won't say that. Wait and see.' He looked to Kylie for support.

'The judge didn't reply to my letter,' said Zoe.

'I guess judges don't reply to letters. That doesn't mean anything.' Stefan was kicking at tiny bits of gravel on the tarmac, scuffing his shoes in the process. Then he looked up and asked the girls, 'Do you want to see the latest game I downloaded on my phone?'

'Yeah,' said Kylie enthusiastically, moving to his side as he fished the phone out of his pocket.

Zoe moved to the other side and the three of them got absorbed in the jumping figures on the little screen. 'Cool,' said the girls. When the bell called them back to the reality of the school day Stefan pocketed his phone and said to Zoe, 'I'll ring you later, to find out.' She nodded distractedly, 'If I can't live with Dad, I won't go back to Mum either, I'll stay with Jean,' she stated.

'Maybe the judge will say you can live with your dad,' Stefan said encouragingly. 'Fingers crossed,' he added, using a bit of adult vocabulary that seemed fit for this occasion, but he knew it wasn't fit. He knew he didn't know the words for this kind of situation. He wandered off to where Max and the other boys were fooling about and joined straight into their banter with the relief of someone who has been swimming out of his depth but can now feel solid ground under his feet. He avoided Zoe for the rest of that day and Kylie seemed to be taking care of her anyway.

*

Even though Zoe had told Jean not to pick her up that day, the woman was waiting outside the school gates at 3.30 with the other mums and grans. She was concerned the girl might run away again if she found out the outcome of the court case and Jean had no doubt that she would find out. Telling a child she mustn't phone her family had seemed naïve to Jean when she could see children on their phones everywhere, and what youngster would refuse to lend their phone to a friend in need? No child would think it was wrong to want to speak to your dad, indeed Jean didn't think so either. She didn't really buy the brainwashing argument and by now she felt she knew Zoe well enough to be clear that nobody could brainwash that kid into anything. She was the strongest, most stubborn child she had ever known. But she was also sensitive and vulnerable, and Jean was concerned. She stood a little way from the other mums, feeling tense about Zoe's reaction when she saw her. She hoped that once they got past the inevitable dose of initial rejection, Zoe would come round and see that Jean was the only person who could offer the emotional support she needed. And the girl was going to need plenty of support. Jean braced herself, feeling important at the same time.

A wave of hostility rose inside Zoe as soon as she caught sight of her foster carer, standing there with an insufferable air of ownership written all over her soft round face. It was an expression Zoe loathed. It made her want to shout at Jean, 'You're not my mum, you're nothing to me, go away, leave me alone!' But then, unexpectedly, memories of Jean being nice to her popped up in Zoe's mind and she felt a pang of guilt. Perhaps she was a bad person for hating Jean, but today anyway she couldn't help it. She pretended she hadn't seen her foster carer and walked straight past with her head down, chatting with Kylie and Michaela. When Jean called her name, she glanced over with a sullen look and said, 'I told you not to come and fetch me. It's not raining, I'm walking back.' She didn't say 'walking home'. She had trained herself never to use the word 'home' when talking of either Jean's house or her mother's flat. It hadn't been easy, but she had done it, and it gave her a kick when people complained.

'Jean is trying so hard,' Gerald had said once, 'it would be nice, Zoe, if you could sometimes refer to her house as home. I know it upsets her that you never do.'

'I've got a home and one day I'm going to live there. It's Dad's house. Nowhere else is home.' And then she stared him out. Gerald was easy to stare out.

On this day, outside the school gates, Zoe knew one thing. She was not getting into the car and she was not giving Jean the pleasure of telling her what the judge had said. In any case Zoe knew the verdict. She knew she would not be allowed to live with her father. She had known it as soon as she got up that morning, she had known it for the last three months, but now she didn't want to hear it, she wanted to hang on to hope for just a little while longer.

'Zoe,' said Jean with a hardened stare, 'I'm asking you to get in the car now.' A few Mums looked around recognising a familiar tone of voice, glad that this time it was someone else's kid who was being difficult.

'I'm walking,' snapped Zoe back, standing next to her friends. Michaela smiled at Zoe. 'Good for you,' she whispered. And the three girls carried on walking as if Jean wasn't even there.

'Micky,' said Zoe, 'Can I use your phone?'

'Pay me back after?' asked Michaela, whose funds were always low.

'Promise,' replied Zoe, holding out her hand. 'If she comes for me, I'll start running, okay? She'll never catch up with me.'

With fast nimble fingers Zoe dialled her grandmother's number and lifted the little phone to her ear. Then she turned around and stared at Jean defiantly. Now, however, she could barely breathe as she listened to the ringing of Granny's phone, and she turned around again, with her back to Jean. If there were tears, she didn't want Jean to see them. The phone got picked up, at last.

'Granny?' Her heart started beating violently as hope surged back out of control. But it wasn't Granny. There was a silence, and then Dad's voice, but before he said anything she knew. The moment of silence had said it all. Prepared as she had been, she couldn't stop the tears. She barely felt Kylie's arm around her shoulders. All she could do was tell her father she didn't want to be in care, she didn't want to go back to mum's, and she would keep running away until she could live with him. Finally, she snapped the little phone shut and handed it to Michaela who thought she wouldn't mention payment just now. That could wait. Zoe brushed her tears away and pulled on Michaela's arm to drag her away from shouting insults at a bunch of small kids who were enjoying the fascinating spectacle of someone else's drama. Zoe grabbed Kylie's arm as well and the three friends walked on down the street, but Michaela, who could be quite a naughty girl, looked back for a second and poked her tongue at Jean. It happened so quickly the woman was not quite sure the cheeky girl had done it.

After watching the girls walk away from her, Jean spun on her heels and marched to her car. Why should she care? Why had she cared? This had been the most unrewarding placement she'd ever had and even if Zoe refused to go back to her mother, she was pulling out. Enough was enough. She started the car and sat there tasting the humiliation that had just been dished out to her. Then she pulled away from the pavement, squeezing into the long line of school traffic, and headed home. Inside her head a vivid little film had started playing, telling the bitter story of all the nice things she had done for Zoe since the beginning of the placement. *'The brat,'* she thought, *'the nasty brat. Deserves everything she gets. But now I'm done. Gerald and Sally can plead all they like, I'm done. Zoe can go to hell.'* She changed gear aggressively and stalled a minute later as the light turned red unexpectedly. Blushing hard she snapped a look at the car next to hers and sure enough, a young man was staring at her with a sneer on his face. Leaning forward over the steering wheel she started her engine again and just before moving forward as the light turned green, she stuck her tongue out at him. *'What is that girl doing to me?'* she thought to herself, but she knew her anger had dissolved when she'd poked her tongue at the annoying man. Now she wondered where Zoe was, perhaps she had run away again, but Jean found with relief that she, for one, did not care. She'd

298

done her bit, now let others take care of the future. She wasn't even going to rush home. She had a bit of shopping to do and if Zoe had to wait on the doorstep all the better.

When Jean got home, Zoe was indeed sitting on the second of the three steps leading up to the front door of the tall, terraced house. The girl looked so frail and lost Jean felt a pang of remorse. But why wouldn't the child let her make her happy? She could, she knew she could. She could come to love that kid, sometimes she just wanted to give her a big cuddle and it hurt not to be allowed to. She slammed the car door shut and Zoe looked up, a blank expression on her face. As Jean walked up to the bottom of the steps, carrying her shopping bags, Zoe hoisted herself up and, looking down at her shoes, muttered a virtually inaudible 'sorry' as Jean went to put the key in the door. It was the first time Zoe had said sorry of her own accord and Jean did not want to spoil the moment.

'I know you're having a bad day,' she said turning the key, 'but don't forget, Zoe, it's not my fault. I'm only trying to help.' She stepped aside to let the girl in and as Zoe brushed past her, she repeated 'Sorry' in what sounded like a genuine apology. Jean followed her down the hallway and when Zoe made for the stairs Jean said, 'Come and talk to me in the kitchen. You can help me unpack.'

Zoe stood wavering, with one foot on the first step of stairs, the other one still on the floor, one hand on the banister, her head bent down looking at her feet. Jean resisted saying any more and just walked to the kitchen. Seconds later she heard the girl's footsteps following her. She lifted her shopping bags onto the surface by the fridge and reached over to press the knob on the kettle. Zoe was standing right next to her, with a packet of chocolate biscuits in her hand, 'I love these,' she said.

'That's why I bought them,' said Jean turning to face the girl. Zoe looked up at her with pitiful eyes and Jean drew her gently to her. 'Let me give you a cuddle,' she whispered in her ear, and the girl collapsed in her arms, sobbing and clinging to her and breathing in rasps. The boiling of the kettle drowned all sound for a moment but when it settled Jean heard Zoe hiccupping into her shoulder, 'I… w…want my dad, I… w…want my dad.'

There was something Jean had to tell Zoe, but she didn't want to wreck this moment of closeness and she didn't want the girl's hostility to flare up again so soon. She glanced at the clock above the door, thinking she probably had half an hour to play with. Time to get drinks and eat a couple of biscuits, then she would tell her. Fifteen minutes passed; they had finished their snack, but Jean was still struggling with what she had to tell the girl. Finally, she took a deep breath and spoke.

'Zoe,' she said, 'I have something to tell you that I suspect you're not going to like.' The girl looked up suspiciously and Jean added quickly, 'It's nothing to do with me, it's to do with your mum. She wants to speak with you today and is going to call after work, in a few minutes I expect.' Her tone was apologetic, her eyes pleaded for a measured reaction and Zoe gave her a look of such hopelessness that she wished she had persuaded Leanne not to come so soon. But there was no way out now.

'I don't want to see her,' said the girl flatly.

'I didn't think you would, Zoe, but you can just listen to what your mother has to say. You don't have to make any decisions now.'

Zoe shrugged as if nothing mattered now anyway, and Jean was relieved. Perhaps the mother and daughter wouldn't fight, and perhaps she could take some credit for that. She finished putting the shopping away and Zoe stayed with her. They didn't speak, but the silence was not hostile. When the doorbell rang Zoe seemed resigned. There was no fuss.

Leanne walked in wet from the rain that had broken in the late afternoon. They sat in Jean's front room listening to the rain pelting against the windowpanes and Zoe told her mother she was not going back to the flat. Ever. Dusk and clouds mingled to make for early darkness and Zoe felt the world outside was a horrible place with nowhere for her to go to feel cosy and safe. She sat slumped in her armchair, refusing to look at her mother, staring at the gathering darkness outside, waiting for her mother to get annoyed with her. But Leanne did not come even near to annoyance. She had rehearsed the whole scene and was prepared for Zoe's mood. She didn't expect results on this day. On this day she was just laying the foundations of her future victory. One day she would have her daughter back and she would show the world she was a good, capable mother who knew exactly how to raise a daughter. A better parent than Joe.

She got up and drew the curtains against the darkness and the rain. Then she sat back down across from Zoe and started to speak. She told her daughter she understood her disappointment with what the judge had said, but she, for one, didn't want Zoe to be in care for years to come. In fact, she would do everything so her daughter could come back to live with her mother, where she belonged. She made it sound as if she was on Zoe's side, fighting with her against the judge's verdict. If Zoe agreed to come home, Ivor would move out again in the first instance so that Zoe could settle in the flat with her mother and sister, and later, when Zoe was happy for that to happen, Ivor could move back in. But only when that felt right for everyone. In due course the visits with Joe and his family would resume. Leanne was trying very hard to be nice and Zoe was almost tempted to agree to go back. She had to steel herself against that temptation however, because this would be victory for her mother, defeat for her father and she couldn't swallow that bitter pill just yet. She slumped further into her armchair, saying nothing, watching her mother from under her eyebrows. Could she even trust these promises?

'*She's putting it on,*' she thought to herself after a brief glance at her mother's face, '*she's very good at pretending stuff like that.*' Her eyes slid back down to her trainers where they settled once and for all. When Leanne got up to leave Zoe didn't look up, didn't stir from her chair. Leanne was sorely tempted to make the girl feel bad about her behaviour, but she had decided on a course of action and she was going to stick to it. She was good at that. As she reached the door she turned and said, 'I want you home, Zoe, because I'm your mum and I love you. I know I'm not a touchy-feely sort of person, I know I've got my faults like everyone else, but I am your mum and that means I care about you in a way nobody else can or ever will. Don't ever forget that.' Then she walked out of the room, pleased with herself. She had delivered her well-rehearsed little speech with perfect timing and in just the right tone of voice. She believed every word in it but rehearsing it in advance had been a very good idea, allowing the words to come out smoothly, like something out of the mouths of actors on TV. Before leaving the house, she headed briefly to

302

the kitchen and popped her head round the door to say good-bye to Jean. In response to Jean's enquiring look, she whispered, 'It's early days, but I think she'll come round. Hopefully you won't have her for much longer, Jean. Thanks for everything.'

*

Leanne was right about Zoe coming around soon but quite wrong to think her little speech had anything to do with it. The girl barely listened to words she had heard many times before and recognised as her mother's way of telling the world about the sort of person she was. When she said, 'I'm not a touchy feely sort of person,' she said it with pride, like it was a quality not to enjoy giving other people cuddles. What Zoe knew for certain was that her mother did not love her. She knew that because there were two people in her life who loved her, and they were her dad and her grandmother, and she could tell the difference. She decided she would stay with Jean.

She was still sitting in her armchair in the front room, listening to the sound of angry rain against the windowpanes when Jean came in to tell her Stefan was on the phone. Zoe perked up and held out her hand quickly, remembering that Stefan had said he would phone later, to find out. She told him what the judge had said and that although her mum was keen to have her back, she was staying in care. Unsure how to respond to that bit of bad news, Stefan quickly switched to another subject and suggested meeting up on the following Saturday afternoon to go skating down the front. 'I'll bring my blades,' he added, and Zoe's heart skipped a beat. Although Stefan had acquired roller blades and had quickly mastered the new skill, he still favoured his skateboard which was infinitely preferable for his image. Boys don't rollerblade, boys walk around looking cool and carefree with their skateboards dangling loosely from under one arm, able to drop them and jump on if they feel like it or pick them back up and run with their friends if that's what they want to do. There's freedom in a skateboard, and there's recklessness and risk. Sit, stand or lie on it, whiz down fast and take your chances, show your pals you're not frightened of anything, not even of a car coming across from a side street and killing you. You can play Russian roulette with your skateboard, you can watch adults go white as you fly past, you can feel invincible and immortal. By comparison blades are about as exciting as making cake.

Which is why Stefan's offer was not your run of the mill offer to get together on a Saturday afternoon. This was special. Like a carefully chosen gift. Zoe felt her heartbeat pick up and her insides go soft and squashy. She prayed he wouldn't mention Kylie. He didn't. They agreed to meet at two o'clock and as Zoe switched the phone off, she noticed the rain had stopped pelting against the window. Perhaps the weather was changing. Three days to Saturday. Just when she had thought she would never look forward to anything ever again. That night Zoe surprised Jean and Owen by being not just civil, but on the edge of friendly. That day of all days. There was no accounting for kids. Or perhaps it was because the girl had said she wouldn't go back to her mother, and thought it was in her interest to be pleasant with the foster carers with whom she now wanted to stay. Only to spite her mother of course, they understood this, but if it meant the girl was going to make an effort, then that was something. Be that as it may, however, Jean was not going to make long term promises to Social

Services. She would carry on looking after Zoe for the time being. Only for the time being.

23. Sunlight on Autumn Leaves

Saturday sprung into life with bright sunny skies but also some distant clouds that Zoe kept an eye on all morning. She knew full well it could be sunny at ten and raining by two in the afternoon. The clouds gathered, some grey ones scudded in, low and threatening, but they passed shedding only a drop or two and by the time she picked up her blades and slung them over her shoulder, hanging by their tied laces, the sky was blue again and the white candy floss clouds that moved gently in from the sea were no threat at all.

She was bursting with excitement and when Jean insisted on walking her down to make sure she was safely over the busy road running along the sea front, she thought she would scream with frustration. Controlling herself however, she fell in with Jean's agonisingly slow pace. They finally got to the lights and Zoe pointed to Stefan already on his skates, doing a tentative backward stride, with his head looking back over his shoulder. Then she noticed with a sharp pang of disappointment that Stefan's dad was also there, skating with a man's powerful push just a bit further down the path. Jean was relieved that Zoe's afternoon on the front hadn't turned out to be a cover up for some escapade or other and decided she had gone far enough. She was particularly pleased to see Stefan's dad there with the children. She stared after him for just a moment whilst Zoe ran across, mesmerised by his graceful body gliding along effortlessly. She had never thought of him before as an attractive man and as her eyes turned to the boy, she noticed that he too was a good-looking lad, with his straight blond hair coming down into his eyes and his supple body spinning and balancing with grace.

Then her heart stopped. Waving and grinning at Zoe the boy had launched into a backward turn without noticing the bicycle coming the other way. Jean's hand shot to her mouth as she prepared for the collision. But in the last second before the crash the bike swerved sharply onto the grass, and all that happened to Stefan was that he got called a fucking wanker. Jean shook her head. The other boy's voice had carried all the way across the traffic, kids had no shame these days, and Zoe, far from shocked was bent double with hysterical laughter. Stefan was grinning away, chuffed at his own indestructibility. Jean shook her head again and started walking slowly uphill with the thought in her head that Zoe wasn't that unhappy after all. Then she felt ashamed. As she stopped to catch her breath, she wondered why everyone was so intent on denying Zoe any right to happiness. As if laughter with her friends in the afternoon belied the tears at bedtime when she desperately wanted her dad or her gran to tuck her in and kiss her goodnight. Jean sighed. How many more years of this for Zoe?

*

Stefan's dad glided up to the children and did a neat stop inches from Stefan's own blades whilst giving his son a smug grin. He was a good skater; he knew it and he couldn't help wanting the world to notice, including his son. Zoe was sitting

307

on the damp grass, tightening her laces as hard as she could, impatient to get going. She stood up, found her balance and stuffed her ballerina shoes in the back pocket of her jeans. The sky had cleared now, and the sun was warm on her face. She pushed off with her right leg, glided away, turned gracefully around and sped back with powerful strides. This she loved, this movement, this energy, the space, the speed, the skill and most of all the fact that Stefan and his dad were watching her. When, a few minutes later, Stefan's dad said he was off to watch the rugby and would pick them up later, she struggled to hide her joy. The children set off on a race along the wide path, they performed tricks and turns for each other's benefit and finally collapsed on the grass just past the playground where kiddies ran around swings and slides and splashed around in the paddling pool even on a cold day.

Zoe sat leaning back on straight arms, her hands sunk in the soft grass. She inhaled deeply. The heady fragrance of freshly cut grass was making her a little dizzy. She noticed they hadn't cut the grass all around the daffodils and those patches were like big round islands of high wild grass with masses of yellow trumpets breaking up the expanse of green. It was pretty. She was acutely aware of Stefan's presence right next to her, and the atmosphere seemed charged with some mysterious electric force. Stefan was lying down, with a blade of grass between his lips and his hands laced behind his head.

'So, what are you going to do?' he asked. And they both knew what he meant, but as Zoe did not answer immediately, he added, 'Go back to your mum?'

'Never,' replied Zoe. 'She'd love that, wouldn't she?'

Stefan's eyes lingered on Zoe's profile. He liked the angry set of her little chin and imagined the look in her eyes. Spirited.

He had read that word in one of the books he'd borrowed from the school library, probably one of the Harry Potter books, and it had instantly matched with Zoe in the way two cards match in a game of snap. He stared off again into the sky, smelling the grass and the salty tang from the sea. Seagulls glided high up in the sky, glinting white in the immensity of blue, looking as if they knew something about the meaning of life that humans didn't.

'What are those?' he asked Zoe, looking forward to her knowing the answer, even from this distance. She shot a glance up into the sky and said in a bored tone of voice, 'Herring gulls.' Tiny specks lost in the blueness and the certainty in her voice. Stefan's heart was beating with a strange force inside his body, filling his mind with a powerful impulse to extend his hand and stroke Zoe's arm. She was beautifully and essentially herself at that moment and he was moved in a way that was new, exciting and a little scary. Why should another person have that kind of power over him? Was it power? She sat there with her eyes lost in the difficulties of her life, her reddish-fair hair hanging down messily to her shoulders, proclaiming her indifference to fashion. He watched in silence frightened to lose the perfection of that moment, intent on hiding how he felt. What if she found out and laughed? With a small shudder he closed his eyes and thought about football. Match of the day tonight. He would watch it with his dad. He was about to ask Zoe if she was going to watch it herself, but she spoke before he did.

'Sometimes I want to be dead,' she said as if it was a simple fact amongst many others she could have chosen to mention.

Stefan understood it wouldn't do to mention football.

'Go back to your mum's,' he said, sitting up so he was level with her now. He wrapped his arms around his bent knees and stared down at his blades.

'Why would I do that?' she screwed up her face in disgust and incomprehension.

'She wants you to go back, right?' He turned his face to look at her.

'Exactly dumb dumb, why would I do what she wants?' Their eyes locked in mutual mockery.

'Because,' he replied slowly, 'because…' his voice trailed off, tantalising, challenging, mocking, and she responded just as he had expected, pushing him over and nailing him down. 'Come on then,' she threatened, 'out with it, and if the reason isn't good enough, you die lovely boy.' His grin broadened and he didn't even try to struggle free.

'How do I die?' he asked with a calculating look in his eyes.

'Smashed by a roller blade,' she replied.

'All right, I give up. I shall reveal all.'

Zoe relaxed her grip and Stefan swiftly wrenched his arms free and caught her wrists.

'Now who's gonna die?' he asked mockingly.

'Go ahead,' she replied closing her eyes, 'I just told you, I want to be dead.' Her wrists went limp and Stefan's mind reeled out of control. She opened her eyes again and a sudden beautiful smile lit up her face.

'Do you know,' she said, 'that your hair is the colour of sunlight on autumn leaves?' Her voice was matter of fact, same tone she might have used to ask something like 'Do you know that Miss Brown is away next week?' Stefan's mouth dropped open, but no sound came out. Chaos of the most disturbing kind had broken up inside him and he was desperately snatching at words for a jokey retort to disarm the bomb about to destroy him. As the right sentence failed to form, he just kept staring at Zoe wondering if she could hear the loud beating of his heart. Pump…pump…pump … He remembered a science class where they had shown them a model of a beating heart and now, he could see his own, flushed pink and alive with the rhythm of his emotion. He let go of her wrists. As if unaware of his embarrassment or perhaps to relieve it, Zoe continued in the same matter of fact voice, 'Back in November Owen took me walking in some woods, and I noticed the sun coming through the branches changing the colour of the leaves. They were like… lit up, yellow with bits of red and light brown and it was just like your hair, blowing in the wind like now.' Her hand lifted as if to touch his hair with the tips of her fingers, but it stopped in mid-air and paused with a flutter of fingers mimicking the breeze. Then she looked at him again and a smile touched her face with shyness. Stefan stopped breathing.

'That's… that's a really nice thing to say about my hair,' he replied, cursing himself for sounding so dumb. 'I like your hair too,' he added, feeling stupider by the minute.

'My hair's rubbish,' replied Zoe, 'it goes all frizzy and wild, and it's red.' The sea breeze was messing it up even more than it already was. Her mum had been right, she should have kept it short, but she wasn't going to back down on that any more than she was going to back down about going back to the flat. 'Anyway, why should I go back to Mum's?'

'I like your hair, and it makes you different. Every other girl has straight blond hair, how boring is that? In the yard you stand out, you're you, unique,' he added pleased to have come

311

up with one good word at last. Unique. He thought she was too, quite different from the others.

'Don't you like Kylie's hair? I thought you fancied Kylie.' Zoe's voice had turned mocking and she was observing him with a slanting look that was a challenge. No messing about now, choose, good boy. Declare yourself. Don't keep me guessing any more. My hair makes me different, ok, but does that mean it makes me better?

'I don't fancy Kylie,' was all he volunteered.

'So why should I go back to Mum's?' repeated Zoe, running away now from the next question in her mind, 'Do you fancy me then?' She wasn't even sure what 'fancy' meant exactly, but it was what people said on TV to mean someone was special, more attractive than others. If Stefan didn't fancy Kylie then he couldn't possibly fancy Zoe who was not half as pretty, and suddenly she wanted out of this dangerous territory.

'You said she wanted you back.'

'So?'

'So that gives you power.' He was leaning on one elbow now, looking up, pensive. 'You could kind of bargain with her, ask for your phone back for instance.' Zoe nodded slowly as possibilities began to dawn on her. Power. She hadn't had that for a long time.

'You say that she doesn't really look after you much when you're there.'

'She doesn't.' Zoe gave a short bitter laugh. 'She wants me there, and then she just wants to go out shopping or to the pub.'

'So, you'll have more freedom.'

312

'That's true,' she mused. Jean took her responsibilities with annoying seriousness. Wanting to know everything. Dropping her off, picking her up. It would be good to get shot of that.

'And then…,' continued Stefan, drawling the words out, like he was telling a story and building up the suspense, 'and then…' his eyes were challenging her now, keeping her waiting.

'And then what?' she laughed, pinning his wrists into the grass again and looking down into his face. He grinned, she pouted, he closed his eyes as if to say I know stuff and how are you going to get me to say it, she shook his arms and repeated, 'And then what?'

'Then,' he said, looking extremely serious, his fair hair falling back from his high forehead, his light brown eyes dotted with darker spots looking straight at her, 'the secret visits could start again.'

She felt the air drain out of her in one swift sweep and all her muscles went limp. She let go of his wrists and gathered her small hands into her lap, sitting back on her heels. How come she hadn't thought of that? Her eyes were still on his face, but she was looking through him, past him and into her own head. Of course. Now the judgement was over she could start seeing her dad again and if she was at Mum's that would be easier. Her eyes focussed again, and she caught a strange expression on Stefan's face. He was looking at her as if he was so interested he wanted to break into the secret of who she was. Their eyes met and a fragile smile broke on his lips. In that moment of total absorption when she had stopped being aware of anything other than the thoughts dancing inside her head, he had seen beauty in his friend's face and as it touched him it also scared him. Beauty that grabbed his insides and did

313

stuff there that was out of control. More powerful than anything he had ever felt, even when Arsenal had beaten Chelsea in that epic drama a few weeks back. Now she was looking at him as if trying to put the pieces of a puzzle together and he wanted to laugh and ask her whether his nose had swapped places with his eyes. Why was she looking at him like that?

Zoe had stopped thinking about her dad. Zoe was thinking about Stefan. Stefan fancying her. A new exciting possibility, but still only a possibility. She realised that. He wasn't going to say it out loud, but wanting the secret visits to start again, now, wasn't that a sign? Wasn't that his way of saying he wanted to be with her more, in that exciting way when they had shared a secret and flouted together the authority of adults? If he wanted that again, then wasn't it obvious that she was special? Or was it just the excitement he was after, not the closeness but the excitement, what boys loved, and she did too of course, but she loved the closeness more. She searched his eyes to find the answer, but it wasn't there, a gently mocking expression was covering everything up, a curtain drawn against the outside world. She remained silent, hating to admit that he'd had a good idea before her.

'Yeah,' she said at last, 'it would be good to see Dad, but Mum would think she'd won. That would spoil everything.'

She saw the disappointment in Stefan's eyes and felt guilty. He had come up with a brilliant idea and she had knocked it on the head, pretending the idea wasn't that great. She felt confused, unsure why she'd done that. She wanted to be friends with Stefan, she knew these days she'd rather be with him than Kylie, and yet now she'd done this, and she didn't know how to get out of it.

314

'You know what my dad would say about that?' asked Stefan, still lying on his back looking up at her with that gently mocking expression. Did he know what was going on in her head? Kylie might have known, but a boy?

'What?' she asked, with a grin. 'What would Mr Wise say about that?' Because Stefan often quoted his dad's views on stuff, she had some months ago coined the expression Mr Wise. It was an open invitation to a fight, and they both knew it. Stefan sprung up to a sitting position and his hands flew to clamp around her wrists. His grin widened with his new position of power and he said with mock menace in his voice, 'He would call it biting off your nose to spite your face, and he would be right.' His eyes held on to hers and she didn't know whether he meant that because she wouldn't let her mum win or because she wouldn't admit he'd come up with a brilliant idea.

'He wouldn't,' she snapped back, pretending to try and free her wrists.

'He would,' insisted Stefan, forcing her to look at him.

'Wouldn't.'

'Would.'

'Ok, he would,' she suddenly admitted, 'but if we have a race to the café, I bet I can beat you.' It was an admission of everything and they both knew it. They burst out laughing, rolling back onto the grass, great whooping gusts of laughter coming from nowhere but shaking them to their roots. Zoe had tears running down her face and Stefan had gone beetroot red with spasms he couldn't control.

'Bet you...,' he hiccupped, 'bet you, you don't...beat me.'

They pushed themselves up and ran awkwardly on their blades down to the path. Zoe had moved slightly faster and had a head start. She pushed off in her sleek way and Stefan saw her take the lead. She was a better skater than him, but he was competitive and reckless. He wasn't going to lose without a fight, and he bent forward the way hockey players do, forgetting all about style and just pumping power into his muscles in order to achieve speed. And suddenly the whole skating thing came beautifully together for him. He seemed to be running and skating all at once, his arms thrusting in perfect harmony with the swaying of his hips. He had never thought it could be this exciting, what with the speed and the risk. A dog running across his path, a kid swerving stupidly on her tricycle, a branch across the path and he would go flying, he knew it, and it would hurt. It would hurt like hell. But just ahead of him Zoe was taking the same risks and she was giving it everything, she didn't care either. The café had appeared into view now and the gap between them was narrowing. He pushed harder and out of nowhere she found the strength to go faster too and regain a little bit of her lost lead. Pictures of rowers in the Olympics flashed through his mind. How to get that last inch, that last extra ounce of effort out of a body that seemed stretched to the limit.

Suddenly he sensed victory. Zoe had slowed down. By very little, but she had slowed down there was no doubt about it and he knew he had some reserves left. But just as he upped his performance by another tiny margin, just the margin that he knew would win him the race, an image flashed in his mind. Zoe's face as she had looked when lost in her thoughts, and to him, at that moment, entirely beautiful. For that split second, he lost his concentration and the margin slipped. Zoe sensed it and she touched the first post of the wrought iron that marked the end of their races about one second before him. But a second is all it takes, and she had won. Instead of turning round triumphantly in her usual throwing out of arms and swaying of hips, she rounded on him accusingly, 'You let me win.' This was unforgivable and they both knew it.

'I didn't,' he replied truthfully.

'You did, you lying toad. You were right behind me, but you still wouldn't have won except I got cramp in my right foot and I slowed down for a second and I know you could have overtaken me, so how come you didn't?'

'I lost my concentration, for just a second I lost my concentration and then you got your speed again and that was that.' He shrugged. His hair shone gold and red and light brown in the sun and Zoe thought it was too beautiful and she mustn't stare like an idiot.

'You lost your concentration,' she mocked, grinning her disbelief at him. 'Yeah, like you normally lose your concentration in a race, for no reason, when you're desperate to win. It's bullshit. What would make you lose your concentration at the crucial moment?' She had her fisted hands on her hips and was looking at him with her head cocked mockingly to one side.

'You,' he answered flatly. He ran his fingers through his hair and let it all fall back with the sun picking up those golden colours again as each hair fell back into place, hardly ruffled.

'Me?' she uttered, not knowing whether to laugh or shout at the outrageous suggestion.

'Yes,' he answered firmly, 'you. There was an expression on your face back there,' he flicked his hand back at where they had just come from, 'and I … I thought it was quite… beautiful.' He stressed the word beautiful as if to show he wasn't afraid of it. 'Stupidly I let that expression come into my

317

mind just as I was about to overtake you and I lost my concentration.' He shrugged again and pushed his hands deep into his pockets, with a small grin that asked her to forgive him for being such an idiot. She was staring at him, open mouthed. 'It just shows that it wouldn't be a good thing for a sportsman to be in love,' he added casually.

Zoe's head reeled. She looked up into the distant blue sky in front of her and glided there with the five or six herring gulls circling above. Was she dreaming? Imagining things. How come he was looking so normal, just standing there with the breeze in his hair and his eyes settled on the horizon? She wanted to put her hand out on his chest and feel if his heart was banging in there like hers inside her chest. Instead, she said, 'Your idea of the secret visits was brilliant.' She paused, then added, 'I wouldn't admit it 'cos I was gutted I hadn't thought of it myself.'

Stefan gave her a big grin. 'I knew that.' Fisting his hands, with his head bent like a boxer, he flexed his arms and sprung them out, touching her lightly in rapid succession on the shoulders and in the pit of her stomach. Delighted, she retaliated with much harder punches in his chest. He caught her wrists and they wrestled, balancing on their blades and supporting each other even as they pretended to push the other one over.

'Ok,' he said, 'I can make up for beating you to the idea, if not to the post.'

'How?' she asked challengingly, as if the offer would have to be a very good one to achieve what he proposed.

'I've got enough money for two ice-creams,' he said, adding for good measure, 'two doubles.'

They bought their ice-creams and went to sit companionably on the low wall opposite the café. The sea was so far out you could barely see it and birds dotted the vast expanse of flat shimmering sand, their heads bobbing up and down as they searched for food. Clouds were gathering now on the horizon and Zoe thought they might get wet before they got home, but she didn't care. Even if she got home soaking wet this would remain one of the best days in her life. Perhaps the best. She licked the last of the chocolate ice-cream and turned the cone to start on the strawberry.

'I'm gonna do it,' she said.

'Do what?' asked Stefan whose mind had been on tonight's Match of the Day.

'Go back to my mum's.' She gave the ball of pink ice-cream a couple of hard licks and then ran her tongue carefully all around the edge, catching the drips.

'Good,' replied Stefan. 'Look at those clouds,' he added. 'We better get going.' He stuffed the end of his cone in his mouth and swung his legs around and over the wall. Zoe did the same and as she stood tall on her blades, ready to push off, Stefan gave her his best grin and said, 'Race?'

She sent a long, measuring look down the path and replied, 'Ok, to the garage.' And before he'd had time to get ready, she was off, laughing wickedly as she left him behind.

24. Back with Mum

Zoe went back to her mother a week later. She got her phone back and all kinds of assurances that life with Mum would be freer and happier in every way than life with Jean, good as Jean had been, and she had been good Leanne was quick to add, but that just went to show that nobody could replace the real parent and Leanne was happy that Zoe could see that at last. She was careful not to blame all the problems on Joe, in fact she was careful not to mention Joe at all. Zoe was careful not to mention unsupervised visits or anything like that. Jessie was under strict orders to be nice to her, she could tell, and hard as it must have been for Jessie to have her annoying half-sister back, she behaved herself. In any case Jessie was now fifteen and wasn't around much to be annoyed or annoying. Ivor had moved out for the time being.

  Power between Zoe and her mother was finely balanced and they both knew it. As long as neither stepped out of line into forbidden territory, perhaps life could be all right. Zoe took possession of her bedroom again and for the first time in her life referred to the flat as home. Food wasn't as good as Jean's meals, but there was more freedom to eat when you wanted and not sit down at the table if there was something good on TV. But the greatest joy for Zoe was having her phone back.

'You know you're not to talk to anyone from your father's family, don't you Zoe? That's the agreement. Can I trust you with that?' said Leanne as she handed a brand-new mobile to her daughter.

'Mum, it's my friends I want to talk to. Not having a phone was like being an alien or something. All my friends were downloading games and stuff all the time, and I'm like "No, I haven't got a phone, no I don't know about the latest game, and I haven't heard the new ringtones, and don't talk to me about mobile phones 'cos believe it or not, I'm not ALLOWED to have one.'

Leanne kept a straight face, but she bit her lip not to laugh. Relief was sweeping through her. Zoe had grown into just another kid. Spoke like one, made the faces and threw the hands about, it reminded Leanne of Jessie when she used to come home from school and speak the latest school speak and roll her eyes in the way every other girl rolled her eyes 'cos you just knew that was the latest schoolyard fashion and anyone who didn't behave in that exact way was either hopelessly out of touch or the most advanced trendsetter who was a step ahead of the rest and waiting for them to follow. Zoe was not, Leanne thought, a trendsetter but she was a quick learner, just as Leanne herself had been. And Jessie after her. Leanne warmed to her daughter. Perhaps things were going to be all right after all. Teenage girls wanted a Mum around, to shop with and talk about lipstick and haircuts, yes, perhaps her time was finally coming, when she would be the number one parent. One day Zoe might decide she wanted to go back to unsupervised visits, but the older she got the less likely she was to be close to a dad whose main interests were football and computers.

Leanne smiled to herself. She had won this battle, just like she won all her battles. Out with that annoying family. She smiled again as she thought of the money this whole business had cost them. She'd received legal aid, but they hadn't. So much for them acting so bloody superior all the damn time, better off, better educated, where did that take them? Her only regret was that she wouldn't have a chance to gloat. She reached for a cigarette out of her handbag and watched Zoe leave the room with her treasured phone nestled in the palm of her hand. Leanne smiled to herself at the thought that not having her mobile had been Zoe's real problem these last few months and yet the girl had been writing to everybody under the sun about wanting to kill herself if she wasn't allowed to live with her dad. Kids! She pushed the kitchen window open and sat next to it as she drew in a lungful of smoke and released it slowly into the outside world.

The first thing Zoe did after leaving the kitchen was lock herself in the bathroom and text her dad. 'Got phone. Call U later. xxx Z.' She entered her dad's number and pressed send with her heart beating fast. She looked up at the door even though she knew nobody could come in and her mum was smoking a fag anyway, which meant she wouldn't move from the window until she'd finished. No smoke in the flat was one big condition of Zoe staying there. With a gratified smile Zoe read her phone's words to her: 'your message has been sent to 07906376557'. She could talk to her dad again, and to her grandparents and to aunty Emma. Her heart was bursting with disbelief. After all those months of being cut off. She deleted all signs of her message to her father. She would have to delete everything all the time and wouldn't be able to have her favourite people in her address book, but it was a minor hassle compared to the joy of her retrieved freedom. She polished the front of the phone with her sleeve, brought it up to her lips for a long heartfelt kiss and stuffed it deep in the pocket of her jeans. She turned the tap on and let it run for the time it would take to give her hands a quick rinse and left the bathroom.

Her double life had just started, and she would manage it with perfect brilliance for the next eight months. The first three months in the flat were almost happy. The contrast with what had gone before retained enough clarity to make Zoe appreciate her gains. Significant freedom, a good measure of power, no longer bearing the stigma of being a child in care, secret visits with her dad, and the excitement of planning and plotting the visits with Stefan. That friendship was better than ever. On the delicious verge of something else all the time, without quite knowing what that something else would be except that it carried all the mystery of an adult world they knew was their future and guessed would be rich in things now difficult to imagine. When talking with Kylie Zoe now felt immeasurably mature and experienced, as if Kylie was still in a childish world fit for babies. Both girls were aware of this, with Zoe having mysteriously become popular with other girls as well. The only downside was that the teachers' reports to the social workers were so positive everyone agreed the move back to her mother was fully vindicated. Miss Brown got closest to the truth when she said to Caroline, one of the teaching assistants, 'I wonder what is going on in Zoe's life to make her so happy, but I'm damn sure it's got nothing to do with a supposed reconciliation with her mum. When I asked her about that the other day, she said life at home was fine and she gave me a sweet smile. But Caroline, that smile was

323

pure acting, and I think she knew I knew. She smiled again, as if to say, "Don't worry, I've got everything well under control." I'd love to know. I like the kid.'

'Boyfriend?' asked Caroline.

'She is friendly with Stefan, but isn't eleven a bit young for that?'

'They start younger and younger these days. Anyway, I had a boyfriend when I was twelve.'

'Did you? I was about seventeen I think, lower sixth as it was called in those days.'

But after that Miss Brown and Caroline both watched Zoe and Stefan closely and came to the conclusion that it most probably was that relationship that was making the girl so glowingly alive. And mischievous, in a nice way. Those big grey-blue eyes looking at you innocently yet so full of secret knowledge.

This state of affairs lasted until the middle of July when Ivor moved back in with Leanne and the girls. And then everything changed.

*

The middle of June was also when Zoe saw her grandmother without supervision for the first time since the day of the Christmas Lights. It happened on a Saturday, without any planning by anyone. At two o'clock that day the bell rang on Joe's front door. He looked away from the TV in annoyance and glanced at his watch. Zoe was about to arrive through the back door any minute now and the last thing he wanted was for someone to be in the house when this happened. He sat where he was in the TV room and carried on watching golf which, in the summer, was his main source of sporting pleasure. It wasn't a patch on football, and he would switch it off when Zoe arrived. The doorbell rang again, with an insistency that made him rise from the couch. He headed slowly for the hallway and edged into the front room, hoping to catch a glimpse of his visitor without being seen. Just as he stepped warily into the room, he met his mother's eyes. She was standing squarely outside the bay window, slightly bent forward to peer into the room. With a sigh he went to open the front door.

Sunshine and summer fragrances flooded into the hallway as he held the door open. His mother pecked him on the cheek and asked why he'd taken so long to answer the bell.

'Not a good time for visitors,' he replied, closing the door behind her as she made her way towards the kitchen.

She stopped in her tracks and spun around, meeting his eyes with the dead seriousness of a mother questioning her little boy about who broke the blue mug and chucked the pieces in the bin without telling anyone. His eyes didn't shift.

'You know why, Mum, let's not play these games. She'll be here any minute, so you can stay or go, it's up to you, but I don't want a lecture.'

Janet stood hesitating. She hadn't planned this and therefore shouldn't feel guilty. The attraction of seeing Zoe unsupervised for the first time since the girl had last run away, months and months ago, was powerful. She felt her pulse quickening. Her mind took her right back to that day in April, ten years ago, when the phone call had come to say Leanne had gone into labour. In that moment she had forgotten her dislike of the woman and had just felt the tugging of deep emotions shared only by women. A man could never quite understand what giving birth meant or the feelings that united a mother to her children. Zoe was born at eight o'clock the following morning and they rushed straight over to the hospital. Leanne had been asleep when they got there but Joe had come out from behind the grey curtains, holding the tiny bundle in his arms. When he deposited the child in Janet's arms the small face framed in white cloths and blankets whisked her back twenty-eight years into her own past. She gazed down, looked up at her son and down again in confusion. Her grown son seemed to have deposited himself into her arms. 'She's beautiful,' she whispered and squeezed the baby a little closer to her chest. Then quickly she handed the little bundle to David, 'You hold her,' she said. Grandmother was what she was, not mother, and it was important not to confuse the two. She smiled in delight as David handed the baby to Joe and they watched their son gaze in wonder into his daughter's face, looking too choked up to say anything. Here was a man who was going to make a good father.

Now Janet and her son stood looking at each other in the hallway. 'Mum,' he repeated, 'I told you I didn't want a lecture.'

'I haven't said a word,' she replied.

'No, but your eyes are giving me a lecture anyway.'

Janet sighed, turned around and carried on walking into the kitchen.

'It's not a lecture,' she said, sitting down at the table and clasping her hands in her lap. 'It's just that these secret visits are not the way forward.'

'They're the only way forward, Mum. I'm seeing my daughter without some social services busybody listening to everything we say. Are you staying?' he asked sarcastically.

'Don't attack me Joe,' she replied, looking hurt.

'Didn't mean to attack you,' Joe mumbled, mechanically putting the kettle on. When he was with his mother, he reverted to being a little boy and forgot that she was vulnerable like everybody else. He still saw her as the mythical being she had been in his child's eyes, the one who knew everything, who comforted others, who was so strong she could never get hurt. Which was why it was all right to get angry with her and have tantrums and say bad stuff to her because she didn't get hurt. It made no difference to her. She would just look down with amused or scolding eyes, but never hurt eyes.

When he had first seen the hurt in her eyes after one of his many attacks on her it had been a shock. As if it wasn't his mother in front of him, but some stranger he didn't know. He had looked away, confused, not knowing how to react, and had observed her from the corner of his eyes, willing her to become herself again so that he too could carry on being himself and they could revert to the familiarity of their long-established relationship. She had on that occasion recovered her composure and the awkward moment had passed. But there had been others, and his father had spoken to him. He had tried to adjust to these new circumstances where the strongest person in his life could suddenly become weak and upset and make him feel horribly uncomfortable. He had tried to learn to comfort her after upsetting her, he had tried to stop upsetting her, but it had been a useless effort.

The only person with whom he could become the comforter and the strong one was Zoe and that was why he loved her so much, she brought out in him a new person, a nicer person than he was with everyone else in his family. There were no bad feelings at all towards Zoe. Being with his

327

daughter was the closest he got to feeling at peace with himself.

'Stay,' he told his mother, putting instant coffee in a couple of mugs. 'She'll be delighted to see you. You know how much she hates contact.'

'I'm just worried, Joe, that if we're not seen to co-operate with the care plan, we'll lose Zoe forever. You know I've been working hard at co-operation and I want to stick with it for at least another few months. Give it a chance to bring results.'

'But you told me it wasn't working,' said Joe, keeping his voice calm. 'Didn't you say they were now accusing you of being strategic?'

Janet nodded, bowing her head under the weight of her undertaking. The loneliness of it. 'You must admit, Janet,' Gerald had said recently, 'that we were right to take Zoe away from the influence of her father. She is happier now than she has been for a long time.' 'If only he knew,' Janet had thought to herself, whilst noticing he had been kind enough not to add 'and from your influence.' Despite everything there was something likeable about Gerald and at times they would talk almost openly. 'Nobody questions that you and David love Zoe, Janet,' he had once said. 'Even the judge said it in his report. Our only concern is that Zoe is also allowed a relationship with her mother.'

'But that's all she's allowed Gerald. Can't you see how wrong that is? Not to allow a child to see the parent she has always said she loves the most?'

'She's not saying that now…'

'Have you asked her?' Janet had interrupted sharply. Gerald had looked away, embarrassed.

'Best to leave well alone,' he muttered, shuffling in his seat.

328

'How do you know all is well then? How come nobody ever wants to listen to her? I've shown you her letters to us. She is desperate to have unsupervised visits with us and with her father.'

'The care plan doesn't rule them out, Janet. Just give the girl and her mother enough time to get back into a solid relationship, and then we'll introduce unsupervised visits again. Be patient. I say it'll take no more than a few months and Leanne will be ready to authorise unsupervised visits.'

'A few months! But in that time, Gerald, I'm only allowed to see my granddaughter once a month, under supervision. That is just cruel.' Tears had glistened in her eyes, and she had added, because she knew she had to for the sake of credibility, 'and in that time she doesn't get to see her dad at all.'

'That's his choice, Janet,' Gerald had replied.

'Well, you know what I think about that, and what's more I know you have some sympathy with what I think.'

'I promise you, Janet, I regard unsupervised visits as the next step in the care plan. They will happen. Trust me.'

He sounded genuine at the time but then nothing happened. Nothing changed. More time was always needed. And now Janet was being offered the unsupervised visit she longed for and why should she turn it down out of loyalty to a care plan that never took her or her family into account? She looked at Joe with a naughty smile and said, 'Do you know, I think I will stay.' He smiled back as he handed her a mug of milky coffee.

They sat silently waiting for the sound of the back gate creaking on its hinges. When the squeak came, they looked at each other again and Joe smiled. The back door was pushed open quietly, then Zoe's face appeared around the door, her eyes cautious and excited all at once. When she took in her grandmother sitting at the end of the large pine kitchen table she froze, looked quickly at her dad as if to ask, 'Is this okay?' and when his smile told her it was, she ran into her granny's arms and buried her face in the hollow between neck and shoulder. The fresh smell in her grandmother's hair was magic, as was the familiar lavender fragrance from the lavender parcels that Granny pushed in amongst the clothes in her drawers. Zoe inhaled deeply and then said, 'Granny, you smell of you.' They all laughed. Zoe thought this was one of the best moments in her life: a surprise better than any she had had under the Christmas tree, and her two favourite people there with her, in what she still regarded as her home, sharing this big secret, all three of them laughing together, no rows, no arguments, nothing bad at all.

In answer to Zoe's first excited question, however, came Granny's explanation that this was a one-off and no, there would be no secret visits to her house as well, it would be much too risky and might lose all the ground she thought she had made with Social Services. Zoe had climbed into her lap and sat snuggled there, looking from her gran to her dad with wonder in her eyes.

'Your hair is lovely,' said Granny, running her fingers through the wavy strands and lifting them lightly so the light picked up the shades of red. She very nearly added, 'I hope your mum isn't trying to get you to cut it.' Janet had become aware of all the negative sentences that invaded her speech when Leanne popped into her mind. She knew it had to stop, even though she felt much of it was justified. 'Just keep Leanne out of your conversation,' David had told her, and she worked hard at doing just that. Not just for Zoe's sake, for her own sake as well. What was the point in poisoning her own mind with all that bad stuff? Leave Leanne alone to get on with her life and just concentrate on getting what was right for Zoe. It sounded easy, yet it was the hardest thing she had ever done. Her dislike of Leanne ran deep into every recess of her mind and blocking it was at times impossible. Words would explode inside her head and demand to be let out. Sometimes she won, sometimes they did. David would then give her the look, and she would glance away, guilty and stubborn all at once.

As if Zoe had read her mind, she suddenly sagged inside her Gran's arms and said plaintively, 'Ivor's come back.' Her father tensed up and leaned forward. 'How come?' he asked with a ripple of anger in his voice.

'Mum said I'd had three months to adjust to being home. She also said it would be good to have Ivor around during school holidays, when she's in work.' Zoe looked unhappy.

'How long has he been back?' asked Dad.

'Three days.'

'What's it like?'

Zoe shrugged. 'He pretends to be friendly, but I can see he hates me the same as before.

'What about you?' asked Gran.

'I hate him too,' replied Zoe quickly in a matter-of-fact voice.

Janet and Joe exchanged a look, and although neither would have admitted to it, they both knew that the other was not displeased.

'Now Mum's going to be horrible,' added Zoe, staring vacantly at the kitchen cupboard on the wall opposite her.

'Is she?' asked Janet, hugging the girl a little closer.

'Yeah,' Zoe nodded. 'When Ivor's around they all gang up on me. Mum's like, showing off to him, look Ivor, I know how to handle Zoe. Jessie will love it too. Saying how ugly my hair is and stuff like that.'

'Has it started happening?' asked Janet again. She glanced at her son who looked sombre but showed no sign of wanting to speak.

'No, not yet.'

'Maybe it won't, Zoe,' said Janet. 'They know they've got to treat you well if they want to keep you there.'

'Gran, they didn't treat me well before, and look what the judge said. That Mum was a great mother. It's their word against mine, and they believe them, not me.'

Zoe shrugged and for a moment her young face looked much older than her age. But then, as suddenly as the sky changes when the sun comes shining out from behind a dark rain cloud, her face lit up and she looked at her father expectantly.

'Dad, did you buy that new computer game we talked about last week?'

'I did,' he replied with a smile. 'It's set up and ready for you, I'll come up now.'

Zoe jumped out of her grandmother's lap and started swaying her hips and singing the James Blunt song of the moment, 'You're beautiful', in the middle of the kitchen floor. Joe smiled. It was so typical of his daughter to move effortlessly between painful and happy thoughts. He pushed his chair back and stood up, looking with amusement at his daughter who was now doing fast dance steps on the spot, telling her gran that Kylie had taught her how to do this. He pushed his chair back, stood up and froze as the doorbell rang stridently through the house. His mother and daughter had turned into statues, Zoe with one arm up in the air and her foot twisted at a funny angle. She shot her father a terrified look and when he nodded, she dashed out the back and disappeared. Looking pale Joe strode off closing the kitchen door behind him. Janet's body had tensed up and she worried that if it was the police, they would detect her nervousness immediately. She got up and went to wash their two mugs, keeping her back firmly to the door. Seconds later a silent pair of hands grabbing her shoulders gave her a terrible fright and Joe burst out laughing from behind. Zoe reappeared.

'Who was it?' she asked

'Delivery man. New bits for the computer.'

'Can I go and play the new game?' asked Zoe, jumping up and down.

'Yes, I'll be up now,' replied her dad.

When Joe came back down after setting up the game for his daughter, Janet had more coffee and biscuits ready.

'Isn't it incredible,' she pondered, 'that we should be so frightened of the police when we have done nothing wrong. When we are doing nothing wrong. Just seeing our daughter and granddaughter.' She looked deeply puzzled and pained. 'It's like living in another country or at another time, when people weren't free. It's like being in a nightmare and never waking up.'

Joe looked at his mother pensively, then looked down at his mug of coffee. She held her breath. He looked as if he was about to say something, and Joe didn't often volunteer any information. She waited, perfectly still.

'I know it's my fault, Mum,' he said at last, 'and I'm sorry. It's affected Zoe, it's affected all of you. If I hadn't gone crazy over Leanne none of this would have happened.' He shook his head in what looked like disgust at himself and now Janet felt sorry for him.

'Still,' she replied, 'you never hurt Zoe and she's told everyone she wants to be with you, and yet here we are, reduced to secret visits and hiding when the doorbell rings. It's not right, Joe. Do you remember a few years ago, a little black girl was killed by her parents in London, I think she was called Victoria Climbie. So, they leave a child like that with her parents and they take Zoe away from the father she wants to live with. Where's the sense in that?'

'Don't ask me, Mum, I hate them all.'

Their eyes met and Janet felt swept by a wave of warm feeling. It was rare to feel closeness with her son and it was precious. The fear of destroying the moment paralysed her; yet saying nothing would end the moment as surely as saying the wrong thing. Joe wouldn't be the one to keep the closeness alive.

'I should go,' she said, playing safe. The wrong word might not just destroy the moment but also destroy the memory of it.

'Yes,' said Joe, draining the last of his coffee, 'and I'll go and play that game with Zoe. She's very good, you know,' he added with a proud nod of the head. His daughter. Good at computer games. Like him.

It was Janet's turn to feel proud of her son. When Zoe was born, she had known he would be a good father, and he had been until the split up. But now she wondered if he would ever be allowed to live the life of an ordinary father, enjoying his daughter's company in private or in public, without fear of the police knocking on the door. Her efforts with Social

Services took on meaning again and she left her son's house with renewed determination.

25. Progress

Ivor's return did change the atmosphere in the flat. It wasn't that he treated Zoe badly, no, he knew better than that, but his presence brought about subtle differences and these impacted the other two, with Mum snapping at her daughter more often and Jessie acting as if she had a license to be annoying.

A big clash erupted about ten days after Ivor had moved back in. It happened over breakfast, on a dull rainy Sunday, when Zoe was feeling a bit depressed that there would be no rollerblading today down the front, nor anything else to look forward to. Kylie went to church on Sunday mornings, and it was a rare Sunday afternoon when she wasn't doing something with her family, visiting her gran or whatever. Zoe shook some Cheerio into her bowl and reached for the milk. Stefan would be watching sport with his dad and on a rainy day there would be absolutely no excuse to phone him. She sprinkled sugar over the crispy hoops floating in milk and plunged her spoon into her bowl. That left Michaela, but Sophie would be round there too, and Zoe wasn't so keen on Sophie. Zoe munched on her cereals wondering whether to phone Michaela anyway. From a distance, she was aware of her family around the kitchen table. Mum looking like death after a late Saturday night out drinking, still smelling of tobacco and booze, her hair hanging down her face in messy strands which she never bothered to brush before breakfast. Ivor sat there in silence, drinking coffee and reading the paper. Mum had decided they would have Sunday breakfast as a family and that was why everyone was in the kitchen instead of doing their own thing in their preferred corner of the flat. Mum and Jessie were talking about hair. Jessie wanted a certain haircut and was trying to get Mum to pay for it. Zoe paid no attention. She was halfway through her cereals when Jessie changed the topic from her own hair to her sister's.

'Anyway, Mum,' she said, intent on winning her mother's attention, 'the one who really needs a haircut here is Zoe.'

Zoe's spoon froze in mid-air. 'Mind your own business,' she snapped, glaring at her sister. Ivor raised his eyes from the sports pages and tut-tutted.

'Jessie's only saying it to be helpful, sweetie,' drawled Mum, her head still blurry from the night's drinking. She looked at Ivor as she plucked a cigarette from the packet on the table. 'What does the man in the family think?' she asked playfully. 'Nice hair or not?'

'No comment,' replied Ivor with a chuckle that raised the hair on the back of Zoe's neck.

'My friends like my hair, so shut up,' she shouted at Jessie, fighting the tears.

'And what about your boyfriend, does he like your hair too? Zoe's got a boyfriend, you know,' Jessie trumpeted round the table. It was as if Zoe's clothes had been stripped off her in one quick sweep and she sat naked inside a ring of mocking eyes. 'He's quite cute, considering,' added Jessie careful not to expand on the idea contained in the word 'considering'.

'Is it that boy Stefan?' asked Mum, lighting her cigarette and getting up to stand by the window which she pushed open with her elbow. She looked down at her daughter with a gleam of amusement in her eye.

'I don't have a boyfriend,' shouted Zoe, banging her spoon on the table, 'so leave me alone.'

Mum's voice cracked through the air like a whip, 'Cut that out Zoe,' she said knowing it was what Ivor wanted to hear.

'I hate you all,' hissed Zoe, scraping her chair back ready to run out of the kitchen. But Ivor beat her to the door, without laying a finger on her of course. Leanne left the window and stubbed her cigarette on her breakfast plate. She then gripped her daughter by the arm, dragged her back to the kitchen table and sat her on a chair.

'Now then Zoe,' she said, sitting next the girl. 'We've been through all this before and you know where it got you, don't you?' She lifted the girl's chin, 'Look at me.' Zoe looked back sullenly. 'Where did it get you Zoe?'

Zoe was silent.

'Into care, that's where it got you. And that's where it'll get you again if you carry on in the same way.' Leanne paused. She didn't look right or left, but she knew Jessie and Ivor were observing the scene with the sharpest interest. Waiting for her to show her colours. Was she going to be soft on the brat or was she going to put her in her place, where she deserved to be? Leanne looked at her daughter and saw Joe. The sullen eyes, the untidy hair, the angry twist of the lips. 'Your behaviour just now was out of order, young lady,' she said coldly, 'and I'm not going to put up with that kind of thing. Nobody was unpleasant to you but…'

338

'You WERE,' shouted Zoe, sitting up but refraining from banging the table. 'You made fun of my hair, and you made fun of my friends.' She couldn't stop tears running down her face.

'Nobody made fun of you.'

'They did,' she said, pointing at Jessie and Ivor, tears flooding her eyes now.

'Jessie said she thought you needed a haircut, she's got a right to her opinion, that's not making fun of you. Ivor said nothing at all. And then Jessie said you had a boyfriend. What's wrong with that? I've heard you mention Stefan, so, if you have a boyfriend what's the problem?'

'I don't have a boyfriend!' Zoe's breathing became trapped inside her chest and she stammered, 'm…m.. my inh… inh…inhaler.' Her eyes had grown big and scared.

'Jessie, get her inhaler from the bedroom, hurry girl. Now listen to me Zoe, asthma attack or not I'm going to say what I have to say. For the last three months you've shown you're perfectly capable of behaving yourself, and I am not going to tolerate tantrums and shouting for no good reason.' Leanne stopped as Jessie ran in holding out the inhaler. Zoe grabbed it and took the deepest breath she could manage. The grip on her lungs loosened and she blinked with relief a few times, before closing her eyes completely. 'All right, Zoe?' asked Leanne. 'Now look at me. We're going to finish this conversation. We know you can control your tantrums, so from now on, any bad behaviour and you get grounded. No rollerblading, no meeting up with friends and no phone. Do you understand Zoe?'

Zoe stared back at her mother's dishevelled face feeling powerfully rebellious. 'Ground me then,' she challenged, 'I don't care. I don't care about anything.' Her face was itchy with tear stains, but she resisted the childish impulse to wipe the saltiness away. She would keep her head up and it helped to think that if she got grounded one of them would have to stay in with her, and the punishment would be nicely shared out.

Once Zoe was back in her bedroom, however, all the rebellious feelings melted away and she lay on her bed crying and holding Flossie close to her chest. The temptation to run away was strong again but she knew from experience that it led to one or two nights away with her grandparents and after that things got worse.

'Remember Gerald and the Witch?' asked Flossie with her silent eyes. Zoe did, and she remembered the threats to move her to a foster family in a different part of town, or even a different town, so she couldn't run away anymore. She would go to a different school, lose her friends, no more rollerblading down the front, no freedom, no secret visits. Whilst putting on her best show of sullen indifference she had taken note. These people had power and she had a lot to lose. Flossie was very good at reminding her that running away was not a good idea.

'And then there's Stefan,' added Flossie. Zoe nodded. She closed her eyes and hugged Flossie tight. Stefan had kissed her the Saturday before last. But it had happened so quickly that now she struggled to remember the feel of his lips on hers. He had given her a quick shy smile and then they had both pretended it hadn't happened. But she still remembered the knocking of her heart inside her chest and the knocking afterwards every time he stood close to her, hoping he would do it again. But he hadn't. She hadn't either. She had come very close two or three times, but at the last second nothing had moved.

Zoe lifted Flossie high up with extended arms watching her ears flop forward in their funny way. 'All right Flossie, I know. Running away would be stupid. I won't do it.' Zoe meant it, and yet soon enough she would change her mind.

*

On that same rainy Sunday Janet had her children around for lunch and they sat at the dining-room table acutely aware that the family gathering was making Zoe's absence more intensely painful than ever. On such occasions small talk never lasted long before someone brought up what was on all their minds, and sure enough, this time it was Janet who broached the subject.

'Don't you think Zoe's losing weight?' she asked Joe. Emma's fork, with a broccoli floret speared through it, stopped in mid-air. It was the first open admission that her parents knew about the secret visits and Emma shot her brother an interested glance. No reaction. As if this was a perfectly ordinary subject of conversation. Emma pushed the broccoli into her mouth and munched slowly. Her brother was silent.

'David thinks so too,' insisted Janet.

'True,' said David as he gripped a chicken leg between finger and thumb, 'but I did say it could just be that she's having a growth spurt.' He lifted the chicken leg to his teeth and bit into it, catching the dribble of gravy with the napkin in his other hand.

341

'She's left to her own devices,' continued Janet, 'and she's not eating properly. I call that neglect, don't you?' She looked around the table.

'Have you heard from those people you wrote to?' asked Emma. She had also noticed that Zoe was losing weight, and with anorexia such a threat for young girls she understood her mother's concern. But their aim was to be granted unsupervised visits again and accusing Leanne of neglect at this point would backfire.

'Yes,' replied Janet, 'but I'm not holding my breath. The MP's got two votes to lose, mine and Leanne's, so he's going to be very understanding and do nothing. The Children's Commissioner has promised to look into it. We'll see.' She piled some vegetables on the back of her fork, pushed it all into her mouth and chewed mechanically. If you asked her, thought Emma, she wouldn't know what vegetables she's eating.

Janet had aged in the last couple of years. When at rest her face sagged with two deep lines dragging her mouth down and giving her a heart-breaking look of thin-lipped old age. A smile would lift her face again, but Emma was aware that her mother just didn't smile much these days. Papery and frail was how she looked.

'Also,' added Janet, 'I don't like the thought of Zoe running wild everywhere. I call that neglect too. A young girl shouldn't have the run of the neighbourhood.' She cast her son a critical look. He looked at his sister and shrugged with his palms spread out.

'My fault,' he confessed, 'I'm all for that freedom and we know why.' He looked down at his plate, lifted a piece of chicken to his mouth and continued between mouthfuls.

342

'She's fine Mum. She's sensible. She's always with one friend or another, and her freedom is what keeps her going. She spends as little time in the flat as possible and when she's there, she stays in her room. Nobody gives a damn. She probably doesn't eat a great diet, but Leanne was never one to cook for the family. I did most of the cooking if you remember.'

'How can they allow this,' protested Janet, 'how can they make Zoe live with someone who doesn't look after her, doesn't care, doesn't love her?' She twisted her napkin between her fingers and dabbed the lower rim of her eyes in small apologetic pats. Silence fell. Eating stopped. The napkin got unfolded, then folded again, carefully, and laid on the table. Without looking up, Janet spoke again. 'Sometimes I don't know why I bother to carry on with my fight. Seems to me you're all happy with the way things are.' She raised her eyes and with her lips tightly pressed together, scrutinised each face, one after the other. There was a catch in her voice as she added, 'I'm not even sure Zoe cares about seeing us only once a month.'

Joe felt the unmistakable warnings of a migraine coming on. His right eye throbbed and a ball of pressure pushed against his skull from the inside. He wanted to shout and bawl or run out of the room, knowing he must do neither. His father was a paralysed figure of indecision, but his sister looked composed. On top even. On fucking top. As women invariably were when emotional shit hit the fan. He watched her with a mixture of relief and rancour. She was about to diffuse the situation. He'd seen it all before. Hated her for it yet had to be grateful. Now he watched her hoping in equal measures that she might succeed and that she might fail.

Emma's hand extended gently and curled over her mother's. 'Mum,' she said softly, 'you're not on your own. It's just that we don't know what to do. There's this brick wall ahead and nowhere to go. What would you like us to do?'

Janet's hand flipped over, and she gripped her daughter's fingers. 'I would like to feel I'm getting some support Emma. And that I'm fighting a cause that others believe in too.' Her eyes bore into her daughter's, but the men knew this was for their benefit. Joe's head pulsated with pain. 'But right now,' she added, 'I feel taken for granted.' There. The words were out. What a relief after feeling the growing weight of that particular type of unfairness for weeks and months. Mercifully Janet could feel that her eyes would stay dry. Emma would now try to manipulate her back into a better mood, but she wouldn't be taken in. Emma could talk till the cows came home but Janet would not lose sight of the fact that they had all organised their lives in neat little ways, leaving her to be the one who kept up the pretence of co-operation with Social Services, and therefore protected the rest of them. She sacrificed herself for the family and didn't even get a thank you for it. Not even from Zoe. In fact, worse than that.

The memory of the last supervised visit tightened her gullet with pain. The girl had asked if they could cut it short by half an hour because she was meeting friends to go into town. Her eyes had sparkled with excitement at the prospect of lunch in McDonalds and Janet had suddenly felt very old and very dispensable. The supervisor's eyes had burned through the side of her face. 'So much for the girl's desperate unhappiness,' they seemed to say whilst the woman scribbled rapid notes. Thankfully David had waited until they made their way back to the car to put his arm around her shoulders. That was when the tears had come.

Now Janet held her daughter's eyes, strengthened by her anger.

Emma sighed. 'Zoe's trying to make the most of her life Mum,' she said, 'but it doesn't mean she's happy in the flat. She's told me that when she's there she pretends she's wearing Harry Potter's cloak of invisibility and they can't see the real Zoe. And if they tease her about her hair or whatever she doesn't answer, because they're not talking to the real Zoe.'

'Really?' said Janet releasing her grip on Emma's fingers. 'Isn't it unbelievable, that an eleven-year-old girl has to resort to tricks like that?' she looked around at her son and husband hoping to rope in their indignation.

'She's got coping strategies,' said Emma, 'but I also think…', her voice trailed off uncertainly.

'Think what?' asked her mother.

Emma tried to back off, 'No, there's no point thinking about that.' She shook her head regretfully. She shouldn't have mentioned it.

'Emma, I'll be imagining all kinds of things if you leave me hanging like that.'

'All right,' replied Emma reluctantly. 'I think… she may be forgetting what it's like to live with a loving family.'

'What do you mean?' asked Janet sharply, deep furrows ploughing her forehead. She glanced at the men to see if it made sense to them. It didn't, nor did they seem to like what they were hearing. Zoe wasn't going to forget their love, surely. Emma was talking nonsense, as she often did.

'Think about it,' said Emma slowly, 'she's been out of a loving environment for how long now, six months with Leanne and how long before that with foster carers? A year?'

'Eleven months,' said Janet flatly.

'So there, seventeen months away from being loved. She's forgetting what it's like.' Emma paused and scanned the faces around the table. Dubious, all three of them. She took a breath and gathered her thoughts before launching into the best explanation she could think of. 'I see it in school. Put kids in with a bad teacher, they'll moan at first then get used to it. But if the rubbish teacher goes off sick and those kids get a good experience with the supply teacher, then watch them go up in arms when the bad teacher comes back. Now they know the difference.'

'Are you saying,' asked Janet deliberately, 'that Zoe is getting used to unhappiness?'

'In a way. I believe she's losing the memory of how good it feels to be living with people who are on your side and want you to be happy.'

There was a silence as Emma's family slowly digested her theory. Knives and forks lay forgotten on the table and what food was left on their plates went cold and soggy. They didn't care. David was the first to absorb Emma's vision into his thinking.

'You know,' he said in his slow pondering rhythm, 'I think Emma's got a point. They said they were taking Zoe away from all of us because we set her up against her mother. And yes, Emma, you're dead right, we were doing that. Not by brainwashing her, that was a silly accusation, but by giving her something she wasn't getting with her mother.'

'Still,' said Janet slowly, 'I cannot believe Zoe is forgetting what it's like to be happy and loved. That,' she added with a tremble in her voice, 'would be too tragic.'

'Remember Mum,' continued Emma gently, 'the other day we were talking about countries with authoritarian regimes, wondering why people put up with their rulers. Same thing. They don't know anything else. And that's why the rulers are so desperate to stop western influence seeping in. Give people a taste of freedom and they'll want more. But take it away and people learn to just survive. I'm convinced that's what's happening with Zoe, she is surviving.'

Janet looked at her daughter pensively. 'That's what people mean, I suppose, when they say children are resilient.' Her voice trailed off. Begrudgingly she had to admit Emma often came up with good ideas, yet nobody in the family gave the young woman much credit for her thinking. Just then Joe did exactly what they all tended to be guilty of.

'You're always looking for complicated explanations,' he said dismissively, 'when what's going on is actually quite simple. Zoe hasn't forgotten anything at all. She still wants to live with me, or if that's not possible, with Mum and Dad. She talks about it all the time.' Joe paused, assailed for a fleeting second by a doubt about what he had just said. But he quickly moved on to his next point. 'What's happening, Emma,' he continued in a slightly condescending tone, 'is that she hates living with Leanne and Ivor as much as she ever did, but she's enjoying the sense of adventure in seeing me, and you, secretly, particularly as Stefan's in it with her.'

Emma shot a concerned glance at her parents. It was typical of Joe to be unaware of their feelings and he'd done it again.

But they didn't seem to have even heard what he'd said. They were lost in their own thoughts.

'So where do we go from here?' asked Janet, looking at her daughter.

'Keep pressing for unsupervised visits. Cooperate. Play the long game. Get Zoe back. Give her a taste of real happiness and see how she responds to that.'

Janet's face lifted and she squeezed her daughter's hand, 'Thank you Emma, I needed to hear that.' She got up and started to clear the plates, scraping the shrivelled-up vegetables and congealed juices down onto her own plate. She picked up the pile, looked at the family and said, 'I needed to get these things off my chest, and I feel much better now. I'm sorry if I got a bit emotional.' She nodded pensively and added, 'Unsupervised visits. That's the first step.' Then she turned around and headed for the kitchen with something close to a spring in her step.

After this conversation Janet re-engaged with Social Services with a vengeance. She felt the hostile vibes coming her way, the doubts in their eyes, the tapping of fingers on desks as they played for time, the veiled accusation that she was being manipulative, that she hadn't really changed at all and was just pretending, in a nutshell that she couldn't be trusted. She smiled patiently, listened without arguing and carried on playing the part they all knew she was playing. But she could sense progress. Repeat the same thing often enough, she realised, and people start to believe you. She said everything they wanted to hear. She assured them she had learned her lessons from the judgement and was acting on the judge's recommendations. How could she be blamed for that? She agreed that Zoe was happy and settled now. She argued

348

that unsupervised visits would be safe. It was just about bringing a balance into Zoe's life and providing some normal family life with the paternal family, although she understood that Joe couldn't be part of that, not until he agreed to supervised visits. She was critical of her son's attitude. Agreed he should put Zoe first more than he did. There were no more criticisms of Social Services, no moans, no mention of the paternal family's rights, no demands. Just patient nibbling away at what had seemed an impregnable opposition. Like a prisoner digging his tunnel an inch at a time and never thinking of the day it would be done, just quietly digging away, knowing progress was being made but never showing the least twinge of satisfaction or expectation in case someone became suspicious. Janet couldn't afford a mistake. She couldn't afford to be exposed for the fraud she was, because the new image was fragile and should it be shattered it could never be pieced together again. Janet knew this. She sat with Gerald and discussed the issues with her hands clasped in her lap and a look of innocent compliance in her eyes. She worked alone. David couldn't be trusted, and it would be harder to maintain the act with him present as a cynical witness.

Finally, victory came. It was a hot day in the second week in July and Janet was sitting with Gerald in the little interview room on the second floor of the building. The blinds were drawn, and the windows were open, but the heat was the same indoors and out, clinging to you relentlessly. Running a finger inside the collar of his shirt, as if that would cool him down, Gerald announced that Leanne had agreed to a first unsupervised visit for the coming Sunday. It took Janet all her willpower to conceal the explosion of triumph in her heart. 'I am so pleased,' she said quietly, 'Thank you Gerald. I know I owe this to you.' He did not deny it.

She walked out of Social Services into that beautiful July afternoon feeling as happy and excited as a young girl going on her first date. She had achieved her aim against all the odds. Couldn't wait to tell David. Janet slid into the stifling heat of her car, opened all the windows and pressed her music on. Joni Mitchell singing Chelsea Morning. Janet sang along all the way home, able at last to see a brighter future unfolding before her eyes. Zoe's visits would turn into happy times again; soon enough they would include Joe and Emma, and with the school holidays approaching, Leanne would be more than happy to let the girl stay with her grandparents for longer periods. Gradually Zoe would find herself sharing her time between her mother and her paternal family and in three years' time she would be old enough to decide where she wanted to live. As Janet veered into her drive and parked the car in front of the white garage door, her mind filled with optimism. She got out of the car and noticed the garden was bursting with gorgeous colours. The Silver Jubilee rosebushes were covered with perfectly formed pink blooms, the grass was densely green and in the middle of the lawn the Japanese acer was as delicately poised as she had ever seen it. There was beauty all around her and she had stopped noticing. But now Janet felt she was coming out of the woods and her eyes could see the world again. She walked into the house with a spring in her step and a smile on her lips.

That same day, however, Zoe made a discovery that would take her and her family straight back into the thickest, darkest parts of those very woods Janet had thought were now behind her.

26. The First Unsupervised Visit

When Janet was offered her first unsupervised visit, she assumed her efforts with Social Services had paid off, and with the school holidays soon to start, Gerald had been able to persuade Leanne to agree.

But it hadn't been like that. Leanne had been the one to come up with the idea. Gerald hadn't pushed her into it, far from it. She remembered the look on his face when she told him her decision. Surprise, gladness, but also concern. 'You know you don't have to do this,' he had said. 'Zoe is very settled now, are you sure you want to take any risks?' She remembered her reply with gratification. 'I am confident, Gerald,' she had said with a bright smile, 'I have a very good relationship with my daughter, and I don't want to deprive her any longer of the affection of her paternal grandparents.' Big time brownie points for her. Uncertain look in Gerald's eyes. But Gerald didn't know everything. He didn't know how much Ivor and Zoe hated each other and she couldn't tell him that. He didn't know sex had taken a nosedive, or that Ivor had threatened to walk out three times in the last two weeks. Leanne felt she was losing her grip. Something had to be done and unsupervised visits would hand Leanne power. Bad behaviour? No visit. Leanne smiled as she thought about that, puffing pleasurably on her cigarette whilst doing the dishes in her kitchen. That was one reason she wanted unsupervised visits to resume. But the greatest benefit of those visits would be to take Zoe away from the flat and give her and Ivor a chance to be on their own. Go out together. Have a good time. That was what they needed and that was the main reason Leanne wanted Zoe to stay with her grandparents again.

On the day Gerald gave Janet the good news, Leanne spoke to her daughter. Zoe had gone to Kylie's after school and would be home around six. Leanne grabbed a beer from the fridge. The flat was like an oven and a beer would cool her down nicely. She went to wait in the front room, looking forward to Zoe's excitement and gratitude. At ten past six the front door opened and slammed shut. Zoe's footsteps trod lightly up the stairs. Leanne heard her bag being dropped by the kitchen door and a minute later her daughter appeared at the lounge door. She stood there looking at her mother with her serious eyes staring disapprovingly at the bottle of beer.

'I thought you didn't drink before dinner,' Zoe said accusingly.

'I know sweetie, but today's a special day. I have some good news for you. Come and sit here with me,' she added, patting the cushion next to her on the couch. Once Zoe had sat herself down Leanne took her daughter's hand in hers and paused for a moment whilst peering into the girl's eyes. Zoe looked down at her trainers.

'Aren't you interested?' asked Leanne.

'Depends,' drawled Zoe in a sceptical voice.

'You're going to have your first unsupervised visit with your grandparents.'

Zoe's head whipped around, her eyes wide and unbelieving. 'When?' she asked quickly.

'Next Sunday.'

'Next Sunday,' repeated Zoe incredulously. 'The judge changed his mind?'

'Nothing to do with the judge,' chuckled Leanne, looking forward to getting credit for the new development. 'I suggested it to Gerald,' she added importantly. 'The judge put Social Services in charge of your life, not me, but of course they listen to what I have to say. If I say I think the time has come for you to see your grandparents again, they're prepared to try it out. Obviously if you were to start running away again, that would be the end of that. But I don't think you will, will you sweetie? You've grown up a lot in the last year.' She ran her fingers through her daughter's hair and added for more brownie points, 'you were right about growing your hair, it does look nice.'

Zoe was thunderstruck. Digesting what she had just heard. Coming to terms with the idea that her mother had been in control all along, not the judge. It was her mother who had stopped her seeing her grandparents and stopped her seeing her dad, not the judge. In a flash Zoe understood that her mother also held the power to decide when she might visit her father again and a powerful mix of hatred and resentment surged inside her.

'Aren't you pleased?' asked Leanne, with a hint of annoyance in her voice.

'When can I see Dad?' asked Zoe, staring at her trainers.

Her mother tensed up and took her hand away to pluck a fag out of the packet. She held the cigarette between her fingers without lighting it.

'Social Services would never agree to that,' she replied, and Zoe knew she was lying. She wanted to scream at her mother,

353

call her a liar, cry tears of rage that she had been subjected to months of horrible, supervised contact when her mum could have put an end to it. But now was not the moment to tell her mother what she thought of her, because if she did, she could forget visits to Granny and Grandad. Anyway, why had her mother suddenly decided she could visit her grandparents? She cast her an oblique glance. Summer holidays. She had often heard Granny give a little sarcastic laugh when Leanne became keen for Zoe to spend more time with her grandparents. 'School holidays,' she would say shooting Grandad a meaningful glance. Zoe understood, but didn't care. If school holidays meant she spent more time with her grandparents, why should that be a bad thing? But now she could see where her grandmother was coming from. Someone was pretending to do you a favour, when really, they were doing themselves a favour, and that's what stuck in your gullet, and it was sticking in Zoe's gullet just the same as it used to stick in Grandma's gullet. She sat silently staring at her trainers, pulling long wisps of wavy hair in front of her face.

Leanne felt her own annoyance rise. Her fingers tightened on the cigarette and after a moment's hesitation, she reached for the matches on the coffee table and lit it. Then she got up from the couch and went to stand by the open window, blowing the first plume of smoke in the direction of the street and not noticing that it floated back in, spiralling gently above her head in feathery grey threads. At this moment all Leanne noticed was the resentment filling her mind. She watched her daughter sitting sullenly on that couch and the itch to smack her across the face was overwhelming. But she knew what she had to lose by indulging that itch.

'Well,' she said coldly, looking down at her daughter, 'there I was thinking you'd be over the moon at visiting your grandparents unsupervised, but I was wrong. Contact couldn't have been that bad after all. Know what, I think I'll give Gerald a ring and cancel the whole thing. If it doesn't make you happy…' Her voice trailed off as she tapped her cigarette out of the window. The ashes floated lightly away in the warm breeze.

'It does make me happy,' Zoe said quickly, flicking her hair back and presenting her mother with a smile and wide innocent eyes, 'it's just that I haven't seen Dad for such a long time, I want to see him too.' She paused to check that her words were having the desired effect on her mother, whilst gloating privately over her lie. One day she would tell her mum how she had deceived her through all those years, and that would be a moment to relish, but for now she had to play her mum's game. 'I hate contact,' she added, 'and I want to see Granny and Grandad at home. We won't have to talk all the time; I can watch TV and do other stuff.' Predictably Leanne liked the news that Zoe didn't want to be talking to her grandparents all the time. Her face softened and she came back to the couch, stubbing the end of her cigarette in the ashtray as she sat down.

'You are pleased then?' she asked, patting her daughter's leg. Now the scenario she had played over and over in her mind was back on track and she could easily push away the little blip that had nearly spoiled it.

'I'm very pleased, Mum, thank you for telling Gerald. I can't wait for Sunday.' She pecked her on the cheek before leaving the room to go and do her homework on the kitchen table.

But in the kitchen Zoe didn't do any homework. She opened one book in front of her, for safety's sake, and stared blankly at the meaningless figures of a Maths problem. Her chest heaved lightly but she knew she was not about to have an asthma attack. What she felt was not the oppressive and threatening feeling of anxiety when something bad is happening or threatening to happen, no, what she felt was a mysteriously good feeling. The air filling her lungs was a positive force which she didn't understand, but which was giving her strength. Strength to do what she had been too weak or too uncertain to do in the last twelve months, but what was now a clear path ahead. Her mother had pretended she had to obey the judge, and it had been a lie. She had had power in her hands, and she had chosen to use that power to deprive her daughter of the company of the people who loved her, her dad, her grandparents, her aunty Emma. That could never be forgiven. Zoe felt suddenly liberated from all the mixed-up feelings she had had in relation to her mum. No more guilt, fear, shame or doubt, because in this moment Zoe knew that what she felt for her mum was simple hatred, clear and brittle as glass, and after Sunday she would not spend another day living with her mother.

*

On Sunday morning Janet awoke to a dim awareness of movement in the room. She extended her arm into the other side of the bed, and sure enough the solid surface of David's back eluded her. In a few minutes he would be back with two cups of tea. She flopped over, sinking into her pillow again, half asleep. Back in their working days the cups of tea heralded the special status of Saturdays and Sundays, and that made them special. But now every day was the same.

Except that today was not the same at all. Her eyes popped open as memory kicked in and she woke up fully to the miracle of today. She sat up, grabbed the extra pillow lying on the floor and tucked it behind her neck. It felt wonderfully cool against her skin. Today was the day she was going to see her granddaughter without a supervisor to wreck the visit. They would sit on the settee, have lots of hugs, read stories and chat freely.

She relaxed back into her pillows, closing her eyes again to shut the tears in. Looking back now, she couldn't believe the months of patient work she had put into this, couldn't believe that her reward had come at last. So close it seemed more unattainable than ever. And then she reminded herself, it would be over quickly. Zoe was coming for lunch and staying until late afternoon – Leanne had said she would pick her up between five and six.

But Janet hadn't spent that much time on her own with her granddaughter since…. her mind went blank as she struggled to work out when she had last seen Zoe. It was when Zoe had run away on the day of the Christmas Lights 2005, which was eight months ago. But before that…, she felt her chest tighten painfully at the memory of Zoe being dragged away to foster carers and tears came to her eyes. That had been around Easter, nine months before the Christmas Lights, and during Zoe's first few months with the foster carers, complete strangers to her little granddaughter, the girl had not been allowed any contact at all with her paternal family because the psychiatrist was assessing her.

357

Wave after bitter wave of pent-up resentment and anger now flooded Janet and tears ran down her face and neck, soaking her nightie. She reached for a handful of tissues on her bedside table and just as David entered the room, slightly stooped as if under the weight of two mugs of tea, she blew her nose loudly. He cast her a worried glance as he bent over to deposit the mugs on her bedside table and sat on the edge of the bed, taking her hand in his and looking distressed. Janet's emotions rattled him. Feeling powerless to soothe them away created unbearable pressure inside his head. As if the tears were a slur on him, as if they accused him of some foul deed he damn well knew he hadn't committed.

'Why are you crying, honey?' he asked. 'This is a good day,' he added hopefully.

'Do you know…?' replied Janet, sobbing her heart out at his use of the word honey, 'Do… do you know,' she blew her nose again, stumbled on the same words a couple more times and finally came out with her sentence, 'do you know that these bastards have stopped us seeing Zoe for seventeen months? SEVENTEEN MONTHS?' she repeated staring at him. He knew she wasn't attacking him, yet he felt attacked; he had to exert all the control he was capable of not to shout back, 'It's not my fault!' Instead, he squeezed her hand and said, 'I know, love, but why think about that today, when today is your victory?'

'A few hours, a few crumbs, you call that victory?' She snatched her hand out of his and buried her face in a fresh handful of tissues.

David felt himself drowning. He shook his head.

'I don't understand, Janet,' he said. 'You've been waiting for this day for months and now you seem to want to spoil it.'

There was a touch of irritation in his voice he knew he should have controlled, but he wasn't superhuman, they both knew that, and he couldn't cope with irrational emotion.

'I couldn't allow myself to hate them until today, can't you see that? I had to cooperate with them, didn't I? On my own.'

Now the accusation had come. He knew it. He had known all along this would be his fault after all and she was not crying because she was upset, she was crying at him. And he couldn't stand it.

'It was your choice Janet, don't blame me. I offered to come with you, and you said you couldn't rely on me to behave myself. You said you would deal with this alone and …'

'I know,' replied Janet, taking his hand in hers and giving him a rueful little smile, which momentarily lifted her ruined face. Relief flooded him, but still he felt some anger that he had been attacked at all. She squeezed his hand, 'I'm sorry,' she added, 'I've bottled up too much for too long, and now it's all coming out and you're on the receiving end. I'm sorry.'

David saw his chance to make a point he hadn't so far had the courage to make. He cleared his throat lightly, causing her to look up sharply.

'Janet,' he said looking down at their clasped hands on the beige duvet cover, 'I think we should be careful not to get into any more fights with Social Services.' She gave him a forlorn little smile, aware that her face must be a mess, with cruel wrinkles and sagging muscles making her look old.

'I must look terrible,' she sighed, bringing a tissue up to dab at her red swollen eyes.

'I don't care about that, and you know it,' said David gently, 'but Janet did you hear me?'

'I heard you,' she nodded.

'We must show Zoe a united front, agreed?'

'David, there's no reason to think she's going to complain about her life with Leanne. She seems quite happy. You've seen it. Lots of friends, lots of activities, she'll be happy to see us, I'm sure, but she's done all right without us, hasn't she?'

David's heart sank. Janet's feelings and moods were so tied up with the children and grandchildren, it was hard to take. Didn't he matter? Their happiness together? But now was not the time to bring up this particular gripe. Anyway, she couldn't help it and he loved her as she was.

'Janet, she's not twelve yet and she's been through a hard time. Give the girl a break. Give yourself a break. And promise me we won't make the same mistakes again. Look what it's done to you.' He held his wife's hand firmly. 'You've achieved what you have, and now we make it clear to Zoe that it's up to her to build on this. If she behaves, she'll have more and more visits with us, and if Joe behaves, he may get part custody again. Leanne will be glad to have some free time, as we know.'

'Joe will never bow to the system,' said Janet, her lips tight with sorrow.

'And that's his problem, honey. He's a grown-up man now.' His eyes bore into hers with absolute seriousness. She had to understand that he wouldn't stand any more destructive behaviour from anybody, especially a son who didn't seem to give two hoots about anyone except himself.

'You're right, David, I know you are.' She paused to give her husband a grateful little smile. Mechanically lifting a fresh tissue to her eyes, she added resignedly, 'To tell you the truth, I'm tired of it all anyway. Tired of fighting, tired of feeling let down.' She took a deep breath and gave David a bright smile

360

which came close to restoring her face. She pressed his fingers between hers, 'No more fights,' she said, 'and let's be glad of what've got.'

'That's my girl,' said David, bending over to kiss his wife. 'Now I'll go and make fresh tea.' He picked up the two mugs of cold tea and left the room, stooping as if concerned he might knock his head on the door frame. Janet smiled fondly as she watched him go.

*

Three and half hours later Zoe ran in through the wide-open front door shouting, 'Granny, Grandad, I'm here, I'm here!' and the sunshine seemed to come in with her. Granny came rushing out of the kitchen, where she'd been pretending to cook, and Grandad looked up from the newspaper he'd been pretending to read. The girl flew into her grandmother's arms and stood in clasped embrace as if she would never come out of it. Over her head Janet looked at her husband with a tortured mixture of pain and gladness in her eyes. 'What a crime the last eighteen months have been,' she seemed to be saying, 'but this is the best moment in my life.' David gazed at his wife holding her granddaughter and thought this might also be the best moment in his life. How Janet deserved this! Janet and Zoe looked like a statue of love, two stone characters entwined for etcrnity, with their arms tightly wrapped around each other as if to stop a possible enemy from trying to wrench them apart. He smiled with relief and a deep feeling of happiness swept through him, brushing aside any twinge of envy that might have tainted the moment for him.

But now Zoe was disentangling herself from her grandmother and rushing to him, then she was on his lap, her arms around his neck, her head buried just under his chin, her breathing just a little too fast but gradually slowing until it became a gentle murmur like the distant sound of the sea on a windless day. His arm tightened around the frail birdlike body of the child and shame cast a brief shadow in his mind. Had he forgotten how much he loved his granddaughter? Shame turned to anger. Had they made him forget? His hand gently stroked the child's head, snuggled against his neck. I belong here. David was silent. Janet was looking down on him and the radiance in her eyes took him back thirty years, when she had been beautiful in young motherhood, when she had proudly handed babies over for him to hold, turning him into a proud dad, and now she was doing it again, turning him into a proud grandfather, reminding him that this was what mattered in life. This above all. She never forgot, but he sometimes got distracted.

Zoe sat up and looked from one grandparent to the other. 'I can't believe I'm really here,' she said in wonder. 'Can you believe it?' Her eyes scanned the room, taking in every detail, every porcelain ornament, every vase, every picture on the wall, checking that it was all just as it should be in all the familiar places. Without leaving her grandfather's lap she swivelled around so she could scan the rest of the room. Then she inhaled deeply and said, 'Granny, I love the smell of roasting chicken,' and for some mysterious reason they all burst out laughing. She fell back into her grandfather's arms and closed her eyes. 'Home,' she whispered.

How can you, in five miserable hours, pack in eighteen months of missed stories, missed cuddles, of working in the garden with Grandad, watching TV with Granny, baking brownies, playing snakes and ladders, making new furniture for the doll's house, drawing on Granny's special art paper, it couldn't be done but Zoe was trying her best. She flitted from one thing to another, getting a taste of everything and quickly moving on to the next, like a child who wants to try every sweet on the sweet counter. Janet watched her with delight. There had only been one difficult moment, immediately after they had sat down to lunch, with the chicken sizzling on the table and the roast vegetables filling the room with their sweet aroma, and Zoe's eyes had suddenly misted over and her little mouth had turned down as she looked at her grandparents and said, 'I wish Dad was here.' But the moment had passed, Janet had replied, 'So do we, sweetheart, and hopefully that will happen soon. We're on the right road now.'

Zoe had not looked convinced, but she had nodded and once she tucked into her food, her happy mood returned. As if she had decided to be happy. Decided not to mull over all the bad things that had happened, that were still happening, as if she'd heard her grandfather that morning and had agreed with him. Yes, let's count our blessings and build on that. Janet was hugely relieved. She didn't want another fight now, what she wanted was more of this. Happy Sundays with Zoe, and soon with Joe and Emma there as well. As she watched her granddaughter lap up the happiness, she felt optimistic. Leanne would be only too keen to offload the girl onto them. Now the woman had the satisfaction of knowing she had come out a clear winner her other needs would come to the fore, and her other needs were not about Zoe. That was when the grandparents would become very useful once again. If they all played their cards right, Janet could visualise whole weekends and holidays with Zoe. Her efforts had not been in vain.

Little did she realise that everything was about to change in ways that she would never have expected.

27. A Summer Storm

The change happened just as the brass clock on the mantelpiece struck five.

Picture a mountain storm in high summer. Sunny skies one moment, darkness and thunder the next. You are unprepared. Unable to believe it is happening. Your energies do not rally as they should and you stare at the sky thinking this cannot be, it will pass now, and by the time you frantically look for shelter the first hailstones are already pelting down on you while thunder and lightning split the heavens above your head. Standing there in your shorts and T-shirt you know that you completely failed to appreciate the unpredictability and indifference of the elements.

Zoe's face went from sunny to dark just like that treacherous sky over the highest peak. The smile left her lips, her eyes turned sullen, and her body seemed to shrink as it turned in upon itself. She had been drawing and Granny had been sitting opposite her at the dining room table, doing a drawing of her own. The girl looked up at the first chime of the clock.

'Mum's picking me up in half an hour,' she said flatly, holding her crayon in the air. Janet glanced up and quickly caught David's eye as he looked up from his crossword puzzle.

'Help', was the message. David put his paper down and waited for Janet to speak.

'But hopefully you'll be able to come back next Sunday, or the one after. Gerald seemed to think that…'

'I'm not going back.'

It was the way she said it. Janet and David shot each other another panicked look. This morning they had been prepared with all the arguments why it would not be a good idea to start rebelling and running away again, but now, caught unawares like this, their minds were blank. As if they'd never seen this coming. Zoe had put her crayon down and she was looking at them seriously, like someone ten years older and with a kind of suicidal determination in her eyes.

'Sweetheart,' blurted Janet, desperately scrabbling inside her head for the arguments that had seemed so convincing that morning, 'I don't think you want to go down that road again. It didn't work the last time, did it?'

'I don't care. I'm not going back. I'm never going back. I'm never living with Mum again. I hate her.' The words came out frighteningly cold and emotionless. Janet frowned and David hoisted himself out of his seat and came to take his place at the table.

'We thought you were getting on all right for the last few months,' continued Janet, 'You hated contact, of course, and not being allowed to see your dad, but all that is coming to an end now. Things will get better and better.'

'Do you know,' Zoe burst out angrily, 'that it wasn't the judge who said I couldn't see you and Dad? It was Mum. If she had said I could see you, everyone would have agreed. That's what happened today. Suddenly she decides it suits her for me to come and spend Sunday with you, probably because she's going drinking with her friends, and so I'm allowed to go. She could have let me see you ages ago, and she could let me see Dad now. But she doesn't, does she? She doesn't care about me and that's why I hate her.' Tears of outrage welled and flowed. Janet and David watched and listened, unable to come up with anything of any use; the girl was right of course, but they knew better than to agree. 'I'm not going back, ever.' She stared at her grandparents who looked back at her with their own troubled eyes.

'Zoe, love,' Granny said at last, 'we understand how you feel, but you know what will happen if you refuse to go back, they'll just make you.'

'If they do, I'll run away again. I'll run away every day if I have to.'

'They'll take you away to another town. They can do that you know.'

'Then I'll run away from there. I'll hitch my way home. Or I'll kill myself. I'll stop eating. Go on a hunger strike. Granny what is the point of my life if I can't live with Dad? Or with you until I can live with Dad again.' Her voice had gone from angry to pleading. 'All I'm asking is to live with my dad, or with my grandparents. If they hate me so much, they won't allow that, then what is the point of my life?'

'The point, Zoe,' said David calmly, 'is that one day you will be able to go and live where you want. When you're fifteen …'

'Fifteen!' interrupted Zoe in outrage. 'I'm not even twelve yet. That's years away. I can't carry on like this for all those years, Granny I can't,' she shouted with such urgency in her voice that both grandparents were suddenly worried that her threats of suicide might come to something one day.

367

'Zoe,' said Janet in a placating voice, 'I know you hate living with your mother and Ivor, but if you are patient, I'm convinced that we can get you to spend more and more time with us, and to start seeing your father…'

'No,' shouted Zoe. 'I'm not going back, I hate them all, I'm never going back. Please don't make me.' She looked at them both pleadingly.

Janet shot David an alarmed glance. What would he say after their earlier conversation, what would he think of her if she gave in easily, and yet how could they turn into Zoe's enemies when they were all she had in her battle against the world? He was staring at his granddaughter, but Janet didn't know this look, she couldn't tell if he was about to lose his patience with the child or if he was thinking something else altogether. But what? She watched his hand move across the table and gently slip under the small hand of the young girl. Then slowly he brought his other hand over and held her little hand in both of his, as he might have a small, wounded bird fallen from the nest, delicately, without much hope of survival but with all the gentleness he was capable of. Zoe was following the movement of his hands and trying to elucidate the mystifying expression on his face with mild wariness. Was he going to oppose her with so much gentleness it would be impossible to fight?

'You know something young lady,' he said looking straight into her eyes, 'you are an infuriating little rebel, but I take my hat off to you. You have more determination and guts inside you than even your grandmother, and I never thought I'd meet her match. You will go far.' He patted her hand and a little smile pulled at the corners of his lips. As she listened Zoe's face began to crumble and when he finished, large fat tears were rolling down her cheeks, one behind the other, playing catch up, gathering momentarily on her upper lip, then riding over that minor obstacle, down and over her lower lip, down again to hang suspended on her jaw line before finally dropping onto her pink T-shirt where a wet mark spread in an uneven blotched shape. Her hand didn't move to brush away the wetness on her face, but once or twice her tongue licked at the saltiness. She didn't want to break the moment. Granny, she knew, would always take her side, but to hear her grandad say these things about her was the sweetest thing at the saddest moment, and she liked the taste of that feeling.

'Will it be the bathroom again?' he asked in a deadpan voice.

Zoe nodded.

'Then you'd better go now, because I'm pretty sure I've just heard a car pull up at the front of the house. Sure enough, a horn tooted imperiously at that moment and Zoe's eyes widened in alarm. She snatched her hand away from her grandfather's hold and after giving them both a scared, desperate look, ran upstairs towards the bathroom.

'Are you going to tell her Zoe's locked herself in the bathroom, or am I?' asked David.

'You better go,' replied Janet. 'Safer. You know what the sight of that woman does to me.'

David stood up and stared at nothing for just a few seconds. The impatient horn honked again, and he walked off slowly towards the street. Janet went to the window and observed the scene from a hidden angle. David always stooped, that was the way he walked, but today she saw a weariness in that stoop that sent a pang clawing at her heart. How different this was from the way he had visualised his retirement, yet he never complained, never tried to make her feel bad about the way things had gone because of her. The way he was now leaning into the car window with his elbow resting on the top of the car, was so essentially him that it brought a lump to her throat. Yet she knew that when he returned, the hug she would give him would fail to convey the poignant intensity of her feelings. When they were young 'I love you' had meant something big and powerful, but now it meant something deeper whilst sounding unavoidably banal.

She watched David straighten up slowly. He stood there for a painful minute, his eyes following Leanne's car as she backed into next door's drive, turned around in an angry screech of crunching tyres and drove off. Then he shuffled slowly back up their little path.

'She said she would send the police over to get her,' he said with a shrug. 'We're at war again.' He looked as if he was already defeated, before any real battles had even started.

*

Leanne drove home trembling with rage, but she knew some of her anger was directed at herself. She had been a fool. Even that wimp Gerald had tried to warn her. But she had been so confident, so damn confident, that even now she couldn't quite accept what she had heard. Maybe the grandparents had locked Zoe in the bathroom. Maybe when the police got there, they would set her free and she would tell them what had really happened. As Leanne stamped furiously on the brake when a pedestrian stepped gaily onto the crossing without looking, vivid pictures of happy outings with Zoe came flashing into her mind, driving her anger into higher and higher gears. Nobody would tell her that Zoe hadn't enjoyed that shopping trip two weeks ago, she got new jeans and a new Gap top for god's sake. Leanne found a parking space quickly, never a problem on a Sunday, and slid out of the car, slamming the door behind her, in the way she told the girls not to do. Although she was still wearing the high heels she'd had on all afternoon in the pub, she ran across the street and up the stairs to the landing where the telephone sat on its flimsy gold table with a chipped black top. She was still trembling as she flicked the pages of the address pad next to the phone and she glared at Ivor when he emerged from the front room to find out what the hell was going on. She hammered the numbers in and waited.

'Sunday,' she muttered, 'the bastards won't be there.' But someone did answer.

'My daughter's been abducted,' she shouted into the phone, 'I want someone to go and get her now.'

Slowly the person on duty managed to get a vaguely coherent story out of Leanne, and then asked, 'Is the girl at risk?'

'What do you mean, is she at risk, she's been abducted,' shouted Leanne at the moron at the other end.

'But you say she's with her grandparents. I take it they don't want to hurt her.'

'Not exactly,' replied Leanne reluctantly, 'but she is at risk of emotional abuse. That's what the judge said. Emotional abuse.' Her knuckles were white from clutching so tightly at the phone. The exchange ended and as she finally slammed the phone back in its base, she looked up at Ivor with that dangerous light in her eyes and said accusingly, 'Why didn't you stop me agreeing to these stupid unsupervised visits?'

'What did they say?' he asked, ignoring her attack.

'It'll have to wait till tomorrow 'cos it's not an emergency. Not in their book it isn't, but it is in mine. Can you believe it?' she shrieked, 'can you believe after all we've been through they would still try it on? On the very first visit? What do they think they're going to achieve? That's it now, they can kiss goodbye to unsupervised visits, in fact they can kiss goodbye to all visits. I'm going to really put my foot down this time, and as for Zoe, grounded for a month, that's what she's gonna get. She can spend her school holidays pent up in the flat.'

She was trembling so much she couldn't get her cigarette to light. Ivor did it for her and she inhaled greedily, one long drag after the other. Ivor went over to the fridge and pulled a beer can out, but she stopped him with a sharp gesture of her hand.

'Get me a whiskey,' she snapped, 'a beer's not what I need just now.'

Ivor sighed quietly and reached for the bottle of cheap Scotch in the top kitchen cabinet. Leanne always wanted whiskey to calm herself down, but all it ever did was make her aggressive. He was in for it tonight, he just knew it, and wondered whether he could think of an excuse for getting the hell out. But much as he scrabbled around in his mind, nothing materialised.

As he listened to Leanne's rants and digested the news that Zoe, instead of spending less time with them and more with her grandparents, was now set to be in the flat all summer, the thought crossed his mind that life with Leanne was possibly coming to an end. He had seen her that afternoon flirting with his friends, and although it was good to be with a desirable woman, the drawbacks were beginning to outweigh the advantages. He needn't have worried, however, about Zoe being a burden to him through the summer, because Zoe was not about to come back to the flat.

*

The following morning Gerald was knocking at the Milton's door at 9.30 exactly. Next to him stood the big policewoman, looking relaxed and unafraid. But this time Janet was ready for them. She had spoken to her lawyer first thing and he had been adamant that without a recovery order they had no right to lay a finger on Zoe. She didn't need to lock herself in the bathroom and he would come over in person if needed. With his hourly rate flashing in her mind, Janet expressed the hope that that would not be necessary. But the only reason she didn't call back to ask for his presence was the cost.

The two hours she and David spent battling with Gerald and PC Harris proved exhausting. They were bullied, threatened, accused of fantastical crimes against their granddaughter, branded with motives they did not have, criticised for loving their son, held responsible for the way Zoe felt about her mother and generally denounced for all the bad things that had happened since Leanne and Joe had split up. Apparently, they were even responsible for the split up because Leanne had depicted them as interfering in-laws who took a dislike to her from the moment they shook her hand that very first time.

Janet and David fought back. But every move they made seemed to sink them further into the entanglements of a debate that was so unfairly weighted against them they let their indignation cloud their judgement. Zoe, who had been sitting tightly wedged between her grandparents, tried to come to their rescue on the issue of her feelings towards her mother, but her statement that 'she had always hated her mother, and that was because of the way her mother treated her and nothing to do with her grandparents, only served to inflame their hostility towards the girl. A creature lacking in all the normal feelings one expects to find in a child, particularly in a girl. Never mind that PC Harris had endlessly rowed with her own mother, she had also loved her. Love was what you felt for your parents, end of story. And if it wasn't, then there was something seriously wrong with you. As there clearly was with this little madam.

All the time the arguments were raging back and forth between the adults, Janet could feel Zoe trembling. It wasn't a tremble in her hand, or in her arm, or in her leg. No, she trembled from head to toe until the man and the woman left, and even after David had taken them to the door, Janet could still feel ripples travelling up and down her granddaughter's body. She hugged her close and the girl burst into tears.

'Gran, can you see how much they hate me?'

'They don't, sweetheart, they're just cross because you will not do as you're told.' But even as she said it, she knew she was not being honest. 'But I can see why you feel they hate you,' she added, 'they seem to want to crush you, don't they?'

'Yes,' nodded Zoe with tears running freely down her face, 'I think they want to kill me. Gran, they make me scared.'

Janet hugged the girl closer.

'We'll keep fighting,' she said as David walked back into the room. He slumped into one of the two armchairs and ran his fingers through his curly grey hair.

'It feels' he said meditatively, 'like a horrible case of déjà vu.'

Zoe didn't bother to ask what 'deejevoo' meant. Not good news, she could tell that much, and she didn't want any more bad news. But it had been her decision to take this course of action, and now she would have to see it through. No good being a cry-baby. Granny surprised her by saying she should see a doctor and have some time off school to recover from the shock of what had happened that morning. Zoe didn't think she needed to see a doctor but staying home with Granny sounded good and she watched in anticipation as Granny phoned the surgery to make an appointment. The receptionist said she would ask Doctor Bates and phoned back a few minutes later to say he was able to fit them in at the end of the afternoon. Granny couldn't believe her luck.

Zoe liked Dr Bates but when they walked into his surgery that day, she thought he gave her a funny look. Had he heard what a bad person she was? He seemed friendly enough as he listened to Granny's explanations, nodding his head every so often, and when he looked at Zoe again, he gave her one of the nicest smiles any grownup had ever given her. It was a smile that said, 'I like you, I'm sincerely sorry to hear of all your problems and now I'm going to do whatever I can to help.' Then he turned to his computer and typed quickly, changing his words a couple of times. The note came sliding out of the printer and he handed it to Granny, saying 'Send that to the school and I'm sure nobody will give you any trouble, specially at the end of term.'

As Zoe left, holding her granny's hand, she thought there had been something else in the doctor's eyes, as if he was saying sorry about something he'd done. But Dr Bates hadn't done anything, so she must have imagined it. The main thing was, he'd written that note saying she was suffering from nightmares and stomach cramps due to shock and anxiety, and she didn't have to go to school for the next two weeks.

They might come and take her away before the end of the two weeks, but she wouldn't think about that now. Maybe something would happen to stop that happening. Maybe this new judge wouldn't give the recovery order, maybe he would say she could stay with her grandparents and she didn't have to go and live with strangers. She squeezed Granny's hand and said, 'Do you think I'll be staying with you for two weeks?'

'Let's hope so,' said Granny. 'Let's take a day at a time and enjoy every moment.'

They did. To Zoe this period felt like the happiest in her entire life. She rediscovered with a sense of wonder what it was like to live with people who loved her. She had known the love had never gone away, her dad loved her, and her grandparents loved her, and Aunty Emma, in a slightly different way loved her too. But she had forgotten what it was like to be immersed in this love from the moment you got up in the morning to the time when the adults tucked you in and said goodnight. The word love sounded big and full of mystery, yet in everyday life it was nothing extraordinary and you didn't even know it was there until it was gone.

Zoe had tried in the past to explain to Kylie what it was like to live in the flat, but she knew that Kylie had not understood. Kylie had never lived with people who didn't love her so she couldn't understand. Stefan knew what it meant to feel unloved, because his mother had left him, and the hurt was there all the time. But he didn't understand what it was like to live without daily love. One day he had even said to Zoe, 'At least your parents both want you,' and she had heard a hint of bitterness in his voice. And as for social workers, unless you told them your mother was beating you up on a daily basis, they thought you had nothing to complain about. That was

376

why Zoe welcomed smacks and threats of physical violence, because she knew that was her only hope of anyone believing she was unhappy. Yet smacks were not the problem. The problem was missing the vital ingredient that made life good. The vital ingredient that everyone else looked for all the time, you only had to watch East Enders or Coronation Street to see that, people wanted love, and if you listened to all the pop songs, you could hear that everyone was looking for love, but if you were a kid and you said, 'I'm not happy here because they don't love me,' the answer you got was, 'what do you mean they don't love you? They don't hit you, do they? You're not abused, are you? What more do you want? And anyway, what do you know about love, you're only a kid. Kids know nothing. If you haven't got any bruises to show us, then get back home and stop moaning, little madam.'

Zoe had tried to think of ways to explain it, and both Granny and Aunty Emma had said useful things like, 'It's hard when people are not on your side,' and 'people who love you want you to be happy,' or 'people who love you never want to hurt you.' All that was true enough, but when Zoe tried to apply those ideas to her mother, she could see that Leanne would come up with perfectly convincing counter arguments. 'When have I not been on your side? When Jessie didn't want you to come to town with us a couple of weeks ago, whose side did I take? And when Ivor said it was time you got a paper round and earned some money, whose side did I take?' And that would be the end of that argument. Taking Zoe shopping, or taking her out for a curry would show that Leanne wanted her to be happy, and if Zoe said that sometimes they made fun of her in the flat, and she was hurt, Leanne would say that if you got hurt because of a little light banter, that was your problem, but it certainly didn't show that other people were out to hurt you. That light banter, Your Honour, she would say, is part of our family life. We all do it to each other, and it's just a bit of fun. But Zoe, Your Honour, will not tolerate any fun. She is the one who doesn't like us, not the other way round.'

Which was why there was no point trying to explain to social workers, guardians, judges or anybody else why she hated living in the flat, the only way to make people listen was to run away. Perhaps if she ran away every day for a year, they would let her go and live with her dad. Or with her grandparents. Zoe knew that the recovery order had been granted and Gerald and the hateful policewoman would soon be knocking at the door to take her away. She had been told she wouldn't be forced to go back to her mum, but she wouldn't be going to Jean and Owen either because they had another child staying with them and they didn't want two. There would be some new foster carers and Zoe was nervous about that. She reflected that she shouldn't worry about it because on the morning they came to get her, she wouldn't be there anyway. She had her plan.

*

Meanwhile Sally Walker, from the fostering team, was tearing her hair out. She couldn't believe that the idiots in the childcare team had decided Zoe needed to be in care again. And that was the problem with childcare social workers. It's easy to remove kids from troubled families when it doesn't fall to you to find a better alternative. And for Zoe Milton, the only place that would be any good was Jean and Owen's. The couple hadn't said outright that they didn't want to take Zoe back, but they came up with one reason after another why they couldn't have her just then. Fair enough, they had another child there at the moment, but they had been known to take on more than one child at any given time. So why not this time? They talked about a summer holiday and not wanting to take two children, they talked of a plan to redecorate the bedrooms, and every time Sally found a way around the problem, they came up with another excuse, all the while saying they wished they could help and agreeing that coming back to them would be best for Zoe. Sally's confidence that she would get the couple to agree began to crumble as she read their latest email. Family visits was now the reason why they needed their spare room for the summer. Sally picked up the phone, dialled Jean's number and hung up after the second ring tone. What was the point? They were not going to have her, and she had better look for another family. The trouble was, there weren't any other families. Well, there were the Davies, but they would be useless with an eleven-year-old girl.

By the end of the day however, it was the Davies she had had to turn to. She told Gerald she didn't think the placement would be suitable, but he wanted Zoe in care as soon as possible and he grabbed the name and address without waiting to hear any more. Sally hung up thinking she would keep working on Jean and Owen, and when the placement with the Davies collapsed, as it would, she might be able to convince them to have Zoe back.

28. Running Away with Granny

When the phone call came to say that they would be coming to take her to her new foster family the following day, Zoe was ready. She shrugged and pretended that she was resigned to it. But after Granny had tucked her in and said goodnight for what would be the last time, she didn't go to sleep. She listened for the sounds of her grandparents going to bed and when the house had gone completely quiet, she crept out of bed and tiptoed to her wardrobe. She pulled her rucksack out and packed it with as many of her clothes as she could fit in, leaving a little space at the top.

Then she went to her door and listened with her ear pressed against the wood. All was silent but there was a danger that her grandparents might be reading in bed. Still their bedroom was quite a long way from the kitchen and if she got caught, Zoe would say she'd had a dream and woken up thirsty. She pressed down on her door handle and when it squeaked, she froze. The house remained silent. She pulled the door open very slowly and stood listening. As all was quiet, she tiptoed to the kitchen, cut across the darkness to where the fridge was and pulled the heavy door open, spilling light into the room.

The shelves packed with carefully wrapped food brought a couple of brief hot tears to her eyes, but this was not the time to be a softie. She looked towards the door again, quickly pulled the cheese and butter out, and pushed the fridge door almost shut, so that only a trickle of light came to help her. She lifted the top of the bread bin and pulled six slices out. She held her breath as she pulled the cutlery drawer delicately and managed to lift a knife out without disturbing anything else. Then she made three big sandwiches. The butter was hard and wouldn't spread, and the cheese was difficult to cut without banging the knife on the worktop, but finally it was all done, and she wrapped the sandwiches in silent cling film.

Then she put the cheese and butter back where they had been and swept the worktop clean with the side of her hand, catching the crumbs with her other hand and dropping them in the bin. On her way out she plucked an apple from the fruit bowl, and carried everything, including the knife into her bedroom. If she left a knife lying about and Granny went to the kitchen in the night, she would notice it and wonder what was going on. You couldn't keep anything from Granny. In her room Zoe had already stashed away a bottle of water and a packet of chocolate biscuits. This would keep her going until Stefan came to the rescue. She had taken some money from Granny's jewellery box, where she kept her cash, and she had a note ready that she would leave on the bed to say sorry, and she would pay her back later. She set her alarm clock for five and stuffed it under her pillow so that nobody except her would hear it. Then she tried to sleep.

When the alarm gave its muffled vibrations from under her pillow, Zoe emerged from her vivid dreams into tiredness and confusion. Why did it feel as if she'd hardly slept and why was the alarm under her pillow? She pulled it out, looked at the time and began to remember. She snuggled up under her warm duvet and closed her eyes again. Perhaps she didn't want to do this after all. The derelict house was where she was planning to hide, and Stefan had promised to bring an old sleeping bag over. Zoe and Kylie had had their secret den in the garden of that old boarded up house and Zoe remembered with pride how well that had worked out when she'd first run away. After that however Kylie had been strictly banned from going anywhere near the place ever again, and Kylie was obedient. Stefan on the other hand, impressed by Zoe's daring escapade, had wanted to see the famous den. The two children had then started nosing around the derelict house and had found a way in by removing a couple of loose planks from a downstairs window. It was an old sash window, stuck in a half open position, and the children had clambered in. It had been too dark to explore properly but Zoe had thought that with a torch it would make another good hiding place. Now she had two torches in her rucksack, and she would have to apologise to Grandad about that later.

Zoe glanced at the alarm clock and was horrified to see that fifteen minutes had passed, and she was still in bed. She kicked her duvet off, got dressed quickly and hitched her rucksack on her back. She grabbed Flossie from the bed, crept out of her room and very quietly made her way towards the front door. She tried to ignore the fast beating of her heart and concentrated on stopping her shoes from squeaking on the wooden floor in the hallway. The key was in the front door and now it was just a matter of turning it and pushing down on the smooth white handle. The front door never squeaked and if Zoe closed it slowly and carefully behind her, the only sound would be a light click which couldn't possibly wake anybody up, especially when her grandparents' bedroom was at the other end of the bungalow. Her heart was racing now, pushing a lump into her throat. Once out of the house, she had a long way to walk to the derelict house and she knew that every adult who saw a young girl like her out and about so early in the morning was a potential danger. She pulled the door open and noticed the swishing sound it made as it brushed against the carpet. Outside the morning air was fresh and pleasant against the skin, cool but with the promise of summer warmth later. The sky was a light airy grey, and the breeze was already tearing ragged gaps between the clouds, revealing pinkish blue fragments. Birds were tweeting busily in Grandad's hedges, but apart from that all was perfectly still and quiet. She stepped out and pulled the door gently behind her. Just before it clicked shut a voice froze her hand on the handle.

'Zoe, where are you going?'

*

Zoe stopped breathing and closed her eyes. After all the care she had taken, after getting so far in her plan, this failure was a bitter blow. End of plan. End of escape. Back to nasty reality. Hateful foster carers. Pointless life. But at least nobody knew about the derelict house and she could try again another day. They couldn't keep an eye on her all the time. Slowly she turned around to face her grandmother who was standing in the hall in her white dressing gown, with eyes full of worry and sadness and hair sticking out in every comical direction. If Zoe hadn't been so anxious, she would have laughed.

'Granny, I'm running away please don't stop me. I don't want to go to foster carers.' She gave her grandmother a pleading look.

'Running away to where Zoe?' asked Granny, shaking her head.

'Dad's shed,' lied Zoe, knowing that any adult in the family, no matter how much they loved her, would have been appalled at the mention of a derelict house.

Granny shook her head in a pitiful admission that she didn't know what to do next. Zoe stepped back into the house and took her grandmother's hand in her own and said, 'Granny, I'm not doing this to make you unhappy, it's just that I can't go back to foster carers again.'

And then Granny changed. Zoe watched the transformation in wonder. Her grandmother straightened up, ran her fingers through her hair and absentmindedly tightened the belt around her waist. Her eyes had come to life again, and behind the eyes Zoe could see some fast thinking taking place. Granny glanced at her watch. A plan was forming inside her grandmother's head and Zoe's heart started beating fast as she watched, holding her breath.

'Remember what you said you'd love to do after watching that nature programme the other day?' asked Granny.

'Go and see the puffins on that amazing island?' said Zoe questioningly.

'Yes,' replied Granny. 'I'm going to take you there today.'

Zoe's eyes widened. For years she had wanted to see a real live puffin and now, on what had threatened to be the worst day in her life, she was going to see one. She was reeling with a mixture of disbelief and enchantment. Granny went off to get ready and Zoe sat on the settee in the lounge with her rucksack between her legs cautiously allowing her excitement to mount inside her chest. She could barely remember the last time she had a day out with her grandmother, and now not just a day out, but the best day out she could have wished for. Granny reappeared, her short grey hair neat and tidy, her rucksack dangling from one hand and her car keys in the other.

'Let's go,' she whispered a little tensely. 'I have binoculars for both of us.'

'What about Grandad?' asked Zoe, slightly disappointed that the bird lover in the family wouldn't be there to share her pleasure at seeing puffins.

'He's still asleep,' replied Gran, 'I've left him a note but didn't say where we were going. Nobody's going to stop us having a good time today.'

'What if they're all really angry with you, Granny?' asked Zoe, running to keep up with her grandmother.

'I've nothing to lose Zoe. They can't hurt me any more than they've already done.'

Zoe nodded as she got into the back of the car. It was good to know Granny felt exactly as she did about all this, and as the car filtered into the early morning traffic Zoe and her grandmother exchanged a look of wicked delight in the rear-view mirror. A day stolen from the authorities. The clock showed 6.45 and by the time Gerald knocked on their door with his recovery order they would be waiting for the first boat to the island. Janet's heart was beating noticeably faster than usual, but she told herself that she wasn't exactly committing a criminal offence, even if their adventure went against the sacrosanct Care Plan. She turned left onto the main road out of town and even though she was in hurry to get to the dual carriageway, she minded her speed. There was often a traffic cop hiding somewhere along that stretch and the last she needed was to get stopped, even if it was only for a speed fine. After they passed the end of the speed limit sign, she opened the throttle and a surge of elation swept through her. They had made it and she felt as if she had just robbed a bank.

By the time they got to the small harbour, where the little boat picked up visitors to the island, the sky had cleared with only a few fluffy white clouds hanging lazily in an immensity of blue. They parked the car in the field allocated for that purpose and Zoe hitched her rucksack on her back, bursting with anticipation. This was pure delight, pure adventure, and after the months of deprivation she had endured, the excitement sent tingles all down her arms, back and legs. She breathed in the salty tang of the sea, and as they walked down to the little jetty, she thought waves had never glittered so brightly in the sun. Her rucksack felt light as she had taken all the clothes out, but she had her picnic, she had Flossie, and Granny had given her a pair of binoculars. Sometimes, Granny had said, the puffins left the islands in July, so they must be prepared for not seeing that many, but it was unlikely they wouldn't see any at all. Puffins, Zoe thought, were the best birds ever, and there had been a time when she had been showered with puffin gifts, puffin cards for her birthday, small ceramic puffins to have on her windowsill in her bedroom, and she had even had a puffin plate and a puffin beaker. But now she was going to see the real thing and she couldn't wait.

As the boat pulled out to sea, Zoe felt a lump rise in her throat. She was sitting on the wooden bench along the side and had to twist slightly to look ahead. The feeling of freedom was exhilarating, lifting her spirit into space where nobody could come and get her, where she could fly like the herring gulls circling above. Her eyes gobbled up the blue, the vastness of the sea and the distant shape of the island on the horizon. One of the gulls following in the wake of the boat emitted a shrill cry and then all the birds squawked and flapped their wings at each other, before resuming their gentle gliding.

And it was then, as Zoe's eyes left the gulls to scan the sea again, that she saw it.

'Gran,' she exclaimed with tremendous excitement, 'look, I've just seen one, oh my god, it's tiny, I thought puffins were quite big, look another one, they're like bullets shooting along. Gran, it's amazing! I've seen a real puffin.'

A young couple of birdwatchers smiled indulgently, and the other heads on the boat followed her extended arm in the hope of rediscovering inside themselves something akin to the enthusiasm of a child.

'You're going to see a lot more,' said the young man, 'they're still on the island, and some are still feeding their young, so you might see some with tiny fish hanging from their beaks.' Zoe looked at him with eyes wide with wonder. The island was getting closer and there were more and more birds as they pulled in near the shore. Plenty of puffins, but also razorbills, guillemots and great black-backed gulls looking like predatory giants next to the smaller birds. Zoe knew that the big gulls were quite capable of eating puffins and she felt a surge of hatred towards them.

They landed, paid their fee and started walking along the path which took visitors to the cliffs that were home to the island's puffins. Zoe would have run up the slope but her grandmother was trudging up slowly, a little out of breath, and the girl had to hold back, watching all the other people walking past them. Finally, they got there, and Zoe stopped in awe. Puffins everywhere. Flying off the cliff edge, coming in to land, standing around unfazed by the people watching them. Wonderfully comical, they were like little clownish people, with their large multicoloured beaks emitting no sound when they opened and closed them, as if communicating in deaf language, toddling along, diving into their burrows, emerging again and standing at the entrance as if mounting guard. A world of strangely endearing little creatures that she could have watched all day, not even needing her binoculars as they were all so close. At Granny's request, however, she agreed to leave puffin land and walk around the rest of the island, holding hands with her grandmother for long stretches. At one point they stopped to watch rabbits running and hopping freely in the expanse of low vegetation. Until then Zoe had only seen rabbits in cages and in petting farms but here they enjoyed their freedom. Janet and Zoe carried on walking up along the path until they reached a high point from where you could see armies of gulls squawking and squabbling on impossibly steep cliffsides. This was a good time to take the binoculars out and Zoe wished her grandad had been there to talk about the birds they could spot.

When they sat down to have their picnic great black-backed gulls circled above their heads threateningly. Zoe thought their wingspan was as wide as she was tall, and their hooked yellow beaks looked like they could do your face plenty of damage. She held on tight to her sandwich and stuffed it down quickly. Gulls were known to dive and try to take your food off you and these huge gulls were scary. Just as Zoe bit into her first chocolate biscuit, one of the gulls landed in a flap of wings just a few feet away. Zoe quickly pushed the packet of biscuits back into her rucksack. Then she hid the biscuit she was eating with her other hand and only relaxed once all her food was gone. The can of coke Granny had bought for her in the garage was of no interest to the gulls, yet they stood there watching. Zoe was glad when Granny finished the coffee in her flask and they could get up, feeling bigger now than the mean looking birds. Slowly the giant gulls opened their wings and in a few powerful flaps took off gracefully towards another horizon holding a different promise of food. Granny and Zoe walked on, admiring the rocky coast and hoping to catch sight of a seal or two from the clifftops further up the island.

'I wish I could come and live here,' said Zoe wistfully as they made their way back towards the area where the puffins had their burrows. 'I would feel safe here,' she added, and Granny gave her hand a squeeze without replying. They had another fifteen minutes watching the puffins and then it was time to join the other people making their way to the jetty where the last boat of the day was waiting for them. Getting back on the boat and watching the island recede in the distance was sad. Puffins skimmed the waters in their bullet like way, getting rarer as the boat made its way towards the mainland. Zoe kept her eyes firmly on the horizon behind her, as if to hang on to the magic of the day for as long as possible.

When they got back to the car Granny phoned Grandad and told him where they had been. There was a long silence as she listened to what he had to say, then she said, 'Well, we're coming home now anyway, and Zoe can start in her new foster placement tomorrow. It's only a day for goodness' sake. She's had the best day in her life, except that you weren't with us. She kept saying, "I wish Grandad was here." We may stop for a bite to eat, but we'll be back in plenty of time for Zoe to get a good night's sleep and be ready for tomorrow.'

Zoe looked up anxiously at her grandmother's back, and the smile she saw in the rear-view mirror failed to reassure her. They sat in the car, clicked their safety belts on and Granny eased out of her space on the bumpy ground of the field. For quite a few miles they were on small roads and Granny had to concentrate as she might have to squeeze by or even reverse if a car came the other way. Silence and tension hung in the car, destroying all the good memories of the day. When they turned onto the main road, Granny gave Zoe another smile in the mirror.

'Don't worry, love,' she said. 'We knew they wouldn't be pleased, so this is no surprise. We'll get a lecture when we get back, or tomorrow morning, they'll tell me I'm a very bad person, they may ground you for a while, but hey, wasn't it worth it? Wasn't that one of the best days ever?' Now Zoe cheered up and they fell into chatting about what they had seen and done. The road straightened out and Granny accelerated, as if she was suddenly quite keen to get home.

'Gran, watch it,' shouted Zoe in alarm, 'there's a police car ahead, over there.'

Granny glanced at the speedometer and said there was nothing to worry about, she was well within the speed limit. But now a policeman had come out of his car and was flagging them down whilst finishing a conversation on his mobile phone. Granny looked flustered and confused. Either her speedometer had stopped working or the policeman was going mad. She had been doing fifty-five. She pulled in, parked behind the police car and pressed the switch to let the window down. She looked up at the police officer ready to argue her case, whilst remaining very polite of course. He didn't give her time to say anything.

'Mrs Janet Milton?' he asked in a neutral voice. He was a youngish man, with fair hair and had he smiled, his face would have been pleasant. But he didn't smile.

'Yes,' replied Janet, her mouth going abruptly dry. She looked at the man in uniform questioningly. Weren't the police supposed to protect you, wasn't that their role, why was this one suddenly so frightening and how come he knew her name?

'Is that your granddaughter, Zoe Milton sitting in the back?' he asked again. Granny's head turned automatically towards Zoe as she answered 'yes' and was shocked at the girl's pallor. 'Are you all right?' she asked, reaching behind to touch the girl's cheek. 'Officer,' she said, turning back to him, 'my granddaughter suffers from asthma, I'm concerned…'

'Have you got your inhaler?' he asked, leaning forward into the window to address Zoe.

She nodded.

'Have it ready,' he said, not unkindly. 'Now take all your things,' his eyes swept the back of the car where her rucksack was, as well as the clothes she had spilled onto the backseat, 'and come over to sit in the back of my car.'

Zoe started trembling. She gave her grandmother a panicked look and shook her head as if to say, 'please don't make me do this.' Janet looked up at the police officer and said, 'Officer, this is very frightening for Zoe, could she…'

'You should have thought of the consequences before taking her away against the order of the court, Mrs Milton. If Zoe is now upset, you only have yourself to blame.' His young face hardened as he said this, and he looked devoid of human emotions.

'Do you realise,' asked Janet, talking with the gentle kindness of the older to the younger generation, 'that you are causing my granddaughter a great fright in the name of child protection? Does that make sense to you?'

'Mrs Milton,' replied the young officer in the voice of an automaton, 'it is not for me to pass judgement on the merit of the case. I'm just obeying orders.' His eyes turned to Zoe as he jerked his head in the direction of his car. 'Are you coming? Or will I have to drag you out?' he asked.

'Just obeying orders,' sighed Janet under her breath, but refrained from adding, 'like Hitler's minions.' She placed her hand on Zoe's arm and squeezed it gently. 'I'm sorry the day has to end like this, sweetheart, but we did have a good time. Now best if you go with the officer and do as you're told. You will be taken to your foster family, where they would have taken you this morning anyway, so …' The sound of a police siren screaming from down the road behind them made Janet and Zoe turn their heads in unison. The young police officer looked up too. Someone else in trouble, thought Janet, with a kind of relief that she wasn't the only one being stopped by the police on this quiet country road when the sun was still shining brightly at the end of what could have been a perfect summer day. Her eyes widened when the police car's siren died as the brightly painted vehicle slowed down before swerving neatly into the lay by and coming to a halt inches behind her own car. She looked up sharply at the young officer. His eyes were fixed on the other car with calm expectancy. Janet became aware of Zoe's hand pulling at her arm.

'What's going on?' whispered Zoe 'Are they going to take us to prison?' Her hand was trembling, and Janet grabbed it firmly. 'Of course not, sweetheart,' she mustered a brave smile from a place inside her where smiles still existed, 'We haven't committed any crime.' At that moment the two policemen loomed up in their dark uniforms by the side of the car, cutting off the sun. The new one was older and something in the lines on his face made him kinder looking, but there was nothing kind in his voice as he uttered his little speech: 'Mrs Milton I am here to charge you with the abduction of your granddaughter Zoe Milton, and I will ask you to follow me to the police station. Zoe,' he added in a voice that brooked no dissent, 'will you please follow Mr Smith here into his car. He will take you to the family where you should have gone this morning.' He stepped aside with military stiffness to let Zoe get out of the car, which she did without further delay. She grabbed her rucksack, stuffed all her clothes in it and said in a pinched voice, 'Bye Granny.' She wanted to add 'Thank you for today,' and show the policemen that they may be arresting them now, but they had failed to stop them having a good day. Show some spirit. Instead fear tied a dry knot in her gullet and she just walked with her head down to the police car in front. Beaten. Again.

29. The Unprofessional Social Worker

Sally Walker, the fostering officer, had been right about the placement with the Davies, except that it lasted even less than she had anticipated. By the end of two weeks the querulous couple wanted to be shot of a girl who was difficult and hostile. You couldn't blame them, except that most foster carers made some effort to give a child time to settle. But not Mr and Mrs Davies. Now Sally sat at her desk feeling depressed. It was obvious to her that the place for Zoe was her grandparents' home, the kid was shouting loud enough from every available rooftop, but no, Gerald wanted her in care, and Sally knew damn well the only reason Gerald wanted that was because he was shit scared of Gail. The ridiculous Care Plan had her signature all over it. Sally herself had moved from the childcare team to the fostering team soon after Gail had been appointed Team Manager. She knew she couldn't work with the woman, but now she had to pick up the pieces in the aftermath of her punitive decisions. She thumbed through her list of foster carers again, but of course nothing had changed in two weeks. Apart from Jean and Owen there were no families in the school's catchment area, and Sally couldn't bear the thought of taking Zoe away from all her friends. She wouldn't change schools, no, a taxi would bring her in, but for the rest of time she would be out in the sticks with no friends, and friends were clearly what had made her life just about bearable so far. Sally stared at her book for a while longer, then snapped it shut and picked up the phone. The number she dialled was Mrs Davies'. The woman picked up and instantly launched into her usual litany of complaints. Sally managed to cut her short and asked if Zoe was there. When told the girl was about to go out with one of her friends, Sally asked Mrs Davies to put her on to Zoe. The girl was never unpleasant with her and she quickly agreed to wait for Sally to come and have a chat. Zoe was as keen to leave the Davies' household as they were to see the back of her, and she hoped the fostering social worker would come up with a solution.

Ten minutes later Sally was ringing the Davies' bell. Mrs Davies opened the door looking offended that Sally was coming to talk to Zoe rather than to listen to her complaints, and she showed the two of them into her small front room without saying a word. Zoe slumped into one armchair and looked at Sally without hostility or hope. When she heard that all Sally had to offer was the possibility of Jean and Owen, except that until now they hadn't been at all helpful, she wasn't surprised. She shrugged, as if nothing mattered any more, but in a hidden corner of her mind there lurked the knowledge that Jean and Owen would be a significant improvement on Mr and Mrs Davies. Sally may have detected some of this thinking because she started arguing that if Zoe made amends and promises, they might change their minds. Sitting in Mrs Davies' chintzy front room, she leaned forward gazing pleadingly into the girl's blank eyes.

'I can't promise I won't run away, Sally,' said Zoe flatly, 'because I will. I'll run away every day until they let me live with Dad or Granny and Grandad.'

Sally sighed and looked down at her fingernails. After a moment of silence, she looked up sadly and said, 'Zoe, if you do that, you'll just get taken away to another part of town or even another town, so you have nowhere to run away to.'

'I don't care,' replied Zoe with a blank stare, 'I don't care about anything. I'll run away anyway, maybe I'll run in front of a train and that'll be the end of all the problems.'

Sally pressed her lips together and carried on looking at the child slouching in the armchair opposite her. Her grey-blue eyes stared back with a scary depth of indifference. Zoe had made many such threats before without carrying any of them out, but Sally knew that you ignored such threats at the child's peril. 'Manipulative' was all Gerald had to say about that. 'Trying to get her way.' Why shouldn't she get her way? wondered Sally. Why shouldn't a kid be allowed to live where she wanted, when she had made it so abundantly clear to the world that it wasn't just a whim of the moment?

'I suppose the plan is still to get you back living with your mother?' asked Sally.

'I'll never go back to my mother,' replied the girl in a flat remote voice. 'It's because of her I'm in care, it's because of her I can't see Dad, I never want to see her again, I hate her.' She reeled this off as if she had learned it by heart. This was her line about her mother and that was all she was ever going to say. No point in engaging in dialogue, you could almost feel her ears shutting off at the end of the little speech, deaf to anything anyone might have to say.

'So, you don't care where you go?' asked Sally tentatively.

'No,' was the predictable answer.

'Zoe,' said Sally, 'I'm really sorry about what's happened to you.' She understood she was stepping into the dangerous territory people called Unprofessional. Where you tell the truth. Where you chuck away the line you're supposed to toe. A knot tightened in her stomach. Was this wise? Zoe was looking at her with a flicker of interest in the back of her eyes. Surely, thought Sally, my salary doesn't take away my right to beliefs of my own? She cleared her throat, even though it wasn't in need of clearing.

'I believe that what has happened to you is wrong, Zoe,' she said, feeling the rapid beating of her heart, 'wrong and sad. You shouldn't be in care.' So there, the words were out, ringing dangerously in her ears, but as she glimpsed the wonder in Zoe's eyes, she also felt a rush of exhilaration. She had touched the girl. 'But you are in care and I want to do everything I can to help you,' added Sally, her voice trailing off as she realised this was not strictly true. There was something she could do to help, but that would be an even more flagrant step in the direction of being Unprofessional, and did she really want to put her job on the line? Zoe must have read the touch of anxiety on Sally's face, because she said, 'Don't worry Sally, I won't tell anyone you said that. I know what they're like.' And she smiled. The sunshine smile that could, in a flash, lift her face and touch it with beauty. A lump narrowed Sally's gullet and she swallowed hard. Would she do the right thing by this little girl?

She left Mrs Davies' house in a daze. Her words of support to Zoe had surprised her as much as they had surprised the girl, and now she had given herself a dilemma. She glanced up at the darkening sky, thinking she hadn't brought an umbrella and if she had to park miles away from the office, she would get drenched. She got into her car and her words to Zoe rushed back to fill her mind. 'I want to do everything I can to help you,' she had said. If she did nothing now, then she would have to live with the knowledge that the words had been pure bullshit. As she parked her car in front of the office, thanking her lucky stars a space had become free just as the rain started pelting down against her windscreen, she knew she had a choice to make. She slipped out of the car and ran to the open door of the Social Services building, getting wet in those few unprotected seconds. From the shelter of the porch, she pressed her remote and the car flashed as the doors locked. Then she went in quickly.

The team room was empty. She went to her files and pulled out the one marked Zoe Milton. She quickly found what she was looking for. Her heart started beating fast again as she picked up a pen and scribbled down Janet Milton's phone number on a yellow post-it. She tore off the post-it from the block and stuffed it inside her handbag. The door into the team room swung open and two of her colleagues crossed over to their desks, grousing about the impossibility of doing their jobs when there were simply not enough fostering families. Quickly pushing Zoe's file out of sight, Sally joined in despairingly. 'Tell me about it,' she moaned with a huge roll of the eyes to the ceiling, and they all laughed, but the laughter didn't quite dispel her sense of guilt. Whatever she did now she would feel guilt, towards her colleagues or towards Zoe. That was the choice, plus the risk to herself.

She pushed these thoughts away. One thing at a time, she resolved, and picked up her phone to dial Jean's number. By now she knew it by heart, and Jean answered after four rings.

'Jean, I've just seen Zoe and I'm desperate,' said Sally. There was a silence at the other end. Then Jean said, 'Does it look like she's going to behave herself?'

'Quite the opposite,' replied Sally with a sigh. 'She's threatening to run away every day and run in front of a train if we take her away from the area. That's why I need you. You're my only hope to avert disaster.'

'But Sally why should Owen and I put ourselves through a load of hassle for a girl who is quite capable of telling us she hates us?'

'Only because she's a child who needs help and you're the only people who can give it. But I can well understand why you don't want to. I'm a beggar here, Jean, and I have nothing to offer you in return. Except perhaps a child's life.' There was another silence at the other end and Sally stopped breathing as she waited for the reply. To her amazement, Jean said flatly, 'All right, Sally, we'll do it. See if we can keep her alive.'

Sally gushed forth with gratitude, but Jean cut her short and said best to get off the phone or she might change her mind. 'Owen will kill me for this,' she added before putting the phone down. Relief had swept through Sally and as her muscles began to relax, she realised how utterly exhausted she felt, and it was only half past eleven with most of the day's work still to do. She had achieved the impossible, yet it would go down completely unappreciated. In fact, both Zoe and Jean would end up resenting her because she had arranged a placement neither of them wanted. But she knew she was giving Zoe the closest thing to a home. Did she owe the girl any more than this? She would think about it later. The phone call she had in mind could only be made from the privacy of her home and her chest tightened at the thought.

The morning passed in report writing but busy as she was her mind would not let go of that wretched phone call. Her mind swung ten times from one position to the other. Perhaps Zoe's grandparents didn't need her help. Perhaps they knew what they could do at this point, what with all the lawyers employed by the family. But perhaps they didn't know. She tapped away at her dirty keyboard whilst her mind played the indecision game. In the afternoon she had to attend a couple of Looked After Children reviews and a team meeting at bloody four o'clock. A brainstorming session, the team manager had announced cheerfully. On how to recruit more foster carers. 'As if…' sighed Sally, thinking she could have finished the last of her reports in that time.

The team meeting finished at ten past five, having produced not one new idea. They all scurried back to their desks keen to put their computers to sleep for the night and go home. The moment Sally was in her car the matter of the telephone call popped up, inexorably. As she sat locked in traffic, she went through the pros and cons methodically. The reasons against the phone call gathered momentum. True, it meant going for the easy option, but why shouldn't she have an easy life, like Debbie and Helen, who switched off their computers at five thirty on the dot, and never gave work another moment's thought until nine the following morning and even then, they'd have a coffee and a chat before they really got going. Why shouldn't she do the same? Treat work for what it was, a way of earning a living and not an endless bloody headache.

The traffic inched forward, and Sally knew that she was nearing the point where she would turn off the main road into clear open side streets. Soon as she got home, she would discuss it with Steve and then make her decision. Except she knew what his line would be, and she would disagree with it, so what was the point in going through all that just to go and make the damn phone call anyway? Why not accept the phone call had become her destiny at roughly nine forty that morning when it had materialised in her head, uncalled for but determined to stay. She parked in front of the house and ran up the three steps to the front door. It was unlocked. She pushed it open and met with the mouth-watering smell of frying onions and garlic. She paused to inhale deeply and then made for the front room. She picked up the phone and shouted in the direction of the kitchen 'Smells wonderful, honey, got a phone call to make, won't be long.' She got the yellow post-it out of her handbag and dialled Mrs Milton's phone number, her heart beating loudly inside her chest.

'Hello, Janet Milton speaking,' came the voice, slightly tense like many voices of a generation who hadn't grown up with the telephone.

Sally explained who she was, and Mrs Milton gushed with appreciation for the way she had always done her best for Zoe. Sally wavered on the edge of changing her mind. She shouldn't be on the phone at all to Mrs Milton, let alone with a view to betraying her colleagues. Anxiety gripped her insides.

'Mrs Milton,' she heard herself say, 'I am phoning to suggest something to you. Strictly speaking I should not be talking to you and I trust you will treat this conversation as confidential.' Sally paused for a couple of seconds, hating the cowardice in her voice, the attempt at protecting herself, wanting to have her cake and eat it. She straightened up, collected her emotions and continued. She wished now she had rehearsed this with damage limitation in mind. She must say as little as possible, not blame anyone, just give the info. She took a quick breath.

'Mrs Milton,' she said, 'I saw Zoe this afternoon and she told me she would never live with her mother again.'

'That is also what she has told us,' replied Janet wondering what this phone call could possibly be about.

'If Zoe's relationship with her mother is seen to have broken down irretrievably, we will be looking for long-term foster carers to take her in. It will probably fall to me to do that.'

'Long-term foster carers,' protested Janet with an indignant shake of the head, 'when we want to have her, and she wants to be with us. It beggars belief.'

'That's why I'm phoning, Mrs Milton, said Sally, clenching the phone, 'just to say that anybody can apply to be foster carers.' The other end went silent.

'Mrs Milton?' asked Sally, checking the other woman was still there.

'But not grandparents surely?' asked a disbelieving Mrs Milton.

'On the contrary, it is not unusual for grandparents to apply to be foster carers for their grandchildren.'

'So, we could apply…' Janet's voice faltered. It was almost too much to take in. The new hope, but also the knowledge they wouldn't stand a chance, not with their history with Social Services. 'How do we go about that Sally?'

'Your lawyer will tell you, Mrs Milton.'

402

'Sally, I can't thank you enough for this,' her voice had a crack in it. 'You're the first person from Social Services to …'

'I know, Mrs Milton,' interrupted Sally, 'The system has not worked well for you and I'm sorry about that, but social workers often do good work too.' Had Sally redeemed herself with the profession by slotting that little sentence in? 'There is something else,' she added quickly, forcing the words out before she had a chance to back out of the next challenge. There were little point telling Zoe's grandmother about applying to be a foster carer unless she gave her the whole picture. She took a deep, quiet breath, aware of the expectant silence at the other end. 'If you decide to go down this road, it will be vital to get the right person to do the assessment.' Sally's heart was beating in her temples, bringing on a tension headache. 'Unprofessional' was flashing in big red letters inside her mind and sweat was rising on her back and under her armpits. Could she lose her job over this? Was she being brave or very foolish?

'You mean someone objective?' said Mrs Milton carefully.

'Yes,' replied Sally. 'When I get your application, I will do my best to get the right person to do the assessment, but if I fail, you may have to demand someone who is genuinely independent, perhaps from another authority, although even then, independence is never guaranteed, people know people and have their own agendas. The person I'm thinking of will be truly objective.' At that moment Steve stuck his head round the door and waved his wooden spoon at Sally with a big grin splitting his face. All she could do in return was wave him away with a mock frown of annoyance.

'Could you tell me her name?' asked Mrs Milton, 'so I know if I need to object or not?'

403

Sally was silent. Did it matter? She would have to tell Mrs Milton when the time came, so why not now? She felt like a spy, disloyal to her side, helpful to the enemy. Except there should be no enemies. Weren't Social Services there to help people? How come the Miltons had become enemies? That was what was wrong, and Sally wanted nothing to do with that. She wanted the right outcome for a young girl called Zoe, and surely that was why she had become a social worker. 'Anne King,' she blurted out.

Janet, who did not boast a good memory for names, knew she would never forget that one. Anne King. Hope came alive in that name. Janet put the phone down and headed for the garden to tell David. He was deadheading in the flower bed and straightened up with difficulty as Janet started to talk. He listened with the scissors in one hand and a bunch of dead flowers in the other, careful to tune into Janet's take on this new development. A good thing or another red herring? He watched Janet intently as she came to the end of her story, '...and this woman is called Anne King,' she concluded triumphantly. And then she smiled, looking ten years younger. *Could this,* David wondered, *be the proverbial light at the end of the tunnel and was travel now moving in the direction of that light?*

30. Anne King

Sally Walker spent the following two weeks waiting for the Milton's application to land on her desk. Every year she spent the first two weeks in August virtually on her own in the deserted office. Her colleagues all had children in school, and she didn't object to going away in June or September when sunny towns and beaches were not so packed. Nevertheless, she never enjoyed the hot and lonely August days in the silent office, but this year it would have one advantage. There would be no one else around to deal with Janet's application, as long as it arrived before mid-August. Every morning she looked through her post with feverish interest, and every morning she was disappointed. Was Janet getting on with it? She didn't dare get in touch again in case she got accused of interfering with Zoe's Care Plan should anyone in the Childcare team find out about her involvement. Instead, she had to sit tight, powerless to calm the impatience that was eating away at her.

On August 16th Brenda Cole, the Senior Practitioner, sauntered back into the office sporting her inevitable summer tan, which Sally suspected to be fake. She had a cup of coffee in one hand and a pile of mail in the other, but clearly no intention of looking at anything until she'd filled Sally in on all her holiday news. She dropped her mail on her desk and it spilled out in a fan like shape, revealing a fat A4 envelope that looked very much like somebody's application to become a foster carer. Sally stared at the envelope whilst nodding and smiling with feigned interest at Brenda's tales of flight delays and perfect beaches. The only thing on Sally's mind was that Anne King might not be Brenda's choice for the assessment. For one Anne's arms did not respond to being twisted and Brenda was a big arm twister. But the greater risk here was that Brenda was friendly with Gerald. Senior Pracs going for coffee together, that kind of thing. Let Zoe come up in the conversation and that would be the end of Janet's fostering hopes. Sally watched Brenda drink the last drops from her cup wondering if the woman was ever going to open her mail. But no, she pushed the pile aside and turned her computer on. Biting her lips in frustration, Sally opened her own emails and tried to focus on the most tedious task of the day.

Brenda finally turned from her screen and reached out for the pile of mail on her desk. Holding her breath, Sally watched out of the corner of her eye as Brenda opened one envelope after another. She grabbed the large one last, pushing her finger in at the top and tearing crisply through the paper. A big wad of papers got pulled out, but Sally failed to glimpse any clue as to what it might be. She stared back at her emails and pretended to work.

'Amazing!' exclaimed Brenda, 'I get back from holiday and what's waiting for me in the in-tray? Someone's application to become foster carers. Can you believe it, in the middle of August, when nobody's even trying to get new foster carers.'

'A family?' asked Sally, her face going hot and red.

Fortunately, Brenda was absorbed in the paperwork. She peered more closely at the additional information given at the end. 'No', she said 'these are grandparents applying to foster their own granddaughter. Zoe Milton.' She read on and added, 'I think I've heard you mention Zoe Milton.'

'Yes,' replied Sally, thinking fast what to say next. 'Zoe's with Jean and Owen Tinsley at the moment.'

'Did you say she was a difficult kid?' asked Brenda, frowning as she tried to bring the case back to mind.

'It's a complicated situation, certainly,' said Sally turning back to her emails, as if she had no desire for further involvement.

Brenda was sitting back in her chair, leafing through the application and the many documents attached. 'It might be best if you deal with this case, Sally, what do you think?'

Sally's heart was hammering in her chest. So close. The next card was risky, but she was going to play it anyway. Looking up from her screen she summoned the most casual tone she could manage, 'I'm happy either way, Brenda. You decide.' Then she turned back to her emails as if the decision was of little consequence. She could barely breathe as she waited for Brenda's reply.

Brenda was still looking at the papers in her hand, thinking it might not be easy to find someone to do the assessment in the middle of August. It wasn't that easy at the best of times, what with the Local Authority only paying a pittance for a job that took about three months of weekly interviews. Private agencies paid double the rate and had all the assessors queuing at their doors. The more she thought about it, the less she fancied chasing after people, having to beg and coax. 'It does look complicated, Sally, and I'm not ready to snap out of my holiday mood just yet. If you're happy to take it on, I'll leave it on your desk.'

Sally nodded and pointed her chin in the direction of her tray. Then she became absorbed in her emails again, not even looking up at the sound of the fat envelope dropping on top of her other files. Inside she was turning cartwheels and somersaults. It would now fall to her to find the right person to do the assessment and she knew exactly who that was. She would phone Anne from the privacy of her home that very evening.

When Sally made her phone call later that day, she was disappointed to get Anne's messaging service. Disappointed, but not concerned. Although Anne was a busy person, she seldom turned anything down, particularly not a case like this one, where she could make a difference. Sally left a message and waited all evening for Anne to return her call. But she didn't hear back until the following evening. When her phone rang showing Anne's number on the screen Sally picked up excitedly. As she was home, she would be able to talk freely and whilst she knew she shouldn't try to influence Anne before sending her the application, she could give her the bare bones at least. She was looking forward to that. Anne would say nothing, but she would think the right thoughts. Sally was sure of that. But before Sally had time to explain anything, Anne turned her down. Against all expectations. Sally barely listened to her reasons, which were to do with being too busy and wanting to do things with her husband now that he was fully retired. The moment Anne stopped speaking she butted in regardless, 'Anne, this kid I'm looking after really needs you. She needs an independent thinker. You're the only one I know.'

'It's kind of you to say so, Sally,' Anne replied, careful not to ask what the case was about, 'but I simply haven't got the time to do a fostering assessment. Try Ruth Elliot, she'll do a perfectly good job for you.'

They said good-bye and Sally sat staring at the silent phone in her hand. She didn't want a 'perfectly good job', she wanted a job done by Anne King. In her need to share the blow of her disappointment, she sent Mrs Milton an impulsive text, 'Anne said no. Sorry.' She promptly regretted this further instance of Unprofessional behaviour which, she knew, would haunt her for days to come. Life was a bitch. She also realised Janet would now be depressed and sent a further text, 'Not to worry, I have other people in mind.'

Janet Milton retrieved Sally's first message seconds after it was sent and felt the instant flare up of acid reflux in her chest. Sally's second text did nothing to calm it down. All she could think was that she was very nearly out of her anti-reflux medication and boy was she going to need more after this piece of news. The trouble was, Dr Bates had been trying to wean her off these tablets and she was worried he might object to another prescription so soon after the last one. It was past six o'clock now anyway and phoning the surgery would have to wait until the morning.

The first thing Janet did the following morning was leave a message on the surgery's answering service. She expected to hear back that a doctor would phone her during the day, but the secretary called back half an hour later to say Dr Bates would fit her in at the end of his surgery and she should come at six. Dr Bates was very accommodating these days, Janet thought, as she put the phone down.

She got to the surgery before six and picked up a magazine from the sorry pile, thinking she would be there a while given the number of patients already waiting. People got called in by the various doctors and by a quarter to seven only three people were left and the other two were sitting near another doctor's door. A patient had come out of Dr Bates' consulting room a couple of minutes ago, and yet it gave Janet a jolt when her name was called out. She quickly put the magazine back on the pile, fumbled her glasses back in her handbag and walked into the doctor's consulting room feeling nervous. What if he argued against more anti-reflux medication? Last time he had given her a spiel about some undesirable side-effects and that they shouldn't be used long-term. It was the main effect she cared about, and the main effect burned her chest and the back of her throat and what was she supposed to do about that if she didn't have her precious tablets? It was perhaps in anticipation of such difficulties that she found herself pouring out to him the story of her frustrations. He didn't try to stop her. Listened with surprising interest, considering the time of day and the repetitive nature of her enduring saga with social services. Janet got so carried away that she let slip the forbidden name – Anne King. Realising her indiscretion, she bit her lip and scrutinised the doctor, who fortunately seemed absorbed in his own thinking at that moment. Best not to attract his attention to the name by asking him to keep it to himself. She cleared her throat and said, 'So that's why I need some more Omeprazole.'

'Of course,' he said, shaking himself free of whatever had been on his mind. He quickly typed the information on his computer. He was quiet as he waited for the prescription to slide out of the printer and Janet felt mounting awkwardness. It was as if he'd forgotten her existence. He snatched the green slip of paper from the printer, signed it with a flourish and held it to Janet, his face still blank with distant and private thoughts.

'Thank you, Doctor,' she said, feeling foolish to have opened up as she had. She left quickly, hoping the Pharmacy in Tesco would have the same opening times as the shop itself. As she started her car, she reflected that Dr Bates must have been jolly glad to see the back of her. She imagined him telling his wife over dinner about this old bat who at quarter to seven, for goodness' sake, thought it relevant to embark on the story of her life as a useful explanation as to why she needed reflux tablets.

But Janet was quite wrong about that.

*

Doctor Bates had not forgotten Zoe Milton or that he owed the girl a favour and as soon as the grandmother had left, he reached for his telephone directory and looked up King, only to realise he didn't know Anne's husband's first name or where they lived. He slammed the book shut in annoyance. This was his chance to put right what had gone wrong in that damned case conference and he didn't doubt he could succeed where others had failed. He would be the hero who got Anne to change her mind, take the case on and alter the course of Zoe Milton's life. He had hoped for instant gratification but now it would have to wait until tomorrow when his secretary would track down Anne King's phone number. Then he would phone her as soon as he had a moment, indeed he would create a moment. He looked forward to it. He had a lot of time for Anne King and had a sense that she liked him too. He wouldn't tell her about the embarrassing case conference when he had failed to speak his

411

mind, she didn't need to know about that, but he would use his position as family doctor to convince her she had a big part to play in this story. Then he would use his charm to gently twist her arm. Satisfied with his plan, Dr Bates got up and walked briskly through the deserted foyer and out into the car park. Only two cars left, a small Kia and his BMW next to it.

As he slid into his leather seat, he pulled his phone out of his pocket and texted his wife to say he was on his way. Then he started the engine and reversed smoothly and quietly out of his space. The beauty of finishing late was that the traffic was thin and the drive home, with Classic FM soothing his nerves, was relaxing. A nice bit of time to unwind, let the mind wander and gradually switch off from the day's demands. He sailed through a couple of green lights, feeling luck was on his side, but the third set turned red on him, forcing him to stamp the brake a little sharply. That action somehow brought Anne's calm and controlled face into his mind. Her clear blue eyes looked straight into his and suddenly he knew he would not be able to twist her arm. With this particular woman neither his charm nor his status would have any impact. The light turned green, and he accelerated gently. His mind veered away from Anne King to thoughts of Zoe Milton. He remembered the small face filled by anxious eyes, the little hand holding fast to the larger hand of the man who had so alienated social workers he was now not seeing his daughter at all. Dr Bates' imagination jumped into that man's shoes and for a brief minute he felt the pain of having his child taken from him. It was unthinkable. A story out of Kafka. He slid quickly back into his own safe life where things like that did not happen. He backed the BM into his drive and switched

412

the engine off. The music stopped and in the silence that followed his mind forced him back to the case conference where he had discovered his own capacity for weakness and cowardice. He shuddered and tried to push the scene away, but it didn't oblige. He could still feel the beating of his heart, the sudden dryness in his mouth and the sweat in his armpits; he remembered clearly what he had wanted to say, and he also remembered the cringing words that had come out of his mouth instead. He remembered the fear. Fear of being alone in disagreement, fear of their judgement, fear of looking like an utter fool. To add to the ignominy of it all, the young school nurse sitting next to him had gaily launched into her truth as if it was as easy as one two three. What would Anne King think of him if she knew this? In a flash he saw a way that might help change her mind. He got out of his car knowing what he had to do that night. It wouldn't be pleasant, but he would do it.

After dinner he retired to his study and went online to search for Anne King's work address. Then he wrote her a letter. In it he told her about the little girl who wanted to live with her dad, and then he told her the exact truth about the case conference. How he had failed the girl, was still ashamed of it and saw Anne as the one person who might be able to stop and reverse what had so far been a tragic course of events. This little girl, he wrote, needs someone to stand up for her because the rest of us have failed. He put a toned-down version of his signature at the bottom of the page and posted it that very night, first class.

*

When Anne King opened her mail two days later, she was intrigued to find a letter from Ian Bates, the doctor who never failed to turn up at case conferences. She liked him, but how could she not like someone who had, over the years, paid her so many compliments? She scanned the letter, sat back in her chair and read it again more slowly. So that was the story of Zoe Milton. She had not wanted to hear it from Sally, but now, with this letter, Ian had cleverly sunk a small hook of interest in her mind. She would show the letter to Paul. See what he said. A small guilty smile parted her lips because she knew damn well what her husband would say.

Sure enough, Paul said this sounded like too important a case to turn down and perhaps their new semi-retired life could start after she'd finished this assessment. It would mark the turning point in their lives, and he had no doubt she was the person to bring about the correct outcome. First thing the following morning Anne phoned Sally to say she had thought about her request some more and would like to see the file. No promises yet, but she would decide quickly. Bubbling with hope, Sally agreed to bring the file to Anne's office by mid-morning. When Sally arrived, Anne took the file without engaging in conversation and put it on her desk. She finished dealing with a few other issues and at one o'clock she walked over to the small Tesco across the road and picked up a low-fat salmon sandwich. Then she came back, closed her office door and settled with the file. Ten minutes into it she slammed it shut and pushed it away across her desk. She munched pensively on the second half of her sandwich, forgetting to taste any of it. She brushed the crumbs off her fingers into the wastepaper bin and got up automatically to switch the kettle on. She extracted no more taste out of the coffee than she had out of the salmon, but by the time her mug was empty, she had decided what to do next. She sent Sally a short email to say she would do the assessment, starting immediately. Then she picked up her phone and dialled the Milton phone number. She couldn't wait to hear the story from the couple themselves.

The phone rang in the Milton household just as Janet and David were finishing lunch.

'What now?' she sighed without moving.

'Shall I get it?' asked David half rising, but she shook her head, waving him back into his seat, and shuffled over. She picked up the phone with the slow reach of an old woman but straightened up and squared her shoulders as she brought it to her ear.

'Hello, Janet Milton speaking,' she said. Then she went silent. Lowered herself absent-mindedly on the window seat next to the phone, just listening. There was no telling from her face what was going on, nor did she give David any revealing eye contact. He felt strangely, annoyingly excluded.

'Yes,' she said at last, 'tomorrow at six will be fine.' She said goodbye and as if in slow motion slotted the phone back in its cradle. Finally, she looked up and met David's eyes. 'You will never guess who that was,' she said impassively. David scrutinised her face, then shrugged, 'No darling, I guess I won't, so are you going to tell me or carry on staring at me like I've landed from another planet?'

'That,' she said slowly, 'was Anne King. And she's coming round tomorrow at six.'

*

Janet and David liked Anne King the moment they shook her hand, but they also felt intimidated, and it wasn't just because her reputation came before her. Her eyes did that to you, blue and clear like the sky, but with the cool depth of the sea. This was a woman who would make her own mind up without any help from anybody. A wise old fox who would find you out if there was anything to find out. Fortunately, Janet and David were not planning to keep anything from her, and that, they realised, was just as well. They showed her into the lounge, pointed to David's seat by the window and went to occupy the settee, within reach of each other's hands. Anne dismissed the file and said what she wanted was to hear their story but first she would explain her role.

'The job of the person doing a fostering assessment,' she said, 'is to get to know the applicants well enough to decide whether they can be trusted with children. A child going into care is often from a background unfamiliar to the future carers, and the child may have all kinds of issues due to their history. Attitudes to race, religion, homosexuality need to be explored as well as views on school and how to bring up children. The applicants' own history and their relationship with each other are also central to the process. There is a lot to cover and that's why it takes about three months of weekly interviews exploring all the necessary topics.' Anne stopped and smiled, giving them a moment to digest all this information. 'This,' she added, 'is my usual introduction. Your case is different as you're applying to foster your own granddaughter and what I want to hear first is your side of Zoe's story.'

Now it was their turn to talk. She listened. Made some notes, but mainly listened. Nodded, asked the odd question, brought Janet back to the point when she got derailed by her emotions, accepted tears and anger, did not take sides or pass judgement. Just listened. At half past seven she glanced at her watch and arranged the next meeting for the following Tuesday at the same time. She said she would arrange to see Zoe immediately after that second meeting. There was a hint of reverence in their manner as they accompanied her to the door, as if she had the power to give absolution after hearing a confession.

Talking to Anne had felt a little like confession. No longer restrained by the need to play the system and snatch points from the opposition, Janet had let the truth pour out of her, without glossing over Joe's bad behaviour or their dislike of Leanne. David had nodded in agreement. It was liberating to dwell in the truth. But now that Anne's reassuring presence no longer filled the room, Janet had doubts. The slim grey-haired woman had said nothing to give them hope.

'She's very professional, isn't she?' suggested Janet.

'By which you mean she didn't say much?' asked David, wrapping his arm around his wife's shoulders. 'No need to worry about that. It's only the first meeting. There are seven to come, plus her meetings with Zoe. You didn't expect her conclusions today, did you?' he chuckled. He gave Janet's shoulders a fond little squeeze, but truth be told, he too had felt uncomfortable during the interview. It was not his style to open up freely about his private thoughts and feelings, and yet this woman had got him to do it. Almost against his will. He wasn't sure whether that was good or not, and she had certainly given nothing away. Time would tell.

31. Zoe Meets Anne King

Zoe knew that her grandparents were applying to become her foster carers and she was glad about that but didn't want to get her hopes up. She had had her fill of disappointment. She stored the information in a corner of her mind, locked it up and went rollerblading with her friends. Zoe was now a class act at not allowing her unhappiness to interfere with friendship and fun. Unhappiness could be switched on and off at will, which she realised made adults doubt that she was unhappy. At times she wondered herself if she was that unhappy. She hated to admit it but going back to Jean and Owen had felt a little like going home. A dull kind of home, but home, nevertheless. Familiar and relatively safe. Secret visits and phone calls had resumed with her dad and seemed now like the only way of life they could hope for, whilst memories of happiness with her grandparents were drifting away from her again. Occasionally she would force herself to remember, closing her eyes and feeling her grandmother's soft papery skin brushing against her cheek or her grandfather's arms wrapping around her whilst they looked together at his big glossy book of British birds. But when she did this her heart ached with such a cruel mix of pain and longing that she quickly killed the memories. What was the point in craving something you couldn't have? Instead, she got used to the shade of grey that was now the colour of her life accepting that the sun only shone through when she was with her friends.

But even being with her friends could cause grief because they had proper parents to go back to at the end of the day and every time they mentioned mum or dad a stab of pain shot through her. Stefan's dad and Kylie's mum were nice to her, but she couldn't respond to the kindness in their eyes because it smacked of feeling sorry for her and she knew with a child's simple intuition that if she allowed herself to ride into her own heart on the wave of their pity, she would drown. Which is why she kept her distance. No cuddles, thank you, no touching; wrong arms, wrong hands, wrong lips. But there was one person who could make the sun shine for Zoe, and that was Stefan. A certain look in his eyes, caught unawares, could send her heart bounding out of control whilst butterflies with claws tightened and twisted her insides. A shy brush of his hand against her cheek could open up a sky so blue she felt she would fly straight into it and disappear like a distant plane whose shredded trace vanishes into nothing. She wanted to kiss him, but she wanted even more for him to kiss her, and she figured that if he felt the same nothing would ever happen. And that was perhaps for the best, because in her heart of hearts Zoe knew that Stefan was only a little boy for whom his skateboard and his football team were the important things. She tried not to think of September when they would all start in the Comprehensive school and maybe ignore each other in the playground, in case the big boys and girls made fun of them. The way Jessie had made fun of her.

Zoe still wrote desperate letters to her grandparents, but she did it without any faith that they would bring about the desired outcome. She still threatened to run away and kill herself or stop eating if she wasn't allowed to live with them or with her father, but her letter writing had become a ritual rather than the fierce expression of despair it used to be. Zoe had stopped expecting good news. She had lost hope. Which is why when Jean told her a woman was on the phone about the fostering assessment, she didn't get too excited. It was after all just another social worker. Zoe took the phone from Jean and listened. The woman explained who she was and asked if she could meet Zoe on Thursday at four thirty. Zoe said yes, she would be home. The woman said she would pick her up and they would go for a walk down the front if the weather was nice. If not, they could sit in the café and have an ice-cream. Zoe couldn't see why they couldn't have an ice-cream either way but refrained from saying so. She hung up unsure whether she had liked the woman's voice or not. Her name was Anne King. She hadn't sounded like a social worker or a teacher, but the voice had not given her a good feeling either. It had been distant, matter of fact, the voice of a busy adult. Of an important adult.

The day came, the sun was out, and Zoe waited by the front room window for this woman to turn up. Inside she felt the kind of nervousness you feel before a test. Fear of making a mistake, of not getting a good mark. Trying to stifle it didn't seem to work. Trying to stifle her hopes didn't work either. What if this woman was different? What if she said Zoe could go and live with her grandparents and they would become her foster carers? Allowing that thought inside her head sent her heart galloping way out of control and Zoe knew this was no good. Disappointment would be too painful if it didn't work out like that, she mustn't even think about it. Zoe turned from the window and sat in the armchair that had its back to the window. Her ears however tuned in to the sound of every passing car. When one finally slowed down, she sat up in the chair gripping the armrests and listening intently. Sure enough, the engine had stopped. Zoe's heart raced, her chest tightened, and her mouth went dry. She was seized by a powerful impulse to run and hide. Instead, she walked into the hallway ready to open the door when the bell rang.

The day before she had broken the ban on phone calls to her grandparents and Granny had said 'Just tell her the truth, Zoe.'

'But Granny, that's what I've done before and they put me in care,' she whispered down the phone as if someone from social services might be lurking among the bushes along the path where kids were racing on scooters, roller blades and bicycles.

'Still, that's what you have to do, tell her the truth and hope this woman listens.'

'Can I tell her I hate Mum?' asked Zoe nervously. She had come to understand that certain truths were so revolting to adults that you could then become a revolting person in their eyes.

'Zoe, sweetheart, don't think about it in advance. Just answer her questions with what your truth is. I think this woman is different from all the other people we've seen so far. I think we can trust her.'

Zoe had switched the phone off and looked at Stefan who was sitting on his skateboard on the grass. 'She says I must tell her the truth,' she informed him.

'I agree,' replied Stefan.

'I don't,' muttered Zoe stubbornly, tightening her arms around her drawn up knees. 'I don't trust her.'

But when Zoe opened the door to the woman with short grey hair and amazing blue eyes, her resistance melted away. The woman's smile did it. It was a big smile, as if Zoe were an old friend she was really glad to see. Then she extended her hand, and they shook hands the way grown-ups do. 'My car's down there,' the woman said, pointing to a very cute sports car. They walked to the car in silence and Zoe felt nervous again. As she slid into the low-slung front seat Zoe cast the woman an appraising side look. Although she was old, Anne King somehow didn't look that old in her smart cropped trousers and trendy black top. As she started the engine she turned to Zoe with another smile, and suddenly Zoe had the strange feeling that they were two kids going on some adventure together, an adventure that somehow the world of adults around them would disapprove of. If they knew. But the woman's eyes told Zoe that they didn't know, and she even wondered if the woman had winked at her. But no, she must have imagined it, because the woman was now looking like a perfectly normal grown-up woman driving her car with the pleasure it gave her to know it was both cooler and faster than most other cars on the road. Zoe shared in that pleasure and felt a little thrill that she was looking down at other drivers in their ordinary cars. When she grew up Zoe decided, she would have a car just like this one. She shot the woman another sidelong glance and decided to take the plunge. 'Cool car,' she said as if she knew stuff about cars. The woman smiled, keeping her eyes on the road. 'I love it,' she replied. 'You're going to think I'm very silly,' she added, 'but it makes me feel young.' She took her eyes off the road for just a moment to meet Zoe's eyes and she chuckled softly. 'Thought you'd think me daft,' she said, pulling smoothly out to turn right and presumably go and find a parking space in one of the back streets. Well, Zoe had been surprised at Anne King telling her what she just had, but it was nothing to do with the car making her feel young. No, a cool car was good for your image, everybody knew that, and Anne King was no different from anyone else in that respect. What had astonished Zoe was that this important grown-up had cared what Zoe might think of her. Mostly adults didn't think kids even had views, let alone care about them.

'If I had a car like this,' Zoe said, realising as she said it that Stefan would have known the make and exact model of the car, 'it would make me feel very grown-up, and I could look down on everyone else. That would be cool.' She nearly added 'specially looking down on Gerald Crispin and Gail Anderson,' but decided against it. It was still early days with this woman. She decided there and then to learn car makes and models, even though it didn't interest her, because she wished she had been able to roll the name of this one off her tongue. She could just imagine Stefan doing it with a superior smirk and hated him for it. 'What is it by the way?' she asked, thinking she could at least boast to Stefan later on about riding in a whatever it would turn out to be.

'It's an Audi,' the woman said as she reversed expertly into the only space in the street.

'What kind of Audi?' asked Zoe, knowing she needed more info than that to impress her friend.

'It's an Audi TT Quattro,' replied the woman as she killed the engine.

Zoe remembered hearing Stefan and his dad talking about some strange sounding quality called brake horsepower. The only reason Zoe remembered it was because of the crazy image of a horse skidding to a halt with brakes on its hoofs. The picture made her smile and she asked, 'What's the car's brake horsepower?'

'250,' replied the woman peering at Zoe with curious interest. But she never asked why Zoe wanted to know, so Zoe felt free to tell her, in a confidential and colluding sort of way.

'It's just that I want to impress a friend. He'll be gutted when I tell him I rode in an Audi TT Quattro that had 250 brake horsepower. What's the acceleration from nought to whatever miles?' she added remembering this other important bit of info about the power of cars. The woman threw her head back and laughed, 'Nought to 62. It's 6.5 seconds, and the only reason I know is because my son drummed it into my head. Me, I like the shape of the car.' They smiled at each other.

'I know,' said Zoe, 'all that technical stuff is really boring, but I'm going to learn it anyway because boys are gutted when a girl knows about cars and sport. I'm learning just to annoy them.' Having announced her new resolution, she opened the car door and swivelled out, slipping smoothly off the shiny leather seat. The woman got out on the other side and locked the car with one smug click of her remote.

'Maybe you shouldn't let other people push you into learning stuff you've no interest in,' she suggested tentatively.

'S'pose not,' replied Zoe, as they walked companionably back down towards the main road. 'But sometimes you find it's more interesting than you thought. For instance, I wasn't the least bit interested in birds, but my granddad kept telling me all the names, and reading his bird book with me, and now I'm glad I know all that, and I am interested. I can't stand it if I think I've seen a bird and I don't know what it is, so I look it up straight away on the Net or in my bird book.'

They had reached the traffic lights, and when the little man turned green they crossed to the middle island, stopped, waited for the other green man and crossed the second side of the dual carriage way. Then they walked across the grass, alongside an old pub with its wooden tables and benches spilling out onto the green and towards a bench that overlooked the path and the beach. Anne seemed to know exactly where she was heading. The tide was a long way out and you could hardly see the water. Birds dotted the wet sand, pecking here and there in what was actually mainly mud.

'So, you could name all the birds on the beach now?' asked the woman as she sat down on the bench.

'Those are easy,' said Zoe, 'they're just herring gulls and black headed gulls. Over there,' she added, waving her left hand towards the other end of the beach, 'you might see oyster catchers and sometimes curlews.' She smiled shyly, but there was pride in her eyes.

'And this is the grandfather you wish to live with?' asked the woman.

Zoe nodded silently, and her eyes welled up because the talk of birds had reminded her how much she missed her granddad. The woman was observing her closely. 'Tell me about your grandparents, Zoe,' she said softly, 'and please call me Anne.'

Zoe looked up into Anne's amazing blue eyes and found it was not going to be at all difficult to tell this woman the truth. This woman was not judging her. Granny had been right; she could trust her with her thoughts and feelings. She knew this with the same simple certainty with which she knew that her father and her grandparents loved her. It was wonderful to know something so good so clearly.

Zoe embarked on her story, and when it came to her feelings about her mother, she said in a flat voice that she hated her. Anne nodded, looking down at her smart summer sandals as if she were seeing them for the first time. 'Yes,' she said pensively, 'when people who should love us don't, we hate them for it.' Zoe was silent for a moment, pondering this new angle on her bad feelings for her mother.

'You think it's okay then?' she asked puzzled.

'I do,' replied Anne.

'But my friend Stefan doesn't hate his mum, even though she left him, him and his dad. I think if she came back, he would be glad.'

'He would if she came back to be a loving mum, because that's what he wants.'

Zoe was silent again. Then she said, 'But I wouldn't be glad if Mum wanted to come back and for us all to live together again.'

Anne was quiet for a minute or two, and Zoe stared at her sideways, waiting for her reply. She had no doubt Anne would have something to say about that, but she seemed to be hesitating. Then she shifted her position on the bench to face Zoe and extended her arm along the wooden back of the bench as if she was putting her arm around Zoe's shoulders but without touching her. She looked at Zoe with great kindness in her eyes, but no pity as far as Zoe could tell, so it was all right, and she said, 'Think about it Zoe, if your mum came back wanting to apologise for everything and wanting

426

to be a good mum to you from now on, wouldn't you be glad too?'

Zoe allowed her imagination to go down that most dangerous path and then nodded slowly, with glistening eyes.

'You see,' said Anne gently, 'you think you hate your mum, but it's more that you want something from her and she's not giving it to you. Maybe she can't, maybe she hasn't got that gene.'

'So, I'm not a bad person?' asked Zoe quickly, holding her breath. She stared at a little girl in pink, pushing hard with her right leg to get her pathetic little scooter get some speed up. Which it never would. Not in a million years of pushing.

'You are most certainly not a bad person,' replied Anne, refraining from putting her hand on the girl's shoulder. Physical comforting was not her brief, but helping a troubled youngster get rid of her guilt was a different matter. 'And,' she added, 'you have a right to your feelings. Feelings have important things to tell us, but in the main we don't listen, we push them away. You're doing well to listen Zoe.' Zoe pondered this in silence.

Anne looked up at the darkening sky. Heavy clouds were rolling in from the sea, lit up around their edges by the late afternoon sun. Colours were beautiful at this time of day, sharp and intense, as if the slanting sun touched them with magic. Her eyes swept from the greens along the path to the shiny metal of the in-coming sea under the ominous darkness of the clouds. Then she remembered her promise of an ice-cream. They got up and walked towards the café against a steady flow of dog-walkers, joggers and cyclists going the other way. In the little café she got Zoe to talk about her friends, and school, and when she brought it all to an end by

427

saying she would like another meeting in a couple of weeks' time, all Zoe wanted to ask was, 'Why two weeks, why not tomorrow?' Instead, she licked the last of her chocolate ice-cream, crunched the cone between her teeth and stuffed it all in her mouth. Then she licked her fingers clean, brushed her wet mouth with the back of her hand and they got up to make their way back to the car.

As soon as she was home in her bedroom Zoe texted Granny, 'Anne is brill. Love Z.'

32. David's Rebellion

'What do you make of Anne?' Janet asked David over breakfast about six weeks into the fostering assessment. She was holding an appetising piece of buttered toast layered with the best organic marmalade, yet she was not biting into it. As Janet hated cold toast David knew her question meant she was not happy with Anne. He cleared his throat, lifted his cup of tea to his lips and drank slowly. Then he said, 'I think she's on our side. But I know what you mean, it's not always obvious.'

Janet put her toast down on her small silver edged plate and sighed. 'I have no appetite,' she commented sadly. She drank her tea, put the cup down and looked at David as if for rescue. 'We've had all these meetings, but we have no idea what she thinks. Is she playing cat and mouse with us, enjoying being the cat?'

'Everybody enjoys power. But I think she's just sticking to her rules, say nothing until she's written the report.'

'I know that,' replied Janet with the mild irritation of someone being told the obvious. 'But does she have to keep us hanging like this? Couldn't she give us a hint? That's why I'm uncomfortable.'

'She's being professional. Fair enough.' replied David, 'What bothers me is something else. I feel as if I've been…' he trailed off, searching for the right word, or the right idea.

They looked at each other, but Janet couldn't help him. 'I know,' he said, 'I feel as if I've been used.' He nodded, relieved to have hit on what had been nagging at him.

Janet picked up her cold piece of toast and bit into it as if it had the power to make her think more clearly. Her eyes fixed David but were really looking through him at the thoughts his words had just sparked off inside her head. 'Used.' The word rang true. She felt that too. But why? Anne was doing her job, they wanted her to do it, and the whole exercise had been giving them more hope of success than anything that had happened for the last three years. She tore off another bite of toast, and as she munched on it pensively a look of new understanding showed in her eyes.

'I think I know why we feel like that,' she said picking her napkin from her lap and rubbing the stickiness off her fingers. She placed the napkin on the table and flattened it absentmindedly, deep in thought.

'Why?' he asked, suppressing a smile. This was so Janet.

She looked up, still silent. Then, as if finally confident of her conclusions, she said, 'Because it's a one-way deal.' And now she was speaking in riddles, which was also very much Janet, enjoying being one step ahead and keeping the other one guessing. The other one being him of course, always that little bit slower, although he reflected that in this case he'd come up with the magic word, 'used'. Now she would give him the analysis. It was often the way it went, that's why they made a good team, as Anne had suggested in their last meeting. They had both nodded enthusiastically. A good team was exactly what they were. His mind dwelled on that little exchange, and he thought that maybe he too could see why they felt 'used' by the whole thing, used and mildly humiliated. But it was Janet's turn to speak first.

'What do you mean, a one-way deal?' he asked.

'Think about it David,' she replied, and as she leaned forward, he could feel the words were about to pour out in a flow of excited interpretation. Suddenly he saw his daughter. Leaning forward in just the same way, with one arm bent and her fist lightly clenched, her whole body giving the message that she was ready for action. Action from the head. He suppressed another smile and listened. 'In a normal two-way conversation,' said Janet, 'one person decides to open up, and then the other one does the same, and on it goes. But if the other one does not respond with the same kind of openness, then you clam up. End of intimacy. Otherwise, it feels like the other one's had a good look at your life but kept theirs a secret. Anne strips us naked and stays fully dressed.' David was frowning as Janet's explanation now fed his own vague sense of humiliation. He took the tea-cosy off the white ceramic teapot and poured himself another cup, adding a little milk afterwards.

'What do you think?' asked Janet, impatient for his agreement and hopefully praise.

He drank his tea slowly, keeping her waiting in his turn while trying to come up with the same clarity she had achieved.

'You're right, but there's more to it than that,' he finally said. 'There's a kind of humiliation, you know, like we're …, like we're being examined. That's it. Like kids sitting a test, wanting to please the teacher. Damn it, I can't believe I'm being made to feel like that at my age, with the kind of life I have behind me.' He banged his cup of tea down in a brusque movement that made the saucer rock. David had been a civil

431

engineer, working on big projects in teams of highly skilled men, and then he had started his own construction company. He took a lot of pride out of that, particularly from his ability to manage difficult men and difficult situations. It hadn't been easy, but he had done it successfully. And yet now here he was, sitting in front of that woman once a week, feeling like a schoolboy.

Janet sat back, a little frightened by David's sudden anger. He could be awkward when his pride was threatened, and the last thing Janet wanted was for him to stop co-operating with Anne, when they were so close to the end. So close perhaps to success.

'David,' she said in a placatory tone, 'we knew it would be like that. Sally told us the person doing the fostering assessment would want to know everything about us, from our childhoods onwards, our relationship, our jobs, and you said…'

'I know what I said,' interrupted David, slamming the table with the palm of his hand, 'I said we had nothing to hide.' He turned his angry gaze upon Janet, 'and that is still true. What I didn't realise Jan, was that I would be made to feel like some delinquent kid having his life examined.' He paused and recovered his breath. 'To establish if I should be allowed to look after my own granddaughter. My own granddaughter, for god's sake!' He barked a short bitter laugh, and Janet wished she had never broached the subject.

At the next interview, due to be the last but one, David was withdrawn and uncooperative, leaving everything to Janet. Anne was taken aback, and at first floundered to find a way of dealing with his strange behaviour. Things had gone so well, and she had been optimistic she could write just the kind of report Janet and David wanted and deserved. She had been staggered by their story, by the wrongness of everything that had happened and in equal measure, by their perseverance. She knew about the mortgage they'd had to take on, they had been frank about everything as if she were a trusted friend. And yet now David was hostile, out of the blue. Anne took a quick look at herself, wondering if she'd said anything in the previous meeting to upset him, but failed to raise any significant memories. In the end, unable to cope with the tension, she turned to David and asked him point blank if she'd done anything to explain his silence. He pretended to be embarrassed, fidgeting with a couple of coins that suddenly materialised between his fingers, but she could see he was pleased she had asked. He had wanted the question, and now he was just killing time in false pretences before launching into the complaint that had been mounting up inside him. She sat back in her armchair and waited, concerned and alert. A quick side glance told her Janet was equally concerned, but she knew what was coming and seemed to think it was best to let him have his say. She would probably apologise on his behalf afterwards. Her eyes were downcast and there was something long suffering about the hunch of her neck.

'It's nothing personal, Anne,' said David, 'pushing his back against the cushions behind him. 'but the system sucks. They send somebody in like you, and don't get me wrong, you're doing a great job, but let's face it the job is about getting us to talk about ourselves, prying into our lives, stripping us naked, from a position of power, and then passing judgement. How do you think that makes me feel?'

Anne was stunned. She shifted in her armchair, clutching at disarrayed thoughts. She enjoyed these assessments for the very reasons David hated the one he was being subjected to. Getting people to open up bordered on exhilarating. Looking into their lives was more fascinating than reading a novel because of the truth factor. And yes, she had to admit that she enjoyed passing judgement, making the recommendation, influencing the course of events. It felt like detective work. In order to find out what applicants might be hiding she had sneaky little questions designed to get prospective carers to betray prejudices or authoritarian attitudes. When she explained this to her husband, she called them cute questions and gave him examples to show how well they worked. But her husband would be surprised to see her now, all tied up in conflicting thoughts and not knowing what to say. David had exposed her as well as caught her unawares and because she saw his point of view with total clarity, she wanted to say sorry. Yet she realised how ridiculous it would be to do that, given she was simply doing a job they were desperate for her to do. Then she remembered her golden rule, when running out of ideas, ask a question.

'David,' she said, 'what would you like me to do?'

A magic wand would not have produced a better result. His anger deflated and Janet's face flooded with relief. 'I know,' he said with an irritated shrug, 'that's why I said it was nothing personal, we're just caught in this.'

'And as David said,' Janet chipped in quickly, 'you are doing a wonderful job.'

From a position of power, thought Anne, cringing. She had all the power and they had to behave or else…

Anne had planned to explore the subject of their relationship with Leanne a little further that day, but in view of David's outburst, she decided to leave that to another meeting and returned instead to the bland topic of their childhoods. Soon they were talking freely again. The beauty of the job had always been that because people love talking about themselves, extracting information had never been painful, until today. Today Anne understood it was a one-way deal, and that she was operating from a position of power. She felt humbled, because wise as she believed herself to be, she had been blind to that unpleasant fact. But then it was also that very power that would enable her to write a report that might bring young Zoe back home. Or at least in her grandparents' home. If it did, all this would be forgotten. For now, she must press on with her report regardless of David's feelings. She knew what her recommendation would be, but there was no knowing if it would convince the fostering panel. Any unturned stones would attract questioning and criticism.

The last interview took place during the October half term. Janet and David had had contact with Zoe the day before and there were tears choking Janet's voice as she talked of her frustration at having to meet her granddaughter in such degrading conditions. David took her hand in his and the look they exchanged said more about their relationship than all their answers to weeks of questioning. Anne brought them round to the subject of their daughter-in-law and whilst they didn't try to hide their dislike of Leanne, they denied that they had tried to turn Zoe against her mother.

'Anyway,' shrugged Janet 'if Zoe had loved her mum, there's no way anybody could have turned her against Leanne. Look how everybody has tried to turn her against her dad and against us. Did it work? Kids know their own hearts, and nobody can change that.'

Anne nodded, 'Children are closer to their feelings than we are.' Anne had a beloved three-year-old granddaughter, and she didn't think much of her daughter-in-law's rigid ways with the child. It was not hard to see why Janet and David had not taken to Leanne, and given how they felt, it was fair to say they had behaved neither like saints, nor like villains. Just like ordinary human beings, but they had been turned into villains. She closed her notebook, gathered her papers and slid her pen back in its loop inside her handbag. Then she looked up and smiled.

'I believe you will make excellent foster carers for your granddaughter and that is what I'm going to say in my report.'

Janet's hand grabbed David's and they looked at each other as if neither dared to breathe. Then slow silent tears gathered along the bottom rim of Janet's eyes and rolled down one by one, leaving long trails that she didn't bother to brush away. David drew her to him and glanced up at Anne, pressing his lips together and hugging his wife close. 'She has been through more than you know to get to this,' he said. Anne felt humbled again. The suffering of others. A bleak uninviting territory where too much empathy tempts your own pain out of its closet. Her eyes strayed down to the papers neatly piled on her lap, rested there for a moment and then came up again tentatively. 'My report,' she said, 'will be a big step in the right direction, but it is not guaranteed to win the war.' She paused, feeling the light beating of her heart and the slight frown gathering between her brows. The last thing she wanted was to inflict more suffering, but she couldn't allow unrealistic hopes go to everybody's head.

They looked up and nodded. 'We know,' said Janet, dabbing her face with a crumpled tissue, 'you told us all about the panel in the first meeting, remember?'

'I do. It is the first thing I tell people because I only have the power to influence the decision. I don't make it. The panel members may not be happy with the report and ask me to look further into this or that. Even though they ask me to do the assessment because of my experience and how well they think of me, blah blah blah, when it comes to the report, they don't seem to trust my judgement. They argue with me, picking holes in my report, whingeing that I haven't done this or that according to the procedures, sometimes I wonder why I agree to do the work in the first place.' She gave a short, self-deprecatory chuckle and stood up, holding all her papers in one hand and hitching the long handles of her handbag on her shoulder.

'Power shifts all the time, doesn't it?' said David, lifting himself up with the slow care of a man whose joints let him down much of the time. 'Now in your hands, now in someone else's hands,' he added with a smile full of friendly sarcasm. Anne grinned back and turned to say goodbye to Janet. Just as her hand was moving towards the other woman, the phone rang. Janet froze, darting her husband a panicked look.

'I'll answer it, love,' he said calmly. He swivelled around slowly and headed for the phone near the window. Anne watched him pick up, then looked away as Janet's gaze suddenly made her feel indiscreet. 'Can you phone back in ten minutes,' he said, and after a brief silence, added, 'No sweetheart, give me ten minutes.' It wasn't the term of endearment that gave him away, nor the tone of his voice, it was the alarmed look on Janet's face when the word 'sweetheart' slipped through his lips. A shift took place inside Anne's mind. Her eyes met Janet's and what she read there widened her own with new understanding. She darted a sideways glance at David who was walking back towards them with his usual stoop, looking down at his feet, absorbed in his own thoughts. Anne's gaze turned back to Janet, quite steady now, and she spoke with deliberate brightness, 'As I was saying we cannot count our chickens yet. The fostering team may ask me to revise the report in this or that way and the panel may need convincing, but the one thing you can be sure of is that nobody will change my views on your suitability as foster carers for Zoe.' She paused and then added, 'I'll complete the report in a week's time, and I need you to gather all the documents that are on the list I gave you a couple of weeks ago. With a bit of luck, we may catch the November panel.'

She leaned forward and shook hands with Janet, her smile as clear as a cloudless sky. Janet shook her hand back, with the warmth of immense gratitude, and searched the other woman's eyes. No there was nothing there. She must have imagined the look she glimpsed before. Her chest relaxed and she gave Anne her broadest smile.

Anne walked briskly out and slipped behind the wheel of her sexy little Audi with the usual pleasure. She drove off without looking back or waving. This was work, not friendship, and it was important not to forget it. But the moment she turned the corner and accelerated down the long avenue lined with the magnificent cherry trees which made such a show in the spring, she threw her head back against the head rest and burst into merry laughter. The laughter kept sneaking back into her mind as she drove. The thought of it!

438

Social workers telling people what they were not allowed to do, people nodding obediently and then doing exactly what they wanted. She laughed again. They had all been in touch all along, on the phone and who knows, visits too, quite possibly. Good for them. Good for the human spirit that will not be daunted.

At the first set of lights on the main road her gaze was drawn to the car next to hers, a little red Clio, and sure enough a youngish man was staring at her with open curiosity. Why was a woman on her own laughing like that, particularly a woman her age? She gave him a big smile, and, as the lights went green, she winked at him, pressed the throttle and went roaring off. She laughed again, enjoying her naughty mood. Yes, good for Zoe for breaking the rules and meeting her needs behind the backs of the power freaks in charge of her case. The more she got to know that girl, the more she liked her. She was relieved to think that father and daughter may not have suffered three years of complete separation. She turned right towards the leafy area where she was fortunate enough to live, a few minutes from the sea, and in no time was driving smoothly onto her herringboned paved drive. She got out of the car with her papers under one arm, thinking she would get on straightaway with the report. It would be nice to make the November panel.

33. Up and Down

Zoe knew her grandparents were having their last interview with Anne King that afternoon and they had agreed Zoe would phone them after dinner from her bedroom, when Jean and Owen were in front of the TV and wouldn't hear who she was talking to. But Zoe hadn't been able to wait. With only a few minutes to dinner and her heart beating madly, she had dialled her grandparents' number. Granddad had picked up and said in a funny kind of voice 'Give me ten minutes.' But in ten minutes Zoe would be downstairs eating and she wanted to know now. Was Anne going to recommend them to be her foster carers or not? Surely Grandad could have given her a clue, even if Anne was still there. Zoe switched her phone off in annoyance and stared at it for a long time with her chest heaving, in and out, in and out. She wanted to scream that she had been waiting years for her life to be put right and, no, she could not wait another ten minutes, not one minute more in fact. She was in the wrong life, with the wrong people and the wrong feelings, she'd had more than three years of it and now she couldn't take it anymore. This was not her life, she didn't want it, she wanted to die.

When Zoe had told the nice fostering social worker, Sally Walker, that she would run away every day until she was allowed to live with her dad or her grandparents, she had meant it. That had been back in July, when she was staying with those horrible people, Mr and Mrs Davies. Now it was October half-term, and she hadn't run away. Not once. Not even thought of running away. But now she was thinking of it again, and she didn't care what happened to her. What was the point of a life where she was not allowed to live with her family? Where random adults had put her in a prison called foster care. For no good reason. Where other random adults had said she couldn't be with her friends anymore. But that was another story, and she couldn't bear to think about that one just now. She could only take so much pain. Only so much pain.

Zoe knew why she hadn't run away in August. First, at the end of July she had met Laura. Sally had told Zoe that Jean and Owen were looking after another child, a six-year-old girl called Laura. Laura was a quiet girl, Sally had said, she had her own room, and her presence wouldn't affect Zoe at all. Zoe didn't care about Laura one way or the other, a six-year-old would not be a friend or an enemy, and this view was confirmed when she met the child. Laura was small with long blond hair and clung to Jean silently, following her around all the time. She had taken one blank look at Zoe and stepped back to hide behind Jean. *Weird kid*, Zoe had thought.

But that night Jean had come to say good-night and she had sat on the end of Zoe's bed. Zoe didn't want Jean in her room, and she knew that Jean knew this, but Zoe was so relieved to have left the Davies household that she accepted Jean's intrusion without hostility.

'I want to tell you a little bit about Laura,' Jean said, pulling on the duvet to straighten it out with the flat of her hand. She seemed a bit stuck.

441

'She's not very chatty, is she?' said Zoe helpfully.

'No, that's why I wanted to explain to you about Laura. You see, Zoe, Laura doesn't have a mum, or a dad, or any grandparents.'

Zoe sat bolt upright and her eyes went very wide. 'What do you mean, she hasn't got a mum or a dad?' she asked accusingly, as if Jean was making this up, perhaps to show her what a lucky girl she was, with a whole family out there, even if she wasn't allowed to live with them. 'Everyone has parents.'

'Laura's mum is a single mum, there was never any dad involved. But Laura's mum has problems with drugs, she's in and out of hospital and has finally agreed she can't look after her daughter. Laura is waiting to be adopted. If there are grandparents, they don't want to know. Laura's never met them.' Jean stopped talking and Zoe was silent too. Here was a child who was worse off than her, and Jean hadn't made up any of it, she could tell. As if to confirm that thought, Jean said, 'The fact Laura doesn't have anybody doesn't make your situation good, Zoe, I understand that. I wanted you to know about Laura, so you don't ask her stuff about her family.'

'Does she have friends?' asked Zoe without much hope. That little girl didn't look like the popular type. If anything, she looked like the kind who got bullied in school. Jean shook her head, 'No friends, but she likes me. Trouble is Zoe, I don't want to adopt anyone, that is not a responsibility I want,' she added as if justifying herself to a twelve-year-old girl. Zoe nodded.

'Does anyone want to adopt her?' she asked doubtfully. Zoe's limited understanding on these matters was that babies got adopted, not six-year-old children.

'There is a couple applying to adopt.'

442

'You don't like them?' asked Zoe, noticing Jean's reticence.

'No, no, I do like them, it's just ...' her voice trailed off as she struggled with the rest of the sentence.

'What?'

'They're two women.' She got the words out quickly, as if to get rid of them.

'You mean they're a gay couple?' asked Zoe easily. And at that moment Zoe became the adult and Jean the child, and they both knew it. 'Are they nice?' asked Zoe naturally, hitting on the one thing that mattered and leaving Jean feeling awkward and embarrassed by her own difficulties with gay couples, who of course were not around when she was growing up.

'They're very nice,' said Jean firmly, finding her grown-up voice again as she got up from the bed. 'Zoe,' she added with a hesitation in her voice, 'I know a six -year-old is not a playmate for you but perhaps you could play with her now and again. Teach her to play. I've tried but she doesn't get it. Maybe another child would know what to do.' And Jean left.

After that Zoe looked at Laura with awe. A little girl who had nobody in her life except Jean. One day, when Jean was out and Owen was reading his paper, Zoe taught Laura to play hide and seek. When the little girl finally got it, she shrieked with laughter every time she found Zoe and the older girl jumped at her out of her hiding place. Another time Zoe let Laura into her room, and she even let her play with Flossie. After that Laura would knock on Zoe's door to be let in. She was no trouble and would sit on the floor quietly, stroking Flossie while Zoe was reading on her bed. Zoe noticed that Jean was very careful not to comment on anything happening between her and Laura, and that was good. Also good was the

443

fact Jean was not on her back all the time. She could spend whole afternoons out and not get interrogated when she got back. She played with her friends and she saw her dad whenever she could. The highlight of the summer had been her three interviews with Anne King. In August Zoe had not wanted to run away because life had had some good stuff in it.

In September however everything changed.

There was a lot of excitement in the air about starting comprehensive school. Fear as well as excitement because the Comp was a big unknown place, and Zoe and her friends knew they would be the smallest kids there. After being the biggest in the primary school, this was a daunting thought, and the Comp was full of bullies and tough kids, everybody knew that. Zoe wasn't frightened but she was nervous and her problems, she realised, were unique to her. She listened to Kylie, Michaela and the other girls talking about going to town with their mums to buy uniforms, cool pencil cases and pretty rucksacks. Zoe was silent. She would have died rather than talk about going to town with Jean. The shame of being the girl in care reduced her to silence. Behind the silence her anger was mounting again, because she should have been doing these things with her dad and her granny, and then she could have chatted and laughed with the other girls.

The next blow came when Zoe and Kylie discovered they were going to be in different classes. Kylie's mum talked to someone in school but was told it was good for children to learn to make new friends, wasn't that the point of going to a new school? But Kylie's mum agreed with the girls that the school was wrong about this. As she poured juice and got the biscuit tin out, she talked of Sarah who was her own best friend to this day and with whom she had been through school from her first year to her last. 'What's wrong with old friends? Old friends are the best.' Kylie couldn't eat her biscuit because she was crying, and Zoe watched her friend discover the pain of losing control over your life. The world of adults was a hostile one, she already knew this, but now she discovered teachers were as bad as social workers. They were all intent on taking her away from the people with whom she felt safe and happy.

On the first day at the new school only the Year 7 students were in, but they seem to fill the yard anyway, standing in quiet little groups in their fresh uniforms. There was a low buzz of conversation, but nobody was running or playing. A couple of teachers came out and addressed the children near the entrance and then they all started to move, trouping into the vast Assembly hall where rows of chairs were laid out. Zoe and Kylie sat next to each other watching the proceedings with trepidation. The headteacher came to stand on the platform at the front, with three teachers on each side of him. Zoe watched them, thinking the young woman with short dark hair looked friendly and hoping she would be with her. The headteacher talked for a while about rules and other boring stuff, and then he said they would call out names by class and the children were to walk up and follow their teacher to their classroom. He emphasised this must happen quietly. No running or talking. Zoe's heart was beating fast, and she listened carefully to the first roll of names. She wasn't in Year 7A and nor was Kylie. Now it was Year 7 B's turn, and the nice woman with short dark hair stepped forward. She called out one name after another and suddenly Kylie's name resounded throughout the hall. Kylie looked at Zoe in a panic

445

and Zoe nodded and pushed her forward. As she watched her friend go off to Year 7 B with two other girls from their old class pain tightened her insides. She managed to keep her tears back but when she saw Stefan get up, a few minutes later, and walk away towards Year 7 C, she lost that battle. Now she was crying, and she couldn't help it. Shame flooded her, and she didn't dare look up to check if people had noticed. She blew her nose, wiped her face quickly and waited anxiously for her own name to be called, hoping her tears wouldn't show. She ended up in Year 7D and as she walked up towards a severe looking man with grey hair her vision blurred with more tears. A quick glance up and down had told her she didn't know a single person in her new class.

As the days and weeks went by Zoe lost her old friends and didn't make new ones. It wasn't that Kylie and Stefan didn't want to know her anymore, no, they said they wanted to get together but they were just too busy to do it. Kylie had started horse riding lessons with a girl from her class, and she was still doing dance of course and now Zoe felt the pain of being one of many friends. A hanger-on. She didn't want that. As for Stefan, he was now playing football all the time, and it was obvious he wouldn't be seen dead rollerblading down the front with a girl. One day she mustered up the courage to phone him at home to ask if he and his dad were watching the game that afternoon, hoping she might get invited. Stefan's dad picked up and sounded embarrassed when he heard Zoe's voice. He said he was watching the game on his own and added with an awkward chuckle that he too was being deserted by Stefan. Zoe switched her mobile off, swallowed her tears and never phoned again.

If Zoe didn't make new friends, it wasn't because she couldn't, it was because she didn't want to. She didn't want the shame of saying she was in care, she didn't want to explain her life to other kids, she didn't want to feel like a freak. She joined the odd game in the playground and at the end of the day, she went home alone. That way, if Jean was picking her up because it was raining, she didn't have to answer awkward questions about the woman waiting for her in the car.

In the summer Zoe hadn't run away because friendship had filled her life, and in the autumn, she didn't run away because she didn't have any friends to give her the strength to even think about it. Her only friend now seemed to be Laura, and that was a bitter thought. Despair was back and was making itself at home inside Zoe's head.

*

Sitting on her bed after her grandfather had asked her to give him ten minutes, Zoe carried on staring at the silent phone in her hand. 'No, Grandad,' she said under her breath, 'I can't give you ten minutes. I can't wait ten minutes. I've waited long enough and now I can't wait anymore. I can't…' Just then Jean called her down to eat.

Zoe chucked her phone on the bed and made her way downstairs sullenly. She sat at the big kitchen table opposite Laura and mumbled that she wasn't hungry even though it was macaroni cheese which was her favourite. Owen talked to Jean about some work issue he had, and Zoe didn't listen. Laura was silent as always. As they were finishing their meal the phone rang and Jean went to answer it. She came back into the kitchen holding the handset towards Zoe and said, 'Your Gran's on the phone for you, Zoe', as if this was a perfectly ordinary thing to say. Zoe looked up in astonishment. She wasn't allowed to talk to her gran, was she? So, what was going on suddenly? Jean nodded for her to take the phone and Zoe grabbed it, getting up quickly in case Jean changed her mind.

'Granny!' Zoe shouted in delight as she jumped onto the settee in the front room, but before she had time to explore the extraordinary thing that had just happened, Granny had launched into the news about Anne King and what she was going to say in her report. Zoe shrieked in triumph, even though Granny was quick to remind her that the panel might yet disagree with the report and reject Anne's decision, and added that it could take a few weeks before they went to panel.

'A few weeks,' groaned Zoe, 'Gran, I'll die if I have to wait a few weeks.'

'Zoe, we're nearly there. Just bear that in mind. Nearly there.'

They said good-bye, Zoe put the phone on its base and walked back to the kitchen to share her news with Jean, Owen and Laura.

'That's good news, Zoe, we're very glad for you,' said Jean. She stood up, reached out for the dirty plates and started piling them in front of her carefully. Then, out of the blue, she said something that nearly knocked Zoe over. 'Also, Zoe,' she said, 'Owen and I have decided…' her voice trailed off as she exchanged a look with her husband, but the look must have told her it was okay to carry on, because she finished her sentence with '…we've decided that from now on you can phone anyone you like from your bedroom.'

Zoe was dumbstruck. She looked from Jean to Owen a couple of times, and finally asked carefully, 'Even my dad?'

'Yes,' said Jean, 'as I said, anyone you like.'

448

'Why?' asked Zoe.

Jean glanced at Owen again, picked up the pile of plates and said, 'Because we don't agree with the Care Plan anymore.' Then she took the plates to the sink, pulled the dishwasher door open, and bent over to start loading it. 'Fucking ridiculous,' was how Owen had described the Care Plan, and he had said it some time ago. 'Everyone agrees the relationship between the girl and her mum has broken down irretrievably, as they put it, but Zoe is still not allowed to phone her dad or grandparents. What kind of world do we live in?' But Jean had been worried about falling out with Social Services and it had taken her a while to agree that they would stop enforcing something they disagreed with. What had decided her in the end, was watching Zoe going steadily downhill during her first half-term in the Comp. The girl seemed totally lonely but wouldn't talk about her friends, wouldn't talk about anything in fact. When Jean had read Zoe's school report, she had known something was very wrong. 'Not one positive comment,' she had told Owen indignantly. 'And you know why that is, don't you?' Owen had replied sarcastically.

'Can I go and phone them now?' asked Zoe, struggling to believe this was really happening.

'You certainly can, young lady,' said Owen, winking at her behind Jean's back. Zoe understood in a moment of stunning revelation that she had had an ally in the house all along and she hadn't known it. She gave Owen a big smile, ran out and shouted back 'Thank you.'

When Zoe went back to school after half-term, she found she could make sense of the lessons once again. Some teachers were not great, but some were very good and the

449

science one was a real character who made everything fun and exciting. She noticed a couple of girls in her class being friendly and was particularly attracted to the one who was naughty and funny. Suddenly she had a little gang to be with at break time, and the next thing she knew, Kylie was gravitating towards her again. Stefan was still immersed in his football but there was a boy in her class she liked. He had dark hair and big Harry Potter glasses and he was very clever. He was quick witted and the two of them cracked sarky jokes at each other when the teacher wasn't looking. The good stuff was back in Zoe's life, and it was kicking despair out of her head.

In early November, however, there was a bit of bad news. Granny told Zoe they had just missed the November panel and would now have to wait until mid-December. Granny tried to cheer her up saying December was a good omen because it would bring her home for Christmas, and wouldn't that be neat?

'But Gran I would've been home for Christmas too if it had been the November panel, and I would've seen the Christmas lights too.'

'I know, sweetheart, I'm just trying to see things in a positive light. I was disappointed too when Anne told me we'd missed the November panel. The wait is just as unbearable for me as it is for you.'

'Good,' replied Zoe, 'so stop pretending it doesn't matter that we missed the November panel. It does matter and I'm gutted.'

Janet hung up and turned to David pensively.

'What is it love?' he asked, looking up from the sports pages of his newspaper.

'There is one thing we have never even thought about,' said Janet.

'Which is?' prodded David gently.

'We don't know how we're going to get on with Zoe when she's here every day, if she's here every day, I should say.'

David lowered the paper slowly onto his lap, still wide open, ready to get back to. 'What makes you say that?' he asked.

'Zoe is so strong willed. What will happen when we're not on the same side of the argument anymore?' Janet hadn't moved from the window seat next to the phone. Her face was all frown and anxiety now and David could have burst out laughing. Three years of fighting, so close to victory and now the doubts set in. He folded his paper and set it aside.

'Sweetheart,' he said without a hint of a smile, 'we'll deal with that when it arises. No point worrying now. Come and sit on the settee and I'll make us a cup of tea.' He patted the cushion next to him on the settee.

Janet came to sit down next to her husband. 'Do you remember all the rows with Emma?' she whispered. 'We're taking Zoe on at just that awkward age, and...' her voice trailed off as she met David's eyes, ' ... and we're, we're kind of...' She paused, hearing the shame in her voice, 'we're kind of inheriting her, with a lot of baggage, and we didn't bring her up, so she won't have the boundaries, she won't know...'

'Janet,' said David firmly, 'stop it. It's too late to think about all that now, and even if you had before, it wouldn't have changed anything. You're right, it may not be easy, and at times she may seem ungrateful. We would never have chosen to raise our granddaughter, but that's what life has handed us, it's not ideal, but we'll cope.' David went off to make the tea and Janet sat thinking of the way Zoe had spoken to her on

451

the phone. When he walked back in with the mugs of tea, she carried on, thinking aloud now. 'She was sharp with me just now, and ungrateful. Not a thank you for all I've done, just her annoyance at missing the November panel. Not a thought about how that makes me feel. But can I tell her off? No, I suppress it. And I know perfectly well why. I'm frightened. Frightened that if I say her behaviour is hurtful, she might stop loving me, might decide she doesn't want to come and live here. David, almost as if she's doing me a favour by coming to live here. Can you believe that? But that's how it feels. When it should be clear to everyone that we're doing her a favour by taking her in, doing her a huge favour in fact, if you think of all the fighting and the money, but subtly, deep down, there's this feeling that she's doing us the favour. Do you feel that?' Janet had pulled a tissue out of her cardigan pocket and was dabbing at her eyes.

David was silent. He had been feeling this all along and he could barely believe that Janet had come around to his wavelength, but it also frightened him. Thinking like that was not Janet, it was him. How would she cope with those kinds of thoughts? He didn't want her to change, didn't want her to get hurt. And he felt that thinking like this would hurt Janet. She was venturing into unknown territory and he sensed the danger.

'Sweetheart,' he said, 'let's not get carried away just because Zoe was a bit sharp with you. Remember all the letters where she says she loves us? And don't forget she's only twelve and has been through a lot. When she comes to live with us, as we both hope she will, we will deal with her behaviour just the way we dealt with Emma. We did fine with Emma, especially you. Let's just take one thing at a time. The panel first. Okay?'

452

Janet nodded obediently. The thought that Zoe's letters were manipulative flashed through her mind, followed by the thought her behaviour had nothing to do with being twelve, because Joe was still capable of selfish and manipulative behaviour, and he was thirty-six. But she didn't like those thoughts and as David was telling her not to have them, she was happy to oblige.

'You know me better than I know myself,' she said, 'and you put me right when I go wrong. I'll make lunch now and put all that nonsense out of my mind.' She stuffed the tissue back in her cardigan pocket and asked David if tinned salmon and salad was fine by him. It was. Life was back on its familiar tracks and it was a relief.

Now all they had to do was wait for the 13th of December and hope Anne King's report would convince the panel.

34. The Panel

The night before the panel Joe and Emma came to eat with their parents. Emma was excited and talkative; Joe was silent, and Janet watched him try not to be sullen as well as silent. He produced a few smiles, but they were forced, and he nodded at the conversation, but it was obvious he wasn't listening. His eyes were absent, and whenever they met hers there was a quick shift away towards an imaginary object of greater interest. Janet struggled. She knew exactly why her son was behaving in this way and she felt ashamed for him. How could he resent the fact that Zoe might be coming to live with them, how dare he resent it? Yet she could read the resentment all over his closed face. Joe had a way of closing his face that told you all you needed to know, all he wanted you to know without having to say it and face the consequences. She walked back in from the kitchen holding her lasagne dish between her gloved hands and bent over to lay it down carefully on the oval hotplate in the middle of the table. Then she straightened up against the stiffness in her back. Janet felt a pang of sorrow for her son, trapped inside feelings he refused to even acknowledge, a prisoner behind his sullen mask, desperately unable to make himself happy. Or perhaps that was what he wanted her to believe. Perhaps with his friends, watching the football or going for a drink, perhaps there he was a different person. She hoped he was.

Emma talked all through the meal, but her optimism failed to spread round the table. Janet could hardly eat, and David watched her with concern. They both knew they had reached the end of the road, there was nowhere else to go. Being so close to victory made the thought of defeat unbearable.

'You're not very talkative, son,' said David amiably enough.

'I can never please you, can I?' replied Joe sarcastically.

'And I can't say anything without you jumping down my throat, it beggars…'

'Stop it, the two of you,' shouted Janet slamming her knife and fork on the table, on either side of her plate. She glared from one to the other and they looked down at their plates. 'Tonight, of all nights,' she added, 'I would expect some friendliness around this table. And you,' she said to Joe, 'should be ashamed of yourself for being so sullen and ungrateful towards your father and myself. After all we've done, all we've spent, we're about to possibly win our battle at long last, and you sit there looking offended. What's your problem Joe?' She stared at her son, but he didn't look up.

'Mum, let's not …' Emma butted in.

'Be quiet,' snapped Janet, flapping her hand at her daughter. 'I want an answer from my son.'

Joe looked up at last and said, 'What have I got to rejoice about?' he said with a hostile shrug, 'my daughter's not coming back to me, is she?'

'What have you done to get her back Joe? Nothing. Worse than nothing in fact. You've alienated everybody, behaved atrociously towards Leanne and for the last two years you've sat in your house sulking and seeing Zoe secretly, taking a risk that would have put an end to ever getting her back at all if you'd been found out. You haven't helped us one bit, and now you haven't even got the grace to say thank you.' There it was, out, and Janet felt a lightness in her heart. It was a good feeling, a soothing contrast to the oppression tying knots inside her at the thought of that wretched panel the following day.

'I'm sorry, Mum,' said Joe. 'I know it's thanks to you there's that panel tomorrow and…'

'Are you sorry Joe?' interrupted Janet peering into his eyes. He looked away. 'Or what exactly do you feel? About the last four years? About tomorrow?'

Joe shifted uncomfortably in his chair and started fiddling with his fork, not looking up at anyone. Janet was still staring at him, waiting for her answer. Emma sat tensely staring into her plate and David looked depressed, hunched over with his elbows on the table and his hands dangling down. What had he done to deserve this family? The silence spun out until the weight of it made Joe look up at his mother.

'I suppose I'm gutted that I've messed up and you haven't. I never thought you'd get anywhere. I thought it was useless. A lost cause. I gave up. You win. You get Zoe.' His eyes strayed down to his plate again.

'Joe,' said Janet firmly, 'I don't want Zoe.' Both Emma and Joe looked up in surprise. 'I want to be enjoying my retirement with my husband, I don't want to be bringing up my granddaughter. That's your job, not mine.' Joe was stunned. Then understanding dawned. Inside his head he'd been barking up the wrong tree these last few months. He stared down at the congealed scraps of pasta and tomato sauce strewn across his plate, feeling very stupid.

456

'Mum,' he said, 'That's what I want too. I want to live with my daughter and bring her up. I know I can do it, but now you're going to be her long-term foster carers, so where does that leave me?'

'Don't speak too soon Joe. Let's wait for the panel tomorrow. If we are accepted as her foster carers, it will be a very big first step, but it doesn't mean we have to be her foster carers for life. We'll have to work on bringing the Care Plan to an end. When that happens, I can't see what's to stop Zoe moving in with you.'

Joe nodded. Pictures were popping up inside his head, dangerous pictures he knew had no business there at this stage. He could see himself walking along the beach holding his daughter's hand, going to town together, having a pizza out somewhere, coming to visit his parents with his daughter. Not coming to visit his daughter at his parents' house. He shook his head to dispel the images before they sent him crazy with hope.

Janet was also struggling with the irrepressible hope ballooning inside her. 'I don't know how to get through the time between now and the moment the panel deliver their verdict,' she said. Tears rolled slowly down her cheeks, highlighting the wrinkles as they caught the light. She smiled at her family through her tears and for an instant she looked young again, the young mother, the young wife they remembered from years ago. The smile went and her face became old and wrinkled again. The brother and sister exchanged a quick glance. One day she wouldn't be there for them anymore. They fell silent. The shrill ringing of the phone broke up their thoughts and Emma rushed to get it. It was Zoe, sounding very excited.

'Emma, I've got something to say to Dad. Is he there?'

Emma passed the phone to her brother.

'Dad?' she asked, 'Will you come over now and we can go for a little walk before I go to bed? I can't bear to be on my own tonight. I'll never sleep.'

'But…' Joe didn't know what to say.

'Owen said he's not going to tell anybody, and Jean didn't say I couldn't do it.'

'I'll be over right now Princess, great idea. I'm on my way.'

He turned to his family, shook his head and said with a flash of bitterness in his eyes, 'I've just been given permission to take my daughter for a walk by a couple of total strangers.'

'After tomorrow you may not have to ask for permission,' shouted Emma at her brother's disappearing back. Joe stopped dead and turned around. He looked at his parents sheepishly. 'Good luck with the panel,' he said. Then he stood there, keeping them hanging for whatever else was on his mind. But all he came out with was a simple 'Thank you for everything.' Then he left quickly to go and see his daughter, grabbing his warm jacket on the way out.

*

At half past nine the following morning, David sat in the lounge in his grey suit, scanning the middle pages of the Telegraph and wondering what on earth Janet was doing. She'd started her ablutions long before him, yet there he was waiting. He folded the paper and shouted they were going to be late if they didn't make a move right now.

'I know,' Janet shouted back in a flustered voice, 'I'm nearly ready. Be down now.'

458

When she appeared two minutes later her cheeks were flushed and her eyes panicky. She grabbed her handbag and looked around feverishly for the reading glasses that were not in it. Then it was her mobile phone she'd mislaid, and finally she was ready and looking at him as if to say, 'What's keeping you?' He rose from the armchair, pushing himself up ponderously and as he followed her to the front door, he asked in a puzzled tone, 'Weren't you wearing your trouser suit a moment ago?'

'I know,' she replied casually, 'but it didn't look right. A skirt is more feminine, you know, more motherly.' She closed the front door behind her.

'Janet, you don't seriously think that the decision is going to hinge on what you're wearing?' He clicked the car doors open and as Janet moved around to the passenger side, she said to him across the car roof, 'You never know. Dress matters.' As they bent and struggled into their seats David decided not to pursue the matter despite a powerful temptation to say that getting there late would create a much worse impression than the difference between a skirt and a pair of trousers. Mercifully traffic was light that morning and they got to the Town Hall ten minutes early. He glanced at Janet as they got out of the car and was shocked to see how white she was. As they walked up the steps towards the imposing building, he reached out to put his arm around her shoulders, but she evaded him. On her face she wore a look that said, 'I'm going to deal with this in my way and on my own, so just leave me to get on with it'. She was staring ahead but David knew she wasn't taking anything in, just forcing herself to breathe, talking to herself in soothing voices, concentrating on the crucial need to win over this new group of people. As they

459

pushed through the stately wooden doors, they saw Anne leaning against the reception counter and chatting with the large woman behind the desk. She must have caught the woman's eyes looking their way because she turned around and nodded at them with a thin, professional smile. She gave the receptionist a quick wave and marched them along towards the meeting room where various intimidating people were already milling around. Heads turned as they walked in and presently everyone settled down in their seats and the proceedings got under way.

Janet felt a knot of sickness at the centre of her stomach and her mouth was so dry she didn't know how she would articulate the words for her answers. Her grim determination to appear relaxed was working against her, but she still clung to the image she had to project. The perfect grandmother. Happy, warm and welcoming. She felt David's hand enfolding her own. Trying to tell her something. She didn't look round. Then he squeezed her fingers gently and her resistance melted away. Her head turned around slowly and when she met with his you're-a-wonderful-woman-and-I-love-you smile, she couldn't help but smile back and her eyes filled with gratitude for the man who never failed to be there when she needed him. As her head turned back towards the panel, she caught three pairs of eyes watching that little exchange, and in that moment, she thought 'We're going to win this.'

The six people on the panel introduced themselves. Sally Walker and her Team Manager were there, from the Fostering Team, the others were from other departments, Education, Health and one woman was a local councillor, all sounded senior and important. The Chair was a Principal Officer in Social Services. Now Janet felt nervous again. The first question came from Sally, and she gave Janet a smile of encouragement as she asked her to describe what kind of child Zoe was. Janet relaxed as she launched into the easy task of telling the panel about her granddaughter's many interests, activities and friendships. The first hurdle was behind her and she answered all the other questions with confidence. She noticed little nods, little glances exchanged between some members of the panel, she saw them thumb back through the report with approving fingers. Her only doubt was about the Chair. He sat there like a judge and Janet was wary of judges. Too full of their own importance to be swayed by the views of others and this Chair had said so little it was impossible to read his thoughts.

'Mrs Milton?' A clerk was standing next to her and motioning her to get up and move towards the exit. Janet saw Anne walking down from the back of the room and remembered that the panel were now going to question her on her report. She followed David out of the room, and they went to sit in the corridor along the wall.

*

Inside the room Anne was now sitting in Janet's seat, facing the panel. She knew the Chair, Andrew Riley, and thought she might have a bit of fight on her hands. He was not one to deviate from the majority view and the majority view so far had been that Zoe should not be allowed anywhere near her paternal family. She spread her papers neatly on the desk in front of her and looked up, bracing herself.

Andrew Riley was a short thickset man in his fifties with an asymmetric face and a bit of a boxer's nose. He had risen to Principal Officer through naked ambition with surprisingly little interest in social work. He also had the reputation of being something of a bully. Anne was not surprised when he spoke first. It would be his way of trying to sway the panel, showing a strong lead and hoping the others would follow. Anne was quite capable of doing the same herself, but she liked to think that in her case it was invariably in the interest of justice and compassion. With Andrew it would be about enforcing the power of the authorities, it would not be about protecting the child.

'Your report surprised me, Anne.' He looked up from the report into Anne's eyes, and she read all the intimidation he had packed in there. She eyeballed him back and said nothing. Let him explain his surprise. 'You seem happy' he continued after a brief silence, 'to dismiss the expert conclusions of one profession after another, social workers, paediatricians, guardians, psychiatrists, lawyers, judges.' He paused. 'All of them are wrong and Anne King is right. They advocate a neutral environment for a troubled girl, but you say she should go back to the paternal family accused of causing her emotional damage. Can you explain this to us?'

Anne did not fail to detect the Chair's patronising tone and knew it was a trap to avoid. The temptation was to jump to the defence of a report that explained these things perfectly well and be drawn into an argument about the validity of the professional opinions instead of an argument about Zoe's needs. Her job was not to convince the Chair, who would never change his mind anyway, her job was to convince the other five. She was pretty sure Sally and her Team Manager were on her side and she hadn't seen much support for Andrew's opening speech on the faces of the others. Nevertheless, her heart was beating faster than normal. A young girl's life was at stake here and her words must win over the local councillor, the man from the Education Department and the woman from the Health Department. Taking a deep, slow breath, Anne broke into her speech.

'Zoe is a twelve-year-old girl who has been caught in a rift between her father and her mother. Her needs are the needs of every child. Children need to feel safe and happy, they need cuddles and bedtime stories, they need family life and traditions, they need Christmas, and Easter, and summer holidays, they need fun; they need family who take them to the pictures, who take them on outings, have picnics in the woods and on the beach, rejoice when they succeed and console them when they fail. This, I would argue, is what we call love. Disagreements and rows will happen too of course, but always in the context of those loving feelings. Food on the table and clean bedding are important too, but that is provision rather than love.' Anne paused to look at her audience and give them a moment to absorb the picture she had sketched in front of their eyes. Sally gave her an imperceptible nod, and Anne continued with increasing confidence. 'For three years Zoe has lived without the kind of love we believe our own children and grandchildren are entitled to. For three years she has been deprived of the freedom to be with the people whom she loves and who love her. A neutral environment is one where there is food on the table and clean sheets on the bed, but not love as we understand it. As Zoe understands it. Which is why she has been protesting about her situation for three painful years, at times threatening to kill herself. Why would we condemn an innocent child to another three years of that kind of life?'

The panel members were silent. One or two of them fiddled with their pens, as if to avoid looking up at the others. They seemed uncomfortable, perhaps slightly ashamed to think that the institutions they belonged to had somehow allowed something like this to happen to a child. At the beginning of the 21st century for goodness' sake! Are we not as enlightened as we thought we were? Andrew Riley, however, thought he was still not enlightened enough, and had another attempt at destabilising Anne's position.

'You talk of love, Anne, but Zoe's father and grandparents have been found guilty of emotional abuse against the girl. Do you dismiss that?'

'I do,' said Anne, firmly. Her clear blue eyes held his until he looked down at the pen in his hand. 'There is not a shred of evidence that they emotionally abused her in any way. The accusation was they turned her against her mother, but there is no evidence of that either. Zoe is adamant her dad always said her mum was a good mum and she must listen to her and behave herself; the grandfather said all along that Zoe should accept that spending half her time with her mum and half with her dad was fair; the grandmother encouraged Zoe to go back to her mother after every visit, but Zoe refused. Her feelings towards her mother are her own. They always were her own. I know. I talked to her in a relaxed environment, on three occasions. I did not probe, I let her speak about her life and she told me she hated her mother. She was clear and she had her reasons. So, yes, Andrew, I dismiss the accusations of emotional abuse. Zoe's grandparents love her very much and they have spent inordinate amounts of energy, time and money to rescue her out of foster care and bring her to a loving home. In fact, nobody has questioned the grandparents' love for Zoe, not even the judge.'

Before Andrew had time to say anything else, the man from the Education Department cleared his throat and all eyes turned to him. He was a good-looking man in his forties, with short black hair and lively eyes. Anne felt a tightening in her stomach. Did she have a second enemy here?

'How do you account for all these professional people getting things so wrong about Zoe?' he asked. Anne glimpsed the twinkle in his eyes and understood he was having a bit of fun. Spinning out the showdown between her and Andrew. Her mouth was dry, and she could have done without this, but on the bright side she could tell this man was with her and perhaps handing her an opportunity to kill any doubts in the minds of other panel members.

'Nobody listened to Zoe,' she replied, making eye contact with everyone on the panel, one after the other. 'Nobody got to know her outside the intimidating environment of an interview room. The child came to see these interviews as traps she got caught in and she became silent. Frightened to talk because whatever she said led to worse and worse outcomes, even though she was telling her truth. Nobody talked to the people who did know Zoe, like her teachers, the school nurse, her friends or her friends' parents. The expression "emotional abuse" was so deafening that nobody could hear anything else.'

Anne was pleased with that last sentence. The good-looking man from the Education Department grinned and nodded to show his appreciation. Something in his eyes told Anne he would have winked if it hadn't been totally inappropriate. She could also see the other two nodding in unison, and she felt the tide may have just turned for Zoe. She breathed a quiet sigh of relief and took a sip of water from the bottle in her handbag. Then she looked up expectantly, in case someone had something else to say or ask. They didn't. She gathered her papers, picked up her handbag and left.

Outside in the corridor David and Janet were waiting, getting more and more nervous. Anne was taking a long time. They were both having similar thoughts, but they didn't want to see confirmation of their own fears in the other's eyes. They sat and stared at the beige wall opposite in silence. The sound of a door opening gave them a jolt and they sat up nervously. Sure enough, Anne was coming out of the room and she gave them a discreet thumbs up as she walked towards another chair further down the corridor.

'What does that mean?' Janet whispered.

'She's pleased with how it went, relax,' said David.

Now the panel were in their closed session, and the almost unbearable tension inside Janet's chest came from hope, not from fear. It didn't take long. Five minutes at most and she heard the door open again and the clerk called them back to their seats. They sat facing the panel, and Anne was sitting further back. Janet's heart was thrumming in her chest and she was holding her breath. She seized her husband's hand; he pressed her hand back and she saw with a glance that he wasn't breathing either. The Chair was fiddling with some notes, gathering his thoughts before speaking. He cleared his throat and a wave of sudden fear swept through Janet. He was going to say that, regrettably, in view of all that had gone before, it would be safer…blah blah blah…. she felt sick in her stomach and looked down at her feet just as the man launched into his first sentence. Her ears couldn't make sense of the words. He seemed to have said they would make excellent carers for their granddaughter, but that couldn't be right, nobody was ever going to say that, and David was squeezing her hand much too hard. She looked up and he was looking back at her with a big smile on his face.

'They've approved us?' she whispered.

'Yes,' David whispered back. 'Didn't you hear?'

The man was still talking.

'Are you sure?'

'Yes,' he chuckled, pulling his wife close.

Then she burst into tears.

*

Half an hour later, having sneaked a glance at the messages on her mobile, Zoe also burst into tears, in the middle of a Science lesson. Mr Palmer was very understanding and asked one of the girls to accompany Zoe to the toilets so she could splash some cold water on her face. From the safety of the toilet cubicle, Zoe phoned her gran.

'Gran, I can't believe it. When can I come?'

'I think when you want sweetheart, Anne said…'

'Today, after school, then.'

Granny laughed, but Zoe didn't think it was funny. 'Gran, I don't want to spend another day with Jean and Owen.'

'I know sweetheart,' said Granny, 'I'll talk to Sally and it will happen as soon as possible, but it may not be today.'

Zoe moved two days later. During those two days she spoke to Jean and Owen from a great distance, as if she had already said good-bye and they were now no more than insignificant dots on the fabric of her past. It was more difficult with Laura who looked so sad and lost. On Zoe's last evening Laura came into her room and watched her pack sitting on the bed. She was silent for a long time but finally dug deep and asked the question that had been on her mind for the last two days.

'Zoe,' she said quickly, looking at the floor, 'will you come back to visit after you're gone?'

Zoe had been forcing her schoolbooks into a space that was too small for them and no matter how much she pushed, she couldn't close the lid of her suitcase. She stopped dead when she heard Laura's question and the lid sprung back up. In that instant she knew that she would never set foot in this house again. Never. She looked at Laura's little face and felt a weight of responsibility.

'Tell you what Laura,' she said, 'I'll invite you to visit me at my gran's.'

Laura shot her a look devoid of any hope. Zoe scanned the mostly empty room and grabbed her second least favourite cuddly friend, Bear. 'Look,' she said, 'you can look after Bear for me and when I invite you, you can bring him back to me.' The promise of the invite carried a little more weight now, but both girls were aware that Zoe hadn't given Flossie to be looked after. Laura nodded and left the room, hugging Bear. Holding on to Bear was something.

Zoe carried on packing, feeling a little guilty about never setting eyes on Jean's house again. It was harsh on Jean and Owen, but it couldn't be helped, it was how she felt, and she hadn't asked to come here in the first place. She sat on her suitcase and managed to zip the lid down. She couldn't wait to forget Jean and Owen. She couldn't wait for her real life to start.

When Zoe's real life started however, it did not turn out as expected.

35. The End

How Zoe had dreamt about going home! Walking out of Jean and Owen's house, not looking back, not even once, running to Granny's car, jumping in, slamming the door, not looking out of the side window, just looking ahead, telling Granny to drive away quickly, and never mind the speed limits. Drive, fly, feel like you just dug a tunnel out of the prison and now you've made it, you're free, you're flying like the gulls in the blue sky, YOU'RE FREE! Then walking into Granny and Grandad's house, walking in with your head high, walking in knowing it's your right, walking in knowing you're here to stay and nobody, but nobody, can take you away. Picking up the phone to talk to Dad, picking up the phone to talk to Emma, inviting them over, inviting yourself over, living in a free world, your new free world. She wouldn't walk, she would dance, she wouldn't talk, she would sing, she would sing and dance all day long and she would be the happiest girl in the world. It would be like the day of the Christmas lights, or the day of the puffins, when time stolen from captivity had filled the moment with vivid colours and intense emotions. Now every day would be like that.

Instead, Zoe found herself back in a new kind of prison. She clung to her grandmother, following her around the house, holding her hand, her arm or the bottom of her cardigan. She was turning into Laura. The doorbell gave her jolts of panic and the ringing of the phone made her eyes shoot wide open with fear. Most nights she woke up in nightmare sweats and had to be taken crying to Granny's bed whilst Grandad moved to the spare room. She found excuses not to go out with her friends, became indifferent to rollerblading down the front and in school her teachers noticed a dip in her work. Had social workers, Janet remarked to David one day, been monitoring Zoe's progress, they would have had her straight back into care.

Whenever her father called, illicitly while the care plan was still officially in place, Zoe was nervous, casting brittle glances towards the window and jumping out of her skin at every innocent jingle of the doorbell. Joe struggled not to feel upset.

'I don't understand you,' he said to her one edgy afternoon, 'you used to gaily flout all the rules to come and see me, and now it seems you'd rather not see me at all.' They were sitting on the couch watching a bit of TV together and he pulled her closer to attenuate the reproach in his voice.

'There was nothing to lose then,' she said. 'But now I'm frightened they'll take me away again.' Her lower lip trembled. Joe nodded, hating the bastards for what they had done to his daughter.

This went on for about three months. Then Zoe's nightmares became less frequent, her need to hold on to Granny less imperative, but with the Care Plan still in place she couldn't shed all her fears. Janet and the new Guardian mounted a joint but diplomatic assault for the ending of the Care Plan, and in May of Zoe's thirteenth year the news finally came, one Friday morning, in a brief letter. Gerald wrote that in view of Zoe being settled with her grandparents and on the advice of Zoe's guardian, Social Services had made the decision to withdraw Zoe's name from the Child Protection Register as she was no longer considered at risk. Being fostered by her grandparents had been a good outcome and the Care Plan would be abandoned as of May 12th. He sent his best wishes, hoping Zoe would have many happy years with her grandparents. Janet was too thrilled to be angry, too delighted to dwell on Gerald's light-hearted tone, too relieved to rage against the absence of an apology. Instead, she invited Joe and Emma over, without mentioning her news, and David put a bottle of champagne in the fridge.

The late afternoon was a lovely time of day in Janet's lounge, with the sun slanting in through the side windows, lighting up the room with warm sunset colours. As the family gathered there, Janet watched them with pleasure. David and Joe were exchanging football predictions across the room and Zoe was animatedly telling Emma about an incident in school. A happy scene. At last. And now for the good news. Janet pulled the letter from her cardigan pocket and said, 'I received this letter today. Listen.' She proceeded to read it out aloud, but instead of the explosion of joy she had anticipated, there was a stunned silence.

'So…,' Joe finally said, 'that's the end of the Care Plan?'

'Yes, son. For the first time in over three years, we are free to conduct our lives as we wish. You can take your daughter out for an ice-cream and not worry about police sirens.' This was met with more silence and Janet's smile faded on her lips. She looked around the room with perplexed eyes.

Zoe was the first to speak. 'So that's it?' she asked resentfully. 'After keeping me in care for three years, they can just write a letter like that, like what they did doesn't matter. They don't even say sorry, or we were wrong, or any shit like that?'

'Zoe,' chided Granny gently.

'Sorry Gran, but I can't believe this. They wrecked my childhood, and they don't have to say sorry?' Zoe's voice rang with outrage.

Janet bowed her head and stared at the letter lying limp in her lap. She had not foreseen Zoe's reaction, but she understood it, Joe and Emma would follow close upon her heels with theirs and the room would clank and shake with the furious sounds of their anger. Not one of them would give an instant's thought to how she felt. She got up and retreated to the kitchen on the pretext of getting food ready. She no longer cared. Her work was done and sorting out the volatile emotions of her impossible family held no appeal. They were what they were, but for now she wanted to be alone.

David watched his wife's back disappear through the door and heard the sound of water running into the sink. Emma was talking now, and although he wasn't listening to her actual words, her voice was giving him a headache. Then Zoe started again.

'Zoe,' he interrupted sharply, looking straight at his granddaughter, 'bad stuff happens in life, and people have a choice. They can wallow in self-pity for ever after or they can put it behind them and get on with their lives.' He saw his granddaughter's face close in antagonism and recognised the look from the days when Joe and Emma were a similar age. 'Tell me Zoe,' he continued, leaning forward on his elbows, 'when you're rollerblading with your friends and you take a fall, what do you do?' He peered at the girl sitting opposite him on the couch.

472

'What do you mean what do I do?' she responded defensively.

Joe and Emma watched with keen interest.

'Do you lie crying on the ground or do you pick yourself up and get on with your skating?' asked the old man.

Zoe shrugged without answering. Grandad had cunningly won that bit of the argument and her mind was busy searching for a suitable riposte when she caught her father's eyes looking down at her. The silent twinkle in them said it all. 'Now you see what he's like. Has to be right, has to have the last word.' The distraction freed some space inside Zoe's head and the perfect answer popped in there as if by magic. With a glint of triumph in her eyes she turned back to her grandfather and said, 'Anyway that's different Grandad, because if I fall on my blades, it's my own fault. Nobody tripped me up. But these people they tripped me up big time, they damaged me, and I'll hate them forever.'

'Suit yourself,' said Grandad with a resigned shrug. He sat back in his armchair and continued, 'I suppose it'll be handy whenever something goes wrong in your life to blame it on the last four years.' It took all his will power not to expand into a more thorough examination of the damage done by the blame culture. Joe, who fully expected the lecture to follow, saw his father decide not to do it. He just added, 'But actually, Zoe, one could argue that you learned a lot during the last four years. Amongst other things, you learned that you could win a battle against all the odds, with your own sheer determination and the help of the people who love you.'

Grandad looked sad and tired, and Zoe felt bad. She knew this last sentence was a reminder that the people who loved her didn't deserve to get attacked and rejected when they were just trying to help some more. Where was Granny? Her absence carved a painful hole in the room. Now Zoe felt tears in her eyes and there was nobody to rescue her out of this stupid row.

'Well,' said Grandad glumly, 'I had some champagne in the fridge, but I guess we'll keep that bottle for another day.'

The sadness in Grandad's eyes uncoiled the muddle of bad feelings inside Zoe and it suddenly became very easy to run into his arms and say sorry, and I love you, and I love Granny, and thank you for having me. Life is a struggle, thought David as he cuddled his granddaughter, and that's just the way it is.

When the bottle of champagne finally came out the family lifted their glasses to the beginning of a new life. Joe told his daughter he would take her for an ice-cream down the front in the morning and they would eat their ice-cream sitting on the low wall looking at the sea, just as they used to do. In broad daylight, he added, and they all laughed and shook their heads. He also said they would discuss Zoe's return home, and he lifted his glass again, in the direction of his parents. They smiled back. It was what they all wanted.

But once Joe was in bed that night, unable to find sleep, what had seemed simple in the light of day, became in the dark hours unclear and complicated. Pernicious thoughts came at him relentlessly. He tossed to the right. Zoe would never come to live with him. Why should she want to anyway? She had a perfect home with his parents, pretty wallpaper everywhere and home cooked food on the table. She was settled there. In fact, wouldn't it be wrong to take her away from all that? He rolled over onto his left side, kicking the duvet off with one angry foot. He could see what was going on, Zoe was just humouring him. Coming home for his sake, not because she wanted to. Trying to make him feel like a good dad. Which he wasn't, they both knew that. He flopped over onto his back and flung one arm out across the bed. The truth was, he stopped being a proper dad four years ago. Didn't know how to do it anymore. The social work bastards could be blamed for that. He would have to tell Zoe. Free her to do what she really wanted, which was to stay with his parents. The three of them belonged together now, that was obvious. Joe shivered. Tugged the duvet back up to his chin and turned onto his side again. His head was bursting under pressure. Tomorrow he would tell Zoe the best for everyone was for her to stay with her grandparents. He'd be okay with that. Perfectly okay. He drifted off into restless slumber.

Snuggled safely in her bed Zoe was also awake well into the night, quietly talking to Flossie. She told her about going back to her real home at last, where she would live with her dad and visit her grandparents same as other kids. She would be like Stefan, and Stefan had a great time with his dad. It would be even better for her, 'cos she wouldn't be missing her mum the way he did. Without Leanne around, there'd be no more rows and no more shouting. No Jessie either to make fun of her. A perfect life. It would be good for Dad too. Wouldn't be lonely any longer. She whispered in Flossie's ear that it would be the best day in Dad's life when she came home, 'cos she knew he'd been a bit gutted when she had come back to Granny and Grandad's instead of coming home to him, where she belonged. But he shouldn't have been gutted because it was everybody's plan all along that she would go and live with him in the end. And now she would. And she would pull his leg about being an old pessimist who never believed it would happen. Had it been down to him, of course, it never would have happened. And that was exactly why Dad needed her. To show him that good things could happen, and the main good thing in his life was her. She drifted off into happy dreams.

The following morning Joe rang his parents' doorbell and waited. It was a cool, dull May morning and he shivered in his light jacket. A chunk of blue sky had fooled him earlier on and now he cast a worried glance at the low grey clouds hanging in the sky. If it started to rain, they could always sit inside the cheerful little café and he would have a hot cappuccino instead of an ice-cream. His chest was tight, and his heart was loud as he rehearsed what he wanted to say to his daughter. The door flew open, and she jumped into his arms. Too old, too tall to do this, but she was catching up on years of not doing it when she would have been the right size. He picked her up and hugged her close.

'Dad,' she whispered, 'I can't believe we can go out together.'

'Let's go and prove we can,' he said. 'My only fear is the rain will stop us this time.'

They got to Joe's car and Zoe couldn't help but notice how dirty it was, with parking slips strewn over the floor amongst the grit and mud from years of no cleaning. Piles of papers and files covered the whole of the back seat and Dad's old raincoat had been chucked over and lay limply with one sleeve dangling on the floor. Zoe plucked a dirty rag from her seat and shoved it down the door's side pocket before sitting down.

'Dad, your car's disgusting,' she said, with the unconscious honesty of the young.

For the first time Joe noticed that his car was indeed a mess, and this confirmed his view that he was not fit to be the kind of father his daughter needed. Without a word he drove off,

476

switched the radio on and pop music filled the space. Beyoncé. Zoe hummed in tune. They parked, got out of the car and went to cross the main road. As they walked on the damp grass towards the sea she slipped her hand in his. This was the moment she had waited for. A drizzle enfolded them, but it didn't matter, it felt cool and bracing on her face, and the wind lifted her hair which she could tell was going wild and frizzy. She didn't care about that either. She held on tightly to her father's hand, letting the feel of his rough warm skin travel deep inside her. They stood for a silent moment looking out at the brown foaming sea, impervious to the gusts of wind on their faces. Then they walked into the small café, empty at this early hour on a wet Saturday morning.

As they waited for their order father and daughter looked at each other in awkward silence. They had no words for this moment, because this moment should never have happened. Instead, there should have been three years of normal Saturday mornings. This on the other hand was unfamiliar and mildly threatening. They couldn't decipher each other's thoughts, had no rituals to bring ease into the situation. There was no supervisor listening in on their conversation and yet they didn't feel free to talk. When the coffee and the ice-cream came, they relaxed.

Zoe was the first to speak.

'Dad, when I come home, do you think…' But Joe didn't let her finish. They mustn't go down that road, because he knew there was no coming home. Quickly, whilst carefully stirring sugar into his coffee, he interrupted her. 'Zoe,' he said, 'I want to talk to you about that.'

'About coming home?' she asked holding her spoon in the air.

'Yes.' He smiled at his daughter. He was doing the right thing and when she showed her happiness at being able to stay where she was, he would not bear any grudges against anybody. It was just the way it had panned out. He knew in any case that part of him would be relieved. 'Zoe,' he said slowly, 'I have thought long and hard about this.' In work Joe hated it when people said they had thought long and hard about something, as if trying to give false weight to their argument, and he couldn't quite believe those despicable words had just come out of his own mouth. He carried on. 'I don't want you to feel you have to come home…' his voice trailed off as he watched his daughter's face. Her mouth fell slightly open, and her eyes swam. Then the tears came, richly silent.

'Zoe, what's the matter love?' he asked stupidly, wrapping his hand quickly over her slender wrist. For a while she couldn't speak. Then she said with profound puzzlement, 'Daddy, I thought you wanted me to come home. I thought this was the best day of our lives.'

Joe's inner world fragmented. It hurt. His daughter's tears hurt. His inability to deal with emotions hurt. Every bloody thing hurt, and he felt useless and wasted. He was a complete idiot.

'Sweetheart,' he said quickly, 'forget I said that. Of course, I want you to come home. For a moment I thought you might prefer to stay with Granny and Grandad, because you're settled there, and they look after you well, but that's not what I want. I want you to come home, and I want to be a good father to you. Make up for the last three years. Four years.' As he said the words, they took on the shape of a new almost exciting possibility. Being a caring thoughtful dad. Would Zoe teach him that?

She swiped her tears away with a quick brush of her sleeve. She had always known her dad needed her. Their eyes met. She smiled and Joe knew there was nothing more beautiful in this world than the smile of a child freely given. She had no blueprint for him.

'What kind of dad will you want me to be?' he asked, his hand still wrapped around her wrist.

'I don't care what kind of dad you're gonna be,' she exclaimed, rolling her eyes in despair at the question. Joe smiled, imagining his daughter rolling her eyes just like that when talking to her friends in the middle of the schoolyard. And probably waving her arms. A fully independent little person, with her ways, her attractiveness, her problems. Hope surged inside his chest. She was still speaking. 'Because, if you remember, I haven't been allowed to have a dad for four years. So now I'm just gonna enjoy it. Think about it, Dad, we can just walk out of here and go where we like, and nobody will come to arrest us. Isn't that going to be amazing?'

'I can take you to the cinema, to football games…'

'Shopping,' chipped in Zoe, slipping her wrist out of her father's hold to pick up her spoon and scoop some melted ice-cream into her mouth.

'I can come and watch the school show,' added Joe, aware he hadn't had anything to do with his daughter's school life for years.

'And give me a row if I'm home late after a party,' her eyes twinkled at him with anticipated defiance.

'And you can moan to your friends that your dad's getting you down with his stupid old-fashioned ideas.' He peered at her with his own version of defiance.

Zoe threw her head back and laughed, her whole body shaking with it. Then she stopped, nodded and said, 'Exactly, we can have a normal life.'

His coffee cup was empty, so was her ice-cream bowl. They got up, scraping their chairs against the tiled floor, and as they walked out into the wet sunshine, she slipped her hand into his again. They walked across the path to the little wall overlooking the beach and stood watching the sea and the gulls circling high, supremely at ease in all that space.

'Daddy,' Zoe started, but let her thought hang in the air.

'Yes sweetheart,' replied Joe with a lump in his throat because he couldn't remember the last time she'd called him Daddy. It was always Dad these days.

'I know what I'm going to be when I grow up.'

'What's that, sweetheart?' Joe asked, mildly startled by the thought of this child so soon to be grown up. In no time she'd be turning up with a boyfriend, then university, then…

'I'm gonna be a lawyer and I'm gonna defend the rights of children.' Her large blue-grey eyes came to meet his, with deep seriousness. He squeezed his daughter's hand, realising that he didn't really know her. So that was his job for the next few years, get to know his daughter and stop being a complete idiot. His eyes followed a couple of gulls gliding high and he felt strangely optimistic. Perhaps he could stop being a complete idiot.

Slowly they turned from the wall and fell into step along the path, merging as they walked into the flow of ordinary people, walkers, children on scooters, runners in shorts, girls on roller blades, women hanging on to dogs.

Father and daughter, hand in hand, taking their first steps into their normal lives.

Printed in Great Britain
by Amazon

71212797R00293